Carrion

A Byrd & Crowe Mystery

J.E. Irvin

The New Atlantian Library

Habent Sua Fata Libelli

The New
Atlantian Library

Manhanset House
Shelter Island Hts., New York 11965-0342

bricktower@aol.com • tech@absolutelyamazingebooks.com
• absolutelyamazingebooks.com

Library of Congress Cataloging-in-Publication Data
Irvin, j.e.
Carrion, a byrd & crowe mystery
p. cm.

1. FICTION / Thrillers / Psychological. 2. FICTION / Romance / Suspense.
3. FICTION / Mystery & Detective / International Mystery & Crime
Fiction, I. Title.
ISBN: 978-1-955036-01-6, Trade Paper

December 2022

Carrion

A Byrd & Crowe Mystery

J.E. Irvin

Other books by J.E. Irvin

The Dark End of the Rainbow
Hopewell 1

The Rules of the Game
Hopewell 2

The Strange Disappearance of Rose Snow
Hopewell 3

A Principle of Light

Broken

Acknowledgments

Alexandra Byrd is a product of my imagination and the fictional embodiment of all young women who overcome difficult childhoods and go on to make a difference in the world. I hope you find her as much of a joy as I do.

My sincere thanks to Jenna Beck, chair of Law and Public Safety at Sinclair College, Instructor Joe Niehaus, and the students in Joe's Introduction to Criminal Justice Class for allowing me to sit in on lectures and discussions and pick their brains. I apologize for changing a few details to fit the fictional narrative. It's what novelists do!

It goes without saying that my excellent editor Donna Laugle makes my work better than it would ever be on its own. I owe her an immense debt of gratitude.

To my Storytellers critique group – Christy, Marybeth, Susan, Roger, Judi, Priscilla, and Shulamit, who amaze me with their talent, instruct me with their constructive criticism, and honor me with their friendship, thank you!

To the communities of Springboro and Franklin, who have graciously allowed me to squeeze Hopewell in between their boundaries, then shared their rich histories and locations with my characters, my deepest thanks.

And to my husband Gregg, who, over the years, has transformed from an observer of my process to an astute and trusted critic. Thank you! I couldn't do this without you!

What flocks of critics hover here to-day,
As vultures wait on armies for their prey,
All gaping for the carcase of a play!
With croaking notes they bode some dire event,
And follow dying poets by the scent.

—John Dryden
Prologue: All for Love (1678)

Preface

The Byrd Files…Case #1: CARRION

June 7, 2058

"For forty years, death was my daily bread. As a patrol officer, a detective, a private investigator, and a consultant, I worked every type of murder scene, and witnessed the most brutal crimes, often amid hostility, backlash, and condemnation. Along the way, I tried to keep my soul intact. Don't know if I succeeded, but this is how it all began."

My partner finished reading the introduction and removed his glasses. "Do you really want to tell our story?"
I touched his cheek. "I have to."
"It reads like fiction."
"But you and I know the truth, love, and that's all that matters."

One

Xandra Byrd stepped out the back door of the Buns N Fries and headed into the wind. Above the drive-thru lane, a vulture circled, its graceful swoop a contrast to the ugliness of its beaked face. Sunset streaked the sky in shades of red and purple, deepening the shadows as the bird hovered, then, joined by a companion, dipped lower. One of the lids on the garbage bins must have blown open, inviting the scavengers to feast on discarded French fries and half-eaten burgers. Goose bumps peppered Xandra's arms. She inhaled sharply.

Along with the odor of grease emanating from the restaurant, the scent of decaying lilacs, now past prime bloom, drifted from the bushes separating the eastern half of the parking lot from the dinner theater next door. She gazed from the hedge to the screen of cedars hiding the trash enclosure and the prairie and the wooded land beyond. The forest called her. She wouldn't mind disappearing into the cool darkness under the trees. A hike was preferrable to gathering used ketchup packets and nagging employees to bus tables. Dragging the trash, Xandra swallowed the unease that had dogged her since the argument with her parents earlier that day. Their suggestion that she return to counseling with Reverend Loving meant she wasn't successfully hiding her unhappiness. But she didn't need counseling. She needed to move on with her life, to leave the past behind for good. A discarded burger bag blew across the lot. When a stronger gust ripped the trash from her hand, she chased it down and trudged on.

Overhead, the raptors wheeled back. They often soared above the Hopewell-Springboro corridor, drawn to the fast-food joints and the Kroger Superstore. Vultures, Xandra recalled, could detect rotting meat up to a mile away. Yuck, and useless trivia. She scurried across the drive-thru lane, threading the queue of vans filled with soccer moms and their kids. Fumes from the idling vehicles made her eyes water. Her parents' request echoed in her mind. They knew her previous years had not been easy, and they supported her decision to enroll in Sinclair Community College's criminal justice program. What they didn't know is she hoped that following in her real father's footsteps, becoming a detective someday, would convince her she belonged in the Zetts family, that Joe and Leah, despite giving her up when she was born, did truly love her. She was trying to fit in. She did her fair share of chores and was paying her way through school, even though Joe and Leah insisted she didn't have to. If her parents would just stop trying so hard to make things right. Screw the past and let it go. Yeah, if only she could do that, too. Shoving a loose strand of hair behind her ear, she unlatched the gate in the fence around the trash cans.

Lost in thought, she yelped when the hasp pinched her thumb, then sucked at the blood blister. The wind caught the door and banged it against the enclosure. She stepped inside and paused, puzzled by a dark smudge on the concrete beneath her sneaker. She detected the faint odor of burning, then shrugged. Maybe one of the other employees had grabbed a smoke during their break. She inspected the bins. None of the lids stood open. The fence slammed shut behind her just as a third vulture glided past, wings spread to slow its descent. Still favoring the bruised thumb, she lifted the lid on the first bin, assailed by an unfamiliar odor. Fighting the urge to throw up, she deposited the garbage and turned to leave. Then she screamed.

A woman in a dark skirt and jacket lay splayed across the concrete apron, her face turned away from Xandra. Low-heeled black flats dangled from the woman's feet. One arm curled around her waist. The other lay at a ninety-degree angle above her shoulder, the hand clutching a scrap of paper that rustled in the wind swirling through the openings in the wooden slats. Xandra clapped a hand over her mouth and swore. Pinching her nose against the smell, she crouched over the body. Blood had pooled beneath the woman's head and neck, spreading around her like a large, malignant shadow. A last ray of twilight leaked between the slats, illuminating the concrete pad. Something metallic gleamed by the woman's shoulder. Xandra leaned closer. A pin in the shape of a bird stared up at her, the beak smeared with crimson. Glancing over her shoulder, she snatched the pin and stuffed it in her pocket.

"Xandra?" Her name drifted, tinny and remote, from the squawk box on the outside order kiosk. Reggie Lynx, one of the night shift workers, shouted again. "Hey, Byrd, you get lost out there?"

She shoved her shoulders against the gate, which rattled but refused to open. When the door slammed shut, the latch must have fallen into place. She backed away from the body and stood on tiptoe to peer over the fence. "Reggie? Help! I'm locked in."

Laughter echoed from the speaker before a car drove by, cutting off the sound. Xandra snaked her hand over the pickets to slap at the latch until it slid free. When the gate swung open, she braced her leg against the wood to prevent it from reclosing. Then she took out her phone.

"911. What is your emergency?" A dispatch officer answered on the second ring.

"Hello? This is Xandra Byrd. I manage the night shift at the Buns N Fries."

"What's your emergency, Ms. Byrd?"

Xandra closed her hand around the bird pin in her pocket. The vultures circled lower. "I'm at the Buns N Fries, 728 Hopewell-Springboro Pike. There's a dead body in the trash shed."

"Did you check for a pulse?"

"No, but I don't have to. The woman's dead." Xandra paused when the sound cut off. "Hello? Are you there?"

"An officer is on his way to your location. Stay on the line, Ms. Byrd."

Xandra gripped the phone so tightly her hand shook. "Hurry, please. I'm not positive, but I think it's Reverend Loving."

Two

Detective Janeece Terl slipped beneath the police tape stretching from the drive-thru order menu to the wooden trash enclosure. She observed the fenced-in area, noting the proximity of the bins to the dinner theater driveway and to an unpaved access road that paralleled the prairie a quarter mile to the south along the border of the wooded land. Hopewell's rural character was a bonus until it came to crime. Then it became a complication. She spoke to the patrol officer guarding the site before pulling gloves from her pocket and tugging them on. Notebook and pen in hand, she made her way to the back of the lot. Xandra Byrd stood in the entrance to the enclosure, shoulders hunched, face an emotionless mask.

"Xandra." Terl acknowledged the young woman, then stepped past her to examine the body wedged between the picket fence and the largest trash bin. "You haven't moved or touched anything?"

"No." Xandra clenched her fist to avoid touching the pin in her pocket. "I didn't want to destroy any evidence."

"They teach you that at Sinclair?" Terl edged around the body, running a flashlight over the cracked pad of concrete that served as a base for the structure.

"Among other things." Xandra bit her lip. The pin she'd retrieved stabbed her thigh. Guilt warmed her neck, but she hunched into the collar of her uniform shirt to hide the flush. She and the detective had a history. Three years ago, Terl had assisted her father in investigating the disappearance of the baby Xandra had rescued from a parked car, a baby that turned out to be the girl's own half-sister, Olivia. The detective, still a patrol officer at the time, had been friendly, even supportive, but Xandra's discovery of this crime scene was bound to remind everyone of her sketchy past. "Can I go now?"

Janeece looked up at the young woman who had her father's height, her mother's curves, and her own unique personality. People tended to judge Xandra on her purple hair, eyebrow ring, and the full-sleeve tattoo of thorns and roses on her left arm, but she had the best scores in her criminology classes and a particular ability to uncover secrets. Janeece had kept tabs on the girl, maybe because her intensity reminded Terl of herself at that age, eager, defensive, determined to survive and succeed. "I'd like you to wait in the restaurant," she said. "Once we finish up out here, I'll come inside."

Xandra met the detective's gaze. "The Reverend…she has something in her hand."

"And you didn't touch it?" When Xandra shook her head, Janeece turned back to the corpse. She directed Xandra to point the beam at the Reverend's left arm. Using the pen, Janeece teased the woman's fingers open. "No rigor yet. And, you're right. She's holding some kind of paper. You sure you didn't read it?"

"No. I didn't get that close." Xandra's hand shook, strobing the light across the body and over the fencing beyond.

"Terl?" Janeece's partner, Pete Stone, called out as he approached. He set a forensics kit down outside the fence and poked his head inside the enclosure.

Janeece took back the flashlight. "Go on, Xandra. Don't allow any of the employees to leave, okay?"

Xandra nodded and slipped around Stone. Unclenching her hands, she took a deep breath as she checked out the rubberneckers already lining the parking lot. The restaurant's night crew huddled near the side entrance, anxiety clear on their faces. When Xandra stepped inside, Reggie yanked her behind the counter.

"What's going on?"

"Somebody killed Reverend Loving and left her body by the trash bins. You don't want to go back there." Xandra turned to the other three employees. Carson, Emilia, and Brenda cast wary looks her way. "I don't know what the boss will decide, but if it's up to me, you'll all get paid for tonight."

"Does that mean we can go home early?" Emilia licked her lips, anticipating a few hours of clandestine make-out time with her boyfriend Chad Helton before she had to show up at home.

"Sorry, Em, but no. The police want statements from us, so start thinking about what you saw or didn't see tonight." Xandra moved to the back of the prep area to dial the owner's number, wondering what she could say to make the news easier to hear. Paul Loving owned the Buns N Fries. It was his sister, Doris, who lay dead behind the restaurant.

Three

Janeece Terl continued to stare at the corpse while her partner walked the outside perimeter of the fence. When he re-entered the enclosure, she wrinkled her nose and motioned toward the bins. "We'll have to go through the garbage. Man, I hate sifting trash." Stone nodded in agreement just as his phone pinged.

"The M. E.'s on her way," he informed Janeece.

"Neruda?"

"On vacation. Stark's filling in."

Janeece rose, dusted her hands on her pants, and stepped away from the body. "Take a good look, Pete. Let me know what you think about the object in her hand. There's blood spatter on the east fence and a stain on the concrete that looks recent."

Pete shined his light over the area. "How did the deceased end up inside this fence without anyone seeing her or the killer?"

"Great question." Janeece scrubbed her chin. "If memory serves, there is a path from the end of the theater portico to the back of the parking lot. Narrow but passable."

"And you know that how?"

Terl shook her head. "Had a part-time job there during high school. We used to slip over to the BNF for lunch."

"Still doesn't explain how no one saw her once she reached the lot."

"No, it doesn't, but it's a working theory. I'm going inside to take statements."

"You find a weapon?" Pete said.

"Not yet. We'll have the team move these bins and examine all of it in daylight. Document everything, Pete, okay?" Without waiting for his reply, she stripped off the gloves and stuffed them in a pocket. Just beyond the crime tape, she stopped to observe the staff of the Buns N

Fries as they huddled near the door. When they noticed her watching, the group retreated, casting nervous glances at each other. Janeece waved to the patrol officer guarding the lot and made her way into the building.

The Buns N Fries franchise catered to Interstate 75 travelers as well as the locals from Franklin, Hopewell, and Springboro. Although Janeece had a pretty good idea who owned this store, she did a quick phone search to double-check. As expected, the name Paul Loving popped up. That could be a lead, or another complication. The Lovings were a Hopewell institution. The family had settled in the area more than a hundred years ago, when everything was farmland. They quickly established themselves in the community, buying up acreage, opening shops, serving as council members and state representatives. Paul had a major or minor interest in most of the city's businesses. Local gossip suggested he had recently partnered with an out-of-town investor to construct houses on undeveloped tracts of land in and around the town. The only parcel he hadn't acquired was the forested acreage behind St. Francis Episcopal, the church where his sister, now deceased, served as minister. Janeece shook off the sadness that always clung to her after the initial visit to a murder scene and put on her detective face.

The workers had moved away from the door. Three now sat huddled together around the first table to the right of the entrance. The tall kid Janeece knew as Reggie Lynx stood by the cash register, idly tapping out a rhythm on the countertop. She acknowledged those in the booth before looking over the dining area, noting the caution cones warning *Piso Mojado*. Wet floor indeed. "Where's Xandra?" she said.

Reggie pointed toward the back of the store. "She's shutting down the fryers. We are going to close for tonight, right?"

Terl rolled her eyes as she moved closer to the counter. Someone whispered *Yes*. There was the sound of high fives. "It's not going to be business as usual, if that's what you're asking, but before you leave, I need to speak with each of you."

"Knew it," a girl's voice whined. Janeece approached the group, turning to the male employee. "What's your name, sir?"

"Carson. Carson Smith." He picked up his drink and followed her to a booth away from the others. In his late twenties, Smith wore a wedding band, a cross on a chain around his neck, and a Steelers tee under his uniform shirt. He didn't have much to offer, only that he had wondered what was taking Xandra so long to throw away the trash when the line to the drive-thru window stretched around the building.

"You're certain you saw nothing out of the ordinary during your shift?" Terl narrowed her eyes. Carson sipped until the cup rattled empty.

"I've only worked here two weeks," he said. "I'm in training for a management position."

Writing down his address and phone number, Janeece dismissed him and motioned the younger teenager over. Emilia Cleary cracked her gum, blonde ponytail swaying as she peppered her answer with *like* and *you know*. Terl went through the same questions she had asked Carson. What time did you arrive at work? What was your job? Did you leave at any time? Did you see anything out of the ordinary or unusual during the shift? Emilia's responses were as noncommittal as Carson's. Basically, the girl was clueless about almost everything.

The third employee, Brenda Wittington, spoke next, but her position at the drive-thru window meant she had no clear view of the back of the restaurant or the trash shed. She did remember Paul Loving stopping by around five or six o'clock. He spoke to Xandra but spent more time with Reggie, Brenda recalled, even inviting the teen outside to sit in Loving's new Cadillac, a recent addition to the vintage car collection the man stored in a warehouse on Pioneer Boulevard. By the time Janeece called Reggie over, her throat was dry. "Xandra," she called, "can you bring over some water while I talk to Mr. Lynx?"

Xandra moved from the fryers to the pop machine. Reggie scuffed his way to the detective's table, hands in pockets, shoulders hunched. Xandra placed two drinks on the table and returned to tidying the cooking area. Snatching one of the cups, Reggie slumped against the back of the booth.

"I didn't do anything wrong." His immediate denial sent up a signal the detective couldn't ignore.

"Why so defensive?"

"Because I know what you're going to say when I tell you where I went on my break."

"Do you?"

"It ain't what you think."

"Well, let's find out. Take me through the timeline from when you arrived at work."

The kid sank deeper into the booth as he recounted his movements from three o-clock on. When he stopped talking, Terl nodded. "So, you left the Buns N Fries on your break. Where did you go?"

"I went to sit in Mr. Loving's new Caddy. And I only delivered the envelope to his sister because he threatened to fire me if I didn't."

"You took an envelope to Reverend Loving so you wouldn't lose your job," she repeated. Reggie nodded. Janeece shifted closer to him. "Where did you go?"

Reggie squirmed. "To the dinner theater. She was standing outside with a group of city biggies. They were celebrating something."

"Do you remember who was with her?"

"No. Well, maybe. The mayor was there, and some dude in a fancy suit. He looked rich."

"But you don't know who he was?" Reggie picked at the faux-wood tabletop. Janeece sipped her water. "What kind of envelope did you take to the Reverend??"

Reggie shrugged. "A long, white one."

"Business size, then." When he nodded, she went on. "When you gave her the envelope, where were you?"

"Outside, at the end of the covered walkway. She told the other people to go on in."

"What did Reverend Loving do when you gave her this envelope?"

"She gave it back."

"She refused to accept it?"

Reggie fiddled with his cup. "Yeah, well, she asked me to burn it."

Janeece Terl looked up from her notes. "Do you know what was in the envelope?"

The boy rubbed his hands over his thighs, glanced around the dining room, sipped more water. "Not then I didn't."

"So, when did you know, Reggie?"

"When I opened it, before I came back inside."

"And?"

"There was money inside. A whole lot of money. So, I, um, didn't burn it."

"Okay, you didn't burn the contents. What happened to the envelope?"

Reggie reached in his pocket, pulled out a stack of bills bound with a bank tab, and set it in front of the detective. Janeece Terl leaned closer to inspect the words scrawled on the tab, but she didn't touch the money. "Did you write this?"

"No, ma'am, and I got no clue what *Bait* means. Mr. Loving's strange, you know?" Reggie shrugged.

"What did you do with the envelope?"

"I threw it away."

"Did you throw it in the trash bins inside the fence?"

"Yeah, and my fingerprints are on the lid, but I didn't do anything wrong except keep those." He started to stand. "I was going to give them back when Mr. Loving returned, but he never did."

"Sit down, Reggie." Janeece waited for the boy to settle. "If I look in the trash, will I find this envelope?"

"No." His head dropped lower. "It's not there anymore. I-I changed my mind and burned it. On the slab. Rubbed out the ashes with my shoe."

"Why did you do that?"

"I don't know."

Xandra approached the booth. She rested a hand on Reggie's shoulder. A look passed between them. "It's all right, Reg. I know why."

"Don't, X."

"All right, Miss Byrd." The detective turned to Xandra. "Why did Reggie burn the envelope?"

"He was trying to protect me."

"Do you need to be protected?"

"Maybe. Mr. Loving asked me first to take the money to the Reverend. I said no, but my prints were on the envelope, too."

Terl rolled a finger over her lips. Xandra peeked at Reggie, angry about the lie he'd told and that she hadn't called him on. She fingered the money on the table, money that hadn't been in the envelope but rather in the register that Reggie Lynx worked.

Four

Satisfied she had gotten enough from the other employees for the night, Detective Terl gave them permission to leave. Xandra escorted her co-workers to the door, then slid the bolt home and pulled down the shade. She returned to the booth and Terl's inquisitive stare.

"Reggie seems a little squirrelly and a lot defensive." Janeece ruffled the pages of her notebook. "Is he telling the truth about what happened?"

Startled, Xandra stared at the detective. Was Terl that good at detecting bullshit? "I never thought he was a liar, but he might be stretching things a bit."

"Why do you say that?"

Xandra stared out the window. "I don't know what Loving sent to his sister, but it wasn't money. The envelope was too thin for that."

Terl watched Reggie race from the building like zombies were chasing him. "Do you know something about the money?"

The sounds of the restaurant ticked in the silent space between Xandra and the detective: the buzz and hum of the overhead lights, the electronic murmurings of the ice cream and drink machines, the occasional burps of ovens cooling. "He took it from the register." She cocked her head toward the counter. "But he didn't write that on the binding."

"Good to know. You think someone left that for him?" Xandra shrugged and the detective went on. "Is Lynx a good worker?"

"Most of the time, but not lately. He's been distracted, even at school. We just handed in a big research paper, and we're supposed to be working on a group presentation, although he isn't doing much with that." Xandra slid lower on the bench and folded her hands. Her earrings caught the overhead light, reflecting iridescent shards across the tabletop. "Why?"

"I'm sure you've already figured that out, X, but for the record, you are not a suspect at the moment, just a witness."

"For the moment."

Janeece ignored the comment. "Here's what I know. Despite the events of three years ago, your teenage escapades are ancient history. As far as the law is concerned, you're clean. Now nineteen, you're studying criminal justice at Sinclair Community College."

"I finished my first year in May."

"In addition to being a full-time student, you manage the three to eleven shift here. That's a heavy schedule, lots of responsibility. Doesn't leave much time for mischief, right?" Janeece smiled. Xandra recognized her attempt to remove the accusation from her statement and smiled back.

"I work so I can pay my tuition. My parents said I didn't have to, but," Xandra spread her hands, "they didn't raise me, you know. I don't expect anything from them. This is my life, and school's my responsibility."

"You think they don't owe you anything?" Janeece steepled her fingers under her chin as she watched the girl shove the hurt from their abandonment down deeper. "Okay, walk me through this evening, especially the part about Paul Loving and the delivery."

"I'm the night manager. I work three to closing, but I usually get here early, around 2:30. There's always a rush after school lets out, so I work the counter while the first shift closes out their registers. Then it gets slow until the moms bring their kids by after practices. This time of year, it's baseball, some soccer. Thursdays are always busy, no matter what's going on. Anyway, Brenda and Carson and Reggie clocked in at three. Emilia's always ten minutes late because she comes straight from the high school and there are always traffic problems. Today we were slammed right before Mr. Loving came by. When he pulled me off the fryers and told me I had to take this envelope to his sister over at the dinner theater, I said no, told him I couldn't leave." Xandra twisted her rings. "I don't know what he was thinking. We were short-handed as it was."

"Short-handed?"

"One of our recent hires didn't show. She didn't call in either, but then she rarely does." Xandra chewed the inside of her cheek, uncertain how much to say about the employees, especially one who hadn't even been here tonight. "Anyway, Mr. Loving didn't like my answer and threatened to fire me, but then a busload of retirees came in and I couldn't talk to him anymore. That's when he cornered Reggie. The man is…difficult to work for."

"In what way?"

"I'm just sharing my observations, you understand."

"Don't hold back, Xandra."

"Well, he used to be more easy-going, even funny at times. He never questioned my work, but around the beginning of March, he started asking for text updates on who was working, what time they arrived and left, things like that. Then he asked me to take a picture of the end-of-the-day tally before I locked everything in the safe. He acted super stressed, suspicious, even."

"Hmm, suspicious. Interesting word. Did he not trust you?" Xandra shrugged. Janeece shifted in her seat. "So, what time did he confront you?"

"I'm not sure. Like I said, we were really slammed. Maybe five-thirty or six?"

"And how long was Reggie gone?"

"Again, because we were so busy, I'm not sure. Maybe fifteen minutes, but it could have been longer." Xandra recounted how she saw him cut in front of the cars waiting to order and disappear through the hedges that separated the restaurant from the theater parking lot. "He looked upset when he came back, but we didn't have time to talk about it."

"Did he sit in Mr. Loving's car?"

"Not that I saw, but I wasn't watching the entire time."

"Did anything else unusual happen tonight?"

Xandra adjusted the collar of her uniform shirt, thought through the afternoon and evening hours. "It was a typical Thursday except for the late delivery."

"What kind of delivery?"

"Our regular supplier drops off extra inventory Thursdays. It's standard stuff, paper goods like napkins and drink cups. Usually, the truck comes during the morning shift, but the driver said weather had delayed him. He showed up around maybe eight-fifteen. We haven't had time to put things away."

"What kind of truck?"

"A semi."

"Where does a truck that size park?"

"In the back. In front of the trash enclosure."

"How long did it take to unload the supplies?"

Xandra shrugged. "Twenty or thirty minutes? Again, I didn't really check the clock, but it must have been at least that long."

"Why is that?"

"Because I couldn't carry out the trash until the truck was gone. I can get you a copy of the invoice if it helps."

"That would be great." Terl pursed her lips, jotted down the possible timeline, then looked up. "Okay, tell me about finding the body."

Xandra closed her eyes, unable to repress a small shudder. "Maybe a little after nine, I collected the trash, stuffed everything into one bag, and went out the back door. Cars were lined up in the drive-thru, four or five scattered around the lot. The wind kept dragging the bag from my hand. I had to chase it twice before I reached the shed. After I opened the gate and tossed the trash, I saw her."

"Take a deep breath. You're doing fine." Terl waited for Xandra to settle before asking her next question. "It was dark inside the fence?"

"Darker than the lot. The overhead light next to the enclosure broke a few days ago. Maybe somebody busted it on purpose, I don't know. Anyway, Mr. Loving promised to fix it, but he must have forgotten. There is a solar-powered lamp mounted above the bins inside the fence. It comes on at night, but it doesn't put out much light." Xandra refolded her hands. "I leaned over to see if she was breathing. That's when I recognized her."

A knock at the door startled both women. Janeece got up to admit Pete Stone, who entered carrying a cell phone in one hand and two evidence bags in the other.

"Does this look familiar to you?" Stone placed one of the bags on the table, then stepped back to watch Xandra examine the contents. Janeece took the second bag from her partner as they waited for the girl to respond.

"What is that?" Xandra said.

"A dead bird." Stone smoothed the plastic. "It was inside Loving's jacket pocket."

"A bird?" Xandra's words echoed in the empty restaurant. Stone waited for his partner to weigh in. When she didn't, he folded his arms and leaned against the wall. Xandra threw up her hands. "That's weird, isn't it? And I saw two vultures, when I went outside tonight. They were circling above the trash cans. Maybe they knew Reverend Loving was down there."

"It's all right to be upset, Xandra. Breathe." Janeece pointed at the evidence. "Any idea what kind of bird this is? Pete?"

"Rather than speculate, I'll wait for the experts to weigh in. So, Miss Byrd, any idea why Reverend Loving would have a bird on her?" Stone's question hung between them.

"No," Xandra said. "But she also had something in her hand. Detective Terl saw it. Is that what's in the other bag?"

"Looks like the same scrap of paper," Janeece said. "So, I'll ask you again, did you touch or read it?"

"No."

Stone tapped his foot, adding another echo in the empty restaurant. "Anything else you can tell us, Miss Byrd?"

Xandra kept her hands on the table and her legs still, all too aware of the bird pin nestled in the pocket of her jeans. "I...no. But I know what you're thinking."

"What's that?" Janeece returned her attention to the young woman.

"You're making a suspect list." Xandra ticked names off her fingers. "Paul Loving. Reggie Sands. And me, Xandra Byrd."

Five

The moon rode a thin layer of clouds as Xandra turned into the driveway and parked on the slab her father had added to accommodate his teenage drivers. She clamped down the horror of the evening's events and shuffled in through the garage door. Her brother lay on the couch, a can of soda between his knees, a rerun of last year's college football championship game playing on the big screen. Ignoring his greeting, she hung her keys on a hook in the laundry room, slipped off her shoes, and liberated a beer from the refrigerator.

"Hey!" J.J. called. "You allowed to drink now?"

Xandra took a swallow from the bottle before perching on the arm of the sofa. "It's been …a shitty day."

J.J. sat up. "You look strange. What's up?"

She tugged on an earring before plopping down next to an empty bowl resting where her brother's feet had been. She dipped a finger into the salt grains at the bottom and licked them off. "You eat all the pretzels?"

"Not all of them. Uh, beer, X?"

"Tonight is an exception to the no-beer-until-you're-legal rule. The parents asleep?"

"They're in their room. Not sure they're sleeping." J.J. wiggled his eyebrows.

"Gross! TMI." Despite the unease pulling at her, Xandra snorted. Thinking of your parents as sexual beings almost felt like a taboo, even though the connection that had resurfaced between Joe and Leah over the last three years appeared genuine. Her chest tightened. Why didn't they love each other enough from the beginning? Why didn't they keep her then? Oh, she knew the story, how her mother, terrified and young and unsure of the brief but intense relationship with Joe, hid her

21

pregnancy from him, went away to have the baby, and put her up for adoption. How Joe insisted he would have made different decisions in his life had he known. Present circumstance erased past history, her mother believed. Joe agreed. Xandra wasn't so sure. She tried to accept it, but the fact remained that if he had married Leah, she would have been theirs from birth. There would have been no crazy adoptive mother, no lost years. Of course, had they acknowledged her from the start, there would have been no J.J. either. Xandra's thoughts always tangled on that reality. She had always wanted siblings, and she did love her half-brother and the sister they now shared. She sipped the beer and dismissed the slide toward self-pity. "What about Olivia? Did she go to sleep without a fight?"

"Three-year-old's are tyrants. I had to read *Sam I Am* five times before she let me turn off the light." J.J. finished his soda and placed the can next to a set of drawings littering the coffee table.

Xandra toed the papers. "I thought you weren't taking any summer classes?"

"And you'd be right. These aren't for a class." His words turned reverent. "Doris Loving asked me to work up a plan for that land behind the church. She wants to turn the property into an outdoor labyrinth, an arboretum, and a bird sanctuary, and, get this, she wants to add a natural burial site. You know, for people who want to turn into trees after they die."

"Reverend Loving?" Xandra swiped at the beer dribbling down her chin and sat up straighter. "J.J., when did you last talk to her?"

Her brother swept his dark hair off his forehead and twisted it into a manbun. His high-school-cute features had morphed into university handsome, and his keen ability to read people had deepened. Swinging his feet off the couch, he leaned his elbows on his thighs.

"Your hands are shaking. What's up, X?"

She took several more swallows before she spoke. "I found a dead body by the trash bins behind the restaurant."

"No shit? Tonight?" He touched her knee. "What did you do?"

"Called the police. That's why I'm so late. Janeece Terl questioned everybody, including me. She knows the Reverend and I have a history."

"Well, our whole family has a history with the woman. But what's Doris Loving got to do with a dead guy?"

"It wasn't a dead guy, J.J." Xandra took a deep breath. "It was Reverend Loving."

"Wait, what?" J.J. stared into space. "That's impossible. I just saw her, like, at noon. We walked the forest, and she explained her ideas. Besides, everyone loves her. Who would kill her?"

"That's what I want to know." Xandra lifted her hips off the couch to dig in her pocket. "She's the kindest woman I've ever met, and she never made me feel like I didn't belong."

"Damn it." J.J. inspected the drawings. "I needed...what's going to happen to the project?"

"I'm so sorry, J.J. I don't know what to tell you."

He punched the couch cushions. "Man, I'll have to take a second job after all. Grunder's Landscaping has been begging me to come back part-time. Crap on a cracker, there goes any hope for a social life this summer."

The desperation in her brother's words unsettled her. Xandra chewed a fingernail, unsure what to say next. Finally, she spoke. "There's something else, J.J. I found this by her body."

She opened her hand. In her palm rested a silver pin in the shape of a bird in flight. J.J. reached for it, then drew back. He stared at the object smeared with blood, then looked up.

"That's one of the souvenirs Mom bought when we took that trip to Hinckley in March."

"It is." Xandra flipped the pin over. "Remember how Olivia insisted we put our initials on the back so no one would confuse them?"

J.J. peered at the twin j's scratched into the surface. "That's mine."

"Yeah, it is." Panic squeezed at her, but she had to ask, had to know. "J.J., how did your pin wind up beside the body of a dead woman?"

Six

Sleep, it seemed, would not be happening tonight. The image of Reverend Loving lying in a pool of blood with a dead bird tucked inside her jacket kept intruding every time Xandra closed her eyes. She couldn't shake the guilt associated with taking her brother's pin from the scene. Of course, there could be a good explanation for how the pin ended up by the body. It may have been dropped there days before the Reverend was killed. Maybe he showed or gave it to her and just didn't remember doing so. Or Loving could have purchased one like theirs, but why would she? No, this pin belonged to J.J. The initials on the back proved that. The only conclusion that made sense also made the least sense. The pin had been deliberately placed by the body. However, as far as Xandra knew, no one outside the family had access to the pin. She curled into a ball, trying to convince herself that she had done the right thing. J.J. wasn't capable of murdering anyone. If someone was trying to implicate him in the crime, she needed to find out who…and why. And what was going on with Reggie? He had lied about the money, which hadn't been in the envelope. He'd taken it from the restaurant, so he was a liar and a thief. But when had he done that? And why? Questions circled her head like the vultures at the crime scene.

After ninety minutes of tangling in the bedcovers, she got up and logged on to the computer to check her class assignments. Summer sessions were shorter and more condensed, the pace brutal. She had five chapters to read for her humanities elective, a performance evaluation in Peace Officer Training, and a group presentation to organize for Criminology. Reggie was in the Soc 2226 class with her, and they usually studied together. She checked the emails and chats to see if he had sent a message. Nothing popped up. He had been acting weird tonight, nervous, eager to leave, strange reactions from a kid who wanted to be a cop. Well, enough stewing over Reggie. Xandra opened the file on the project, rearranged a few responsibilities, and sent a revised plan to the group. She was reaching for the off button when a new email popped up from her English Comp II instructor, August Penderson. It must be important if he was awake this time of night.

Ms. Byrd: Please see me during office hours this morning. I have a concern about your research paper. Professor P.

What the hell? She had turned that assignment in last week, complete with footnotes and citations. It was a good paper. Joe had pronounced it solid. Leah had checked for grammar and punctuation errors. Confused by the note, she agreed to meet at ten a.m. and closed the screen. Still unsettled, she opened a textbook to read about the Ohio penal code. Three pages in, her eyes drooped. She burrowed into the blankets, only to startle awake when her cell phone chimed at 5:40 a.m. The events of the past hours stacked themselves one on top of the other. Unable to shake off the anxious feeling, she scrolled to the message.

meet me Beck Park Overlook asap need help

Xandra recognized the number as one Reggie had given her to use if she couldn't reach his cell. Why wasn't he using his own phone? Shifting the curtain over the window, she stared into the backyard. Wind rustled through the willows along the fence, rippling the surface of the koi pond Joe had installed for Leah. Although the past three years hadn't been easy, her parents, long separated by fate and circumstance, had found their way back to each other and built a life together, one of which included a water garden with fish. Resentment warred with guilt. Xandra wanted to believe she had a place in their hearts now, in their lives, but she still had moments when she wanted to run back to West Virginia, to the place she once called home, and to Vander Byrd, the man she'd called Dad. Mimaw, the grandmother who had been her lifeline, was gone now, as was the home where they'd lived, burned to ashes by the woman who could never accept Xandra as her own. But running was no longer an option. Despite misgivings, she felt connected to her brother and sister, responsible for her role in their happiness. Her sense of duty outweighed the homesickness, eased the tug of the past. Everyone was trying hard to make this blended family work. They had each pledged not to give up or turn away. Reverend Loving had offered help to all of them and provided counsel as they struggled to find their bearings. Now that the woman was gone, Xandra wondered if all the progress her family had made would evaporate.

Her cell chimed again. Reggie, insistent, practically begging. **X where r u?** Xandra dragged on shorts and a sweatshirt, laced her tennis shoes, and pocketed the phone.

The house slumbered. She peeked into Olivia's room. The girl slept sprawled across her *Frozen* bedspread, blonde curls pasted to her forehead, a copy of the Dr. Seuss book J.J. had read to her clutched in one hand. The nightlight, Xandra's gift for her second birthday, swirled bands of colored light across the ceiling. She blew her sister a kiss before hurrying to unlock the back door and scamper across the lawn. Dew soaked the toes of her sneakers. An animal rustled in the hedge beyond the trees at the back of the property. Crossing her fingers that she didn't startle a skunk, Xandra considered her options before deciding against taking her car. The faulty muffler would announce her departure to the entire neighborhood. Instead, she liberated J.J.'s mountain bike from the storage shed and pedaled out of the development.

A half-mile beyond the City Limits sign separating Hopewell and Springboro, Xandra turned onto Pioneer Boulevard, raced down the bike lane, and coasted into the parking lot of E. Milo Beck Park. Eighty-five acres that once comprised a sizeable farmstead, the natural preserve slumbered in the pre-dawn dark. Fog hugged the winding banks of Pleasant Run Creek as the waterway murmured beyond the trees. Among the shadows that enveloped the overlook area, Xandra spotted a figure slumped against the brick wall that guarded the steep slope leading down to the park itself. She leaned the bike against one of the support beams for the pergola and took two cautious steps forward.

"Reggie?" When the figure didn't move, she wondered if she'd made a mistake in coming. Prepared to run, she called his name again.

The figure turned. In a sudden flare of moonlight, Xandra realized that it wasn't Reggie who waited in the dark. Shorter and heavier, Stuart

Lynx, Reggie's younger brother stumbled toward her. She folded her arms and hissed. "What are you doing here?"

"Xandra." Stuart held out a hand. "It's all right. I'm not here to scare you."

"Don't come any closer, Stu." She pulled out her cell and placed her thumb on the 0911 button. "Where's Reggie?"

"He's... somewhere else."

She backed away. "Why are you here? Why did you send me that text?"

"Look." He put up both hands, palms open. "No weapons, no bad intentions. I learned my lesson in juvie and I'm not looking to go back. I just have a message to deliver."

A breeze drifted over her, fluttering the ends of her hair. "You're wasting my time. I need to talk to your brother."

Stuart took another step closer. "You know he saw Reverend Loving tonight...I mean, last night. She asked him to tell you something."

"Right, like I believe that." Xandra settled onto the bike. Stuart grabbed the handlebars. "Stuart. Let go."

He backed off, arms shaking. "Please, X. I need you to listen. It's important."

"If it's so important, why can't Reggie tell me himself?"

"Because." Stuart's voice shook. "The police are looking for him, and they're not the only ones."

"Why do the police want Reggie?"

"They want to arrest him for murder." Stuart cocked his head, listening to the land stir as light crept over the horizon.

"Who else is after him?"

"I can't tell you that, but I swear it's true. You have to believe me."

"No, I don't."

"I'm not lying, Xandra. The cops came to the house, like, an hour ago. Reggie took off while Grandma and I kept them talking. But he made me promise to tell you what the Loving woman said."

"Why didn't he say something earlier when we were still at work?"

"He was scared, and he didn't think it meant anything. Now he does."

"Fine." Xandra jerked the bike from Stuart's grip. "Tell me."

Stuart glanced around. His arms twitched, then wrapped around his middle. "Loving said to tell you birds of a feather fly together."

"What the hell does that mean?"

"I don't know." He shifted from one foot to the other. A car passed along Lower Springboro Road, heading west toward Hopewell. It slowed as it approached the park entrance, then continued down the hill. Stuart waited for it to disappear before he spoke again. "I'm out of here. Just remember what I said. And don't trust anyone."

The lights of a vehicle washed over the fence along the road, illuminating the entrance to the park. "Go!" Stuart yelled. Ignoring the path down to the parkland below, he vaulted the wall and, arms flailing, scrambled down the steep slope. Xandra flattened herself against the damp grass. As soon as the car passed, she mounted and pedaled out the entrance. The roadway was empty. She raced down the bike lane on Pioneer, skidding to a stop to drag the bike behind a hedgerow that bordered the lawn of the DayCon Medical Arts Building. The same vehicle that had passed twice before, an outsize, dark-colored SUV, returned, coasting up the road and into the park. Headlights swept the lot. The driver exited the vehicle, scanned the overlook, then proceeded to motor slowly up the boulevard. Xandra hugged the grass again, hoping her dark clothing would hide her from the car's occupants.

Once the taillights disappeared down the road, she doubled back to Milo Beck, hoping to catch Stuart and finish the conversation. From the overlook, she watched wisps of thick white fog rise to hide the prairie and the path along the streambed. If Stuart was hiding by the water, no one would see him. Remounting the bike, she turned left out of the park and coasted down the Clearcreek-Franklin connector before veering right into Hopewell. Her legs shook. She wiped her muddy palms on her shorts. Straining to balance on the narrow berm, she approached the subdivision. At her back, the rising sun angled through the trees, illuminating the carcass of a deer along the side of the road. She slowed, then dropped the bike on the gravel to place a hand on the animal's flank, still warm but not pulsing with life. A shadow slid by overhead and passed on. Xandra looked up. In the sky, a vulture circled lower, anticipating a chance to feed.

Seven

The sun stretched pink fingers through the fist of clouds, pushing away the night. Morning emerged in Hopewell Hills, and the neighborhood yawned to life. Sprinklers whirred. Across the street from the Zetts's home, Mr. Spruce putzed around in his garage, the sound of tapping a clue that he was framing another noir film poster. Xandra spotted her family through the sliding doors that opened from the deck to the kitchen. She stashed the bike in the shed and went inside.

"Xandie!" Olivia reached out with oatmeal-covered hands. J.J. frowned, telegraphing his concern. Leah lifted an eyebrow as she sipped coffee from the mug she had purchased in Hinckley. Xandra shuddered at the *Vultures Clean Up Well* motto printed on the side.

"Alexandra." Joe pulled out a chair. "We need to talk."

Xandra acknowledged her father's request, but she didn't sit down. "I have to change." She hurried down the hall to her bedroom, dropped her muddied shorts in the hamper, wriggled into a clean pair of jeans and yesterday's tee, then washed her face and hands in her bathroom. She inhaled, held her breath, exhaled to the count of ten. Calm restored, she returned to the kitchen. Ignoring her parents' stares, she scooped granola into a bowl and added milk. She dropped a tea bag in a cup and settled onto a bar stool. It occurred to her that this was the first time this month the family had all been together for breakfast.

"Why are you up?" J.J. poured a glass of orange juice and set it by her place. "You should still be in bed. We all should."

"Why aren't you?" Xandra spoke around a mouthful of almonds and oats.

"Joe." J.J. aimed his spoon at Dad's head.

"Don't call me Joe." Her father carried his empty plate to the sink. "Where have you been, Alexandra?"

"I couldn't sleep." Xandra spooned more cereal into her mouth, buying time. "I went for a ride."

"On my bike." J.J. narrowed his eyes. "You never do that."

Her father rested a hand on her shoulder. "J.J. and I are off to Caesar's Creek Flea Market on a fishing expedition."

"A new client?" When Joe nodded, she frowned. "You're taking J.J. with you?"

"Someone has to keep me company, so, yeah. You could come, too." Joe waited for her to respond. When she didn't, he shrugged. "I'm not leaving until you tell me what happened last night and where you were this morning. My house, my rules, daughter."

Leah leveled an intense stare at her before she settled Olivia on one hip. She juggled her briefcase and keys with her free hand, tension evident in the set of her shoulders. "I have to get going," her mother said, "or I'll be late dropping Livvie off at daycare, and I have a meeting with the school board in half an hour. You can tell me about your adventure tonight."

Her mother's need to regain the respect she'd lost during the kidnapping incident three years ago resonated with all of them. Xandra's involvement in Olivia's disappearance and return had uncovered many secrets. They all carried significant guilt and remorse. Leah had suffered the most when some members of the community judged her unfit to be a mother and, therefore, not an appropriate leader of a high school. The Hopewell Board of Ed had insisted she take a leave of absence, then released her from her contract. Luckily, the neighboring Franklin School District had a vacancy at the junior high, one they had been unable to fill. The new job had proven beneficial for Xandra and J.J., who no longer had to endure comments from other students regarding their connection to the disgraced principal.

"You could go with your father, Alexandra. Some time off would do you good."

"I can't," Xandra mumbled. "I have a meeting, too."

Leah rattled the keys, but she didn't push for more information. "Are you okay?"

"I'm fine." Leah asked that every day, her attempt to show she cared. Joe relieved Leah of the briefcase and took her mother's elbow.

"Let it go, Lee. We'll all talk later." He escorted his wife and child to the garage. When he returned, he speared Xandra with his best interrogative look. "Now, tell me about last night first. Then you can fill us in on this morning's adventure."

With a quick glance at her brother, she emptied her bowl before relating the events of the previous evening – finding the body, talking with Janeece, what the others saw or didn't see. She didn't mention the pin.

"So, you spoke to Janeece and the new guy, Pete Stone. What about this morning?" Her father crossed his arms. "Where were you?"

"I'm not ready to talk about it yet," she said.

"Alexandra," Joe laid a hand on her shoulder, "secrets can be toxic. I thought you learned that lesson already."

"Don't push, Dad," J.J. said.

Joe held up a finger to forestall his son. "You know I'm right. Are you sure you don't want to talk about it now?"

Xandra set her empty mug and bowl in the sink. She sighed. "I need more time."

Her father steepled his fingers under his chin. "Don't take too long, daughter. Secrets are like wounds. They fester when they sit too long unaired. You sure you won't come with us?"

"I can't."

After her father and J.J. left, she rinsed the dishes and loaded the dishwasher. She lingered over Leah's mug, rubbing her thumb over the logo. *Vultures clean up well.* Was it all just a coincidence? Remembering Reverend Loving's message, Stuart's cryptic warning, the birds overhead at the crime scene, Xandra decided the saying wasn't always true.

Eight

The parking ramp of Sinclair's Parking Garage wound up to the fourth level, the muffler on Xandra's Civic rumbling at each turn. Promising herself to stop by Gerspacher's Garage soon, she pulled into a space near the stairs, scampered down two flights, and crossed the covered walkway into Sinclair Community College. Renovation work had closed off the usual walkways, forcing her to detour up a flight, then down and around several bends until she reached the floor where the media center dominated the central area. From there, she took the hallway to Professor Penderson's office, passing several classrooms before she reached his room. Bracing a hand against the wall, she squared her shoulders and took a deep breath.

The door to Penderson's room stood open, displaying the overflow of books and student papers that were a fixture of every teacher's space. Xandra knocked, then leaned into the tiny office. The professor looked up, his ubiquitous yellow Oxford shirt as rumpled as ever, and waved her in. She perched on a high-backed wooden chair opposite his padded swivel seat. Her flight or fight reflexes kicked in when she spotted two folders on the desk. Her non-fiction report on the Rhonda Richey murder investigation rested on top, a note bearing a question mark in heavy black ink attached to the outside. Penderson tapped his fingers on the folder, then handed it over.

"Miss Byrd. Thank you for meeting me so promptly."

"My grades are very important to me." She held up the report. "Is there something wrong with my research?"

"Actually, no. The research is solid. I have another concern, and not a minor one." Penderson shuffled the papers on the desk, then picked up the second folder. "This is the paper Reggie Lynx submitted. It seems that your work and his have more than a few similarities. Can you explain how the same phrases and sentences show up in both papers?" Xandra handed over her report and he laid the folders side by side. Using a highlighter to mark her paper, he scored the similar lines in Reggie's work. Xandra leaned forward to examine the sections he'd selected.

"That's not possible. We wrote about different topics."

"So I thought, but I assure you, Miss Byrd, that not only is it possible, it appears certain. Reggie Lynx submitted a paper identical to yours."

"I swear," Xandra fisted her hands on her knees to hide their trembling, "the research and the paper are my work and mine alone. Reggie told me he was working on the case involving Officer Roger DeFiles."

Penderson frowned. "Curious, then, isn't it, that he handed in an account of the Richey case that mirrors almost word for word the information in your paper?"

Xandra stood up so fast the chair fell over behind her. If the college accused her of plagiarism, she would be thrown out of the program, even dismissed from Sinclair itself. Her goal of becoming a peace officer would die before it had a chance to come true. She rested a hand on the desk.

"I don't cheat. Ever."

"Please sit down, Miss Byrd." He waited for her to resettle the chair. When she was seated again, he folded his hands over the accusatory pages. "As it happens, I am inclined to believe you. But the evidence says otherwise."

"Please, Professor," Xandra blinked back tears, "what can I do?"

"Well, I have been unable to contact Mr. Lynx, so, for starters, do you know where he is?"

Xandra glanced at the posters of classic mystery films, *Black Orchid, Psycho, Blade Runner,* decorating Penderson's walls. She inspected her nails, frowned at the peeling polish, the ragged thumbnails. She checked her phone to see if Reggie had responded to her texts. "I have no idea. I haven't seen or heard from him since last night after he talked to the police."

"The police?"

"Yes." Xandra met his gaze. "There was an incident at the restaurant where we work. Someone left a dead body by the trash bins. I found her."

Penderson toyed with his pen, then tossed it aside. "That's ... disturbing, but not relevant at the moment. Did Mr. Lynx have access to your research?"

"Not that I'm aware of. He did ask to see my final draft to be sure he was formatting his correctly." She raised a thumb to her mouth, dropped it back in her lap. "I'm so stupid."

"Do you believe Mr. Lynx copied your work?"

"He must have."

The professor sighed. "Well, given the egregious nature of the plagiarism, I'm afraid I must send you to the chair of the department. Professor Pierce will determine what, if anything further, is to be done."

Xandra resisted the urge to see a conspiracy at work, but it was unavoidable. Someone tried to frame her brother for murder. Someone was trying to get her kicked out of school. So not a coincidence. While Penderson contacted the chair of the department, she scrolled her phone, checking the dates she had contacted sources and when she finished the draft. Her mom and dad would vouch for her, she was certain, but they were family. Everyone expected them to take her side. The professor bobbed his head as he scribbled instructions on a notepad. When he hung up, Xandra leaned forward. The instructor handed over the note.

"Dr. Pierce is stopping by her office tomorrow before leaving for a conference. She will see you at eleven o'clock. I will send copies of the papers to her prior to the meeting. In the meantime, you really should try to find Reggie. The young man is in serious jeopardy of suspension or dismissal."

"Thank you, sir." Xandra crumpled the note and shoved it into her pocket, where it rasped against the bird pin. "I'll be there, and I'll do my best to find Reggie."

She hurried back through the renovation maze to the car, trailing curses. Last night, Reggie had lied to the police about what was in the envelope Mr. Loving gave him. He'd attempted to steal money from the restaurant. And he'd copied her work to pass off as his own. The guy she considered a friend turned out to be a thief and a liar. "You son of a bitch, Lynx," she said to his phone photo. "You owe me big time, now." Her cell rang. Hoping it was Reggie, she answered before the call could go to voice mail.

"Xandra? Detective Terl. We need you to come to the station this afternoon for a formal statement. Can you be here by two?"

"I have work at three," Xandra countered.

"Not today you don't. The Buns N Fries is still officially a crime scene. See you at two."

Phone in hand, Xandra stared at the city of Dayton skyline, feeling like a rabbit on the run from an unseen predator.

Nine

Xandra inked in the Saturday appointment with Professor Pierce on the calendar in her room. Then she collected dirty linens from the bedrooms and started the laundry. The chore kept her mind off the hearing with Pierce as well as the looming interview with the police. She wondered how hard Detective Terl would press her. Over the past three years, Janeece had been a welcome visitor to their home, especially after her promotion to detective. Joe served as a sounding board for the various cases she was working on. And Xandra liked Janeece. She admired the woman's persistence and determination to succeed in what had been a man's domain for a long time. In fact, Xandra hoped to snag a mentorship with the female detective. Now, Reggie may have stolen that dream, too. What a disaster, made worse by the fact that Xandra had been the one to find the body, had taken evidence from the scene. But she didn't regret her action. The murder of Doris Loving made no sense, framing J.J. for it, even less. And the sheer logistics of the crime remained enigmatic. How did someone dump the body inside the fenced area without being seen? Why did they place it there and not back in the woods where it was less likely to be found? She pushed the run button on the washer and listened to the water filling the tub. Just as the cycle engaged, she heard the garage door roll up.

"Alexandra?" Her father's call rumbled down the hall moments later. Closing the pocket door to muffle the noise, Xandra joined him in the kitchen.

"You weren't gone very long. I thought you'd be on a day-long stakeout. And where's J.J.?"

"Right behind you." J.J. straggled in with a cooler, banging the wall as he muscled past her and headed toward the refrigerator.

"Did you catch anything on your 'expedition'?" Xandra reached around him to grab a container of leftover pizza.

"As a matter of fact, we did." Her dad dropped his ballcap on the counter and held up his camera. "Lots of photos. But today, our goal was strictly reconnaissance. I wanted to be back in time for your interview."

Xandra glanced at the clock on the stove, then slid the pizza into the microwave. "How do you know about that?"

"Janeece called me first. When do we leave?"

"She asked me to be there by two."

"Great. We have time to eat and discuss your statement."

"I don't need a chaperone, Dad." She slid the heated slices onto three plates and set them on the table. "What do you want to drink?"

"I'm good." J.J. twisted off the cap on a root beer and slid into a chair. "And you should take Dad with you. It can't hurt."

"You want to come, too? Maybe I should ask Mom to bring Olivia. That's bound to make me look responsible."

Her brother threw up his hands. "Well, call me bad. Joe's just trying to help."

"Don't be so defensive, Alexandra." Joe Zetts eyed his lunch. "I thought you might appreciate a little support. Interviews can be intimidating."

"Yeah, you sound a little anxious." Her brother finished off his drink with a burp.

"Gross." Xandra joined them at the table. "I'm not upset about the interview. I had a meeting with Professor Penderson this morning. He accused me of cheating on my research paper."

Joe drummed his fingers against his plate. Her brother shook his head. "He doesn't know you, does he?"

"How well does anybody know anybody?" Xandra fingered the pin in her pocket. "It looks like Reggie stole my work and tried to pass it off as his own. He didn't even change the words. I'm beyond pissed."

Her father steepled his fingers beneath his chin. "Reggie's that kid you work with at the Buns N Fries? J.J., you know him, right?"

"We hang out sometimes." Her brother scooted closer. "Is that who you met this morning?"

"Who says I met anyone?"

"Process of deduction." Xandra rolled her eyes, but J.J. kept going. "You and Reggie are friends. He was working last night when you found Loving's body. This morning you took my bike, not your car, so you went somewhere close. And you're working with him on that group presentation, aren't you? It's a logical guess."

"He's your friend, too."

J.J. lowered his eyes. "We're not that close. You know him better than I do."

"You think? Because right now, I'm certain I never knew him at all, but, heck, maybe you should be studying criminology instead of landscape architecture." She glared at him. Joe patted her arm.

"Your brother's not entirely wrong, is he?" She shook him off. He leaned closer. "What did he want this morning?"

"I didn't meet Reggie. It was his brother Stuart. Said he had a message that Reggie got from Reverend Loving, something about birds flocking together. Didn't make any sense to me."

"What about Reggie?"

"I don't know where he is."

"Maybe he's hiding because he knows your prof found out about the paper." J.J. helped himself to a second slice of leftovers.

"It's possible, but I didn't see Penderson's email until this morning, and he only sent it last night, although he did say he tried to contact Lynx." Xandra began to chew a thumbnail, dropped her hand to her lap. "I think there's more to it than that."

"Alexandra, are you telling us everything?" Joe raised a hand to forestall her denial. "Okay, interview with Janeece first. By the way, does Stuart know where his brother is?"

"If he does, he wouldn't tell me."

Joe got up to clear the table. He shook his head over Xandra's uneaten lunch. When J.J. snatched her pizza and finished it off, her father sighed. "Fine, for now. You talk to the police. Then we'll look into Lynx's disappearance."

Returning to the refrigerator, Xandra grabbed a yogurt. She ate standing at the sink, Reggie's betrayal chipping away at the friendship she thought they'd shared. No wonder she had trust issues. She chugged a glass of lemonade and grabbed a notebook. If the detective was going to interrogate her, Xandra was going to record their talk. Janeece might reveal something that would help her piece together a reason why Reverend Loving ended up dead with J.J.'s pin by her side.

* * *

The glass panels fronting Hopewell's police station shimmered in the afternoon sun. Joe parked his work car, a nondescript compact with tinted windows, next to one of the police cruisers and escorted his daughter into the lobby. Local photographer Ron Levi's recent works decorated the walls, the over-large prints detailing the stark beauty and grandeur of the national parks of Arizona, Idaho, and Montana. Xandra gave her name to the officer behind the bullet-proof glass, then strolled from one print to the next, admiring the landscapes of the American west.

"I'd like to own one of these someday," Xandra said.

"Maybe you will." Joe paused in front of a shot of wild horses galloping past a sandstone outcropping. "I wouldn't mind having that one myself."

"Miss Byrd?" Janeece Terl interrupted their conversation, her greeting and demeanor formal. "Good to see you, Joe. You can wait in the lobby."

"I know Alexandra's not a minor, Janeece, but I'd like to sit in. I won't interfere, I promise."

The detective considered for a moment, then motioned them to follow her. Xandra trailed Janeece through the locked door and down the hall to the first room on the right. Terl's partner, Pete Stone, stood when they entered. He raised an eyebrow at Joe's presence, then left to drag in another chair before inviting Zetts and his daughter to sit. Janeece offered water or coffee. Xandra declined. Joe grimaced.

"That's one thing I don't miss about the job. Bad coffee."

"We've made some upgrades since you left," Pete said. "Thanks for coming in, Miss Byrd."

Janeece cleared her throat. "You're not a suspect at the present time, Xandra. However, you were the first witness at the crime scene. Anything and everything you remember may have a material bearing on solving the Reverend's murder. Now, we know Doris Loving was stabbed and that the killer placed or left her in the enclosure. I need you to walk us through the events of last night one more time. Don't leave anything out, no matter how insignificant it might seem. Ready?"

Xandra opened her notebook. Following the timeline she had reconstructed, she detailed her Thursday schedule: morning classes, an hour of research in the school library, work at two-thirty p.m.

"What, if anything, happened during your shift that seemed out of the ordinary?"

Xandra bit her lower lip. "Yes. Two things, actually. First, the normal delivery didn't arrive until eight o'clock or later."

"That's the semi that parked behind the restaurant, screening the fenced trash bins from the drive-thru and the building itself?"

"Yes."

"The boxes were taken in through the rear door?" Pete said.

"Yes. We intended to put everything away and break down the cardboard, but then, I found Reverend Loving."

"All right." Janeece turned a page. "Tell us what else happened that was unusual."

"The owner, Mr. Loving, stopped by sometime between five and six-thirty."

"Can you be more specific?"

"I'm sorry, I can't. We were really busy. One minute it was five, and the next I checked, an hour and a half had gone by."

Stone rested his elbows on the table and leaned toward her. "Why was Loving's visit unusual?"

"He rarely stops by during my shift. Since I'm the night manager, he expects me to run the restaurant in the evenings. He does come in on the weekends to make sure everything's in order and to check the receipts."

"How old are you, Miss Byrd?" Stone asked.

"Nineteen."

"That's a big responsibility for a young person." He exchanged a glance with Terl. "Are you also responsible for depositing the day's earnings at the bank?"

Xandra shook her head. "No. I lock the money in the safe. Mr. Loving opens it every morning and takes the previous day's receipts to the bank."

Terl scribbled a note, punctuated it with exclamation points, and passed it to Stone. "Okay, let's go on. What happened when Mr. Loving came to the restaurant?"

"He asked me how the night was going. I told him we were short-handed because one of the girls called off. He didn't act upset. I thought he would be when he saw how busy we were, but instead, he asked me to take an envelope to his sister at the dinner theater. I told him I couldn't leave. We argued about it, actually. That's when he asked Reggie Lynx to go outside and look at his new car."

Another exchange of glances between the detectives. Joe moved his chair closer to Xandra, but he didn't say anything.

"Did Reggie go with him?"

"Yes. I asked Mr. Loving not to take him, but they went anyway."

"How long were they gone?"

"I'm not sure. Mr. Loving must have left the property soon after they went outside. As for Reggie, I thought he was only gone fifteen minutes, but now I think that was wrong." Xandra looked at her notes. "I've gone over everything in my head a million times. I think it was more like forty minutes."

"That's a long time to look at a car."

"He didn't just look at the car." Xandra took a deep breath. "Mr. Loving made him take that envelope to Reverend Loving."

Detective Terl cocked her head. Her braids rustled as they slid to the side. "And you know this how?"

"Reggie told me, after I found the body and while we were waiting for the police to show up."

"Alexandra, do you know where Reggie Lynx is?"

Xandra tucked her hands into the sleeves of her cardigan and shook her head. "I don't have a clue."

The detectives checked their notepads. Joe inspected the ceiling.

"Reggie could be in trouble, Miss Byrd," Pete Stone finally said. "Maybe he saw something or knows something that puts him in danger. If so, we can protect him."

Xandra folded her hands on the table. "I don't know where he is."

"All right." Stone folded his hands. "When you discovered the Reverend's body, did you see a weapon of any kind? Anything that might provide clues to the identity of Doris Loving's attacker?"

Janeece followed Stone's questions with one of her own. "Xandra, when you entered the enclosure, did you notice anything on the ground? Did you kick anything or stumble?"

Out in the hall, shuffling feet and low voices announced the arrival of officers for the afternoon shift change. Xandra closed her eyes, thinking about J.J. and the pin and the possibility that her brother was involved in Loving's death. When she opened them, she looked directly at Detective Terl. "Not that I remember, and I didn't see anything resembling a weapon on or near the body."

"That's pretty definitive, Miss Byrd," Stone said. Joe stretched an arm across the back of his daughter's chair. The room grew thick with tension.

"All right." Janeece stood and stretched. "Let's take a break. You want anything to drink now? Joe? Xandra? Pete will get it." Stone left the room, returning with bottled water, a soda, and two cups of coffee. Joe made small talk while Xandra drank her water. The vulture pin poked her from the pocket of her jeans. She should tell them she found it, but the words refused to come. J.J.'s reputation, maybe his very life, depended on her making the right decision. So did her future. She inhaled the sweat and dust odors of the enclosed space and decided she would only reveal it after she talked with J.J. again. After she learned who had taken it from him and how it ended up beside the Reverend's dead body. She watched the officers in conversation with her father, their camaraderie evident in the relaxed set of their shoulders. She wanted to be part of that, to be one of them, yet here she was, concealing evidence from a crime scene. Stuart's warning at the park popped into her head. She decided to keep that a secret, too, until she could speak with Reggie. The detectives took their seats. Joe stood behind her, one hand resting on her shoulder. In that moment, she was glad of his presence.

"You ready to talk about Reverend Loving?" Janeece settled into a chair.

In slow and careful detail, Xandra related collecting the trash and dragging it out to the bins, how the gate banged closed, locking her in, how the shadows seemed to shift to reveal the Reverend's body.

"Did you touch her, Miss Byrd?" Stone said.

Xandra shook her head. "After I screamed, I crouched down to listen for breathing. Her chest never moved. Then Reggie called me from the drive-thru speaker, asking if I got lost. He couldn't leave the counter, so I stretched my hand over the gate to open the latch. Then I called 911."

"Alexandra, did you see anyone?" Joe spoke for the first time, his tone soft but determined.

"No. But the overhead light on the pole outside the fence is burned out. Only the sensor light on the fence by the bins is working, and it only illuminates a small area. If someone were hiding outside the fence, I wouldn't have seen them."

Janeece went over the rest of Xandra's initial statement, then ended the interview. Reminding the girl to call if she remembered anything more, the detective escorted them out. The day had heated up. Joe removed his jacket before they reached the car.

"You did good, Alexandra. How do you feel?"

She shrugged. The pin weighed on her, as did Reggie's disappearance. "Do you think they'll look for Reggie?"

"I would." Joe pulled onto Hopewell Pike and headed home. "Right now, he may be the last person to have seen Reverend Loving alive."

"Is he their main suspect?"

"Main suspect?" Joe rubbed his chin. "Maybe, but I'd say Paul Loving has a lot of explaining to do."

Ten

Back home, Xandra and Joe found J.J. asleep in his room. She needed to talk to him, but she didn't know how to do that without making him angry. Any suspicion she voiced could strain the bond they shared. But what if he knew more about the Reverend's last day than he was saying? She hated the doubts swirling in her head, so she let him rest while she considered what the loss of Doris Loving meant to him. It made no sense. J.J. had no reason to kill the woman. Unless she changed her mind at the last minute and canceled their contract? Would the Reverend do that? Unable to shake the uncertainty, Xandra retreated to her bedroom. She forced herself to work on the class project. Now that Reggie was gone, the group was down a member, which meant more work for her. Maybe she could ask the instructor to add someone to the team.

Down the hall, the click of the answering machine told her Joe was checking for messages related to his new PI business. When his phone chirped, He put it on speaker. "Joe Zetts Investigations. How can I help you?" A female voice spooled out, the words muffled, the anger shrill. Her father reassured the client he was working on her case, then came to Xandra's room to say he was going to wash her car. He turned away, patted the doorframe, turned back.

"You did well today, Alexandra. You were concise and thorough. If you recall anything else, remember any new detail, contact the detectives and let them handle it. Okay?"

"Got it." Xandra concentrated on the computer screen. Already he suspected she was holding something back. She stuck her hand in her pocket, felt the wings of the vulture press against her palm. "Do you want me to start dinner?"

Joe cocked his head. "That's the first time you've offered to do that in, oh, forever."

Xandra stood and stretched. "It's time I carried more weight around here."

"Hmm." He checked his watch. "It's four now. How about you put the casserole in at five? After I clean the car, I'm going to work on J.J.'s fishing gear."

"Not ready for prime time?" Xandra said. Her brother was notorious for tangling his reel whenever they went fishing together. Joe laughed, then banged his way into the garage, bucket and sponge in hand. She checked the oven temp on the recipe Leah had set out before heading to her brother's room. She couldn't wait any longer. They needed to talk.

"Hey, J.J." Xandra knocked before she opened the door. "You awake?"

When he mumbled permission, she pushed her way in, wading through the clothes scattered across the floor to stand by his desk. Her brother lay staring at the ceiling, the plans for Reverend Loving's land spread out on the bed. "Can we talk?"

He crumpled all the drawings against his chest and patted the comforter. "How'd it go with the police?"

"All right, I guess." Xandra flopped beside him, grabbed the plans, and examined each page. "These are amazing, J."

"Yeah? It's a beautiful dream, and a dead one, even before it gets off the ground. I thought this would be a good thing for my career. I mean, if I had a project completed before my sophomore year, how much weight would that carry? I even contacted one of my professors for his input. He offered to be my mentor."

"I'm so sorry, but maybe it will work out yet. The church is still interested, right?"

He opened one eye to stare at me. "The land doesn't belong to the church, X, it belongs, belonged to Reverend Loving. She told me it was part of her inheritance, that she hadn't gifted it to St. Francis yet. She wanted to surprise the congregation with a *fait accompli*, whatever the hell that means."

Xandra poked his chest. "Don't play dumb. You know perfectly well what that means. And the Reverend was smart. She must have a will, or maybe she wrote down her intentions somewhere."

"I doubt it will make any difference. I'm pretty sure her brother will inherit everything."

"Well, you can talk to him about her plan." Even as she said it, Xandra knew how unreal that sounded. Paul Loving could give a rat's ass about a labyrinth and an arboretum, and he certainly wouldn't want a living burial plot on prime real estate land. She fiddled with her rings, trying to tease free some gossip she'd overheard at the restaurant. Something the newest hire, Millie Stanfield, said about new houses and the planning board. Paul Loving served on that city committee, which meant he had a conflict of interest about the development. What a mess. "Okay, that was stupid of me. Duh. He wants to build houses there."

"It's okay." J.J. rolled onto his side and propped his head on one hand. "You meant well. And since I won't be getting paid for this plan, I need a second job. But screw that. What did you really want to talk about?"

Xandra held up the vulture pin. "This."

"You didn't tell the police you found it?"

"No, and I'm not going to until I know how your pin ended up next to a dead woman."

J.J. lurched forward, causing the headboard to bang against the wall as he stared at the pin, his eyes shiny with grief and despair. "I swear, X, I have no idea. The last time I remember seeing that was when I tossed it into my junk box. Maybe Olivia took it out and somehow lost it?"

"No. She can't reach the top shelf in your closet. That is where you keep the box, right?"

J.J. massaged his temples. "Yeah, but I took it out last week when I was looking for my hacky sack."

Xandra scooted next to her brother. "Are you sure it was last week? Was that when Reggie was here?"

"Wait, you're right." J.J. stared at his hands. "He said he came over to hang out, remember? He followed me into my room."

Reggie Lynx. Everything led back to him. Xandra's mind raced, trying to connect Reggie's duplicity regarding the research paper, the envelope and money, the murder, and the missing pin to Stuart's warning about vultures and the suspicions swirling around her and J.J. She forced herself to consider the possibility that the person she had considered a friend had murdered Doris Loving, then planned to implicate her brother in the crime.

Eleven

"Shit, shit, shit, shit, shit!" Xandra pounded the steering wheel. Construction on I-75 had slowed traffic to snail speed. She'd be late for the meeting with Professor Pierce and ruin her chance for vindication. Her conversation with J.J. last night left her more conflicted and wary of everyone around her. Despite her innate distrust of people, she had believed Reggie worthy of her friendship. He had admitted to being by the bins before he returned to the restaurant. Had he stolen J.J.'s souvenir from the family trip and planted it at the murder scene? Why? And why try to shift the blame onto her brother? Or had the pin been dropped by accident? Was its appearance next to the body just a coincidence, or was it a red herring intended to lure the cops away from the real killer? Xandra's head hurt thinking about it. A worker flagging cars through the impasse rapped on the window, rousing her from her musings. She shook off the questions to concentrate on her driving.

When she finally pulled into Sinclair's parking garage, she found the lot mostly empty. She located an open slot close to the walkover. Once she exited the car, she glanced over her shoulder, nagged by the feeling she was being followed. That was crazy. Only her family knew she was coming here today. On the way to Professor Pierce's office, she thought about the weeks since the family outing in March. Reggie hadn't seemed overly interested in her Hinckley stories, although he did ask to see the pins. Who else knew about the minivacation? The realization hit her as she started up the stairs. She had taken the stupid souvenir to work. Everyone had laughed about the kitschy gift, but in the end, even the often-absent Millie Stanfield agreed it was a cute idea. Xandra thought cute was stretching it, but her mother had insisted the pins would be a clever reminder of perhaps their final road trip as a family. Of course, Olivia loved both her souvenirs, the pin and the stuffed vulture she kept by her pillow every night. Xandra thought about that day she brought the pin to the restaurant. Mr. Loving had been there. So had the mayor and most of the council members. They claimed to be conducting impromptu visits to all businesses prior to the Hometown Expo planned for Hopewell's high school gym in April. Buns N Fries was a supporter of local sports teams and contributed door prizes to be awarded during the exhibition. Xandra stopped dead when she recalled that even Reverend Loving had shown up. Did the Reverend hear the employees talking about the vulture souvenir? Did it matter? Anxiety pinged like static in her brain.

"Alexandra Byrd?" The department secretary looked up from her desk when Xandra walked in. "Professor Pierce will be with you shortly."

Xandra took a seat between a potted plant and a table covered with recruiting brochures. If this accusation of plagiarism turned into a career killer, maybe she could join one of the armed services and become an MP. The possibility of losing her chance to follow in Joe's footsteps stabbed at her. She grabbed a few of the flyers, then startled when the secretary tapped her shoulder.

"Miss Byrd? The chair will see you now." Xandra followed the woman into Hannah Pierce's office. The professor sat at her desk in front of a window overlooking the downtown skyline. Shelves bearing books on the law, policing, and forensic topics lined two walls. Pierce motioned Xandra to take a seat.

Perched on the edge of a leather-cushioned chair, Xandra folded her hands and waited for the interrogation to begin. Pierce turned to a minifridge behind the desk. "Are you thirsty, Miss Byrd? I'm having water, but I also keep a selection of sodas and Gatorades. You're welcome to one."

"No, thank you. I'm anxious to clear my name."

Pierce took a swallow from her water bottle, set it aside, and flattened her hands on the desk. "Professor Penderson has informed me of his suspicions. He is inclined to believe your version of the affair, as am I, especially since Mr. Lynx appears to have dropped out of his classes. Have you been in contact with him?"

"No, I haven't. None of this is like Reggie." Xandra leaned a hand on the desk, returned it to her lap. "I never shared my work with him, ever. Except this time, when I finished my paper, he asked if he could look at it to see if he had formatted it correctly. I let him read it on my computer. I never thought he would steal the actual work. I don't even know how he did it."

Professor Pierce focused her calm gaze on Xandra. "It is unsettling that the young man hasn't responded to any calls or texts. I assume his family hasn't reported him missing?"

"Not as far as I know." Reggie's betrayal hurt more now than when Xandra first learned what he had done. She failed to keep the bitterness from her words. "Not that I care all that much at this point."

"I understand. However, we need Reggie's confirmation or denial of this matter to clear you of this accusation." Pierce leafed through a folder bearing Xandra's name. "You have a perfect four-point average and outstanding assessments from all your first-year teachers. Once we locate and speak with Mr. Lynx, I believe we can put this episode behind us."

"I'll do whatever it takes to make this go away." Xandra held her breath. She had left herself open to a wide range of punishments. Such capitulation could end up God knew where. Still, she didn't see another way out.

Pierce held out a single sheet of paper. "I need you to sign this acknowledging your conversation with Professor Penderson and now with me. You may record your version of the incident in the space below your name. Then, I want you to help us find our missing young man. Once Reggie admits his guilt, you will no longer be involved. Any questions?"

Xandra signed her name, then wrote a denial of the plagiarism and reaffirmed her innocence before handing the document back. "I have no questions. Thank you, Professor." When she rose to leave, Pierce motioned her to stay.

"Can we talk for a moment?" Pierce unwrapped an energy bar as she talked. "I understand you discovered a body at your work last Thursday."

"How did you hear that?" Xandra gripped the arms of the chair. "I mean, my name wasn't in the newspaper or on TV."

Pierce admired a diamond on her left ring finger. "Let's just say I have a personal connection to the Hopewell Police department."

Xandra wanted to ask what that meant, but she kept her questions to herself. "It was unsettling."

Pierce cocked her head. Her hair slid to the side, revealing triple piercings in her right ear. "I think you have the makings of a fine police officer, Miss Byrd. Let's clear this little hiccup and get you back on track, okay? Remember, my door is always open if you need or want to talk about your future."

Xandra thanked her again, then scooted down the hall past the secretary. As she headed for the media center, a new question occurred to her. Mr. Loving wanted to develop his sister's property. The man had multiple business investments in Hopewell, even as rumors swirled about his precarious financial dealings. She'd overheard city leaders talking at the restaurant about venture and vulture capitalism, concepts she barely understood, but the terms intrigued her. Did they have anything to do with the Reverend's message to her through the Lynx brothers? Birds of a feather. Had she stumbled on a clue to deciphering the woman's cryptic message?

Twelve

Xandra left the media center an hour and a half later with a stack of business articles and a growing understanding of venture capitalism. She immediately sent J.J. a text asking if they could talk that afternoon before work. She was so focused on the message that she failed to notice the wide-receiver body ahead of her until she collided with him. Strong arms wrapped around her. An amused voice whispered in her ear.

"Xandra Byrd, woman of dreams ...and nightmares, walks right into me. You in some kind of damn hurry?"

Xandra pushed free, a blush creeping over her cheeks, as she eyed Shawn Crowe, the dark-haired man-boy who was her main competition for top honors in their class. Figures she'd run into him now.

"Crowe." She took a step back. "You trying to take me out before the term ends?"

"Stop, Byrd. I'm in too good a mood to argue with you today."

Xandra snorted as she shouldered past him, but the urge to score some points had her turning around. "So, you're capitulating? Must've caved to my superior brainpower."

"Nah, rivalry's still on. I enjoy seeing you squirm."

She poked his chest. "So brash, Crowe, and so deluded."

He threw up his hands, but he didn't back away. "Bring it on, woman, but not today."

Xandra pursed her lips. The edge was gone from his banter. "What's going on?" she said.

"I don't want to spar with you." He ran a hand through his hair. "I heard what happened at the restaurant. You okay?"

This was not the Crowe she knew, not the cocky guy determined to win, no matter who he had to run over to do so. This guy sounded sincere. She choked back a snarky comment.

"I'm coping." She noted bruising on his cheek, tape around his ring and index fingers on his right hand. "How about you?"

"Better, now that I see you're all right."

"Why wouldn't I be?" She pointed at his face. "Who'd you piss off?"

"Damn, girl, you always this prickly?"

"Suit yourself, Crowe. I rescind my concern." She turned to leave. Shawn grabbed her elbow to slow her down, then kept pace all the way to the stairs.

"Now, see, that smart mouth of yours is going to serve you well on the streets. Not so much on the dating scene."

She tried not to laugh, but he was right. She didn't have to bite every hand that reached out, not even his, and he did have a killer smile. Trouble was, he knew it. "Who hit you?"

Shawn steered her away from the walkway to the garage, tugging her down the stairs toward the snack machines. "Would you believe Reggie Lynx?"

Xandra stopped walking. "When did you see Reggie?"

"Ran into him at a street party over by the University of Dayton Friday night."

"Reggie was partying at UD?" Xandra shook her head. "When I see him, I'm going to box his ears."

"Yeah, well, I've got first dibs. The dude's crazy. He tried to steal the keys to my car. When I called him on it, he came at me." Shawn rubbed his jaw. "Got in a few licks before his brother pulled him off and they both ran. But enough of the typical macho bullshit. I hear you found a dead body."

Xandra stumbled, smashing into Shawn's rock-solid back. "Ouch. Do you spend all your free time at the gym?"

"When I'm not studying." He smirked, then pulled her sleeve to keep her moving. "Dead body. Restaurant. Spill."

"How do you know about it?"

He looked at her and shrugged. They both said Reggie at the same time. "I wish he'd kept his mouth shut. It wasn't my choice to stumble over a corpse."

"I understand you know, er, knew the lady."

Xandra's eyes misted. She looked away until the moment passed, then retreated up the stairs. "Doris Loving was a good person. Hard to understand why anyone would want to hurt her."

Shawn rested a hand on the railing. Students flowed past them, trailing curiosity and smirks. "Don't go yet. Let me buy you a drink and a snack while you tell me all about it."

Xandra glanced at her phone. J.J. hadn't responded yet, and her stomach threatened to growl louder. It might help to talk it out, although Shawn was the last person she would have sought for a heart-to-heart. Still, despite their competitive natures, Xandra couldn't fault his intelligence. Maybe he'd pick up on something she missed. "All right, I can spare fifteen minutes."

"I'll take it." Shawn made his way to the machines, returning with sodas, chips, and a package of double-stuffed chocolate cookies. Xandra hadn't realized how thirsty she was until he handed over one of the cans.

"Here. How about we call a truce?" He held on to the snacks, a tentative grin lifting the corners of his very kissable mouth. *Byrd, stop. Guys are off-limits for the foreseeable future,* she lectured herself as she accepted the peace offering. "Now, I want to hear everything about finding the body."

Between sips, Xandra gave an abbreviated version of what she'd told the detectives. When she stopped, Shawn rested his elbows on his knees. "Man, that's rough. You really think you're a suspect?"

 "Let's just say I'm a bad luck magnet and leave it at that."

Shawn balled his empty chips bag and aimed it at the trash. It sailed into the can without touching the rim. "Is that why you're always frowning?"

Xandra took a long drink. "I don't always frown."

"Yeah, you do. And you never stop to talk to anyone after class. Why is that?"

She crammed a chip in her mouth, swallowed, and met his eyes. "I'm working toward a goal. I can't afford any missteps."

"Making friends isn't a misstep."

"Isn't it? I trusted Reggie. You see how that turned out."

"No, I don't see. Why don't you tell me?"

Xandra shook her head. "Look, Shawn, I have trust issues, had them since I was a little kid, and especially now that Reggie Lynx screwed me over, big-time."

"How?"

"I thought he was a friend. Turns out I was wrong."

Shawn glanced at the research materials peeking out of her backpack. "That's a ton of research. I thought you turned in your comp paper last week like the rest of us."

She considered ignoring his veiled question, then opted for the truth. "I did."

"But," he rolled the drink can between his palms, "you're not smiling, and you went to see Pierce."

"And you know this how?"

A muscle ticked in his jaw. "I happened to be in the office when Penderson came by. He forgot to close the door when he went in to talk to the chair."

"Huh." Xandra wondered who else knew about the professor's accusation. She squared her shoulders. No point in secrecy now. "Reggie copied my paper and submitted it as his own. I don't know why he thought Penderson wouldn't figure it out. Anyway, Pierce gave me one chance to clear my name. I must find the elusive Reggie and get him to confess. You see the problem here, don't you? Xandra trusts Reggie. Reggie cheats. Xandra pays the consequences. Story of my life."

Shawn shifted to rest his arms on the table. "Look, X, I get it. You had a shitty childhood. Trauma's written all over you, but you're also brilliant, clever, and, don't hit me, you have a killer glare. It's a deadly combination for someone aiming to make detective someday. No, don't say anything yet. I know we've butted heads over the past year, but I'm not your enemy."

Xandra smoothed the seams of her shorts. "Does wishing something make it so?"

Shawn met her gaze without flinching. "It might, especially if I have a way to help you."

"How would you do that?"

"First, I could go to Penderson and Pierce, tell them I saw him printing off the report."

"Did you?"

"Maybe. I just can't prove that's what he was doing?"

"How? Where?"

"Does it matter?" He rubbed a thumb along his lower lip.

Xandra shrugged. "Probably not. He did it. Even if I didn't give him permission, I'm in trouble, too."

Shawn rested a hand on her knee. "Can I ask you something?"

She narrowed her eyes, wondering where he was going with the conversation. "What?"

"Are you always going to push me away?"

"Why does it matter?"

"I'm tired of you thinking I'm nothing but a jock." He crossed his arms. "I'm more than that, Xandra, a lot more."

"Hey, I know you want to be the top student."

"That doesn't mean—" He paused. The silence grew awkward. "Let me help you. Give me a chance to do something that matters."

He leaned toward her, coiled and expectant. She gulped the rest of her drink. "You're serious?"

He grinned. "As a heart attack, Byrd, so give me a break here. Say yes or shoot me. My preference, however, is the first one."

"I don't want to shoot you, Shawn."

"All right." He reached for her hand. She pulled back. "I know you've got a lot going on, and I know you don't trust me yet, but I want to help you figure this out. Okay?"

"I don't have a lot of free time." She pursed her lips and thought about the few empty spaces on her calendar. "If, and that's a big if, I manage to free up some time, will you not pressure me?"

"I can agree to that."

"All right. How do you feel about breakfast?"

"My favorite meal. When?"

She worried her lower lip until, looking up, she saw Shawn staring at her mouth. "Um, Monday?"

"Deal. You have a place in mind?"

"How about here, before class." Xandra paused. Might as well go all in. "If you're really serious, you can help me find Reggie."

"Deal." He held out a hand, waited for her to shake. "What time?"

"Seven-thirty. Give me your number. In case something comes up."

They exchanged phones. When she entered her info, she glanced down the names in his contacts list until she found Reggie's number. Interesting. No recent calls from the missing Lynx. The thought made her snort. Shawn looked up.

"You laughing at me, Byrd?"

"Not at all, Crowe. Keep an eye out for our missing Lynx, will you?" He groaned. She smirked. "Monday, breakfast. Don't be late."

They retraced their steps to the upper floor. As she turned toward the garage, he brushed his fingers over her wrist. "See you Monday morning."

Xandra felt his eyes on her until she turned the corner. Her skin tingled where he'd touched her. She'd vowed to avoid entanglements, yet she had agreed to meet him, her rival for the top honors in the class and at the police academy. Their breakfast meeting felt like a date, which could lead to complications she didn't want or need. By the time she reached the car, she had decided to table the Shawn conundrum. She had other problems to sort out. Hire new workers at the restaurant. Keep up with her coursework. Stop resenting her parents for the past. Find Reggie Lynx. Most importantly, she was determined to clear J.J. of the murder of Doris Loving. Someone had set her brother up to take the blame. She closed her eyes against the image from Friday morning's bike ride to Beck Park, of the vultures circling closer and closer above the fallen deer.

Thirteen

The rest of Saturday dragged by, leaving Xandra physically exhausted and mentally wound up. J.J. never did respond to her text. Her parents and Olivia were gone when she went home to change and hadn't left a note. No one at work talked about anything except the Loving murder. Locals lingered over their burgers, hoping to gather bits of gossip dropped by the employees. Patrons from out of town raised eyebrows at the yellow caution tape that remained strung around the trash enclosure, wanting to know what happened. Xandra was forced to lug the garbage bags to the Fishy Flavors drive-thru next door. Well, the real name of the restaurant was Cap'n Sam's Seafood Shop, but no one called it that.

Reggie remained a no-show. Xandra dialed his number at every free moment, chafing at the repetitious *This voice mailbox is full*. She sent texts urging him to report in. Those also went unanswered. To add more stress, Millie Stanfield phoned to say her fever had returned, and she wouldn't be back until the doctor released her. Great. Another night short-handed. During the afternoon lull, Xandra shuffled through job applications, setting aside several to schedule for interviews the following week. By closing time, all she wanted was a shower and a beer. Before leaving, she triple-checked all the doors, turned off the work lights, and slipped out the back.

The broken pole light had not been fixed. Among the shadows behind the building, Xandra detected movement. She waited for her eyes to adjust to the dark, then started toward the taped-off area. She had only taken one step when a raccoon bolted across the lot, a burger bun dangling from its mouth. Xandra stifled a cry as the little bandit dropped the bun, chittering wildly, and scampered into the hedges. As the animal rushed past, a form detached itself from the far side of the trash enclosure and lumbered after the raccoon. The plants shuddered as the intruder plowed through them.

"Hey!" She sprinted after the escaping shadow. "Reggie?" By the time she reached the bushes, whoever had been hiding there had disappeared. Xandra backpedaled to her car, keys between her fingers to use as a weapon in case the lurker returned. She slid inside, punched down the door locks, and screeched out of the lot. She didn't stop shaking until she reached home. Dashing into the house, she could hear Joe and J.J. watching a rerun of a Bundesliga soccer match and arguing about a fish knife.

"I told you, Dad. I put it in the tackle box, like I always do."

"Well, it's not there, J. I need you to look for it."

Xandra stripped off her BNF shirt, tossed it into the laundry room, and headed for the kitchen, collapsing across the counter. Her father looked up from the game.

"Alexandra? You okay?"

She whirled to the refrigerator, grabbed a beer, and twisted off the cap. "I will be."

Joe frowned at the bottle, but he didn't admonish her. Instead, he muted the TV and rose to join her. "What happened?"

"There was a raccoon. By the trash bins. Scared the sh—, startled me." She gulped down a third of the beer before speaking again. "And someone was hiding behind the fence."

Joe cursed under his breath. "Did you see who it was?"

She shook her head as J.J. joined them. "Hey, X, you don't look so good."

"You think? It's not every day I surprise a stalker."

Her father rapped his knuckles on the counter. "Tell me exactly what happened."

"Everyone had gone home," she said, "and I was locking up. When I stepped outside, I heard a rustling noise. Then a raccoon ran past me, followed by a person. Someone was there, hiding in the shadows, watching me."

"You think it was Reggie?" J.J. helped himself to her beer.

"Eew." Xandra snatched back the bottle. "Gross. Get your own."

Joe settled on one of the stools at the counter. "Can you describe this person?"

"It was a man, I think. Without the overhead light, that part of the lot is super dark, especially on moonless nights. He looked about medium height, thick through the shoulders." Xandra closed her eyes to conjure up the scene. "Dark clothing. Long pants and shirt, and a hood over his head. I smelled something, too."

"Yeah, raccoon poop and garbage." J.J. snorted.

"No, you idiot." Xandra slapped his arm. "Let me think. A spicy smell, maybe like that aftershave Leah got you last Christmas."

Joe wrinkled his brow. "Did you hear anything, a car or motorcycle?"

"No. Well, the traffic on the road, faint music from the theater." She closed her eyes again, recreating the moment, overriding the panic that threatened when she thought about the place where Reverend Loving died. "There was a chime, like a cell phone ping, maybe?"

"You didn't cross the tape?"

Xandra shook her head. "No, Dad. I know better than that."

He pulled out his phone.

"What are you doing?"

"Calling Janeece. If your intruder was looking for something, he or she may have been inside the fence, left fingerprints or something else behind." Joe moved to the front of the house, his words muffled. Xandra turned to her brother. "What was that about your fishing knife?"

"Dad says it's missing, but I remember putting it in the box the last time I took it to work."

"You took your fishing stuff to your city job? Why?"

Her brother grinned. "We had to check the stocking of the new pond by that old railroad track they turned into a hike and bike trail."

"Maybe you should look under the clothes heap in your bedroom." J.J. rolled his eyes. She took a few more swallows from the bottle. "Why didn't you answer my texts today? We need to talk."

"Honestly, I forgot." J.J. rested his forearms on the counter. "I went to see Grunder. One of his new hires quit, like, today, and he needed me. I'm not sure I'll have time to talk this summer. I might not even find time to sleep."

Xandra reached into her pocket as Joe wound up his conversation with the detective. "You better make time, J.J., because this pin says you were with Doris Loving when she died, and we are both in deep trouble if you can't prove otherwise."

Fourteen

The neighborhood settled into evening, lights winking off as the hours passed, the stray fox rambling among the less -manicured lots. An owl hooted from the cottonwood tree in the yard next door. Inside the Zetts's home, Joe murmured goodnight, peeked in on Olivia, and joined Leah in their bedroom. J.J. trailed behind him, leaving Xandra to put the house to bed. She wandered around, restless, uneasy, her head buzzing with speculation about Reggie's plagiarism and his lie about what was in the envelope. Even when fatigue overtook her, she found it difficult to fall into sleep, dozing off just as daylight slipped in through the blinds. When Leah knocked to wake her, Xandra groaned.

"Alexandra? You up?" Her mother placed an armful of clean clothes on the dresser before perching on the bed. "I finished your laundry. I know it's been a rough couple of days."

"Thanks, Mom." She bristled as the word slipped out. Mom. Did the woman who had birthed and then given her away deserve the title? Leah pretended not to notice.

"Dad told me what happened last night."

"I'm all right."

"Of course, you are, Alexandra. You're a strong, resilient young woman. You'll get through this, and we'll be here to help you."

Xandra turned away. "It isn't so much actually finding the body that bothers me. It's that it was Reverend Loving. I don't understand. Why would anyone kill her? And why stalk me?"

"Evil never makes sense, even when we know a reason. Maybe the man didn't expect to find you there." Leah paused. When Xandra didn't respond, her mother stood up. "Want some breakfast?"

"Don't you have to iron or prep something for next week?"

Leah smoothed a hand over her daughter's hair. "I finished everything up while you were gone yesterday, and summer hours start Monday, so it's dress down for the interim. I'm not putting on a suit again until August. Unless I go to church. We could go together this morning."

"No, but thanks." Xandra thought about the service without Reverend Loving and sighed. "Hey, that'll be a first. Leah Zetts in jeans and a tee shirt."

"Hey, I was a teenager once. That girl still lives inside me somewhere."

Xandra offered a small smile. "Is Olivia awake?"

"Of course. Your sister refuses to sleep a minute longer than necessary. Always afraid she'll miss something."

Xandra started to ask if she had been like that, then swallowed the question. Leah hadn't been there to watch her grow from a baby to a toddler. A familiar sadness tugged at her. She willed it away. The past was the past. No changing it now. Pulling on a pair of cut-offs and a purple top that matched her hair, she followed her mother into the kitchen.

J.J. was chowing down. "Hey, X," he sputtered around a mouthful of Wheat Chex, "I have some free time tomorrow. How about walking the land behind the church with me? It'll probably be the last time I get to show my actual landscaping plan to anyone."

"I have classes and a meeting in the morning, but I could get there around one or one-thirty."

"I thought you had a meeting yesterday."

"I did." Xandra dumped two pieces of whole wheat toast in the toaster. "With Hannah Pierce."

"Pierce? The department chair?" Leah finished cleaning strawberries and wiped her hands on a towel. "Is there a problem, Alexandra?"

"Nothing I can't handle." She poked her head in the refrigerator to avoid more questions. Locating the cream cheese, she pulled out the container and closed the door. "Where's Dad?"

J.J. carried his bowl and spoon to the sink, eying her as he stepped around the counter. "He's with those detectives. Terl called him early. They may have found something at the restaurant."

"What?"

Her brother shrugged. "I don't know, but he sounded upset when he left."

"What did he say?"

"He told me to look for your vulture pin."

Leah turned to them, eyes narrowed, mouth stretched thin, but she didn't say a word. Xandra joined her brother at the counter. "Did you find it?"

"No. It's missing, just like mine."

Fifteen

"Xandra," Shawn called. "Over here."

She followed the sound of his voice to a low table and two chairs tucked in an alcove to the left of the snack and soda machines. Two bakery bags perched next to a pile of books and two cups of coffee. Xandra's mouth watered. Coffee was her kryptonite. Shawn slid one of the cups toward her.

"Rough night?" He nodded at the bags. "Your choice."

Xandra opened one, inhaled the sweet smell of glazed donuts before swooning over the cranberry orange bagels in the second one. "One of each, yes, please. And thank you for noticing. I'm exhausted."

"That doesn't mean you look bad, Byrd, but you could probably use some down time." He gestured at the surroundings. "Care to share?"

Not ready to talk, she spread cream cheese on the bagel and took a bite. Did she really want to tell Shawn what had happened? This détente between them unsettled her. She reminded herself she had reasons for her trust issues, then capitulated. "I surprised a stalker after work Saturday night."

"That's…unexpected." Shawn set down his donut. "Details, X."

"Not much to tell. When I left the restaurant, someone was hiding by the trash bins. I spooked him, or the raccoon did, and he took off."

"There was a stalker and a raccoon?" At her nod of agreement, he polished off his pastry and shook his head. "That's disturbing."

"It is." She sipped the coffee, strong and black, savoring the caffeine jolt. "How did you know how I like my coffee?"

Shawn raised an eyebrow. "You startle an intruder at the restaurant where a woman was murdered and that's what you want to know?"

"Well, it wasn't you, was it?"

He tilted her chin with his hand, forcing her to look him in the eye. "I don't have to stalk women."

"I've noticed." She shook off his hand and took another bite of her bagel. "You didn't answer my question."

"I didn't think you were serious."

"Don't get pissy. I retract the insinuation. Maybe it was Reggie or Stuart, but I don't think so. The man I saw looked bigger, broader than both of them. He was wearing a hoodie and it was dark, so I didn't see his face. And if it was Reggie, why wouldn't he say so?"

"Apology accepted. Maybe Reggie didn't want you to know he was there, and —" Shawn brushed crumbs off the table, "you always bring a thermos to class, and it's always undiluted."

"You might make a detective yet, Crowe." Xandra tapped the lid on her coffee. "Listen, here's the thing I don't understand. You've been contentious with me since we started this program, even churlish."

"Churlish? What does that even mean?"

Xandra started to explain, then rolled her eyes. "You're doing it again, treating me like one of those fangirls always swarming your ass, and I'm not, so don't play dumb. First you challenge me, and now you want to be my friend. Help me understand the change of heart."

A look equal parts chagrin and regret passed over his face. Shawn rubbed his lower lip, a tell Xandra recognized from their earlier encounters. He was about to speak the truth. "Look, I've been an ass, plain and simple, and I'm tired of having you look at me like I'm gum on the bottom of your shoe. I've seen how hard you work, how everyone respects you. Even Reggie, who talks about you a lot."

"You're really friends with him?"

"We're not BFFs or anything, but, yeah. At least, I thought we were." Shawn touched the fading bruise on his cheek. "Until this."

"How close of friends?"

"We were sports rivals in high school, football, baseball. Then, when I started at Sinclair, I ran into him again on campus and at parties. He seemed like a good guy, and he shared stories about working with you. He admired your work ethic and your drive, and I paid attention. Frankly, X, you fascinate the hell out of me."

Xandra choked. When Shawn moved to pat her back, she held him off. "You're serious."

"I am. But the past month or so, something's been off with Lynx. He started cutting class, stopped coming to the bro meetings."

"Bro meetings? Is that secret code for guy talks?"

Shawn's cheeks colored. "We have game nights, you know, video wars and bragging rights to the latest version of *Fortnite*."

Xandra stifled a giggle. "My brother plays that, too."

"I've been worried about the guy, and now I'm worried about you. So, give me a break here and tell me more about what happened."

"There isn't much to tell." Xandra went over the events in the same order she'd told her father and brother.

"Did this man say anything?"

"No, but he gave off this vibe. I don't know how to explain except it was menacing." She shivered. "Totally creeped me out."

"Maybe you should take some time off work until the police find the Reverend's killer."

"I can't. Your parents probably pay your tuition. Mine don't. At least, I don't expect them to."

"You mean you won't let them."

"They only found out I existed three years ago."

"See there, that's what I mean by fascinating. A beautiful woman with a chip on her shoulder and a giant stick up her—"

Xandra grabbed the table. "Stop right there, Crowe, before I walk away."

Shawn scooted closer. "You're not walking away. I won't let you. We're going to work together, Byrd."

Xandra leaned back, the smell of his aftershave messing with her resolve. "Not if you insult me again."

"It's not an insult, it's a compliment. You're a badass, Xandra Byrd. Let's do some badassery investigating together."

She examined his face, his posture, the way he waited for her next move. For whatever reason, Shawn Crowe was determined to insinuate himself into her life. Should she let him? *Keep your enemies close*, a little voice sniggered. Was he an enemy? "If you're serious, Crowe, you can start by finding Reggie Lynx. Then we might have something to discuss."

Shawn tipped his seat back, but his eyes never left hers. "Deal," he said. "Now, when can we meet for breakfast again?"

Sixteen

J.J., wearing his Aussie bush hat and a determined look, waited under the shade of the solitary maple overlooking the parking lot of St. Francis Episcopal Church. Only a few cars were scattered over the asphalt, which baked under the intense midday sun. When Xandra arrived, he rose from the grass to greet her.

"You all right, X?"

"Why does everyone keep asking me that?"

J.J. draped an arm over her shoulder and guided her toward the field behind the church. Several elders waved a greeting as they exited the building. One of the men stopped to call out, "Need anything?" When J.J. explained what he and Xandra intended to do, the man wished them a good walk and went on his way.

Xandra applied an extra layer of sunscreen, tugged on a ballcap, and followed her brother along the edge of the field. A large area had been mowed, then marked with chalk lines for soccer practice. A shelter occupied the north end of the expanse, a grill mounted on a stand beside it, recycling and waste cans nearby. A path circled the field before veering into the wooded acreage beyond the manicured lawn. The traffic noise faded as the siblings neared the trees. Xandra brushed a hand over the foxtails lining the path. Bird song, desultory in the afternoon heat, accompanied them as they struck out through the brush. J.J. stopped at a towering oak with a trunk so large Xandra could barely wrap her arms a third of the way around it.

"I had no idea trees grew this big in Hopewell."

"This," J.J. patted the tree, "is one example of the heritage trees on the property and another reason Reverend Loving didn't want to see this land cleared for housing." He unrolled the plan he carried and pressed it against the oak to point out their location. He drew out a compass, consulted it, and motioned toward their next stop. "We, Reverend Loving and me, decided to preserve this particular stretch of forest as is. She wanted a path to lead there."

Xandra swatted at the midges swarming her. "To what? Where?"

J.J. pushed ahead, following a faint animal trail that opened onto a stand of cattails edging a small pond. "See the flat ground on the other side? That's where we planned a labyrinth with a small stone altar in the middle made from local stones. The Reverend explained about labyrinths, how they provide a meditative place for people to leave their burdens and return to the outside world without carrying so much stress. Sounded a little new-age-y to me, but she wanted it."

Xandra gazed over the water. She imagined a path circling back and forth along the far side, carrying the prayerful into the interior of the labyrinth and back out again. "This is a beautiful spot, J. No wonder you were so eager to help her."

Her brother frowned. "Yeah, that's all gone now. I'm pretty sure Paul Loving doesn't intend to honor her wishes."

"Can the church fight him?"

"How? The man owns or has an interest in half the businesses in town, and he has the people who matter on his side. The Reverend told me the council and the city planning commission were in favor of her brother's proposal. According to her, the mayor even has a financial stake in the project."

"Doesn't that create a conflict of interest? I mean, you can't vote on something to enrich yourself, can you?"

J.J. rolled up the schematic and secured it with a rubber band. "Powerful people with money do whatever they want. Come on, I want to show you where the living tree memorial garden was supposed to go."

Xandra followed her brother along another trail that meandered along the bank of the creek that fed the pond. The stream had carved a channel through the moraine deposits that underlay the town, burbling over a scatter of rocks and, if she had her directions right, flowing all the way to Springboro's Clear Creek. Violets and bloodroot had bloomed and wilted, but wild geraniums and celandine still graced the fringes where light penetrated the canopy. She followed J.J. into the interior. Picking their way through briars, they reached a prairie brimming with the rising stalks of sunflowers.

"Wow." Xandra moved beside her brother. "This is where she envisioned the burial ground?"

Once again, J.J. unfurled the plan. "See the red circle in the northwest corner? That's where we are now."

From their vantage point, the design took on a reality that the scaled drawing didn't possess. Xandra marveled at her brother's talent. He had taken Reverend Loving's ideas and turned the dream into a workable plan. What a shame to surrender it to commercial development. All the trees they had passed would be cut down for roads and homesites, the last of Hopewell's rural heritage transformed into a crowded subdivision. More development would destroy the remaining unspoiled land that had initially lured settlers to the area. If Paul Loving had his way.

"Is there any possibility of keeping the developers away?"

J.J. rerolled the drawing and stuffed it into the cylinder in his backpack. "I don't know."

"Don't give up yet, okay?"

Her brother stared at the sky, then checked his watch. "We better get back. You have work and I'm on my lunch break, which is about over."

They retraced their steps, skirting the pond, and headed back toward the church. They had almost reached the end of the forest when they heard voices. J.J. held a finger to his lips as he crouched behind a screen of invasive honeysuckle.

"Who?" Xandra mouthed. J.J. shook his head. She listened more closely, surprised to hear the voice of Paul Loving. Why was her boss here? The conversation grew louder as the group approached their hiding spot.

"I'm not interested in walking any farther this afternoon, Loving," a man said.

"I just want to show you what we're going to have once the will is processed."

Xandra tugged J.J. lower and whispered Loving's name. Her brother snorted.

"Hey! Tell your muscle to let go of me," Loving said.

"I said I didn't want to do a walkabout this afternoon."

Loving cursed, then retreated, his words fading as he turned away. Before long, the voices rose again.

"I need more time," Loving said. "You swore you wouldn't call in the debt until I secured the land."

"Our contract is almost up, Paul. Like it or not, you agreed to have the deal finalized by," the man paused, "the end of this month. You signed the papers."

"Look, Coulter, I'll have the money and the title to the property, I swear it. I just need to get through my sister's funeral."

"I'm inclined to disagree. You're overextended."

"All this is going to be mine. The city wants houses built here, too, for the taxes and the economic boost they'll bring to town. I'll make a ton as the developer, and then I'll have the money to pay you back. I have a few weeks yet."

"You know, I can sell all your assets today and recoup my investment and more. Besides, the city will work with whoever holds the paper. My track record is better than yours."

There was the sound of scuffling, curses. "You can't do this. I'll—"

"You'll what? Kill me? Like you killed your sister when she wouldn't agree to your proposal?"

The argument subsided. A twin-engine plane roared overhead, drowning out Coulter's next words. Then Loving shouted. "I didn't kill my sister, and you know it."

"Now, I don't know that, do I? You, my friend, are almost out of time and money." Laughter rose. "Tick, tock, Paul. Tick, tock."

"You're a vulture, Coulter, you know that?" Loving said. "I never should have trusted you!"

"No, but you did. You have until the end of the month. Pay up or say goodbye to your little development dream."

Coulter and his companion moved off. J.J. shifted his weight. Xandra held her breath. Ragged breathing preceded the sound of a stick whacking a tree, each stroke accompanied by the ugly curses of a desperate man. Paul Loving was in trouble. Had his desperation led him to kill his sister?

Seventeen

Heat shimmered off the asphalt at St. Francis, reflecting the unseasonable warmth of the late-spring afternoon. Pete Stone exited the church, followed by Janeece Terl, fanning herself with her notepad. Their cursory examination of the Reverend's office had yielded more questions than answers. She made a note to request a search warrant as soon as she returned to the station. Shrugging out of her jacket, she paused to survey the athletic field and the forest beyond. A man in a suit appeared at the far end, accompanied by a second, larger man, who trailed the suit toward the parking lot. She shaded her eyes against the sun's glare.

"Hey, Pete." She tugged her partner to a halt. "Who's that?"

Stone fisted his hands on his hips. "No clue. Doesn't look familiar. Want to find out?"

"I do." She checked her watch. "But I have court on that burglary case in half an hour."

"Maybe it's one of those developers connected to Paul Loving. Wonder what he's doing out there."

"Snap some photos, Pete. We'll identify him later."

Pete took half a dozen shots before peering into the tree line. "Heads up, Terl. Someone else is out there, too, in the trees."

"Interesting. I can spare ten minutes." She led the way to the Crown Vic, started the engine, and cranked up the air conditioning. "Peanuts?"

Pete accepted a package of snack nuts, chugged a bottle of water, and flipped through his notes. "Too bad we don't have time for a more thorough search of Loving's office today. Why was the secretary so insistent we produce a warrant?"

Janeece chuckled. "Marta Obregon is a stickler for the rules, but you're right. We need to do a deep dive into the Reverend's affairs. So much to do, so few hands to do it."

"Soon as we get the warrant, I'll go back." Another handful of peanuts. The pages of his notebook rustled. "What's the status of Doris Loving's hundred acres?"

"Town gossip says that her brother is desperate to gain control of the property. You know he owns a lot of businesses in town, right? That Buns N Fries, for example, where Alexandra Byrd and Reggie Lynx work, belongs to him, plus the hardware store, the rental equipment center on Placer, and the real estate office on Main. I did some research last night on the county tax site. It seems Loving owes back taxes on all his properties."

"Sounds like a motive."

"He does stand to gain the most from his sister's death, for sure. Still, I can't see him as a knife guy. He's the type who hates to get his hands dirty."

The man in the suit and his companion crossed the lot, heading for a gray Lexus. The bodyguard got behind the wheel. Pete double-checked the plate number as the vehicle turned down Greenway and headed toward the Interstate. Five minutes later Paul Loving stumbled from the grassy area, head down, hands in pockets.

"Now there's a dejected man. What do you suppose that's all about?" Janeece said.

"I'm writing down questions as fast as you ask them." Pete paused to grab another bottle of water. "How about we meet after your court case and hammer out a plan going forward?"

Janeece put the car in drive, preparing to leave, when Pete tapped her arm. "Look who else was checking out the property today."

The detectives watched Xandra and J.J. skirt the field and jog back to the church. Janeece was already sending a text to the attorney on the burglary case to say she'd be late. When the siblings stepped onto the lot, Terl and Stone met them.

"Officers." J.J. nodded. His sister frowned.

"Have you found Reggie?" Xandra said.

"Not yet." Janeece said. "Why are you here today?"

"Before she died," J.J. said, "Reverend Loving asked me to develop a plan for her land." Casting a glance back toward the forest, he shrugged off his pack, took out the blueprint, and spread the drawing over the hood, wincing when his bare arms touched the hot metal. Terl and Stone inspected the drawings. Xandra remained where she was, arms crossed, toe tapping. She had less than a half hour to get to the restaurant. She hoped the boss wouldn't show up today. She needed time to process all she'd overheard.

"Why did Reverend Loving ask you?"

The wind blew J.J.'s hair over his face. He shoved it back. "I'm studying to be a landscape architect. The Reverend knew about my plans from my, from Leah, and over spring break, she called me, asked all kinds of questions. When I told her I needed a project to include in my portfolio, to help me get accepted into my major, she offered me the job."

"You're not in the program yet?" Stone asked.

"I've indicated my interest and talked with some of the professors. One of them suggested I work for the city, which I'm doing this summer, and that I investigate opportunities to do landscaping. Reverend Loving, she did more. She invited me to help her."

"Impressive." Terl handed the drawings back. "Can you copy these for us? Might be helpful in the investigation."

Xandra gnawed a fingernail, unable to escape the current that was dragging her and her brother deeper into the mystery surrounding Reverend Loving's death.

Eighteen

Midnight, soft as fleece, seductive as sin, settled over Xandra's shoulders. Cool air whirled up from the floor vent as she shuffled through the articles spread over the table, searching for anything that might help her interpret the Reverend's cryptic message. Venture versus vulture had something to do with business, and she recognized the old saying, birds of a feather flock together, but what should she be looking for? Did Paul Loving and that Coulter guy count as a flock? A murmuration? A murder? Snorting at the direction her tired brain insisted on pursuing, she concentrated on jotting down facts while the ghost of her younger self sulked. She had no time to read for pleasure or to practice her skateboarding skills. Her plan to win big money doing what she loved had been tucked away, along with her high school diploma, the clothes she'd outgrown, and the memories of days when she didn't have enough to eat or a place to sleep. Joe and Leah provided stability, a way to move beyond the abuse of her adoptive mother, a safe space where she could believe she had worth. She didn't regret taking Olivia from that parked car nor the ruse she and J.J. had devised to return the child without revealing their involvement. She was grateful for the support her biological parents provided, but anxiety still dogged her. She needed to prove she was more than a rebellious teenager skating through life without direction, and she'd been well on that course correction until the Loving murder. Now she and J.J. stood in the spotlight again. Someone wanted the police to think her brother was a murderer and she an accomplice. It was enough to make her want to run away again. Shaking off the urge, she selected an article from *Lippitt's Policy and Politics Blog* and began to read.

"Alexandra." Leah shuffled into the kitchen. Xandra jumped. "It's late. Why don't you give it a rest?"

"I can't. Too much to do."

Leah picked up one of the articles. "What is all this?"

"School work. Hey, did Reverend Loving collect dead birds?"

"Maybe. She had one mounted on the wall of her office." Leah set the pages down to scrub at her eyes. "It was a little weird, but even ministers are entitled to hobbies. Doris was a birdwatcher since she was a kid. But, Alexandra, you are not to involve yourself in anything concerning Reverend Loving's murder. It's not your job."

"If J.J. and I are suspects, I'm already involved." Xandra rose to fill the tea kettle.

Leah opened the tea canister and set it by Xandra. "Why would you or your brother be suspects?"

"There's more going on than you know."

"What more?" Joe entered the kitchen, his slippers scuffing over the tiles.

"Did you know," Xandra confronted her father, "about J.J.'s landscape plan for the property behind the church?"

Joe tightened the belt on his robe. "Your brother mentioned it. I knew he was meeting with Doris. Why?"

Xandra glanced out the window. She didn't want to share what she and J.J. had overheard in the woods. Her parents didn't need more stress. But the murder was already wrapping its talons around their family. Maybe they deserved to know. *No more secrets*, her father had said.

"He took me to see the property this afternoon, J.J., I mean. Now that the Reverend is dead, he thinks Mr. Loving intends to build houses there."

Joe and Leah exchanged a glance, but neither spoke. Xandra dropped tea bags into three mugs and poured water over each. The tea steeped as unspoken questions swirled in the air. Xandra's phone chimed, but she ignored it, waiting for her mother or father to say more about the Reverend's land. The cell pinged again. The third time it sounded, she pulled up the messages.

Taking a chance ur up...im hungry...breakfast tomorrow? J I have news

"Awfully late to be texting." Her dad blew on his tea. "Anything important?"

"What?" Xandra blinked up at him. Her mother wrapped an arm around her father.

"Joe, when our daughter almost smiles, it has to be serious."

"No big deal," she said. "Just a friend checking in." She scrolled to the second text from an unknown number.

sorry bout the paper She frowned. *Reggie.*

"Alexandra." Joe grabbed her arm. "What is it?"

She held up the phone so he could read the third text. **CHECK MAILBOX NOW…don't trust nobody!!!**

Joe leaned over her shoulder as she re-read Reggie's texts. She exchanged a glance with her mother, then sprinted for the front door, Joe at her heels. Leah trailed behind, concern on her face. When Xandra pushed at the screen door, her father held her back.

"Are you sure that text came from Reggie?" He tightened his grip. "We need to be careful here."

"I know, Dad. But Reggie wouldn't hurt me."

"This is the same kid who stole your research paper, then took off, right? Think it through, daughter."

"I'm not worried about Lynx."

"Okay. What if Reggie didn't send that message?" Her father asked Leah to fetch a flashlight and his gun. Shielding Xandra with his body, he switched off the porch light. The night crouched over them, stars littering the sky like sparks from a campfire. Leah returned. Joe swept the light over the yard and the street, squinting into the shadows. Once he was satisfied that no strange cars or stray teenagers lingered in the vicinity, he ventured toward the mailbox. Xandra followed. When they reached the curb, she held the light while Joe searched the yard and street, weapon in hand. He gave the all-clear, and she yanked the box open and jumped back, swallowing a yelp. A rubber snake exploded from the opening. When she was certain no other surprise awaited, she reached for the thick manila envelope stuffed inside.

Back in the house, Xandra set the envelope on a cloth her mother had spread over the table. She stared at the mailer, hesitant to proceed.

"Go ahead, Alexandra," Joe directed, setting the safety on the weapon and laying it aside. "And document everything."

Xandra snapped pictures while her father slipped on plastic gloves, then offered her a pair. She held her breath as he gently shook the package. No powder drifted out. Nothing rattled within. He inspected the flap, which had been sealed with multiple strips of packing tape.

"It doesn't appear to be compromised," Joe said. "No evidence of explosives or toxic substances. You can open it."

"Isn't this evidence?"

"It is," her father agreed. "And we'll turn it over to Janeece, but let's see what's inside first. It could be a prank, like the snake."

"Reggie always liked pranks." Xandra eyed the package. "But his first text said he was sorry. Maybe he sent something that will clear my name. I hate being labeled a cheater."

"Open the envelope," Joe said. Xandra slit the tape and pulled out a sheet of paper encased in bubble wrap. She took one more photo before she peeled the wrap free to read the note.

X, I'm sorry. The cops are after me. So is Loving. And some mean-looking dudes came to my grandma's house Friday looking for me. Freaked me good, and I ran. I told Stuart to warn you and J.J. Be careful who you talk to, especially at work. Don't look for me. Don't tell the police. Don't tell your father.

Xandra glanced up. "Guess that last one is off the table."

"Your friend is in serious trouble. Too bad he didn't tell us why." Joe settled on a stool by the counter. Xandra shoved Reggie's letter back in the envelope. A yawn escaped.

"Joe," Leah picked at the edge of the table, "do you have to call Janeece tonight?"

Joe fingered the towel where the envelope rested. "No. Whoever dropped this off is long gone. Morning will be soon enough. Wrap that carefully, Alexandra, and slip it into a bag. There may be trace evidence that can help us verify the sender."

Leah shook out a trash bag. Xandra slipped the cloth-wrapped letter and the rubber snake into the bag and stowed it in the pantry. Then, prodded by her mother, she scuffed her way to the bedroom, fatigue trumping curiosity. She slipped off her shorts and crawled into bed, but not before sending a text to Shawn.

Can't do bf today, but could do lunch I have news too

Tomorrow she'd find out what Shawn had discovered about Reggie, and tomorrow she would question her brother again about Doris Loving's plans for the wooded acres. She also intended to locate the missing vulture pin. Something told her she wouldn't like where it turned up.

Nineteen

Janeece ignored the phone vibrating on her desk. Head in hand, she flipped through the murder file on Doris Loving, checking each entry against her notes. She laid out the photographs taken the night of the murder, lining up those of the concrete pad in front of the trash bins. When Pete arrived, she waved him over, then went to the break room for coffee. He settled in her chair to read through the pages, barely noticing her return. She scanned the notes over his shoulder, hoping to catch something she'd missed. Pete set the papers down to examine the photos. He picked up the magnifying glass she'd been using to peer more closely at one particular shot. Then he rapped it with his knuckles.

"This is why you asked Xandra Byrd if she'd kicked anything or stumbled over anything when she found the body."

Janeece nodded. "Blood spatter indicates an object was there. Maybe it was gone when she arrived."

"Or maybe our Miss Byrd took it."

"Makes you wonder, doesn't it? Evidence or a random piece of trash? Either way, we need to talk to her again."

"Then there's this." Pete picked up the bag with the scrap of paper found in the Reverend's hand. "How did Joe's business card wind up in a dead woman's hand?"

"We're certain it was planted?" Even though Janeece knew the answer, she waited for her partner to concur. "No way she could have held on to it and struggled against her attacker, which it appears she did. The card was shoved between her index and middle finger. A clumsy attempt to implicate Zetts. Which begs the question, why?"

"We keep asking until we find out," Pete said, placing the evidence back in the storage box. They returned to the murder book, drawing up a list of witnesses still to question, when her former partner strolled in. Henry patted her shoulder, nudged her side, and winked.

"Stone." He nodded at Pete. "Thought I'd stop and say hi. Know you're busy. See you at home later?"

Janeece failed to hide her delight. After they'd eloped last spring, she and Henry had requested separate duties to avoid any conflicts, political, professional, or personal. But it made her happy that he found reasons to drop by.

"Indeed, you will, my man," she murmured back. He headed toward the Community Policing Office. Pete laced his hands behind his head and stretched. Xandra approached the whiteboard.

"Here's what we think we know." She tapped the board with a marker. "Either our killer is one lucky bastard, or the crime was not premeditated. He or she gets Doris Loving to walk along the narrow path from the dinner theater to the Buns N Fries and, because the delivery truck shields it from view, into the trash enclosure where he slits her throat, stabs her in the back, and leaves no clues except Joe's business card. He leaves no shoe prints and no weapon. All we have at the scene is an unstained spot where a small object had lain prior to the killing. Did the killer take it?"

"Or did Xandra Byrd kick or stumble over it? Worst case, the girl took it herself, which leads to why." Pete toyed with his phone. "Where do we start today?"

"Joe called earlier. Xandra received a text, purportedly from Reggie Lynx, late last night. It sent her to their mailbox, where she found an envelope with a note that appears to be from the kid."

"And he didn't think to contact us last night?"

Janeece bit her lip. "He didn't see the point. Whoever left it was gone. Xandra photographed and bagged everything. We'll stop there first. Then, I want to take a harder look for our missing Lynx. Pun intended."

Stone snorted. "Lead on, ma'am. I trust your instincts. I drive today, right?"

She picked up the keys, hesitated, then dropped them in his palm and followed him down the hall. They crossed the lot and settled into the aging Crown Vic.

"Why don't we take one of the new SUVs?"

"New isn't always better. I trained in this car. It's like an old, comfortable pair of sweatpants, tattered but still serviceable. Besides, it's a classic."

"You got that right," Pete muttered, slamming the door. "Any report on the murder weapon?"

"Not yet, other than it was a knife with an eight-inch blade, not serrated. Maybe a fish knife."

"Could it have come from the dinner theater?"

"Maybe." While her partner drove, Janeece perused her partner's notes, comparing his observations and findings to her own. The Lynx kid could be long gone, but her gut said otherwise. She decided to check all the local hangouts on the off chance he'd holed up close to home. Patrol officers in all the adjoining municipalities had the kid's photo and stats, but so far, no one had spotted him.

"You know, Reggie's brother, Stuart, is also keeping a low profile. Something about that bothers me. He's got a reputation as a cocky kid who doesn't mind the spotlight, yet he hasn't been seen or heard from since Friday when he spoke with the Byrd girl. I think he's involved in whatever's going on, and I think he's scared. We need to find him, too."

"I agree," Pete said, "although it's difficult to see a connection right now. I realize Doris Loving was well-known, and she knew almost everybody in town. Still, the Lynx brothers don't seem like church-going types."

The neighborhood where the Zetts family lived drowsed in the burgeoning heat. A sprinkler sprayed water against the side of the Vic as they pulled into the driveway. Joe met them at the door, his youngest child, Olivia, snuggled in his arms. When she recognized Janeece, the girl launched herself from Joe's arms, her tiny hands patting the detective's cheeks. The two carried on a quiet conversation until Janeece returned the girl to her father, but not before she promised to come back and play another time.

Xandra joined them, and Terl found herself comparing the woman before her to the girl she'd met three years ago. The slender, half-starved teen had filled out, grown taller. Her hair was a brown curtain, highlighted with streaks of purple, that emphasized her olive skin. The nose ring had disappeared, replaced by a few more wings on the tattooed sleeve that covered her left arm. She had her mother's beauty, although more earthy than ethereal. Her eyes conveyed Joe's intensity, that look that sized someone up in a blink. The brash teen had matured into a blend of tough and sexy, a dynamic young woman who now wore three bead necklaces around her slender throat. She ushered everyone in, and they settled around the evidence bag resting on the table. Xandra cleared her throat and read Reggie's texts aloud, then handed over a printed copy of each one.

"Dad and I found this in the mailbox last night." She tapped the bag with the envelope stashed inside.

"What time?" Pete said.

Xandra opened her phone. "No later than ten minutes after I received the texts, so 12:37?"

Joe confirmed the time. "I checked the area before we opened the mailbox. No strange cars. No suspicious shadows."

"So, the envelope could have been placed in the box much earlier?" Pete said.

"Yes," Xandra said. "We wouldn't have had a reason to go out there unless we had something to mail the next day. No one touched the envelope except me and only by the corners. When we came inside, I placed it on the cloth in there and used gloves."

Janeece examined the bag. "Do you believe Reggie put it in the mailbox?"

"I do, because this popped out when I opened it." Xandra pointed out the rubber snake. "Totally a Reggie thing."

"Does anything he wrote suggest to you where he might be hiding?"

"No."

"Do you have any ideas about that?"

Xandra shook her head. Her hair fell forward, shielding her face. She pushed it back. "Reggie had a thing for that nature park in Springboro, Milo Beck, at the end of Pioneer Boulevard. He liked to smoke a joint by the creek. But he's not really an outdoor guy. I can't see him hiding there. He could be with one of his friends from Sinclair. His brother might have an idea."

"Even if it seems a long shot, do us a favor and write down the names of anyone you can think of who might know his whereabouts. We can also take a ride to the park, maybe do a walk through." Pete slid a piece of paper toward her. Xandra eyed the blank sheet, hesitated, then wrote four or five names and handed it back. "Thanks. I'll contact Springboro PD and city services to see if their maintenance people have noticed anything out of the ordinary."

Janeece turned from the evidence to the girl. "Can you tell us anything more about the incident at the church?"

Xandra exchanged a glance with her father. "Not really. You know that J.J. showed me the land behind St. Francis."

"What about the night of the murder? Anything new come to mind?" Janeece noted Xandra's body language, her intuition buzzing. The girl had a secret. Whether it was relevant or not, Janeece wasn't sure. The interview concluded, she thanked Joe and Xandra, gathered the evidence bags, and peeked into Olivia's room to say goodbye. On the way back to the station, Pete drove through the neighborhood, scanning for anything or anyone who might provide a lead on the midnight intruder. There were no traffic cams in the residential area, although several homes had installed door cameras. It was worth looking into.

"We need to canvas the neighbors, see if anyone saw something or captured images on their home security systems." Pete idled at the stop sign before heading onto the Hopewell-Springboro Pike. "Which way, boss?"

Janeece tapped her notes, fueled by the prospect of fresh leads and a new direction to the case. She wanted to know how the Lynx boys fit into the equation, but first they had to find them. "Let's go to Beck Park. I've got the urge to commune with nature."

Pete fiddled with the radio. "Miss Byrd is holding something back."

"You think?" Janeece worried her bottom lip. "Maybe she is. The question is why." Four stoplights later, Stone turned right onto Pioneer Boulevard. At the end of the road, he triple-checked for traffic at the dangerous T intersection, then pulled across and into the park. A few vehicles were scattered around the lot. On the path leading down the western slope into the park itself, a woman struggled to hold on to the leashes of four dogs, a husky, two schnauzers, and a bloodhound, determined to drag her toward the lone picnic table under the pergola.

"Might as well start with her," Janeece said. "After you, partner."

Pete climbed out and approached the dogwalker. The woman was mopping her forehead, muttering to herself as the dogs crowded around her.

"Ma'am." Pete held up his badge. "Pete Stone. Hopewell PD. And you are?"

"Elise, Elise Brennan. Is there a problem with me being here?"

Pete hurried to reassure her. "You're fine. Looks like you've got your hands full, though."

"Don't know why I do this job. My arms are about to fall off, and I have to walk them two more times today."

Janeece moved up beside her partner. "Janeece Terl. Hopewell PD."

"You're a bit out of your jurisdiction, aren't you?" The woman's tone shifted from exasperated to suspicious.

"Just enjoying the scenery on our lunch hour." Janeece crouched to pet the schnauzers. Baying, the bloodhound strained at its leash. "You come here often?"

"Once a week. Other days I take them to the dog park down at Hazel Wood."

Janeece pulled out a photo of Reggie Lynx. "Any chance you might have seen this young man while you were walking?"

The woman braced her feet against the bloodhound's thrashing. "Otho, stop! What's he done?"

Pete replaced the photo. "The young man is missing. We'd like to find him. Any help will be appreciated."

Before she could answer, the hound jerked the leash from her hand and bolted toward the picnic table. The woman tottered and fell, landing with a thump on her backside. The other dogs raced after Otho. Janeece helped her up while Pete corralled three of the animals. Handing their restraints to Brennan, he followed the bloodhound to the far side of the picnic table. Otho sniffed the pavement, growled twice, and barked at a stain on the concrete. Pete grabbed the dog's collar. "Terl," he said, "you need to see this."

Reminding the woman to stay where she was, Janeece joined Stone. Two feet beyond the end of the picnic bench, a blood smear appeared, the Rorschach pattern tapering to droplets as it disappeared into the grass.

Twenty

Rush hour traffic had lessened as Xandra, brooding over Reggie's letter, wove her way downtown. A pop-up shower spackled the windshield before darting east, causing the car in front of her to slow. She adjusted her own speed, content to remain in the right-hand lane while other, less patient drivers, screeched their way down the Interstate. Had she presented the evidence to the detectives clearly? Had she made the right decision in keeping quiet about the vulture pins? She tried to ignore the tremor in her chest at the thought of concealing evidence, but she'd waited too long to reveal it now. And should she have included Shawn Crowe on the list of Reggie's friends? A tension headache loomed. Where was Reggie, anyway? Locating him had become priority number one.

Brooding over her friend's disappearance, she headed into Sinclair, surprised to find herself outside the media center without remembering exactly how she had arrived. She located the librarian who had helped her before to request a new set of articles. The woman returned with a bin full of journals and magazines. She cleared a space on the counter and set it down.

"You have plenty to work with here, Miss Byrd."

Xandra thanked the woman, then wandered toward a copy machine. She selected an article, placed it face down on the machine, and pushed the button. She had worked through half the materials when movement among the stacks caught her eye. A guy in a hoodie and jeans slipped from behind a shelf and ran toward the exit.

"Reggie?" Xandra's shout earned a reproving glance from the librarian. Abandoning the copier, she hurried to catch the door before it shut. By the time she stepped into the stairwell, the figure had disappeared.

"Miss Byrd?" The librarian beckoned her back into the center. "You need to calm down or I'll have to ask you to leave."

Xandra apologized, then scuffed her way back to the machine. Another student stood waiting, arms crossed, foot tapping. She grumbled about inconsiderate people.

"Five minutes and I'll be done, promise," Xandra said. She tried to hurry through the remaining material, but the paper feed kept jamming. Exasperated, the student left, curses trailing behind her. Xandra sighed. She wasn't adding to her friends' list anytime soon. Relieved to reach the end of the stack, she opened the final journal to a piece titled *"Venture or Vulture?: The White-Collar Crime No One Knows About"* by Archibald Swartz. She copied the article, added it to her backpack, and returned the materials to the desk.

On the way to her next class, she recalculated the hours remaining to complete the general studies requirements for her degree. If all went well, she would complete the ATS requirements by the end of the summer. But first, she had to remove the cloud Reggie had hung over her head. Had it been him in the media center? Her anger and frustration grew. He had stolen her work, passed it off as his own. She couldn't understand why. The guy had it all. He wasn't stupid, despite sometimes acting the fool. His uncle paid the tuition, and Reg made enough money at Buns N Fries to cover his other expenses. He and Stuart shared his grandmother's car, so he didn't have the insurance, maintenance, and fuel bills Xandra did, and he bummed a ride whenever he could, although he never offered to pay for gas. She hadn't cared. It had been nice to listen to him talk about his family. They had dysfunctional mothering in common. Now, she saw everything as a betrayal.

She slid into her seat just as Professor Kate cued up a PowerPoint on revising written work. Xandra started to take notes, but her mind kept circling back to Reggie. Why had he changed from outgoing charmer to reticent and secretive thief? Xandra sketched two timelines, one listing her actions last Thursday and Friday and another with Reggie's known movements. What connected them? Besides the restaurant, the only other common denominator was his delinquent brother. Wait. Stuart had been arrested for breaking into Paul Loving's office. Was that a coincidence? She searched her memory for details.

He'd been sent to the detention facility in Warren County but had only served a month before his sentence was reduced due to good behavior and because nothing had been stolen or vandalized during the break-in. That made Xandra wonder what was behind Stuart's escapade. The next time she saw him, she was going to ask.

The room grew quiet. Xandra looked up. Professor Kate had paused the presentation to move around the room, knocking on desks as she strolled by. Uh-oh. Sliding the timelines into her backpack, Xandra sat up. She didn't need another teacher on her case.

After class, she checked to be sure she hadn't left anything behind, then thumbed on her phone, hoping to find another message from Reggie. Intent on scrolling, she didn't notice Shawn until he touched her shoulder.

"Holy hells!" Xandra jumped. "You scared me."

Shawn opened his hands in apology. "You all right?"

Xandra shifted the pack on her shoulders. "Yes. No. I don't know. My brain is fried, and this damn murder just gets more complicated every day. I think they're after my brother."

Shawn pressed close to avoid being overheard by passing students. "I saw Reggie."

"Where?"

"Just now. In the courtyard. He took off when I called his name."

Xandra matched his steps as he headed down the hall. "I think I saw him, too. In the media center. What's he doing hanging around here? And where's he been for five days?"

"I don't know, but we're going to find out."

"We?" Xandra tugged him to a stop. "You shouldn't get involved, Shawn. This thing's getting crazy, and it could be dangerous."

Shawn looked her over. "Aww, Byrd. You're worried about my welfare."

"Don't get cocky, Crowe. I'm worried about everyone involved in this case."

"Good to know I'm part of that group." He reached for her hand. "Let's get lunch. You can tell me why you're so jumpy. Maybe I can help."

They threaded their way along the crowded hall. Instead of turning toward the snack area, Shawn led her outdoors. She pulled her hand from his. "Whoa, where are you going?"

"No need to go all psycho on me, Byrd. I'm not abducting you." He grinned. She shook her head. "I'm starving, and the Spaghetti Warehouse is just down the block."

She considered saying no, but the prospect of Italian food and a chance to settle the chaos in her head won her over. They made their way down Fifth Street. Once enveloped in the aroma of pasta and sauce, Xandra felt the stress lift a little. Shawn requested a booth in the back. Tucked away from prying eyes and ears, they perused the menu, then ordered the lunch special.

"No wine?" Shawn spread his napkin across his lap. She rolled her eyes.

"Not in the middle of the day before work. Besides, I'm not legal yet."

"So, next time we go out for dinner, bring a fake ID."

Xandra smirked. "How do you know I have one?"

"C'mon, Byrd, what college kid doesn't?"

"Me." She laughed. "Why are you so confident there'll be a next time?"

Shawn blinked away the question. "You're upset. What's going on?"

Xandra toyed with the silverware. "Lots of things. Answer my question."

"There will definitely be a next time. Why? Because I want to see you, and I think you want to see me, too, maybe just a little bit, and I'll take whatever time you can give me." He grabbed her hand and refused to let go. "Okay? Now that that's settled, we have news to share. Want me to go first?"

She nodded.

"Reggie surfaced over the weekend, showed up at that hip-hop concert in Levitt Pavilion Saturday night. He talked to some of the guys in our computer crimes class but took off when the cops strolled in."

"Did you see him?"

"No, I wasn't there. My grandma had an emergency appendectomy. We were all at the hospital. But Leandro, you remember him? Tall, skinny, face like the dark side of the moon?" Xandra inclined her head, and he continued. "Leandro said Reggie told him he was fucked ten ways to Sunday and had to lay low until, Reggie's words, 'they catch the motherfucker trying to take me out.'"

"Really?" She gnawed the inside of her cheek. "So, someone is after him. Why? What does he know that puts him in danger?"

"I don't know the answer to that. The good news is if he's alive, we can find him. In fact," Shawn hunched over the table, "Leandro's having a party tonight. Reggie's invited, and I am, too. Come with. Between the two of us, we ought to be able to corner him."

"I don't know, Shawn. Sometimes I don't get home until eleven. And I have homework."

"I'll pick you up at the restaurant and drop you back afterward. We only need to stay long enough to corner Lynx."

"Where does Leandro live?"

"Centerville. That apartment complex by the Dollar Store along Forty-eight." Xandra fiddled with her napkin. "Why are you frowning, Byrd?"

"I'm walking on the edge here, Shawn, trying to keep work and school going and my family safe. Especially after last night."

"What happened last night?"

Xandra sighed. Shawn watched her as she related the text message, the envelope in the mailbox, Reggie's warning not to involve anyone else. "I need to talk to him. But everything's so screwed up. I know the police think my brother had something to do with the murder. Everyone's telling me to stay out of the investigation, but I can't. I know J.J. He would never…" She stopped when the waitress approached with their meals. They ate in silence, caught up in their thoughts and the questions hanging over them. Finally, Shawn spoke.

"There's more, isn't there? Xandra?"

She hiccuped, wiped her mouth, and rubbed her forehead. "If I push too hard, I could jeopardize my chances of getting into the academy. My past isn't exactly a Pollyanna story. And Penderson's accusation has placed a hold on my career path. In fact, if you hang around me, you could be implicated. You're better off staying away."

"Stop saying that," Shawn said. "I don't know your history, and I don't need to. You're smart and more honest than anyone else. Pierce is going to clear you of that plagiarism charge, especially after Reggie admits what he did. And we'll get him to tell us what he knows about the Reverend's murder."

"Yeah, well, we have to find him first."

"We will." He escorted her to the register, paid the bill before she could object, and excused himself to go to the restroom. Pushing through the revolving door, Xandra narrowly missed running down an old man pushing a grocery cart. She clenched her fists and howled into the heated summer air. Shawn surprised her by slipping an arm around her. "What are you mumbling about?"

"What if he isn't at this party? How am I going to track him down and stay out of Terl's way?"

"With help." Shawn extracted a paper from his shirt pocket. "This is a list of the guys at the concert. I've spoken to most of them, and I wrote down what they said. Maybe you'll see something that will help us figure out where he's been hiding and what he's so afraid of."

Xandra ran a finger down the notes. "Doesn't sound like he's hiding in the woods."

"Agreed."

"But maybe Stuart is."

"Reggie's brother?"

"Yeah." She led the way back to the parking garage. "He's mixed up in this, too. I don't know how yet. And there's this." She pulled the vulture pin from her pocket. Shawn turned it over in his palm before handing it back.

"What is it?"

"A souvenir from a trip my family took in March. My little sister insisted we all get matching ones. So, you may think I'm honest, but," Xandra drew a breath and went on, "I found it at the crime scene."

"You took it?" When she nodded, he folded his hand over hers, hiding the pin. "It's your brother's."

"Yes."

"Is yours missing, too?"

"It is."

"And you're afraid it will turn up where?"

"Somewhere it shouldn't. Now do you understand? Walk away, Crowe, before it's too late."

Shawn rubbed a hand over his face. "I'm not going to tell anyone about this, and I'm not going to quit. We're going to figure this out together."

"Why?"

"Because you're not the only one hoping to make detective one day." Shawn ran his knuckles down her cheek. "I'll see you tomorrow."

He pulled his keys from his pocket as he headed toward his car. Xandra waited until his taillights flashed, warmed by his touch but uneasy at his fierce declaration. Charm and smarts, a killer combination. What, she wondered, was Shawn Crowe's end game?

Twenty-One

Three cars pulled into the park while Pete was calling in the request for forensics. He explained the situation to the new arrivals, then directed them away from the overlook before gathering his kit and gloves from the car. Janeece returned the hound to the dogwalker.

"You said you come here once a week?" Terl said. Elise Brennan mumbled her agreement, eyes riveted on the stained patch of concrete. Janeece stepped in front of the woman to block her view as Stone took photographs. "Please think again about your walk today. Did you see or hear anything unusual or out of the ordinary?"

The dogs yipped and pulled to get moving. "Can we talk by my car?" Brennan licked her lips. "The dogs need water."

"Pete?" Janeece called. "I'm going to walk Ms. Brennan to her car." She followed the woman to a maroon van near the sidewalk that led to the overlook. She waited while the dogs lapped at their bowls. After the animals were loaded into the van, the woman dabbed her forehead with a towel.

"Whoever said this job was easy? Now, what did you want to know? Oh, did I notice anything strange? I already told you I didn't. I rarely encounter more than one other person on the path, although sometimes the school cross country team practices here."

"The teens run this path?" Janeece made a note to speak to the coach.

"Well, yes, I've seen them once or twice. Noticed their jerseys. Occasionally, I'll see another woman walking a dog." Brennan tapped her chin with a finger. "Sometimes I hear things."

"What kinds of things?"

"Shouts. Water splashing. Not in the morning, but if I come late in the afternoon, especially when it's hot. I've spotted teenagers down by the creek. Look like punks to me."

"What," Janeece said, "do punks look like?"

"Oh, you know, pink hair. Or purple. Dark clothing and studs on their belts, dog collars around their necks. Dog collars! And lots of tattoos."

Sounds like Xandra a few years ago. Or today, for that matter. Janeece dismissed that thought. Judging kids by their looks instead of their hearts wasn't her thing. "White? Black? Girls? Boys?"

The woman flushed. "All of the above. They just seem rough."

"Can you spell your name again and give me your address and phone number? In case we need to follow up with you." While Brennan wrote down the information, Janeece sized up the van. Rust spots on the lower panels and the smell of unwashed dog emanating from the open doors testified to the woman's profession and her financial status. In her fifties, hair already gray, pudgy around the waist, Brennan had a hesitant demeanor and a soft voice. Not polished or outgoing, pet sitting for money, the woman exhibited a lifetime of learned stereotypes. Janeece wrote down the plate number of the van, thanked the woman, and returned to assist Stone. A Springboro black and white pulled into the lot next to the van, which exited soon after.

"Hey, Johnson." Pete tugged off a glove to shake hands with the patrolman. "Thanks for working with us on this."

"Chief says to let us know if or when we need to ramp up our involvement."

"We may need your help in scouting the park," Janeece said. "The dog walker who just left claims to have heard shouting and observed a number of teenagers down by the creek."

Cy Johnson scratched his head. "Even when it was a farm field, this place attracted the teen crowd, especially at graduation. They've managed to kick the hell out of an old shed down the hill. The entire area was part of the Beck farm originally. Shame to see history destroyed."

"You have any names to offer?"

"No, only suspects, which change from year to year. We can do a canvas if you like."

"Need you to cordon off this blood trail so our guy can collect samples." Pete led Johnson over to the stained patch of concrete, then pointed across the grass. Thick brush and trees interrupted their progress. The grassy expanse meandered up and around a dry water course, then angled down the hill, merging with the walking trail. "Whoever got hurt went into the park."

Johnson agreed. "I'll ask the park maintenance guys if they've noticed anything. I can bring my dog, too, see if he picks up a trail."

"You have a canine?" When the officer nodded, Pete pulled out a picture. "This is mine. Name's Soldier."

"A Shepherd?" Johnson handed back the photo. "My Callie's a springer spaniel. She was in training when we had that lost child scare in Franklin last year. Found the kid in time to save her from hypothermia. She's a great tracker."

"Sounds good. Let me know if you want me to bring my dog in, too. He's proven his worth in battle."

"I hear you." Johnson thumbed his radio. "I'll alert our forensics guy."

Janeece, accompanied by Pete, returned to the Crown Vic. "Hold up, Pete. Before we leave, I want to check my messages. Maybe there's a Reggie update."

Pete stowed his gear as he waited for Janeece. When she climbed in, he joined her. "Anything?" When she shook her head, he started the car. "What next?"

"A more in-depth talk with Paul Loving."

Loving's business office occupied the bottom floor of a three-story red brick building in a quiet area known as Siever's Walk, a complex that included private storage buildings as well as a government research facility doing contract work for Wright Patterson Air Force Base. It was lunch hour. Employees exited the buildings at a run and jumped into their cars, heading for the fast-food restaurants that lined the Hopewell-Springboro Pike.

"The Buns N Fries will be busy today," Pete said. "Might be worth checking later to see if Reggie Lynx returns to work."

"Good idea." When Janeece yanked the door open, the receptionist looked up from her computer, eyes wide behind oversized glasses. Pete introduced himself, flashed his badge, and asked to speak to her boss.

An angry voice erupted down the hall to the right, followed by a crash, and Paul Loving rushed into the lobby, face blotchy, knuckles white from gripping his phone.

"Not yet. I told you. I'll make it happen, and everything will be all right." When he spotted Terl and Stone, he turned his back, whispered something unintelligible, and hung up.

"Mr. Loving." Janeece blocked the way back to his office. "We'd like a few minutes of your time."

Loving clutched his chest, his eyes shiny. The receptionist hurried over with a box of tissues. He held up a hand. "I need a moment," he said. Slipping past Janeece, he retreated into his office. The receptionist shook her head.

"Poor man. He hasn't been himself for months," she said. "It's worse since his sister died. He has a lot on his plate."

Pete glanced at a nameplate on the desk. "Ms. Waller? What seems to be the problem?"

Gloria Waller raised her head, looked from Pete to Janeece to the locked door, and leaned toward them. "I'm not supposed to say until after the city council meets. It's kind of hush-hush right now."

Janeece scooted a chair closer to the woman's desk and sat down. "Gloria, whatever you say will be held in confidence, but what you know may help us catch Reverend Loving's killer. I'm sure her brother would want that."

Gloria blotted her eyes with a tissue. "Doris was a dear soul. She and I went all through school together. She got me this job after my William passed away so young."

"The council meeting?" Pete reminded her.

"Oh, yes, well, it's this land deal. Doris didn't want Paul to do it, but he's determined to make it happen. He's been working for months with investors and the mayor. I've been up to my ears in paperwork."

Janeece exchanged a look with Pete. "I understood the land belonged to the Reverend."

Gloria glanced over her shoulder. "Mr. Loving said she was going to change her mind."

"When did he tell you that?" Pete asked.

"Last Thursday." Gloria teared up again. More eye dabbing. "The same day the poor woman was killed."

Before they could ask another question, the door to Loving's office banged open. "Sorry for the outburst. My sister and I were very close. Come in, please. Have a seat. May I offer you something to drink?" Loving gestured toward a small refrigerator beneath a shelf bearing assorted snack items.

"No, thank you. We're very sorry for your loss, sir, and for intruding during this sad time. But it's important to find the person who harmed your sister."

"Yes, yes. I understand." The obsequious man staring at them barely resembled the rattled one they had witnessed minutes earlier. "How can I help?"

Janeece sat opposite Loving. Pete examined the wall plaques announcing realtor of the month awards. "You've been quite successful in Hopewell, Mr. Loving," Pete said.

Loving waved away the compliment. "One can never do enough for one's hometown. My sister felt the same."

"Did she?" Opening her notebook, Janeece ruffled through the pages. "I understand she was planning to convert the acreage behind the church into a labyrinth, an arboretum, and a natural burial plot for parishioners."

Loving sniffed. "Well, my sister had her share of fanciful notions. Not many people knew how, um, far out they were. But I convinced her it was in our best interests to develop the land for more practical uses."

"And she was on board with your plan?"

"Of course. We discussed it the morning of her passing."

Janeece waited for him to say more. When he didn't, she went on. "Then why did your sister ask the Zetts boy to draw up a landscape plan incorporating her ideas? J.J. claims he met with her that Thursday afternoon to finalize the designs."

"I can't speak to that. Perhaps Zetts is confused. He was pressuring her about that foolish idea. He wanted the attention it would bring him."

Pete cleared his throat. "Funny. J.J. doesn't seem like that kind of a person."

"Perhaps you need to look closer at that family."

"His sister, Xandra Byrd, works for you, doesn't she?"

"Yes."

"She must be a valuable employee. You trust her with closing the restaurant and counting the receipts for the day."

"I have cameras in place to keep all the workers honest."

"Are they aware of that, Mr. Loving?" Janeece leaned in.

Loving fidgeted in his seat. "I don't owe them an explanation."

She let that go for the moment. "Have you ever observed Ms. Byrd doing anything unethical?"

Loving stood up. "I thought you were here to discuss my sister."

"So," Pete took over, "you and your sister planned to do what with the land, then?"

Visibly relieved by the change in subject, Loving helped himself to a soda from the refrigerator. "My investors and I have proposed a housing development there. We are presenting the initial plans at the next council meeting."

"Who are your investors, Mr. Loving?" Pete said.

"I'm not at liberty to divulge that information, Detective."

"And just for the record, where were you the night your sister was murdered?"

Loving's face flushed. He braced himself against the desk. "How dare you suggest I would hurt Dorie? To be clear, I was at the dinner theater that night with everyone else of importance in Hopewell. It will be easy to check."

"I see." Pete nodded, closed his notebook, and placed a card on the desk. "Thank you for your time. We may need to talk with you again. In the meantime, if you think of anything pertinent to the investigation, please contact us. Oh, and you might want to inform your employees about the hidden surveillance cameras. Unless you have a reasonable suspicion of wrongdoing, it's illegal for you to use them."

Loving ignored the card and Stone's final statement. "I'll speak to my lawyer. Close the door when you leave." He picked up his phone, dialing before they stepped out of the office.

Back in the car, Pete rubbed his chin. "Funny Loving didn't mention that Coulter guy Xandra and J.J. told us about."

"Suspicious minds think alike." Janeece punched in a Google search for a real estate investor named Coulter. It took several spellings before the address of a Cincinnati firm called Coulter Equities popped up. Listed as a venture capital firm, Coulter Equities had a reputation for buying businesses, gutting the resources, then making money when the firms imploded.

"Find anything?" Pete drove toward Hopewell's historic downtown.

"Maybe. If it's the right man, he specializes in cannibalizing failing companies, and our Paul Loving is a very financially troubled man. I'm sending you the links. What concerns me is Loving's insistence that we investigate Joe's kids."

Twenty-Two

During her lunch break, Janeece paid bills online and caught up with her personal emails. Then she spent an hour logging details about Clark Coulter and his venture capital firm. An article in *The Cincinnati Enquirer* examined the firm's support for Republican politicians as well as Coulter's donations to local artistic and charitable organizations. Additional stories in various publications mentioned his "tough approach" and "predatory business acumen," neither of which seemed like flattering assessments. All the stories tallied his personal wealth and holdings, which were extensive. Coulter had briefly contemplated running for an Ohio congressional seat, a detail Janeece found intriguing. Was he jockeying for support in Hopewell with his backing of Paul Loving's project?

While Janeece worked on the equity connection, Pete dug into Loving's financial situation. What he found raised more alarms. When Janeece looked up from her computer, he handed her a printout.

"We'll need a warrant to take a closer look," he said, "but it seems Loving is not quite the success he would have everyone believe."

Janeece skimmed the summary of the man's activities over the past year. Multiple investors had pulled out of a project he backed in the neighboring city of Lebanon that bore an eerie similarity to the one he now proposed for the church land. The state liquor board had cited him twice for underage sales violations at his drive-thru carry-out before shutting it down, and a brewery venture with a Dayton conglomerate had collapsed when Loving's investment capital failed to materialize.

"The man has serious financial problems," Janeece observed, "but there's nothing yet to suggest a connection to his sister's murder."

"Worth following?" Stone stuffed the printout into a binder.

"Absolutely. You know that old saw."

"Where there's smoke," Pete said.

"Something's burning." She checked her watch. "It's too late to visit Coulter today. Let's put that on the schedule for tomorrow."

"Want me to make an appointment?"

"Yeah. Wednesdays are half days for the corporate set. I'd hate to go all that way only to learn he's golfing."

"On it."

Brooding about the relationship between the Loving siblings, Janeece headed to the break room for a coffee. Last year, the local Rotary had donated Keurigs to the police and fire stations as well as a year's supply of K-cups to use in them. It was a real change from having a rookie brew a fresh batch every shift. She remembered her first years on the force, the awful sludge in the carafes, the stale bagels they ate while working the night shift. Joe had always busted her about the coffee, but he'd been a great mentor. She'd like to stop by and pick his brain over this case. While she was there, she could spend time with Olivia. Except the involvement of his son and daughter complicated things. What if one or both of his kids had a hand in the crime? When Henry's arms snaked around her waist, she squealed.

"Hey, gorgeous, what's for dinner tonight?"

Janeece checked for onlookers, then leaned into his embrace, blushing at the memory of last night's meal interrupted by a very carnal need. Meeting and marrying Henry Watson had changed her life in countless ways, erasing the bitter taste of her first unfortunate marriage. Henry was kind, thoughtful, and unusually observant. He always knew when she needed a diversion. Planting a kiss on his cheek, she pushed him away.

"How about take-out from Arepas or China Hut?" Janeece said, her usual fall-back when she was preoccupied with a puzzling case.

"Let me guess. The Loving murder?"

"I can't wrap my head around a motive, unless it's the land behind the church."

"If it walks like a duck and quacks like a duck…"

"Yeah, yeah." She sipped from her mug, then tapped his cup. "We have suspects but no evidence linking anyone to the crime."

"Any strong leads?"

Janeece shook her head. "We had an interview with her brother today. He insinuated Joe's kids might be involved."

"Are you following that thread?"

"Of course they're involved, but criminally? I doubt it, and if I know anything about Xandra, she'll be doing an investigation of her own, despite my warning not to." She savored the aroma of hazelnut and took another sip. "Especially if she thinks she's a suspect."

"Is that a good or a bad thing?"

"A scary thing, Henry. If someone wanted Doris's land badly enough to kill her, they won't hesitate to go after anyone else who stands in their way."

"You think J.J. and Xandra are in danger?"

"Maybe. Something's off. I just need to figure out what. So, you pick dinner. We'll stop over to see Joe later." They shared a quick kiss and returned to work. Itching to re-examine the diagram Xandra had provided, Janeece pulled out the girl's timeline and glanced at the clock. The feeling of time running out dogged her. Every hour that passed increased the difficulty of identifying the killer. They needed to find Reggie Lynx, and they needed to talk to Clark Coulter and everyone else connected to this land deal. That included the mayor of Hopewell and the members of the city council. Which one of them had the deepest interest in sealing the land deal?

Twenty-Three

Headlights raked the front façade of the Buns N Fries, casting Xandra's shadow against the wall as she moved from the registers toward the back of the building. Ignoring the grease burn on her thumb, she unlocked the safe, stashed the day's receipts inside, and repositioned the roll-top desk to hide the contours of the wall-mounted, fire-proof box. She exited out the back, checked that the lock was secure, and scooted into Shawn's Camaro. In the glow of the dome light, his dark eyes sparked with mischief. "You ready for some action?"

Xandra wrinkled her nose. "I stink like burgers and fries. Sorry about that."

"You're making me hungry." Shawn leaned over to sniff her hair. She stilled, aware of the double meaning behind the words. In a few days, Shawn Crowe had insinuated himself into her life, his casual invitations and obvious interest an unnerving complication. Damn the man! Pushing him away, she buckled her seat belt.

"You're in luck, then." She extracted two double-wrapped B&F specials from her backpack. Handing one to him, she balanced a sleeve of fries on the dash, peeled back the foil wrapping on her sandwich, and bit into the deluxe cheeseburger. "We were slammed tonight. I didn't have time to eat."

Shawn pointed to the bottles of water in the console between their seats. "Good thing," he mumbled around a mouthful of burger, "I brought drinks."

They ate quickly, music from a Dave Matthews CD filling the car. When they finished, Xandra stowed the trash in a bag and stuffed it in her pack. "Cookie?"

"Later. Can you hand me a napkin? In the glovebox."

She released the catch and fumbled among the stuff stashed in the box. When her hand closed around a familiar object, she pulled it out, held it up to her face. "Why do you have a fishing knife in your car?"

Shawn snatched it and stowed it in under the seat. "Forgot that was there."

"It looks like my brother's. Except his is missing."

"It is? Well, this is my granddad's. Napkin?" She handed one over. He wiped his mouth, shooting her a quick look. "He gave it to me for protection. My family worries. Not everyone's keen on people like me."

"What's that mean?"

"I'm a quarter Native American. Cherokee. Dayton's racist roots don't discriminate when it comes to skin color or cultural heritage."

Xandra looked away, then back. She touched his arm. "I happen to like your skin color."

"Do you?" He rubbed his thumb over the back of her hand, the air charged with more than restaurant odors. She lowered the window, resting her head so the wind blew through her hair. It felt like they'd crossed a bridge. Finally, Shawn spoke. "Well, that's settled. Let's go crash a party."

Careful to observe the speed limit, he cruised past the housing developments lining the road out of Hopewell. They reached Leandro's place in the Hidden Glen complex shortly after eleven. Inside the townhouse, the living room was packed with gyrating bodies. A rapper Xandra didn't recognize screeched out lyrics from a platform next to a bookcase. The odor of marijuana made her sneeze. She followed Shawn around the writhing bodies and into the kitchen, where they found Leandro hunched over a cell phone, cigarette in one hand, beer in the other. His backside swayed to the thumping of the bass. When he spotted Shawn, he shoved the phone in his pocket.

"My man!" Leandro eyed Xandra as he and Shawn exchanged an intricate fist bump. Watching their hands dance, she wondered how long they had worked on perfecting the moves. Then he looked her way. "You brought a lady. Classy, Shawn, classy."

Opening the refrigerator, their host lifted his chin at the IPAs, the Mexican beers, and the ubiquitous cans of Bud Lite. Sodas crowded the shelves on the door. Shawn shook his head. "I'm designated tonight, Lee." He slipped an arm around Xandra, who opted for a soda, and pulled her close as a trio of Rihanna wannabes and a dark-haired Shakira sidled by. The siren eyed Shawn and mouthed an invitation. He ignored the overture. The rapper in the living room paused for breath, the crowd hollered for more, and the rhythm picked up again.

Leandro shooed the girls out before he addressed Shawn. "He was here, bro, but he ain't here now. Said he had a meeting with, and I'm quoting here, "the son of a bitch trying to get me killed." I tried to stall him, but you know Reggie. Twitchy as a forest fire."

"I appreciate you trying, Lee." Shawn surveyed the group jumping up and down beyond the doorway. Xandra confronted Leandro.

"Did Reggie say where this meeting was taking place?"

"I do not recall, pretty lady, but he was totally worked up, said Stuart was going with him as wingman."

"That," she said, "does not sound safe to me."

"You got that right. Hey, I hear he jammed you up with Penderson. I chewed his ass about that move. For what it's worth, he seemed contrite."

"Yeah, but he didn't step up, did he?" She swallowed hard, looked away. "Sorry. Didn't mean to take it out on you."

"No worries." He grinned as he poked Shawn in the chest. "This guy ever lets you go, you come find me. We could have some fun, you know."

Shawn tightened his arm around her waist. "You okay?"

Xandra finished her drink. "I guess tonight's a bust. No Reggie, no idea where the meeting is."

"You want to leave?"

"Yes. No." She placed her empty can on the counter. "Doesn't seem right to leave without at least one dance."

Shawn's face lit up. "Maybe while we're dancing," he said, "you'll think of a place where the Lynx brothers would meet up with a killer."

"You think that's who he's meeting?"

"Don't you?"

"I hope not. I'm not keen on finding another friend dead."

"Was Doris Loving a friend?"

The crowd pushed in, forcing Xandra against Shawn. His arms circled her waist, drawing her closer, sealing them off from the others. She considered the question, overwhelmed by the loss all over again. "The Reverend was more than a friend. She believed in me when I didn't believe in myself. She brought my family back from a dark place. I owe it to her to find out who killed her and why."

"Thank you, X, for sharing that." He tightened his embrace, swaying with the music until she relaxed into his chest. The song ended, but he didn't let go. "So, what's our next move, Sherlock?"

"Breakfast, tomorrow, early, at the park where I met Stuart. You in or out?"

"I'm in."

She wrapped her arms around his neck and pulled him closer. "Don't call me Sherlock."

Twenty-Four

"You're up kind of late tonight, X." J.J. yawned as he leaned over the computer screen. "Why are you working on a spreadsheet?"

"It's a school thing." She slammed the lid down and pushed away from the table. "Do you know anything about venture capitalism?"

"Venture or vulture?" He rubbed a hand through his hair. "I've heard the terms, but I've got no clue what they mean. However, ask me about trees, and I can tell you everything you never wanted to know about the life cycle of baobabs."

Xandra kicked her feet up on a chair. "Why are you up?"

J.J. opened the refrigerator. "Jonesing for one of Livvie's juicees. Want one?"

Xandra giggled and J.J. tossed one to her. She pulled an article from the stack beside the laptop, highlighting several lines. After a few minutes, she looked up. "You still upset about the Loving project?"

"More like pissed. I was so excited to be working with Reverend Loving on such a great project. She had this vision of what could be done with that land, a dream that was beautiful and ecologically sound, that gave back instead of taking from. Now that she's gone, it looks like we'll get another housing development."

"Why do you say that?"

J.J. retrieved his phone from the charging pad and scrolled to a news item in the Hopewell City Bulletin. *Council To Consider Loving Housing Proposal.* Xandra read the announcement and handed the phone back. "They're discussing it tomorrow?"

"Looks like it."

"According to what we heard in the forest," Xandra drained the rest of her juice, "Loving doesn't have the money to finance this plan. Where's it going to come from?"

"You're the one researching venture capital." He gestured toward the stack of reading material. "You tell me."

Xandra drummed her fingers. "Maybe tomorrow. I'm too tired to think anymore tonight. Plus, I have a breakfast meeting at 6:30."

"You never get up that early unless Mom wakes you. What's up?"

"Well, tomorrow I'll be up by six."

"This meeting have a name?"

"No. Yes. Maybe, but no way I'm telling you."

"All right, big sister, keep your secrets. I'll find out sooner or later." He moved toward the hall. She called him back.

"How's your job at Grunder's going?"

"They're working me hard. The guy I replaced quit without giving notice, and he took off with a truckful of tools, leaving them backed up on jobs, but, hey, they're desperate enough to pay me full-time wages for part-time work."

"Is it worth it?"

"The money's good, and they'll give me good references. Add that to my city connections and it might be enough to admit me to the OSU program."

"Joe will help, little brother, with tuition."

J.J. clenched his fists. "You think you're the only one who can pay her own way?"

"Sorry I touched a nerve. You're right."

J.J. rubbed his eyes. "Have you found your pin yet?"

"I'm working on it." Xandra listened to be sure their parents were still asleep, then took his hands. "I'll figure this out. I promise."

"With a little help from your breakfast meeting?" When she ducked, he tousled her hair, then slouched off to his room, unable to resist a parting shot. "Tell him to treat you right or he'll answer to your bad-ass brother."

Xandra grinned despite the dread roiling in her belly. She and J.J. had been through too much together not to have each other's backs. Maybe she should ask him to help find Reggie. *But,* a voice inside chided, *then you wouldn't get to see Shawn.*

The following morning, awake before the alarm, she showered, then slipped on a white tee and jean shorts. In the kitchen she popped cinnamon rolls into the oven. While the aroma snaked its way through the house, she packed a cooler with granola, milk, and apple slices, adding a towel and napkins as an afterthought. They could pick up coffee at The Brew Shoppe, her treat. She had reached the front room when Olivia sneaked around the corner to whisper-shout good morning. Then Leah peeked out, too. "Got a date, honey?"

"No, just a school thing." Xandra ignored her mother's smirk, alerted by the purr of an engine. When Shawn pulled up, she darted out the door, lugging the cooler with her. He sprinted up the walk to take it from her, his knuckles brushing against hers.

"Feels like you packed a feast." He stashed the cooler in the trunk and opened the passenger door. His grin turned wolfish. "Meeting someone for breakfast?"

"That depends," she met his gaze, "on how soon that someone supplies me with caffeine. There's a coffee shop on the way to the park. You drive, my treat."

A single car idled in front of them at the drive-thru window. Coffee secured, they reached Beck Park in time to watch the fog lifting off the prairie. Settling the cooler on the picnic table, Xandra led Shawn to the overlook wall. To the left, trees screened most of the development named after the park. To the right, another line of trees and brush hid the creek that flowed north to the Little Miami River. Shawn rested his forearms on the wall.

"I had no idea this existed. But it's not in Hopewell, right?"

"No, it belongs to Springboro, but it's so close to the dividing line that we claim it as ours, too."

"It's amazing, and I'm hungry. Are you?"

"Famished. Let's eat." Xandra returned to the table. She unwrapped the rolls, doled out the cereal and the fruit, and offered Shawn a napkin. The coffee steamed in the air, the aroma enticing. She was about to slide onto the bench when she spotted stains on the concrete. She crouched to examine them. Shawn joined her.

"That looks like blood," Xandra said.

"It does." Shawn pointed to the scatter pattern that led to the grass. "Not fresh."

"No. Looks like someone took samples," Xandra said. "There are scrapings there and there."

"The police have been here." Shawn freed a scrap of yellow police tape from the wall where the wind had flung it.

Returning to the table, Xandra helped herself to a roll. "I hope it's not Reggie's. Or Stuart's."

Shawn snagged an apple slice. "You want to explain what that means?"

"If I tell you, you'll be even more involved. That may not be a good thing."

"You're giving me a choice, right?" He waited for her nod. "I want in."

"Why?"

He circled his spoon in the granola. "Because whatever's going on in your life regarding this murder has you seriously off your game at school. It must be important if it's distracting you this much. I want to help because, number one, even if you think I'm an asshole, I'm as good as you at this police stuff. Number two, you need my help, and number three, I like you. A lot."

"You were doing okay, Crowe, until that last part." The silence lengthened between them. She had to admit that having someone to talk to helped. That was who the Reverend had been for her. Now Shawn wanted to fill that void. Any rivalry between them took a back seat to solving the murder and clearing her brother. "This may be wrong on so many levels, but you're only in if you follow my lead. We need to figure out how Reggie, Stuart, and Reverend Loving were connected."

"You mean beyond the obvious that all three lived in Hopewell, and Paul Loving just happened to ask Reggie to deliver an envelope to the lady?"

"No such thing as coincidence, right?"

"Agreed. What else?" When she didn't say anything, he waited for her to look up. "If I'm in, X, you have to talk to me."

"The land behind St. Francis belongs, belonged, to the Reverend. She asked my brother to develop a landscape plan for the property. Her brother wants to build houses there." Shawn helped himself to another roll while Xandra explained all that she had learned since she discovered the body of Doris Loving. She described the encounter with Reggie's brother and the conversation she and J.J. overheard at the church. "I already told you about the pin I found by the Reverend's body and the one I got on that family bonding trip to Hinckley in March. I have J.J.'s. Mine's missing."

"Why did you go to Hinckley?"

"My sister watched some kid documentary about vultures, which, by the way, are butt ugly. When she heard they return to Ohio every spring, she pestered my parents until they decided we'd all go see the damn things."

"You think someone left your brother's pin at the crime scene on purpose."

"I do."

"You sure he's not involved?"

She glared at him. "I know J.J. There's no way he had anything to do with this. Besides, it makes no sense for him to harm his benefactor. No, someone wants one or both of us to be suspects."

"Maybe it's about revenge."

"Why do you say that?"

"Planting a clue that leads directly to a particular person is more than coincidental. It's personal."

"But why?" She began to pack up the remnants of breakfast.

"You said all three of you got pins. Is your sister's missing, too?"

"I haven't looked, but why would they take hers? A three-year-old can't kill anyone."

Shawn rubbed his chin. "Did they all have initials on the back?"

"Yes. Olivia insisted, so they wouldn't get mixed up."

"Who had access to them?"

"That's the curious part." Xandra finished her coffee and stowed the recyclable in the cooler. "Reggie might be the only person close to us who knew about the pins. Well, and a few others from work."

"Do you know who?"

Xandra sat back, trying to remember everyone she had talked to at the Buns N Fries. "Reggie must have taken them. He was at our house the night we put our initials on the backs. He knew where we kept them."

Shawn strolled back to the wall. When Xandra joined him, he nudged her shoulder. "Dead body. Missing friend. Vulture pins as clues. Blood spatter at a park. You don't do simple, X. We've got a lot to sort out."

Xandra leaned against the stone, grateful that he hadn't confronted her about withholding evidence. "After all I've told you, you still want in?"

"I do. You don't get to solve this yourself."

"It could get dangerous." She glanced at the blood smears. "I could lose my chance to enter the Academy. I don't want to jeopardize yours."

"Hey." Shawn turned to her. "I like danger, and I like you. Might as well kill two birds with one mystery."

Xandra groaned. Shawn waited for her to look his way. "Okay, that was bad. But I mean it. How about you stop worrying about me getting in trouble, and we see what we can find out?"

"All right." She held out a hand. Instead of shaking, he folded it between his and held on. Xandra stood beside him, staring out at the prairie, and wondering if she had made the right decision. Shawn Crowe was a bloodhound when he wanted something. His help could make the difference in finding out what happened. He was also a serious distraction she couldn't afford right now. She had a plan for her life, one that didn't include entanglements. She wondered if he had a plan of his own, one that might run contrary to hers.

Back at the house, she hurried to gather her books for class. Shawn waited outside until she returned. "Follow me?" he asked. When she nodded, he moved toward her. "What's our next move?"

"I think we need to walk the park. Soon."

"Tomorrow?"

"All right." Xandra groaned. "Another early morning wake-up call."

"This time I'll bring breakfast," Shawn said. "That will give you an extra half hour of beauty sleep. Not that you need it."

She opened her mouth to reply, but he had already turned away, his words fluttering in the air. *Don't get mushy*, Byrd, she whispered, but the fact that Crowe thought she was beautiful settled like a caress among all the past moments when her adoptive mother, crazy Mary, had told her she was not.

Twenty-Five

The sign at the entrance to the business park indicated that Coulter Equities occupied space in Complex C. Pete drove the tree-shaded lane while Janeece scanned the addresses. Six buildings fanned out around a broad, circular boulevard, the median planted in red, white, and purple petunias. American flags hung at every entrance. Signage announced medical practices and legal firms. Building C sat at the very back of the circle, its landscaping as lush and well-tended as the rest of the complex.

"Can't you just smell the money?" Pete said.

"Mind your manners, partner," Janeece said. "I get the impression we better be on our best behavior in this place."

Pete angled the Vic into a parking space next to a brand-new Tesla. He cracked the windows to let in the breeze ruffling the leaves of the honey locust trees in the yard. At the front door, a placard ordered visitors to press the button on the intercom and state their business. Janeece stepped up to the wallet-sized device. When a feminine voice requested identification, she and Pete held their badges up to the camera's eye. A buzzer sounded and the latch disengaged, admitting them to the air-conditioned atrium.

The interior decorations mirrored the exterior embellishments. Large canvasses of modern art decorated the eggshell-colored walls. A fountain gurgled soothingly in a far corner, and various potted plants claimed space next to leather couches and chairs. Overhead, a window filtered light across the atrium. A woman in her early forties, wearing a tailored grey suit and oyster-colored silk blouse rose from behind a cherrywood desk.

"Officers Terl and Stone. Marilyn Gugino, Mr. Coulter's personal secretary. He'll be with you shortly. May I offer you something to drink?"

The woman cocked her head in the direction of a cabinet that obviously housed more than office supplies. Rejecting the wine, scotch, and brandy on display, the detectives accepted bottles of Evian but declined the invitation to take a seat in the leather chairs. They strolled the room until the phone on the receptionist's desk pinged.

"Detectives? Mr. Coulter will see you now." She guided them down a carpeted hall to a private office, rapped lightly, then opened the door. "Detectives Terl and Stone from the Hopewell Police Department,"

An imposing figure well over six feet, Clark Coulter rose to greet them. After shaking hands, he skimmed a hand down his tie and gestured toward the chairs that fronted his desk. When everyone was settled, the secretary took a seat behind the officers, a minitablet resting on her lap.

"Ms. Gugino will take notes." Coulter said. "If you provide an email, she will forward a copy to you at the conclusion of our talk. No objections, I trust. I find it prevents discrepancies in accounts after the fact."

Janeece raised her eyebrows but nodded agreement. "Thank you for seeing us, Mr. Coulter. We're investigating the death of Doris Loving, the former pastor of St. Francis Episcopal Church in Hopewell. We understand you are in a partnership with her brother, Paul Loving, regarding a proposed development on land behind the church."

"I am aware of Reverend Loving's passing."

"Good." Janeece uncapped her water, watching Coulter as she did so. The man folded his hands on his desk and cocked his head. No sign of nerves or tension. "We are simply following up with anyone who might have knowledge of the Loving siblings and their relationship."

Clark Coulter spread his hands. "I have had absolutely no contact with the deceased, but I have extended my sympathies to Paul. My business," he emphasized the word my, "deals with capital investments, not personal disagreements between relatives."

"So, you were aware that Reverend Loving and her brother disagreed about the use of the land?" Pete returned Coulter's stare. The man barely blinked before leaning back in his chair.

"Paul indicated to me that his sister had unusual ideas for the property but that he, Paul, was confident she would change her mind."

"When was this, Mr. Coulter?" Pete rested his elbows on his knees.

"Some time ago, I believe, Detective Stone. Very early in our discussions regarding the possibility of developing the property, I believe."

Janeece consulted her notes. "In a recent interview with *Business Week*, you describe yourself as a venture capitalist, Mr. Coulter."

The man smiled. "You say that as though it's a bad thing, Detective. My firm and similar ones provide much-needed financial backing to businesses. Although most of my dealings are with larger corporations, I have a particular interest in smaller companies in local towns. I like to keep the regional economy growing."

"You have also bankrupted a number of those small-business owners," Pete interrupted, "or forced them into selling to you."

Coulter shifted his gaze to Pete, his eyes narrowed. "I believe you are misinformed, Detective Stone. I save companies, give them new life. Without my money, many of these owners would lose everything they've invested. Now, I have a very busy afternoon. What other questions do you have for me?"

"How long have you and Mr. Loving been working together?"

"Marilyn?" Coulter looked at the secretary. She consulted the tablet.

"You had an initial consultation with Mr. Loving on December fifth of last year. A second meeting took place January twentieth of this year, with follow-up phone calls on a bi-weekly basis until," she paused, tapped the screen, and resumed speaking, "April fifteenth, when both you and Mr. Loving met with Ray Eisner."

"Who's Ray Eisner?" Pete said. Coulter smirked.

"Really, Detective? I'm certain you know the name of Hopewell's mayor as well as I do."

Pete shifted in his seat. Janeece scribbled a note and looked up. "Were you meeting with the mayor in regard to the housing development proposal?"

Coulter leaned back. "That, Detective Terl, is probably a question for the mayor to answer."

"Just one more thing today, sir." Janeece tapped her notes. "You say you didn't know the nature of Reverend Loving's plans for the acreage?"

Coulter placed his palms on the desk. "I fail to see that matters. As I indicated previously, Paul assured me that his sister had changed her mind and would agree to our proposal. Whatever her initial plans were for the land, they had changed and had no further bearing on our deal."

"When, exactly, did Mr. Loving tell you his sister had changed her mind?" Pete continued to stare at the man.

Gugino spoke up. "May 30. Mr. Coulter had a video conference with Mr. Loving."

"Interesting timing," Janeece said. "One day before Doris Loving was murdered."

Twenty-Six

The sky glowered at the land as Xandra hurried to meet Shawn. Dark clouds drifted together, threatening rain before noon.

Shawn, jeans low on his hips and a short-sleeved tee with the words *Solitary Man* stretched across his chest, handed over a steaming cup of coffee. "Want to change your mind? We might get wet."

Xandra elbowed him, then launched herself into the passenger seat. "What's the matter, solitary man, afraid of a little moisture?" As soon as the words left her mouth, she wanted to take them back. The regularity with which she made inappropriate comments was embarrassing.

Shawn snorted but didn't say a word until he slid behind the wheel. Her brother, she realized, would like this guy. The thought that she already did worried her.

"How's your vulture research going?"

"Slowly. There's so much I don't understand, especially how this all ties together, but it's too late to turn back now." She directed him through four stoplights, then down Pioneer. Shawn checked for cross traffic before coasting into the parking lot. Raindrops speckled the windshield, although the storm appeared to debate the wisdom of a downpour. They sat in the car, discussing their classes and the timeline for graduation. She avoided talk of the police academy, losing her chance to attend there too difficult to consider. When she finished the coffee, she grabbed her backpack and checked that her phone was fully charged. Then she headed down the hill.

"This trail could use an upgrade." Shawn stepped over several rotted timbers that lined the slope.

"The Eagle Scout who first installed them has gone on to greater things." She followed him along the switchbacks. At the bottom, the trail split, the western branch heading down along the creek, the eastern skirting the prairie. A sign at the junction displayed the various walking options. Shawn studied it, then tapped the farthest point.

"What's on the other side of the creek?"

"More park land, but it's undeveloped. Joe said it needs a bridge, but that section is part of a flood plain. Construction costs run too high to fund it."

He scanned the distant horizon. "Looks like it would provide good cover for wildlife, and for anyone trying to hide."

Xandra started down the path to the right. "Be careful," she said. "There's a steep drop-off ahead. One of the warning signs fell into the water last year."

The threatening skies muted the usual birdsong, although the land hummed with insect noise. Squirrels rustled in the underbrush. Woodland flowers graced the path, wild geraniums, a few late spring beauties, white and purple clover. Xandra breathed in the green-ness, savored the rich earth smells. Memories of her childhood in West Virginia assailed her, the days spent wandering the mountain, the view from Grandfather Rock, the tales Mimaw spun before the dementia took hold. She paused to inspect a dying spruce, unsure of the disease claiming it but certain that J.J. would know and care enough to seek a cure. Shawn placed a hand on the middle of her back.

"You okay?"

"I love it here. It reminds me of where I grew up, the way things were and never will be again. Which, by the way, isn't necessarily a bad thing."

"Will you tell me about it someday?"

Xandra tossed her head, causing her ponytail to bob. Shawn let it cascade through his fingers before he stepped back. She leaned down to inspect a cluster of spring violets, the last of the season. "You don't want to hear all the sordid details."

Instead of responding, he captured her hand and walked beside her. By the time they reached an abandoned shed, all that remained of the farm that once prospered here, she had grown comfortable in his quiet presence. She followed a dirt trail to the remains of the eroding structure.

"Snakes?" Shawn picked up a stick as he circled the shed, pushing through the briars and weeds.

"Maybe. But nothing poisonous." Xandra inspected the sagging structure before stepping inside. Cellophane strips, aluminum beer tabs, and a used condom littered the floor. "Eeew, gross."

Shawn poked at the remnants of a fire in the only corner still intact. "Someone was here."

"They weren't into healthy eating." Xandra kicked at the snack wrappers that littered the ground. "Let's check out the lower field and the creek. If anyone did wander into the thicker forest, they might have left a trail."

"Want me to bag anything?"

"No. The police should be doing that. I'm surprised Janeece hasn't already been here."

"Maybe she hasn't had a chance yet, or maybe she knows something we don't."

"Wouldn't surprise me. My dad taught Terl to keep her cards close." Xandra returned to the main path. Twenty minutes later, they stood on the sand and gravel banks of Pleasant Run, the stream curving away to the north. Across the water, she spotted broken branches and trampled weeds.

"Something's been through there. You game?" Xandra removed her boots and socks and rolled up her pant legs. Shawn grinned and did the same. They held hands for balance as they groped their way over the rocky streambed, water running cold and clear over their feet. Overhead, thunder rumbled.

When they reached the other side, Shawn released her hand to inspect the steep uphill climb. "How much farther do you want to go?"

Xandra dried her feet, then offered the towel to Shawn. She sprayed insect repellent over her pants and arms. When Shawn declined, she narrowed her eyes. "You'll be sorry when you have to pick ticks off your private parts."

"All right, hit me. Can't take chances with private parts," he said, grinning at the color staining her cheeks. A ridge of dark clouds crept closer.

"Ten more minutes, and then we'll head back. We'll be cutting it close, but I think the rain will hold off a while longer." Shawn scrambled up the slope, reaching back to help her climb. At the top, she searched for more evidence of a trail, swatting at the gnats and listening hard for signs they weren't alone. The path climbed upward in a series of ridges. They had reached the end of their allotted time when Shawn spotted something off to the left. They edged past a cluster of thorn bushes and halted. Ahead lay a small clearing. A weathered tent sagged beside a stone-rimmed firepit. A shallow hole, filled with trash, buzzed with flies.

"Looks like we found the litterer." Shawn picked up a candy wrapper identical to the ones in the old shed. "Do you think it's Reggie?"

"Maybe." Xandra checked the firepit, walked the perimeter of the campsite, and peeked inside the tent. "Whoever it is, I bet the blood on this bandage," she used a tissue to hold up the discarded cloth, "matches the stains on the concrete." She emptied her backpack, shook out a plastic bag, and, stuffing the bandage and food wrappers inside, zipped everything into the pack. In the distance, lightning crackled. More rain spattered the clearing. Shawn scuffed away their prints as they retraced their way to the creek. Xandra hurried to follow. After they crossed, Shawn grabbed her elbow.

"What now, X?"

Xandra shivered as the wind increased. "We'll call Detective Terl as soon as we're back in the car."

Twenty-Seven

Paul Loving marched into the police station like a man on a mission. He barked at the officer manning the reception desk, refusing to leave until he talked to Detective Terl. Informed that neither Janeece Terl nor Pete Stone was available, Loving pounded the counter, then slammed out the entry door. Pete watched the tirade from inside the station. When Janeece joined him, he pushed **Replay,** and they watched together.

"What are you thinking?" She zoomed in to examine Loving's face.

"Let him stew a while longer. He's definitely on edge, but we need more information before we confront him." Pete waited for the recording to end, then surrendered the controls to the desk sergeant. "Thanks, Garrett."

Back at her desk, Janeece shuffled through the file on Doris Loving's murder, extracting a recent news article on the development proposal and handing it to Pete. "Let's see what the mayor has to say about the deal Loving and Coulter are proposing."

Pete skimmed the page. "Any news on our missing suspect?"

"No. And we don't have the official coroner's report on the Reverend's cause of death yet, other than an approximately-six-inch blade with a curved tip. Hypothesis: a fishing knife."

"Well, that's something. Oh, and I checked out that business card. Seems Joe Zetts distributed them widely throughout Franklin, Hopewell, and Springboro. The dinner theater had a stack on their counter. Anyone could have taken one and placed it on the Reverend. You look...upset. What's up?"

"While we were in Cincinnati, Xandra left a voice mail. She's discovered evidence of a campsite south of the creek in Beck Park."

"A homeless camp? In Springboro?"

"Only one tent. Bloody bandages. Food wrappers. She dropped them off, emailed photos of the site." Janeece handed him her phone. "Henry is processing the items before sending everything to BCI."

"You suspect our boy's hiding in the forest?"

"Perhaps, or maybe our murderer is or was out there. Either way, this might be the break we need. I'll text Boro PD about the discovery. It might be important, or it might not be related to our case at all." Janeece checked for her badge in the pocket of her jacket. "I don't like the idea of that young man in the wind. He may be an innocent pawn in a larger scheme. Or he may be our murderer."

"If he's injured, he's more than a pawn," Pete said. "He's a target, one we need to find first."

* * *

The city building occupied several acres east and south of the property Paul Loving wanted to develop. While Pete jockeyed with drivers queueing up to deposit water bills in the outdoor drive-thru window, Janeece studied the landscape that served as a border between Hopewell and neighboring Springboro, the area defined by the majestic, old-growth deciduous and pine trees that made up the forest there. *A shame to cut them down to build more houses.* Pete noticed the look on her face.

"You thinking about the land?"

She sighed. "Why must we destroy everything that makes this a good place to live just to line someone's pockets? I like the rural feel of small towns like Hopewell. Too much development spoils the character."

"And brings more crime." Pete led the way into the building. "Have you studied Reverend Loving's plan yet, the one the Zetts kid drew up?"

"Not closely." Janeece acknowledged the greeting of the woman at the reception desk and asked to speak with the mayor, then reviewed her notes while the woman contacted the mayor's secretary. "I think we should talk to J.J. again."

The receptionist gestured toward the stairway at the end of the hall. "Go right up," she said. "He'll see you now."

In the second-floor foyer, Sharon Roilert greeted them and motioned them to go in. They entered the mayor's office to find Ray Eisner, a former martial arts instructor with the shoulders of a weightlifter, crouched over a mahogany desk, the surface dominated by a calendar heavily inked with scheduled meetings and city events. On the wall behind him, enclosed in glass, hung a collection of weapons used in his former business – knives, nunchaku, blunt clubs. Two polearms hung suspended from the ceiling. Eisner came around to shake hands and motioned toward a trio of chairs in front of windows overlooking the coveted land.

"Beautiful view, Ray." Janeece said. "You remember Pete Stone?"

The mayor chuckled. "Indeed, I had the pleasure of interviewing him prior to his hiring. How are you settling in?"

"It's been a good year, sir," Pete said.

"Glad to hear it. Always a pleasure to hire a veteran."

Janeece rolled her eyes, preparing to lift her feet above all the bullshit soon to fill the room. Eisner settled his powerful frame into a chair and steepled his fingers. "You ex-military guys are just the kind of people we need here in our lovely town. Apologies, of course, to the distaff side of our force. We're glad to have your kind here, too, Detective Terl. How can I help Hopewell's finest today?"

"We're investigating Doris Loving's murder, and we're curious about the property," Janeece eyed the view, "that her brother and Clark Coulter want to turn into a housing development."

The mayor looked out the window, then glanced at her, his forehead crinkled in thought. "I'm afraid I don't see how that concerns me."

"Mr. Coulter suggested we speak with you. He indicated you will be voting in favor of the proposed development soon."

"Well, look, detectives, this is city business, not police work. Both the zoning board and the planning commission have studied the plans, and recommended we proceed with the project." The mayor consulted his calendar. "You're right, Stone. A discussion on the proposal is on tonight's agenda."

"And you're on board with this proposal, Ray?" Janeece raised an eyebrow.

"Well, there's certainly no commitment yet. But when it comes to what's best for our town, you know, the council and I," he paused, emphasizing the personal reference, "have only the welfare of the residents in mind when we entertain new ideas."

Pete rubbed his chin. "Were you aware of Reverend Loving's desire to establish a memorial park on the acreage?"

"You know, I believe I did hear a rumor about that, but when she, Paul, and I spoke last Thursday, I understood she had changed her mind."

"You spoke with Doris Loving the night she was murdered?" Janeece said.

"Oh, come now, Detectives, don't play games. You're aware that the Chamber of Commerce had a celebration last week to acknowledge twenty-five years of success for the dinner theater. Everyone who's anyone in Hopewell was there. If you're accusing me of something nefarious, you'll have to include most of Hopewell's business community."

Janeece fiddled with her badge. Eisner was shoveling bull fast and furious today.

"Mr. Mayor," Pete said, "we're not accusing anyone of anything. However, if you care to describe your interactions with the Reverend that night, it may shed light on what happened to her."

"Doris was already at the theater when my wife and I arrived."

"What time was that?" Janeece said.

"Around six, I believe. I went straight from here to the theater. I met Lena in the parking lot, and we mingled with the others in attendance. Doris was outside under the overhang rambling on about her latest birding adventure."

Janeece pursed her lips. "The Reverend was interested in birds?"

"Well, yes. She has quite a collection of them stuffed and mounted somewhere." He smirked. "Everyone needs a hobby, right?"

"Did you notice anything different or out of the ordinary about Doris that night?"

"Not that I recall. Her brother joined us at one point, but he didn't stay long. They may have disagreed about something, but you know how siblings can be. I've known Doris and Paul since we were in grade school together. They've always had a prickly relationship."

"Do you think they were discussing the land proposal?"

"Well, Detective Stone, I wouldn't know. I was busy seeing to my wife and talking with council members. Doris followed us inside, then left at some point to go back out. I didn't see her again after we sat down for dinner."

"Did she seem upset or unhappy when you saw her last?" Janeece said.

Ray Eisner pursed his lips. "No more than usual."

"What," Janeece said, "does that mean?"

"Exactly what it sounds like, Detective. To be perfectly blunt, Doris Loving was not a popular figure with the Chamber. She refused to see the potential in many of the business proposals for the downtown area. Like many old Hopewell families, Doris was quite rigid in her thinking."

"But you're not," Pete interjected.

Eisner gave him a side-eyed glare. "I am not. Hopewell isn't a sleepy rural community any longer. The sooner the old-timers accept that, the more the economy will thrive."

"Do you have a financial stake in this proposed development, Mr. Mayor?"

"I don't intend to talk further about something that hasn't been approved yet." Before Janeece could ask another question, the mayor returned to his desk. "Now, I have a backlog of work to accomplish before this evening's meeting. Please see yourselves out."

Pete remained seated. Janeece closed her notebook and banged it against the edge of the desk.

"Thanks for your time, Mr. Mayor." She narrowed her gaze at the smirking man. *Doris Loving had enemies.* As they exited the building, she showed the note to Pete. He gestured toward the second-floor office and the window overlooking the contested acreage.

"Beginning," he said, "with Mayor Ray Eisner."

"Who, despite his equivocations," Janeece said, "definitely has a financial stake in the proposal. I think we just added a new name to our suspect list."

Twenty-eight

"Xandra?" Leah set the basket of Olivia's toys on the kitchen table, careful not to disturb the index cards next to the laptop. Xandra continued entering data.

"What do you need, Mom?" The word slipped out more easily today. Xandra shook off the feeling of *déjà vu*. Technically, Leah was her mother, a fact that continued to startle her. After three years, she should be over it, right? But the taste of abandonment lingered.

"The Ladies Auxiliary has been tasked with cleaning out Reverend Doris's study."

"Which means," Xandra stopped typing, "you."

"Well, I am the president, and no one else can spare the time this week. I've asked for a personal day to take care of it, and I know how busy you are, but I could really use your help." Leah held her breath, the weight of her mother's hope warring with the possibility of rejection.

"I haven't had much sleep." Xandra scrubbed her eyes. "I don't know how much good I'd be."

Leah covered her daughter's hand with her own, then withdrew it. She moved to the window to stare at the wildflower garden lining the back fence. "The thing is," her mother tapped the screen to dislodge a mosquito trying to get in, "you're the best organizer I know, and I, as you well know, am not."

Glancing around, Xandra had to agree. Despite her mother's best efforts, working full time at a high-stress job and keeping the family in clean clothes and home-cooked meals meant letting the routine cleaning chores slide. Joe helped when he could, but his fledgling private investigations business demanded constant attention. Xandra acknowledged the guilt that nagged whenever Leah asked for assistance, although neither she nor her brother had more hours to give either. J.J.'s work for the city maintenance department kept him busy from seven until three, and his second, part-time job with Grunder's Landscaping ran from four until twilight. He rarely made it home before nine o'clock.

"Why don't you hire a cleaning service?"

Leah slumped against the counter. "We just don't have the money right now."

Xandra knew they were paying for Olivia's daycare and her brother's Ohio State tuition. She had refused their offer to cover hers. Her other dad, the one who raised her until she was sixteen, offered to help with expenses, but she turned him down, too. He had a new wife and child to care for. The legal bills from her and J.J.'s adventure three years ago had depleted both families' savings. The least she could do was pay her way through Sinclair. She banded the notecards and shut down the laptop.

"When do you need me?"

"After your class tomorrow. If you come, I know we can finish the job in a few hours. Then, you have time to nap before work."

Xandra dropped her head in her hands. "I can't take a nap. I have a ton of projects due, and I kind of have to meet someone."

"You have a date?"

"Just a friend from school." Xandra didn't want her mother to know she and Shawn were searching for Reggie. She'd tell Joe. Her parents didn't keep secrets anymore. She wasn't supposed to, either.

Leah circled the table. "Is it that guy who picked you up this morning? He's cute. Does he treat you well? Do you like him?"

"Undecided." Xandra opened the pantry to stare at the snack shelf. "I have no idea why he wants to hang out with me."

"If you feel like talking about it, I'm here." Leah remembered how her heart raced the first time she saw Joe Zetts. She recognized that interest in her daughter's blush. Should she warn Xandra to be careful? Down the hall, a snore erupted, sending them both into giggles. No, Alexandra deserved to find her own way through love's twists and turns, except she couldn't remember the girl being interested in any boy before now. This one must be special. "At least tell me his name."

"Shawn Crowe. His parents own a barbecue restaurant in Trotwood, and he plans to attend the police academy. We have a couple classes together." Xandra returned to the table, a bag of chips in hand. She toyed with the index cards.

"Why don't you invite him for dinner next week on your day off? Let him see what an amazing family you have." Leah picked up the basket and headed for Olivia's bedroom. "I'll make sure your father doesn't interrogate him too much."

"I'll think about it. Dinner might be a step too far," Xandra said. "But, if you really need me, I'll go with you tomorrow."

Alerted by their laughter, Joe shuffled into the hall to whisper in Leah's ear. They shared a kiss. Her mother slipped into Livvie's room. Her father nodded as he approached, settling his shoulder holster against his chest and shrugging into a hoodie.

"You're going out now?" The words stuck in her throat. What her father did was dangerous. "Alone?"

"It's just surveillance, honey. I'll be sitting in a motel parking lot eating trail mix and drinking coffee."

"You're taking a gun." She waited. He shrugged.

"It never hurts to be prepared. You look tired, Alexandra. Go to bed. Tomorrow's time enough to do what you need to do." He tousled her hair and tugged on her ear. "Be good to your mama. She loves you, you know."

Xandra moved to the front window, watched as the headlights swept left then right and her father's car faded into the night. Worry prickled beneath her skin. She shrugged it off, restarted the laptop, and got back to work. It was after midnight before she turned off the lights. She was almost asleep when her phone pinged. **good night, X.** A second followed. **looking forward to our next adventure** She typed in a quick response: **busy tomorrow**

The cell pinged a third time. **Might have another lead on our missing lynx**

See you in class? She sent back and waited.

Minutes ticked by. No response. She waited five more, then hit **Do Not Disturb**, wondering if Shawn's silence was a sign she shouldn't trust him after all.

Twenty-nine

A flurry of ornamental pear blossoms drifted over the driveway as Xandra and Leah arrived at St. Francis. Leah brushed the petals from her shoulders with a sigh, her reluctance a reminder of how close she and Doris Loving had been. Hands full of boxes and packing tape, Xandra followed her mother to the Reverend's office. None of the instructional rooms they passed were occupied. Xandra spotted a caretaker, kerchief in place, scrubbing the floor in the nursery. When they reached the office, Leah inserted her key, tugged the handle forward, and waited for the lock to release. The door squeaked open, emitting stale, heated air. No one except the police had been inside since the Reverend died. Xandra stacked the boxes in the hall, then cranked the window open. Leah flipped on the overhead fan and looked around.

"Always neat and organized, just like Doris." Her throat closed, chopping the Reverend's name in two. "I can't believe she's gone."

Xandra set the rolls of tape on the desk. "I know. She did a lot for our family."

Leah faced her daughter. "She helped me stay strong when Olivia was missing, and she was there when I needed to sort out my feelings about your father and about you."

"Do you regret how things turned out?" Xandra's hair fell forward, shielding her face. Leah tucked the strands back behind her daughter's ear.

"No. I regret letting you go in the first place." The breeze from the fan washed over them. Xandra chewed her lower lip. How should she respond to her mother's naked sorrow? Leah shivered and stepped back. "We better get started. I wonder what happened to all the birds?"

"What birds?"

"Doris collected stuffed birds." Leah gestured at the walls. "Several were on display. I wonder who took them down."

Xandra shuddered at the memory of the bird Detective Stone had recovered the night of the murder. Was it connected to the crime and the Reverend's message to Xandra or simply a red herring? She circled the room, returned to the desk. "What should I do?"

"Why don't you pack her books? Look for the ones with her name inside. I'll work on her papers."

Xandra studied the bookshelves. "What's her system? It's not alphabetical."

Leah sorted the mail, fanned through a binder of sermons, and picked up the Reverend's appointment book. "You'll figure it out. Fetch me a box?"

"Give me a sec." Xandra dragged a few boxes in from the hall, then sat down to tape them together. Leah joined her.

"Here, let me help, and don't pack your boxes too full or they'll be too heavy to move. The custodian can store everything in the basement until her brother claims them."

Xandra pointed at the datebook on the desk. "Anything interesting in there?"

Leah frowned. "Not yet. It's mostly routine meetings with church groups and the board, hospital calls, home visits, medical appointments. There's a recurring note to *'Call P'* every two weeks, starting in," she returned to the desk to shuffle through the appointments, "January."

"Must mean Paul." Xandra finished taping the box, handed it over, and returned to the books. Five minutes later, she snapped her fingers. "I figured it out."

Leah marked several pages of appointments with sticky notes and set it aside. "Let's hear it."

"Each shelf holds books related to various church functions. The top contains scriptural and theological books. The one below holds self-help, psychology, and sociology works. There's one for bibles, liturgical sermon books, that kind of thing. The bottom," Xandra giggled, "is a collection of whodunits and Sandra Brown novels."

Leah laughed with her. "Doris was a very grounded person, honey. She never denied her human side."

"Do you think she regretted never marrying, never having children of her own?"

"Maybe. But she seemed happy with who and where she was." Leah looked out toward the field and the forested land beyond. "She really wanted to create something special on this property. And J.J. was so excited to help her."

Xandra sorted through the books. When she pulled the final volume from the bottom shelf, she spied a small door mounted into the wall. She tugged on the brass handle, but the bookshelf prevented the door from opening.

"Mom?" Leah looked up. "There's a door behind the shelves."

"What?" Leah joined her. "I had no idea. What do you think is in there?"

"Let's find out. Help me move this." Xandra pressed her shoulder against one end of the heavy shelving unit. Leah grasped the other end, and they angled it away from the wall. Finally, Xandra had enough room to slip behind the unit. She grabbed the handle, braced a foot against the wall, and yanked. The door sprang open, coating Xandra in a flurry of dust. A musty odor assailed her. She sneezed three times and rubbed her arms. "Creepy, isn't it?"

A collection of stuffed birds stared out at them, their glass eyes accusing. Leah stepped closer to inspect the mummified remains. "Why hide them?"

"Maybe they're valuable enough to hide." Xandra took out her phone and thumbed on the camera, thinking about the bird in the Reverend's pocket the night she died. "But it is weird."

"Before we pack these away, maybe we should inform Janeece."

"If the police thought they were important," Xandra sank to her knees to get a better look, "wouldn't they have taken them?"

"I don't think they found them." Leah pointed to the dust on the floor. "It doesn't look like anyone has opened this door in a while."

"I'll send these photos to Detective Terl right now," Xandra said. "They must mean something, but what?"

"Didn't J.J. say she wanted to designate part of the land as a bird sanctuary?"

Xandra heard the sadness in her mother's voice, a feeling she shared. Her brother may not be Leah's biological child, but she loved him like he was her own. Of course, J.J. had that effect on people. Everyone loved him. Which made her wonder who would want to frame him for the Reverend's murder? Xandra fingered the vulture pin in her pocket. She carried it with her everywhere now, afraid to lose it or to give someone the chance to use it against her brother again. If only she could find the one that belonged to her. Damn. She bit her lip. She had forgotten to check for Olivia's, to see if it was missing, too. And damn Reggie, again. Why had he disappeared?

"Xandra?" Her mother held up a sheet of paper. "Doris wrote a sermon about money-changers using the temple to further their own ends."

Xandra skimmed the Reverend's speech. When she finished, Leah handed over an article from a Cincinnati paper. "This was with it."

"Clark Coulter's latest projects outside his own county. Should we copy this?"

"No one is here to say no."

Xandra fed the speech and the article through the machine next to the desk, stuffed the copies into her purse, and returned the originals to her mother. "Can I see the datebook?"

"You think it's important?"

"Could be." She snapped photos of the pages detailing the contacts with P, as well as two notations in late April regarding missed calls to C and to E. When she finished, she returned to packing the bottom shelf, surprised by the number of books signed by authors. Reverend Loving was more than a bird collector. Tears threatened. The woman deserved a better fate than bleeding out behind a dumpster.

Leah continued to inventory the contents of the desk. Invoices for church supplies, mortgage papers for the building itself, lists of parishioners and their individual concerns. These last she returned to an accordion file without looking too closely. In the bottom drawer, catalogued alphabetically among other folders, was one labeled *Inheritance*.

"Xandra," her mother called. "Look at this."

Leah spread the contents of the file over the desk. A legal survey of the land behind the church. A scaled-down version of J.J.'s plan for the labyrinth, the memorial seating, and the arboretum. An envelope with no return address and inside a letter with no signature. Xandra read the note aloud.

> *Your going to be sorry if you don't change your mind*
> *Im watching you so watch your back*

"This is a threat." Goose bumps raced down her arms. "Are there more?"

Leah searched through the remaining papers, then shuffled through last week's mail, still sitting in the inbox on the desk. She pulled out an envelope addressed by hand and bearing no other identification.

"Your hands are shaking. Put it down, Mom," Xandra said. "We need to call the police right now. Reverend Doris was being threatened. Whoever wrote these notes might be the one who killed her."

Thirty

Janeece Terl re-read the file regarding Doris Loving's murder, uneasy at the dearth of information available. No finger or shoe prints. No DNA hits yet, although a single blond hair had been found on the Reverend's jacket. Doris Loving was a brunette, and her brother had little hair left, period. None of the persons of interest was fair-haired. Eisner shaved his head. She couldn't shake the feeling she might never solve this case.

Henry kept urging her to stay calm and work through the possibilities, but she didn't feel patient. Their best witness, Reggie Lynx, was on the run, maybe hiding in the woods, which reminded her that she and Pete planned to hike out to the campsite Xandra had discovered later this afternoon. The bloody bandages were being processed. Pete was interviewing Chamber of Commerce members who had attended the celebration at the dinner theater. They were stretched too thin, but Hopewell's budget didn't permit hiring additional personnel. She considered asking Joe to consult, but besides the obvious conflicts, with his new PI business, he had little time to spare. She and Pete were on their own. Janeece yawned, stretched, then rubbed her forehead. The intercom buzzed. "Terl?" the duty officer said. "Paul Loving is back. This time he's got Franco Sorelli with him."

"Thanks, Pat. I'll be right out." Great. A high-priced lawyer who enjoyed besting the police. Janeece stowed the murder file in the top drawer and prepared for a confrontation. Paul Loving not only resembled a bulldog, he acted like one. She wished Pete or Henry were here to temper her. She didn't want to say anything to antagonize Loving or his lawyer and, in her current frame of mind, she might do just that. When she stepped into the atrium, a red-faced Loving, accompanied by his solicitor, rushed over.

"Where have you been all day?" The lawyer placed a hand on his client's arm. Loving shrugged it off.

"Doing my job, sir, investigating your sister's murder. Shall we go to a more private room to talk?"

Loving moved into her space, spraying saliva as he spoke. She backed away, one hand on her taser, the other raised to warn him off.

The lawyer grabbed Loving's elbow. "Apologies, Detective. Take it easy, Paul."

Loving confronted Janeece again. "What's taking so long? It's been a week."

"I'm aware, sir." Janeece said. "All autopsies have been delayed due to a staffing shortage. Of course, we have the initial findings, but we anticipate the formal report later today."

The lawyer nudged Loving aside. "Franco Sorelli, Detective Terl." He handed her a card. "I'm sure you understand my client's state of mind. He simply wishes to put to rest the rumors circulating about his sister's passing. Your conclusions will help. Catching the person responsible is, of course, the most important thing."

"What rumors are you referring to, Mr. Sorelli?" Janeece flicked his card with a finger before stowing it in a pocket.

Loving waved his arms. "People are saying I had something to do with Doris's death."

"It's essential that we quash these unfounded claims. No one wants a lawsuit for defamation or dereliction of duty, right?" Sorelli interrupted. "I'm confident, Detective, that you and your partner will do that soon."

"Mr. Sorelli, if your client has information that might assist us, anything that would help the investigation move more quickly, he should share that with us now." She folded her arms and waited. Loving huffed. His eyes skittered around the foyer.

"Paul?" Sorelli cocked his head.

"I'll come back tomorrow. You better have something more to tell me." Before Janeece could respond, Loving shoved through the front entrance exactly as he had after his last visit. Sorelli raised an eyebrow, murmured, "Later, Detective," and followed his client out. Watching them engage in a heated conversation, she twisted her wedding ring, curious about the gold band Loving was wearing, the one that hadn't been there yesterday. On the way back to her desk, her cell phone rang.

"Janeece?" Xandra Byrd cleared her throat. "Detective Terl? You need to come to St. Francis Church right now."

"Xandra? Slow down, girl, and tell me what's going on."

"My mother and I are cleaning out Reverend Loving's study and we found some things that might be important."

"What things?"

Xandra cleared her throat. "A collection of stuffed birds, like the one you found in the Reverend's pocket."

"Birds." Janeece clipped her badge to the waistband of her slacks. "Interesting."

"And my mother found letters threatening the Reverend."

"You're at the church now?"

"Yes, but I'm leaving soon. I have class and then work."

"You might have to cut class today, Xandra. Stay put until I get there."

"The thing is," Xandra added, "I think the Reverend knew who sent them."

Thirty-one

The in-ground sprinkler system sputtered as it shot water across the parched church lawn. Xandra listened to the wick-wick of the sprayer heads, her eyes drawn to the athletic field and the woods beyond. She considered returning to the meditation place J.J. had shown her, to spend time unwinding the tangle of dread inside her, when her phone lit up.

Sorry I missed class family stuff:(I have news see you later?

The sad emoji made Xandra wonder if something had happened to Shawn's grandmother. She shoved the cell into the pocket of her jeans. She needed to return home and gear up for work. The atmosphere at BNF had been tense for a week. Emilia's parents were worried about her safety. Carson had grown pensive, and, in a surprise move, Millie Stanfield was returning to work tonight. She wondered if Paul Loving would show up and yell at everyone again. Over the past six months, the man had become distant, argumentative, and short-tempered. He wasn't a very good employer. If the Buns N Fries belonged to her, she would treat her personnel better. Droplets peppered the window, rousing her from her thoughts. She checked the time again as Leah joined her.

"If you need to leave, honey, I can handle things here."

"I know, Mom." Mom. How had that slipped out? "But I need to be here."

Leah wrapped an arm around her daughter's waist. "You're such a good person, Alexandra."

"I don't know about that." She touched the pocket holding the vulture pin.

"I know so." Leah hugged her tighter, then returned to the desk. It was already past two. Fifteen minutes more and Xandra would have to leave. She was leaning on the window ledge, re-reading Shawn's message, when Detective Terl stepped into the room.

"Xandra. Thanks for waiting for me," Janeece said. "Leah."

Her mother gestured toward the items on the desk. The detective moved closer. "Is this what you wanted to show me?"

"Part of it," Xandra said.

Janeece sifted through the papers, pausing to reread the first threat. She nudged the envelope containing the second threat with one gloved finger. "Did either of you touch this one?"

"I did," Leah said, "before I realized what it might contain. I don't know who brought the mail into the office, but I'm guessing their prints will be on it, too."

"And the sermon?"

"We both did." Xandra remained by her mother. "There's more. The Reverend had copies of my brother's drawings in the bottom drawer, along with the deed to the land, a surveyor's report, and a copy of her parents' will naming her heir."

"No mention of her brother?"

Xandra exchanged a look with Leah. "We didn't read it all. It seemed personal, and we really didn't intend to pry. But I don't think the Reverend ever intended to change her mind about the land."

Janeece pursed her lips. "You may be right, Xandra, but that's for me and Detective Stone to find out."

"Where is he?" Xandra said.

"Interviewing all the people who saw or spoke to Doris Loving the night she was murdered."

Xandra gathered her purse and keys. "Why didn't you find these when you searched the first time?"

"We just did a preliminary walk-through to be certain she wasn't attacked here. We intended to return sooner, but it's been a busy week. Now that you have uncovered these threats, we have cause to do a more thorough search."

"There's one more thing." Xandra led her to the closet.

Janeece inspected the stuffed birds. "That's curious, and more than a little unsettling, but it might explain the bird on her person."

"I have to go to work." Xandra edged toward the door. "Is there any news about Reggie?"

"No. He's still missing. If you hear anything, you'll let us know, right?"

"Definitely." Xandra turned to her mother. "Are you coming with me?"

"No," Leah said. "Janeece or one of the cleaning ladies can take me home."

Xandra accepted a hug from her mother, shook hands with the detective, and hurried to the car. On the way home, she mulled over the discoveries she and Leah had made. What did she know? What did she need to find out? Should she keep pushing for more? Janeece had been adamant about her staying out of the investigation. But with Reggie still missing and the attempt to frame J.J. with the pin, Xandra refused to stop digging. Shawn agreed with her, and even if she wasn't sure she should trust him, she wanted to know what he'd found out. She'd text him from work. When they met, they could figure out how to protect themselves as they continued investigating. Unless he was somehow involved in this whole mess. Her stomach clenched. She didn't believe Crowe had anything to do with the Reverend's death, but his connection to Reggie remained suspect. She thought about the dead bird in Loving's pocket, the pin dropped or placed next to the body. Everything must be connected, the pin, the land, the murder, the Reverend's message, Reggie's disappearance. If only she knew how.

At the Buns N Fries, she checked the news feeds for updates on the case, then messaged Shawn to meet her after work. She scanned her school emails, so engrossed in the project updates that she almost missed Millie Stanfield climbing out of Paul Loving's car. Millie was frowning. Loving looked anxious, his mouth pinched, his face flushed and sweaty. He reached toward the woman, fingers plucking at her blouse, but she shrugged free and skipped away. She didn't glance back even once.

Xandra's phone buzzed with a new text. **Sorry, Byrd can't make it tonight… tomorrow?**

Thirty-Two

Shawn's unexplained cancellation left Xandra disappointed and uneasy. She needed to see him, had counted on it, and that made her angry. He was upsetting her emotional balance, interfering with her plans for her future. And she couldn't help wondering if he had a secret agenda, something she didn't know about and couldn't anticipate. She clenched her hands at the disconnect between her mind and her body. Damn hormones! Before she could regret it, she sent a quick note agreeing to meet for breakfast, then hurried into the restaurant, surprised to see Millie Stanfield already working the drive-thru window. Usually, the woman begged for a break right before the dinner rush.

The evening was crazy rushed. No one had time to discuss last week's events. Mr. Loving did show up, but not until nine-thirty. Preoccupied and curt, he sent Xandra home before she could finish the receipts, an event as rare as it was unexpected.

The rest of the night passed in a blur of homework followed by a hurried cleaning of her room and a load of laundry. J.J. went to bed as soon as he returned from his landscaping job. Joe left for an evening surveillance of a subject suspected of cheating on her spouse. Xandra felt dizzy from the day's events, first at the church, then at the restaurant, and finally at home. Lack of sleep didn't help. Olivia woke around three, complaining of a sore throat and fever, which meant she and Leah took turns sitting up with the child. Joe stumbled in at six a.m., preoccupied and testy. He apologized for leaving Leah to deal with their sick daughter, gulped a cup of coffee, and headed out again for a meeting with a client north of Dayton. When J.J. slouched into the kitchen, he grumbled about a message from Detective Stone asking him to come to the station for an interview.

Xandra was grateful for the chance to escape the tense atmosphere. On the way into the city, she tried to clear her mind of all but the most pressing items: pass the computer crimes midterm, work on the group project in forensics, sort through the clues about the murder. More importantly, she anticipated meeting Shawn, curious if he would explain why he canceled their meeting last night. Maybe he hadn't stood her up, but once planted, the thought refused to die.

Janeece hadn't called to update the family about the discoveries in the Reverend's office, so Xandra had no way of knowing whether the information she and her mom had discovered aided the investigation or added more complications. She worried about J.J. being questioned again. She refused to consider her brother as a suspect. Three years ago, he had saved her. Now it was her turn to rescue him.

* * *

Shawn was already seated when Xandra, out of breath and dizzy from the lack of caffeine, arrived. She sank into a chair, popped the lid on the cup he shoved into her hand, and concentrated on not burning her tongue.

"That bad, huh?" Shawn shifted his own drink from hand to hand.

"I have a lot on my mind." She broke off a piece of sour cream donut and stuffed it into her mouth, then blew on the coffee before taking another large swallow. "Terl and Stone called my brother in for more questioning."

"They're working the case?"

Xandra raised an eyebrow. "You knew that."

Shawn ran a hand through his hair. "Yeah, I just…have a lot on my mind, too."

They spent the next ten minutes devouring the baked goods Shawn had brought. Xandra didn't intend to be snarky, but the comment slipped out before her brain engaged. "My breakfast was better than yours."

"No shit, Byrd. Everything you do is better than me." Anger and something more underscored his words. She looked closer, at the bloodshot eyes, the narrowed lips, and backed off her next comment.

"I'm sorry. That was out of line. But what you said, it's not true." She waited for him to look up. "You're a way better dancer than me." The reminder of their night at Leandro's party softened his gaze. He leaned forward, elbows on knees, and reached for her hand.

"As if my grandma's appendicitis wasn't enough, she had a heart attack last night and had to have another emergency surgery. We've been at the hospital the past two days."

"You haven't slept, have you?" She softened her tone. "Maybe we should postpone our info sharing another day."

Shawn grabbed her other hand. His grip tightened. "No," he said. "The Lynx brothers are running all over Dayton trying to elude whoever's after them. Last night they stopped back at Leandro's place and asked him to get them guns. I can see Stu carrying, but Reggie? He's into some bad shit, X."

Xandra settled the new information next to the pieces she'd gathered. "Is that everything?"

Shawn shook his head. "The brothers argued while they were at Lee's. Reggie wanted to leave the state. Stuart said they couldn't until they got what was owed them."

"What's owed them? Like money?"

"Maybe." Shawn released her, sat back, stared into space. "What's your news?"

"My mother and I cleaned out the Reverend's office yesterday," Xandra began. She told him about the threatening letters and the stuffed birds. "Not too crazy, right? I have snapshots of the appointment book, but we don't have time to examine them now. And you have more important things to do. Go be with your grandma, Shawn."

"Are you trying to get rid of me?"

"No. I want you to do what matters most, and I don't want you getting hurt because of me."

Shawn pulled her from the chair. "You tell me to leave after I share important clues with you? Seems like you want all the glory for yourself, Byrd."

Xandra tugged, but he was stronger than her. "Let go of me. You know that's not true."

"I don't know anything when it comes to you." His voice, pitched low, cut her like a blade. "Maybe this was a mistake. I'm all give, and you're all take."

"That's not what I meant."

Shawn heaved his backpack over one shoulder and picked up his empty cup. "When you figure out what you do mean, give me a call. Better yet, send a text. That way, when you dismiss my help, I won't have to hear your voice."

Xandra watched him storm off, his broad shoulders hunched, his hair shifting over his shoulders like the currents of their relationship. Blinking back tears, she deposited the rest of their trash in the recycling bin and headed in the opposite direction, bereft in a way she'd never felt before.

Thirty-Three

J.J. stared at the ceiling, his stomach in knots, his mind roiling with questions. Why had the detectives requested another interview? The bare walls, scuffed floor, and spartan furniture telegraphed a disregard for comfort intended to persuade a reluctant witness to talk or a guilty one to confess. Except he had no idea who killed Doris Loving. He hoped his dad, waiting in the lobby, still believed in his innocence. He shoved his sunglasses to the top of his head and rubbed his eyes. He hadn't slept much, too anxious to do more than doze off once or twice. *Don't fidget*, Joe had instructed. *Stay positive*. J.J. rested his elbows on the table. Had they found out about the missing vulture pin? If so, Xandra was in trouble, too.

The door clicked open. The detectives filed in. Stone carried drinks and a notebook, Terl a thick binder. They placed everything on the table. Pete shook his hand. Terl did a fist bump.

"Sorry for the delay. It appears someone rammed a car through the window of Papa Pio's Pizza, then took off, while another bozo tried to rob the Hopewell Community Bank. Hot weather brings out the crazies."

"I understand, but my employer might not. I was supposed to be at work an hour ago."

"I called the city," Pete said. "You're clear for today."

For today. J.J. didn't miss the implication. Stone offered him the choice of drinks. He chose water. The last thing he needed was to burp his way through an interrogation. Terl cleared her throat.

"We need to clear up a few things about Reverend Loving's last day. You stated you met her at St. Francis Church and the two of you walked the property."

"Yes. We spent about an hour and a half going over the sites of the labyrinth and the meditation garden. Then we went to her office to discuss costs and a timeframe for completing the work. We finished just after three o'clock."

"How did the discussion go?"

J.J. frowned. "I don't know what you mean. She was pleased with what I had done and asked me to work up more detailed drawings."

Janeece unfolded the copy of the plan found in the Reverend's desk. "Show me."

J.J. pointed out the existing athletic field and the entrance into the forest. He traced the path to the clearing where the labyrinth would be installed, then indicated where the meditation garden would be. "I have pictures if you want to see them."

"That would be helpful," Stone said. He scrolled through the shots on J.J.'s phone before handing it to his partner.

"Forward these to me." While the boy worked on sharing the pictures, Janeece studied the plans more closely. "When did you take these pictures?"

"That Thursday. I planned to send copies to Reverend Loving, but, well, you know." He spread his hands on the table and sighed.

"So, Reverend Loving didn't disagree with the ideas you proposed?"

Startled by the question, J.J. sat back. "No. She said I had captured her vision perfectly."

Janeece leaned forward. "Then how do you explain that someone saw you arguing with her in the parking lot at," she checked her notes, "four that same afternoon?"

"That's not possible." J.J. rose from his chair. Janeece laid a hand on his shoulder, forcing him back down. "I'm telling the truth. Anyone who says different is lying. We didn't argue. I left St. Francis about three-fifteen. Since I had the afternoon off from my city job, I offered to pick Olivia up from daycare and take her home. You can check with Goddard's. You have to sign the kids out when they leave."

"Details." Pete wrote down the address and phone number J.J. supplied, then stepped into the hall, returning five minutes later. He nodded at Janeece and sat down next to J.J. "Why would someone say they saw you when they didn't?"

"I don't know," J.J. said. "Who told you that?"

"Several people we've interviewed indicated they saw a young man arguing with Reverend Loving that afternoon," Stone said.

"You checked with the daycare, right?" He looked at Stone. "My mom will know what time I got home, and you can check the phone records. I called her as soon as we got there."

"Take a breath, J.J.," Janeece said. "We'll check with her. Better yet. Let me see your phone again." The detective sifted through the calls to and from J.J.'s phone. When she found last Thursday's date, she held the screen up to her partner.

"Can you at least tell me who said that about me?" J.J. stood up again. This time no one stopped him. "When I left the church, no one was there except the organist. I heard her practicing."

"I can't give you that information right now, J.J., but I can promise you we will look into it. Was there anything else different or strange about that day? Did Reverend Loving seem anxious, distracted, upset?"

"She was excited. She kept saying this would be the best way to right the wrongs her ancestors had perpetrated. Her words, not mine."

Janeece pursed her lips. "Any idea what she meant by that?"

"Nope, not a clue."

Pete checked his watch. "J.J., we don't believe you're involved in her murder. However, you are a person of interest. You need to stay close to home until we clear up these conflicting reports."

"I'm not going anywhere."

"Your sister has a history of taking off for parts unknown." Janeece smiled to take the sting from the words, but J.J. wasn't buying it.

"My sister wants to be a police officer. She wouldn't do anything to jeopardize her future."

"Not even to save her brother?"

"No, not even to save me." J.J. moved to the door. "But I don't need saving. I didn't do anything wrong. Can I go now?"

Terl inclined her head. She and Stone accompanied J.J. to the lobby, where Joe greeted him with a hug. The detectives returned to the interview room. While Pete cleared the table, Janeece reexamined the landscape plan.

"So, an anonymous female caller swears she saw J.J. Zetts arguing with Doris Loving around four o'clock the day of the Reverend's murder. The custodian at the church claims he saw a young man in a hoodie arguing with the Reverend about the same time that afternoon, but he can't identify the stranger other than he looked thick, whatever that means. Do you believe the Zetts boy?" Pete asked.

"I don't disbelieve him," Janeece said. "What bothers me is this push to blame Joe's kids. What are we missing here?"

Thirty-four

The day shift had filled out reports and gone home while Janeece sat at her desk, buried in the details of a case as frustrating as any she'd worked. Nothing added up. It was like a skeleton without tendons, muscle, or tissue. She had no way of connecting the bones with the information before her.

Henry popped in, offered to get dinner, and popped out again. Pete had gone home to his wife and kids. Janeece imagined herself and Henry with two kids at home, then dismissed the moment. Growing their family would have to wait. She needed to catch a killer. She shuffled through the notes once more, hoping to spot something she had overlooked. The pressure from the community was immense. The violent death had left them stunned and fearful. They wanted proof that Loving's murder was an aberration, a pointless killing by a transient opportunist. No one wanted to believe that one of their own would harm a woman who lived among them, led them in worship, counseled them in troubled times. But the deeper Janeece dug, the more she suspected a local perpetrator. She rubbed her temples to fend off the headache forming there. Despite the insinuations directed at the Zetts siblings, she didn't believe either capable of murder. However, if the accusation by the woman on the phone or that of the custodian leaked, everyone from the mayor down would be calling for J.J. to be arrested. Janeece dry swallowed two aspirin just as Henry returned with Chinese takeout and a bag of fortune cookies. The front desk buzzed him in.

Her husband pushed through the door of the squad room, tie loose, hair sticking up in spikes, eyes narrowed in affection. She set aside the murder files to retrieve napkins and plasticware from the bottom drawer of her desk.

"You look exhausted, Neecie." Henry set the food on the desk and kissed her forehead. "Why don't you take the night off? We're overdue for a movie. Besides, I miss cuddling with you."

Janeece snorted. "You never say that, Henry. I must really look like shit."

He opened the cartons of moo goo gai pan, moo shu pork, and rice, and handed over chopsticks.

"You know I can't use those." Snagging a fork, she filled her plate with a little of everything.

"You're getting better. My mother will be pleased."

Janeece swatted at him with her utensil. "Hush your mouth. Your mom will never be pleased no matter how much I improve. No woman is good enough for her son."

"Not true. She told me just this morning how much she liked the birthday gift you sent."

"It was our gift, and you're just trying to sweet talk me."

"Is it working?" They exchanged a look. Janeece still found it difficult to believe that kind, compassionate, and passionate Henry was so totally in love with her. After the debacle of her first marriage, she had stopped believing in happy-ever-afters and then there he was. She scooted closer until their knees touched. Henry placed a large cup of tea in front of her and patted her knee. They settled into the quiet as they ate. When she finally sat back, her headache and anxiety eased, he handed her a fortune cookie.

"Here. Maybe there's a clue inside."

She giggled as he winked with both eyes. The cookie cracked apart, the message fluttering to the desktop. She crammed a piece of cookie in her mouth and picked up the paper. **Beware the vulture bearing gifts.**

"Vultures again." She tossed the fortune onto the crime folders. "Can't get away from those damn carrion eaters."

"About that." Henry wiped his mouth as he reached into his pocket. "Thought you might be interested in this updated report from the coroner. I asked him to examine the object you found on her."

"It wasn't a real bird?"

"No, it was real enough, just stuffed, as in taxidermy. I checked with the local shop in Hopewell. Not his work, Starling said."

"Wait." Janeece almost choked. "The taxidermist's name is Starling?"

"Swear to God." Henry drew an X over his chest, then read from the report before handing it to Janeece. "He indicated it was an amateur job. But here's the real kicker. Guess what they found inside."

Janeece snatched the paper and scanned down the page. "Wait. A vulture pin? That is too weird to be coincidence."

"The pin was crammed inside the bird's throat. The only fingerprints on it belonged to Doris Loving."

Janeece rubbed her temples. "Why would Reverend Loving hide a pin inside a stuffed bird?"

"An appropriate question, and that's not all." Henry pointed to a sentence at the bottom of the report. "The pin had initials scrawled on the back. AB. Anybody you know?"

Terl shook her head, jarring one of her braids loose. Henry tucked it back in place, his hand lingering on her cheek before he sat back.

"Someone is going to great lengths to make us believe the Zetts kids are involved in this murder," Janeece said. "Why is that, do you suppose?"

Henry gathered the empty food containers and shoved everything into the carry-out bag. He moved the tea closer to Janeece, then crossed his legs and sighed. "Motive: revenge, greed, anger, or distraction. All, some, or none of the above. I'd look again at the people you and Pete have interviewed. Maybe you can find someone with a reason to implicate the kids."

"No need to look that hard. I can tell you right now." She ticked them off on her fingers. "Paul Loving. One of the employees at the restaurant, maybe Reggie Lynx. Clark Coulter. Ray Eisner. Several council members also seemed especially interested in blaming the boy for Loving's intransigence regarding the housing plan."

"There's a council meeting soon, isn't there, a second vote on the proposal?" When Janeece nodded, Henry rested his elbows on his knees. "I think you and Pete should attend. Observe and record anyone and everyone who speaks for Paul Loving's deal. Also, you need to find out why Doris Loving had a stuffed bird in her pocket when she died. A random red herring or something more sinister? Now, are you coming home or staying here?"

"Actually," Janeece tapped the folder to settle the papers inside and stuffed it into her bag, "I can work at home just as well as here."

They left together. Outside, dusk slipped over the land, settling into shadow as they headed west on Hopewell Pike. The last rays of sunlight streamed across the western tree line, turning the clouds red and orange, backlighting a bird of prey circling the horizon.

Thirty-five

When the timer on the fryer beeped, Xandra lifted the basket from the oil and flipped the off switch. Out in the closed dining room, Carson wiped down the tables. Emilia still manned the drive-thru window and in the lobby, Brenda was ringing up the last customers of the evening. Millie Stanfield had asked to leave early again, this time claiming a headache due to her period, a ploy to avoid the cleanup required at the end of the shift. Enough was enough. If Xandra had the authority, she would fire the woman, who didn't have the work ethic or the personality to deal with people. And Xandra was sick of Millie's snarky comments and veiled threats about moving on to better things. Their latest encounter grated more than usual.

"You're not the boss of me," Millie had shouted when Xandra asked her to take out the trash.

"Actually, I am."

"No," Millie replied coyly, "Mr. Loving is." The way she said it made Xandra pause. When Stanfield first hired on, she had been meek, reserved, content to do as she was told. Over the past two months, the woman had morphed from mousy to bleached blonde valley girl, sporting salon manicures and a tanning booth glow. What the new look meant wasn't clear, but Xandra had her suspicions. She noted the woman's early departure in the time log and checked her watch. Two minutes to closing. When the hand clicked on the half hour, she told Carson to lock the doors while she totaled the registers, collected the money, and carried the receipts back to the office area. Once the girls and Carson filed out through the back door, she rechecked the locks, then placed the money into a bank bag and stowed it in the safe. She had stepped toward the rear entrance when a rustling near the front drew her attention. Everyone had left. Maybe that pesky raccoon had found a way inside the restaurant. She tiptoed past the grilling station and the fryers, rounded the corner, and bumped into the barrel of a gun.

"Not a word," a muffled voice ordered. "Go back and open the safe." Xandra peered into a mask, noted the broad shoulders, the thick torso. The man could overpower her easily. A second intruder, also masked, was trying to pry open the registers.

"There's no money out there," Xandra said, "so you can tell your friend to stop looking."

The man shoved a gun into her ribs and a cloth sack into her arms. "Empty the safe, now, or I'll make you bleed."

Xandra swallowed the fear rising like bile, replaced it with anger. She considered her options. She could grab the fire extinguisher on the wall beside the door, swing it at her attacker. If she moved fast enough. If the man's accomplice didn't have a gun, too. Too many ifs. Her father's advice came to mind: *No life is worth any amount of money.* Joe never said what to do if they were going to kill you anyway.

"All right." Her hands shook. She clenched them into fists as she pulled back the panel that concealed the safe. She spun the dial slowly, stealing glances at the robber, looking for identifying characteristics. A star tattoo peeked from beneath the sleeve of his gun hand. When he looked back at his accomplice, the ski mask rode up, revealing an inked strand of barbed wire circling his neck.

"Ace," he called. "Check the parking lot."

"Driver's here," Ace replied, his voice higher than her captor's. Younger then, early teens. Who were these guys?

Xandra grabbed the money bag, removing the deposit slip from the front pocket. The thief snatched it from her, glanced at the figures, and tossed the paper on the floor. "Seven hundred? That's chump change. Put the paperwork in, too."

"Sorry about the money, sport. Most people use cards these days." Xandra stood and backed away. "Your loss."

"No, bitch, yours." He shoved her back down. "Put everything in the bag."

"Why do you need this?" Xandra fingered the manila envelopes Loving must have added to the safe last night.

"None of your concern." The thief grabbed the sack from her, raised the gun, and slammed it against her temple. She fell backward, catching herself on the desk before slipping to the floor. Blood trickled down her cheek.

"We gotta go." Ace scooted up to the man with the gun and tugged at his sleeve. "She's blinking the lights."

Stuffing the bag inside his jacket, the thief followed his companion down the hall toward the lobby. As they ran, he bumped against the prep counter, scattering condiment packets and straws over the floor. Woozy, head throbbing and hands sticky with blood, Xandra pulled out her phone. The numbers on the screen zoomed in and out of focus. She pressed 0911 first.

"Xandra?" The duty officer barked out. "You find another body?"

Xandra gasped out the facts of the robbery, and despite being asked to stay on the line, hung up. Hoping her father was home, she dialed his cell. When the call went to voice mail, she left a message, then gagged and threw up. Bracing herself against the desk, she managed to text Shawn right before she passed out.

Thirty-six

Case notes covered the cherry wood of the table that overpowered the small dining room, Henry's concession to Janeece when she moved in with him. Despite the drawbacks its size created, the family heirloom had proved an important carrot in advancing their relationship. She smiled at the memory. It had taken months, but when he finally acquiesced to her demand to bring the ancient, overlarge piece of furniture with her, she had no excuses left. After the missteps of her first marriage, she vowed not to make a second mistake, so when she committed to Henry, she meant it to last forever. Listening to him brush his teeth, she welcomed the fierce protectiveness that washed over her, then pondered the evidence one more time. What new perspective would she gain tonight?

The bird in the Reverend's pocket remained a mystery. Why was it there? Had the Reverend carried it to her death, or had her assailant planted it on her? Doris had belonged to several birdwatching clubs and had taken Audubon-sponsored trips since her college days. Although her ministry at St. Francis left little time for her avocation, her vision for the undeveloped land included habitats that attracted birds and birders. Which explained the collection found in her study but not the bird on her person, nor the pin belonging to Xandra Byrd stuffed inside. Janeece moved to the photographs Xandra had taken of the campsite in the nature park.

In addition to the bloody bandages, the forensics team had discovered a shirt inside the tent, both belonging to an unidentified male. One of the Lynx brothers? How were Reggie and Stuart connected to this whole bizarre incident? She paged through the copies of Loving's daybook, then pulled on gloves to re-examine the threatening notes. She unfolded the first and studied the script.

Your going to be sorry if you don't change your mind
Im watching you so watch your back

No signature, although the writing matched that of the second note. She placed the two next to each other and read the second aloud.

Stop what ur doing or the other one gets hurt

Next she traced the imprint of an object that matched the outline of the pin found inside the bird. Janeece steepled her fingers above the evidence and considered the possibilities.

One: the killer stole the pin from Xandra and sent it to Loving.

Two: If this pin belonged to Xandra, did J.J. have one, too? Neither of the Zetts kids had mentioned a missing pin.

Three: Either Xandra and J.J. didn't know the pin was missing, or they knew and had deliberately chosen not to reveal the information. Indication of guilt?

Four: Reggie Lynx had stolen the pin. Was he the mystery boy who argued with the Reverend? Was it about the pin?

Janeece continued to jot down theories. Maybe Reggie stole the pins, then passed them to someone else. Who and why? And how did his brother factor into any of this? Last and most curious of all, only Doris Loving's prints were on the pin inside the dead bird. Why would she implicate Xandra? Or was she sending a message only the girl would understand?

Janeece underlined each hypothetical, then sat back. Due to public interest, the council meeting to consider Paul Loving's proposal had been moved to Monday. Unless the case broke over the weekend, she and Pete would attend. Perhaps their presence would rattle some nerves. She stretched, then placed everything in the binder, clipping the list of questions and hypotheses to the cover. Her cell buzzed.

"Terl?" Pete said. "You still awake?"

"Unfortunately. What's up?"

"I got a call from Miami Valley Hospital. Stuart Lynx was the victim of a hit and run down by the University of Dayton."

"How bad is it?"

"Bad. They don't expect him to last the night. He also had a bullet lodged in his right calf."

"I'm on my way."

Henry shuffled from the bedroom. "What's going on, Neecie?"

"Our missing boy's brother was the victim of a hit and run. The kid's not doing well. I have to go."

Henry wrapped his arms around her. "Give me a minute to change. I'll go with you."

"You don't have to."

"Stop. You're not going out there alone." He slipped away, returning minutes later carrying his evidence kit. They set the house alarm and opened the garage door. Janeece's phone rang again.

"Detective Terl?" The duty officer from the station barked into the phone. "Robbery at the Buns N Fries. Injuries to Xandra Byrd. Ambulance on its way."

Henry took one look at his wife and grabbed her elbow. "You better sit down."

"I'm okay. Someone robbed the Buns N Fries. Xandra Byrd's been hurt. Call Pete and tell him I'll meet him after I deal with this."

Henry pressed the keys in her hand, but he didn't let go. "Are you sure you're up to driving?"

She touched his cheek. "Go help Pete. I'll be there as soon as I can."

The warm night embraced them, its shadows hiding the ugly heart of man. Janeece looked at the sky, unsettled once more by the truth that, in her world, humans were prey. What vultures, she wondered, had come for Stuart Lynx?

* * *

By the time Xandra regained consciousness, police and emergency services filled the building. An unfamiliar EMT was taking her blood pressure while a paramedic she recognized but whose name she couldn't recall, taped a clean compress to her head wound. A third emergency tech hovered just outside the door. Janeece Terl stood over her, the detective's face a study in concern and determination. The medic checked her pupils and spoke to Terl.

"She needs to go to the hospital, but you can have a word while we fetch the gurney." He squeezed Xandra's hand. "You're going to be fine."

"Xandra?" Janeece crouched beside her. "Do you feel up to giving me some information?"

Xandra touched her head and winced. "Two males, one older, maybe late twenties? The other sounded younger. They wore masks. The guy who hit me had tattoos, a star on his right wrist and barbed wire around his neck. He, um, he was wearing red Asics. His jeans were frayed around the bottom. He had on a Blue Jackets windbreaker. He cleaned out the safe."

"Slow down, X." The detective offered a cup of water. Xandra sipped as she talked.

"The younger one wore a pullover with Abercrombie printed across the front. Jeans. I couldn't see his feet. They took," Xandra picked up the crumpled receipt, "seven hundred and twenty-six dollars and fifty-three cents and a handful of envelopes I'd never seen before. I don't know what was in them."

"Great details, Xandra," Janeece said. "Rest now. We'll talk again after you see the doctors."

When the detective stood to go, Xandra grabbed her ankle. "I checked all the doors before I counted the money. They were locked. I didn't hear glass breaking. The only way they could have gotten in was if they had a key. Someone let them in."

The ambulance crew returned with the gurney. As they exited the lobby, Xandra spotted her father pacing the lot and Shawn leaning against his Camaro, arms crossed, eyes narrowed. Her headache eased, and her heart swelled. She wasn't alone.

Thirty-seven

The full moon climbed higher, flirting with wispy clouds, its brightness reflecting off the Emergency sign above the entrance to Sycamore Hospital. Janeece waited for Pete to approach before rolling down the window. He offered her a handful of chocolate-covered peanuts, which she accepted gratefully. In addition to disrupting her sleep, these late-night callouts made her hungry. While she munched, she read over the notes he'd taken at the scene of the hit-and-run.

"Crazy night." Pete brushed his hands against his trousers. "Xandra Byrd gets robbed and beaten at the Buns N Fries. Stuart Lynx is injured in a hit and run."

"And still no sign of Reggie," Janeece said.

"No. So, random events or more than coincidence?" Pete waited for his partner to exit her vehicle. "Do you think the robbery is connected to Loving's murder?"

Janeece tugged on her lower lip. "That's the question, isn't it? All these disparate elements – Doris's plan for the land in opposition to her brother's desire to build houses there, a dead bird with Xandra's pin inside, a robbery at Paul Loving's restaurant. After we check on Stuart, I want to interview Byrd again. Her account of the robbery was very detailed and specific."

"Most witnesses have less than accurate recall, especially after a physical assault. Is she always that sharp?"

"Yes. Alexandra Byrd is a survivor. She grew up with an adoptive mother who abused her, then ran away from her husband with Xandra and the grandmother in tow. X rescued a baby from a parked car and took off with the child, only to find out the kid was her half-sister, and Joe Zetts and his present wife, Leah, her birth parents."

"No shit."

"Wild, isn't it? Yet she graduated from high school with an almost perfect four-point, manages a restaurant forty hours a week, and is paying her own way through college. She has set her mind on following in Joe's footsteps."

"So, you don't see her as a murderer?"

"Never say never, but no. I don't see her brother that way either, although he does have a motive and perhaps the opportunity. Somewhere in this nest of facts," Janeece held up her notebook, "is a loose twig. We pull that, and we'll find our killer."

"But not tonight."

"Not tonight. I'm exhausted, Pete, and I'm sure your family would like to see you for more than a few hours sometime before the next millennium."

"You got that right."

"Let's check on Xandra, then head to Miami Valley to see the Lynx boy."

Pete shuffled his feet. "I'm uneasy leaving the two unguarded. What if the attackers return to finish the job?"

"I share your concern, partner. The chief contacted Miamisburg PD, since they have jurisdiction here. They've agreed to place a patrolman outside Xandra's room. Dayton PD is in charge of guarding Stuart when he comes out of surgery."

With a nod for the ambulance crew on call, Pete hurried through the ER and up the stairs to Xandra's room. The cop in the hall assured them the girl was sleeping, so they headed to Miami Valley Hospital.

"How was Stuart?" Janeece asked as the elevator headed up.

"Still in surgery when I left."

"Okay, quick update and then home. We can write up the reports tomorrow. A few hours' sleep may put all this in perspective." Terl preceded him into the surgical waiting room, empty of all but two detectives from Dayton also waiting to interview the injured boy. They exchanged names and cards and promised to keep each other informed of developments. Then Janeece and Pete returned to Hopewell, grateful for the solace offered by moonlit cornfields and wooded country lanes, the nighttime quiet masking the violence beneath.

Thirty-eight

Moonlight embraced every opening between the slatted blinds, strobing light across the bed where Xandra dozed, only to be roused by a nurse checking her vitals. Unable to fall back to sleep, she replayed the attack over and over, nagged by the feeling that she had forgotten something important. Restless, she punched the pillow, each strike a reminder of the blow to her head. And then she had it. The young guy had spoken, his words revelatory. He had referred to the waiting driver as a "she," which meant one of the female workers, Emilia, Brenda, or Millie, had helped the thieves. Of course, someone from the morning shift could be guilty, but no. Whoever was in on the robbery had shared things only the night workers knew. Xandra touched the bandage covering the stitches in her forehead. A soft rapping followed by the hiss of the door opening interrupted her revenge planning.

"Hey, you." Shawn Crowe leaned into the room.

"Hey." She clutched the covers to her chest. "What are you doing here?"

He shuffled closer, settled into the chair by the bed. "I asked your dad if I could stay."

"You did?" Xandra raised the bed to a sitting position, tucked the sheet tighter around her.

Shawn touched his chest. "He told me to behave, or I'd answer to him."

"Have you been here all night?"

"I have. You okay?"

"I think so." She switched on the light above the bed. "I want to sleep, but they keep checking to make sure I haven't passed out. In fact, it's about time for the nurse to come back."

Shawn eyed the clock on the wall. "Before she does, tell me what's bothering you?"

"Who says anything's bothering me?"

"Your frowny face. Your restless legs. You're all wound up, X. Why?"

"I'm a little freaked that you think you know me that well."

He reached for her, careful not to disturb the IV line. "I thought we were a team. Am I wrong?"

"Last time we spoke, you told me off."

"You wounded my pride, woman. But I'm back, and I'm asking you to accept my apology."

"I don't know, Shawn. I told you I have trust issues. Product of my mucked-up home life, you know?"

"I don't, but I'd like to." He rubbed his thumb over the back of her hand, then released her. "C'mon, spill."

Xandra smoothed the sheet over her legs. She wanted to believe Shawn, to trust the way her heart warmed when he looked at her, but she needed to examine those feelings later, alone, without the distraction of his smile. She sucked her bottom lip. "The guy who hit me didn't speak much, but his partner said a woman was waiting, that she had signaled them to hurry. It has to be someone from work. I've been going over what I know about Emilia, Brenda, and Millie, trying to figure out who would help those assholes rob me, and I'm pissed."

"I love it when you get all badass," Shawn said. She stuck her tongue out. He laughed and leaned his elbows on his knees. "Tell me about your co-workers."

Xandra ticked them off on her fingers. "Emilia Kline, seventeen, still in high school. She's working so she can buy a car. Brenda Rojas, a single mother looking for a sugar daddy to rescue her and provide a stable home for her and her kids. Money is tight. She could be desperate enough to try stealing. And Millie Stanfield, a disaster of an employee and a first-class bitch."

"Why is that?"

"Mr. Loving hired her before I started working there. At first, she wasn't so bad, but then she started calling off at least twice a week. The woman hates working second shift, hates working period, and yet has made no attempt to move on. She's older than everyone except Carson. She grew up in Hopewell and claims she's only working to save enough to relocate to California. But she blows her paychecks on mani-pedis and salon foils and goes clubbing, so she says, on the weekends."

"Does she do drugs?"

"I've detected marijuana a few times, but I don't think she's on anything harder."

"Aren't there female workers on the morning shift?"

Xandra toyed with the straw in her water cup. "Yes, but they aren't likely to know the routine or to have access to the keys. Mr. Loving always opens the restaurant in the morning. The day manager is an older guy with three kids and a decent salary. He'd be stupid to risk all that for seven hundred dollars and a jail sentence."

"How many guys work with you?"

"Four, including Reggie, share night shift duties, but two are teenagers with sports and school obligations. They only work a few days a week, and only until nine o'clock. Carson Smith is older and training to be a manager. He's diligent and dedicated."

"Female suspects it is, then."

Xandra raised her hand to forestall his next question. "There's one more thing. I don't think they were after the money."

"Why not?"

"Because they took other stuff. Paperwork, envelopes, a ledger I'd never seen before."

"You think that's why they were there?"

Before she could reply, the night nurse pushed through the door, followed by Leah. Shawn introduced himself and offered his seat, then kissed Xandra on the forehead. "Later, X?"

He skirted the nurse and disappeared down the corridor. Leah waited while the nurse checked Xandra's vital signs, entered the results on the computer, and, rewinding the pressure cuff, left as quickly as she had arrived.

"Hey," Xandra said.

"Is Shawn the friend you've been meeting?"

Xandra bit her lip. "Maybe. Mom, I'm sorry about all this."

"Alexandra, you have nothing to be sorry for." Leah blinked away tears, hands clenched in her lap. "You've been through a lot, and you need to rest, but your dad and I think you should know a few things that have happened since you got here."

Xandra sat up, kinking the IV tube. The monitor beeped. She winced, hit the reset button, and lay back. "Tell me."

Leah took a breath. "Stuart Lynx passed away early this morning from injuries sustained in a hit and run."

"Oh, no." Xandra closed her eyes. Two deaths now and her own near miss. The knowledge hardened her resolve to find Reggie and force him to reveal what he knew. She had to protect J.J., keep Shawn safe, and find the person who killed the Reverend and maybe Stuart, too, before he went after someone else. She peered out the window. Somewhere beyond the hospital floodlights, a predator circled, picking off prey and leaving them as carrion for the vultures. It was only a matter of time before the beast turned its eye back to her.

Thirty-nine

The chirp of an incoming message woke Janeece at six-thirty a.m., the news from the hospital another blow to the investigation. Despite the surgery to repair the damage to his internal organs, Stuart Lynx had died from his injuries. She sat on the edge of the bed, head in hands, and mourned the loss of the young man, frustrated and angry about the direction of the case. Someone was working hard to prevent her from solving Doris's murder, and now she had a second death to consider. Were they connected? What might she have done to prevent either one? Instinct insisted that Xandra's attack was part of the puzzle, although she couldn't see how. She started to rise. Henry pulled her down.

"Tell me," he said.

"Stuart Lynx is dead." Tears coursed down her cheeks. "He was only sixteen. If he had talked to us, we might have saved him."

"You can't save everyone, Neecie, though I love you for trying." Henry tightened his embrace. "What about the car that hit him?"

"Dayton PD is checking all the camera footage from the area. We should have something to go on by mid-morning."

"Want me to get up with you?"

"No. Go back to sleep. I'll see you at the station." She kissed him, then stumbled into the bathroom to brush her teeth, a list of to-dos buzzing in her head. She sent Pete a text asking him to meet her at the coffee house across from the station before heading to the basement workout room. Three miles on the treadmill should clear her head.

Thursday traffic was light along Franklin-Hopewell Pike. Janeece spotted Pete's SUV, the latest concession to his growing family, and pulled in next to it. She smiled at the memory of his sister's child, Bridget, whom Kelly and Pete had adopted, sketching Janeece's portrait last month. No question the girl had inherited her mother's artistic talent. Little Mikey, almost three, was further proof that some genes carried more influence than others. Despite his mother's quiet academic nature, the boy already exhibited the strength and agility that had helped his father become a SEAL. *Maybe it's time for me and Henry to think about having a kid.* She didn't know if she had the stamina to work and be a mom, but she was willing to consider it. Time, as her mother frequently reminded her, did not favor procrastinators.

The aroma of brewing coffee permeated the air around the building. Pete waited just inside. They ordered, and he led the way to a table with a view of the street.

"I'm sorry about the Lynx boy." Pete stirred his coffee.

"Me, too." Janeece stared at a reproduction of Edvard Munch's "The Scream" hanging on the opposite wall. She felt like screaming herself. "We should get the camera footage from DPD this morning. I also want to talk to Xandra and J.J. today about those vulture pins."

"You believe there's more than one?"

Janeece showed him the photo of the second threatening note. "This reference to the 'other one' makes me think of the pin we found."

"Did you determine where it comes from?"

"Check my browser."

Pete found the link to the vulture festival in Hinckley, Ohio. He read the description and scanned the listing of memorabilia, then handed the phone back. "Reverend Loving was a bird watcher. Maybe she purchased a pin, too. But why put Xandra's initials on the back?"

"I'll ask Xandra after we talk to the second-shift employees of the BNF, especially the females. One of the robbers mentioned a female accomplice. She thinks an employee is behind the robbery."

"How about I check with Paul Loving this afternoon, see if I can persuade him to be more forthcoming?"

Janeece finished her coffee, then rose to order one to go. "You want a refill?"

Pete waved her off. "Of all the mysteries swirling around this murder, what's the most important one?"

Juggling the to-go cup and her badge, Janeece considered his question as they headed outside. The morning greeted them with a hazy face, the temperature once more climbing quickly into the 80s. "Where is Reggie Lynx?"

Pete nodded in agreement. "We have to find him before whoever killed his brother does."

"Right. He could be the key to solving this whole thing."

When they reached the station, Janeece booted up her laptop to check emails. DPD had sent footage from the city cameras mounted in the area of the hit-and-run. A Sergeant Whittaker had narrowed the selections to the time of the accident. Advancing the film frame by frame, Janeece observed a dark-colored car with tinted windows idling by the curb a block down from the party house. The car trailed Stuart, who, inebriated or drugged, stumbled to the corner to push the crosswalk button. The following frames recorded the vehicle speeding up, veering toward the boy, and the impact itself. More cameras captured the car racing away. No rear license plate was visible. Whittaker included a description of the car itself, a black or navy Hemi Coronet with a 440 engine, rare, expensive, and none registered in the area.

Janeece printed the email and the still photos from the video, then added the new information to the case folder before she and Pete headed out to interview the restaurant employees.

* * *

Brenda Rojas answered the door in a mint green bathrobe, cigarette dangling from one hand, a young child sucking his thumb cradled in her arms.

"Ms. Rojas?" Janeece held up her identification. Pete did the same. Rojas motioned them in.

"I heard it on the news. Little Burl woke me up super early this morning, coughing his lungs out. Then, I couldn't go back to sleep, so I turned on the TV and there it was. Is Xandra all right?" Brenda drew in a lungful of smoke and exhaled in Pete's face. He batted away the smoke. She directed them to the sofa, bending to sweep a mound of toys and blankets onto the floor. "I can't believe they did it, but I knew you'd be coming to talk to me. You want something to drink?"

Pete took out his notebook. No need to prompt this one. "Who are 'they,' Ms. Rojas?"

"Well, you know, whoever robbed the place. They as in low-lifes with no more sense than to threaten a business giving people a chance to work and better themselves. I'm going back to school, you know, on account of the employee compensation they provide after you work there three years."

"I didn't know about that." Janeece said. "It's a generous perk."

"That Mr. Loving, he's not such a good boss, but Xandra's the best. You sure she's all right?"

"She suffered a concussion, but the doctors think she'll be fine."

"That's good." More inhaling and exhaling. Little Burl continued to suck his thumb, his eyelids drooping as he drifted toward sleep. "That's real good, because I don't want to lose my job, least not until I'm ready to move on, and I sure don't want to work for that Stanfield bitch. Are you, like, new to the department?" She leaned toward Pete, sizing him up.

Janeece called her back to the conversation. "Millie Stanfield, you mean? I didn't know she was going to be in charge of the place."

"Well, you know, like not right away, but Mr. Loving likes her, so who knows what will happen there?"

"What's Stanfield like?"

"Snotty. Thinks she's the queen bee and always trying to get out of doing her job, but, hey, other than that, she's all right." Rojas snorted. The snort morphed into a cough that rattled her chest.

"Do you have a key to the restaurant, Ms. Rojas?"

"Me? Hell, no. Only Mr. Loving and the day and night managers have keys. Although," her voice turned sly, "I might have seen someone sneaking one."

"Really? Who?"

Rojas stubbed out the cigarette to pat Burl's back when he started to wheeze. She glanced away, suddenly aware of what she implied. "Well, I don't know for sure."

"This is important, Brenda." Pete leaned toward the woman, his voice soft, words cajoling. "You might help us catch the person who hurt Xandra and stole money from Mr. Loving."

"Yeah. Maybe." She rocked her son. As soon as the boy's eyes closed, she carried him into a bedroom. When she returned, she was wearing an off-the-shoulder sweater and jeans.

"Ms. Rojas?" Janeece prodded.

"Reggie's a prankster. He was always clowning around with the keys. He'd swipe them and dance around the restaurant when we weren't busy. Claimed he was planning a rave party there after hours. Drove X crazy."

"So, Reggie Lynx handled the keys. Anyone else?"

Brenda Rojas pursed her lips. She batted her eyes at Pete again, this time with less enthusiasm. "There was this one time. Millie Slutfield," she spit the name out like a bad taste, "took the keys with her on her break."

"Did she leave the restaurant?" Pete said.

Rojas shrugged. "Could have. I didn't see her again until later, 'cause I was, you know, busy working. She put them back where Xandra kept them. I don't think she knows I saw her. Does that help?"

Janeece proferred her card. "Thank you for talking with us, Ms. Rojas. If you think of anything else, be sure to call, okay?"

Emilia Kline lived with her family in a newer subdivision a quarter mile from the Zetts home in a traditional brick and cedar two-story with a wide front porch and a wreath of faux sunflowers on the door. The girl answered their knock in a tank top and short shorts decorated with ice cream cones and balloons, her hair in a high ponytail. She held her hands out like she was drying a fresh manicure. "Police officers? Detectives? My parents are at work. Um, I don't know if I should let you in."

Janeece nodded. "It's all right, Emilia. You're not in any trouble. We can talk here on the porch if you like."

"Well, I guess that'll be okay. Um, do you need to read me my rights or anything?"

Pete ducked to hide a smile. "No, Miss Kline. Perhaps you heard about the robbery at the Buns N Fries last night?"

Emilia jumped, her freshly painted nails gleaming in neon orange. "What? Oh, my God, no. Was anyone hurt? Did they, like, steal money and stuff? Oh, my God. I could have been there. When did it happen? Oh, my God." She snatched her phone from her pocket without using her nails. Janeece closed her hand over the screen.

"That can wait, Emilia. Please, sit down." Janeece waited for the girl to stop shaking. "We need to know if you saw anything last night that you would call suspicious or out of the ordinary."

Emilia collapsed into one of the rocking chairs on the porch. She placed her feet on the railing and wriggled her fingers to speed the drying process. "Um, suspicious, no, unless those grungy construction workers who came in around nine and ordered, like, forty hamburgers or something. I was working the drive-thru, so I only caught snatches of their conversation. And, of course, Millie left early, but she always sneaks out before the work is done. If I were Xandra, I'd fire her ass. But then she can't, can she? I mean, like, she's tight with Mr. Loving. Millie, I mean, not Xandra."

"How do you mean, tight?" Janeece waited for the girl to continue.

"Emilia?" Pete nudged the rocker with his foot. Emilia's feet slipped free of the railing.

"Well, Millie and Mr. Loving are always whispering to each other when they think no one can see them. I work the drive-thru, mostly, but sometimes I've seen her in the back, bending over his shoulder, her chest, you know, touching him. Ew. He's so old."

Janeece nodded. "Do you have a key to the restaurant, Emilia?"

"Nope." The girl replanted her feet on the rail and rested her hands on the arms of the chair. "Don't want one. Too much responsibility."

"Do you know who does?"

"A key?" She tapped one orange nail against her teeth. "Reggie Lynx, maybe. He's always kidding about throwing an after-hours party for his friends at the BNF. Xandra used to get after him about it. Said not to even joke in case somebody heard him. But he said he could do it. And," she paused, her eyes moving from her nails to the driveway to the sky.

"And?" Janeece prompted.

Emilia leaned toward them. "Millie, maybe. Now, I may not know much, but I know girls like her, always chasing money. She'd probably show up after hours, I think, like, to bang Mr. Loving."

"You think Millie Stanfield and Paul Loving were having a relationship?"

"Duh." Emily stood to tug at her shorts. "I don't know about a relationship, but I'm pretty sure they were having sex."

"How do you know that?" Pete asked.

"I saw them coming out of that fenced area where we keep the trash bins. Millie's blouse was, like, buttoned wrong, and Mr. Loving was tucking his shirt in his pants. Ew again! If I wanted to have sex with my boss, it sure wouldn't be by the garbage cans."

Janeece and Pete avoided eye contact as they thanked the girl. Pete reminded her to call if she remembered anything else. As they settled into the Crown Vic, waiting for the interior to cool down, Pete shook his head.

"You believe the girl?"

Janeece snorted. "Hard not to. Her disgust was palpable. Plus, she has nothing to gain by lying."

"Unless she stole the key and is trying to shift blame."

"There is that."

Back on the road, they headed toward Franklin and the home of Carson Smith. Carson lived in a tidy brick ranch on Melon Road, the plat an early sixties-era sprawl of broad lawns and mature trees. A tricycle peeked from behind the garage. A tire swing hung from a limb of the tall oak in the front yard. Mrs. Smith, a petite redhead wearing an apron over a nurse's uniform, greeted them with a smile.

"You're here about the robbery, aren't you? Carson is beside himself worrying over Xandra and the money and his job. You come right in and make yourselves at home. I'll be leaving for the hospital soon. I work at Sycamore. The children are in their rooms playing games on their little screens. Carson?"

Smith rounded the corner separating the living room and kitchen, his thinning hair combed carefully over his forehead. He wore a shirt with the sleeves rolled up and a pair of chinos that bore paint stains.

"Detectives." He checked their identification, then led them into the kitchen. "I'd rather the children not hear our conversation. Six and five is too young to find out about the evils of this world."

The Smiths exchanged a glance. His wife rested a hand on her husband's shoulder and offered drinks. When they declined, she removed the apron, grabbed her purse, and kissed her husband. "I'll leave you to it, then. Call if you need me, Carson."

Smith gazed after her, his devotion clear. Janeece's heart squeezed a little at the proof that goodness and real love still existed. In the world she and Pete inhabited, those qualities rarely revealed themselves.

"Can you give us a run-down of your activities last night? When you got to work? When you left?"

"Certainly. I arrived at the restaurant at 2:45 and left at 9:35. I came straight home, didn't even stop to fill the gas tank, so I'll have to do it today. Merry and I like to spend at least a few minutes together. She works nights Monday through Thursday, but on the weekends, she works days. We try to schedule it so one of us can always be home with the children."

"Did you notice anything out of the ordinary at work over the past few days?"

Carson shook his head. "Nothing's been exactly normal since the murder. And we're short-handed because Reggie hasn't come back. Of course, we get a lot of curiosity seekers, people trying to sneak inside the trash fence. Don't know what they expect to see. Xandra had me put a special lock on the gate after she found kids sorting through the garbage for souvenirs. Can you picture that? Anyway, yesterday went about as usual. You should know the Byrd girl is a good boss, tough but fair. Works hard to treat everyone the same."

"Sounds like there's a but in there," Pete said.

"She lets one woman, Millie Stanfield, push the rules, but then Millie's cozy with the big boss so, you know, Xandra's hands are tied."

"How exactly," Pete said, "does Stanfield push the rules?"

Carson cleared his throat. "I'm not one for telling tales, but she calls in sick or leaves early three days out of six. She never comes back from her break on time, and she weasels out of cleanup at the end of every shift. If I had the authority, I'd fire her ass." Carson glanced toward the room where the children were playing. "Sorry about the language."

Janeece checked her notes. "Tell me, Carson, do you have a key to the restaurant?"

A squeal followed by thumping distracted the man. "Excuse me," he said and strode down the hall. The detectives listened as he chastised the children, promised a snack as soon as his friends were gone, and returned.

"What were you asking? Oh, keys. No, only the day and night managers have keys. Xandra hangs her on a hook by the back door. I think that goofy Lynx kid used to clown around by taking them and promising to hold parties after hours. Where has he been anyway? Xandra took him off the rotation after Reverend Loving was killed. Is he a suspect?"

"That's a question we're still trying to answer. Do you have any idea where he might be?"

"None at all. I hope he's not in any trouble, though. He's a little immature, but I think he has a good heart."

"One last question," Janeece said. "As far as you know, does anyone else have a key?"

"I don't think so. One of the girls, maybe, but Brenda and Emilia, no. Millie, she's in a whole other category."

"Why is that?" Pete said.

"That woman is devious. Anyone who avoids work the way she does yet comes all dolled up like she's got a hot date to flip burgers has a whole lot of other going on."

"Other?"

"Other, Detective Terl, as in sharing her favors for money. I know what she makes at the Buns N Fries, and it doesn't begin to pay for the clothes she wears, the jewelry, the mani-pedis." He shook his head again as he ushered them to the door. Janeece offered a card and thanked him for his time.

"My turn," she said, settling into the driver's seat. Pete tossed her the keys.

"I don't know about you, Janeece," he said, "but Millie Stanfield just shot to the top of my suspect list."

Forty

The hospital discharged Xandra shortly after ten a.m., with instructions to stay home from work until the following day. Joe returned, Olivia in tow, to pick up her and Leah. During the drive home, her sister insisted on listening to Xandra's heart with a toy stethoscope. Then she asked to see the stitches. Her curiosity kept them all laughing, though every time Xandra giggled, her head hurt. Once settled on the couch with an ice pack and a bottle of pain reliever, she turned her attention to her investigation of the Reverend's murder, beginning with Paul Loving. Since he operated multiple businesses in Hopewell, he must have started with some money. Now he was planning to become a developer. Didn't that require even more capital? She was so engrossed in speculation that she failed to hear the doorbell chime. When Leah answered the door, Detective Terl's greeting startled her.

"Did you find Reggie?" Xandra closed the laptop. Janeece shook her head. "Then why are you here?"

"I thought I'd stop by and see how you're doing."

Xandra tapped the bandage covering the stitches. "It appears my head isn't as hard as everyone in my family thought."

Leah frowned, then motioned for Janeece to sit. "Are you thirsty, Detective? I have some fresh-brewed sun tea."

Janeece agreed to a glass, then returned her attention to the injured girl. "How long are you going to be home?"

"Until tomorrow. Stitches come out in a week, but the doctor said the headache might linger for a while. Nothing's fractured, though, so that's good." Xandra set the laptop aside. "Do you have any new information about the robbery?"

"Nothing yet, but we do have a lead on one of the suspects. The tattoos and physical description match those of a parolee by the name of Ryan Tinscher. He's served time for receiving stolen property, burglary, has had a number of DUIs through the years. The younger guy is still a mystery, but once we pick up Ryan, I'm sure we'll find his accomplice."

Xandra rubbed her temple. "Did I tell you about a woman waiting for them in a car?"

"You did. Do you think one of your co-workers is involved?"

"I don't want to," Xandra propped her head in her hands, "but it seems likely. I know I checked the doors before I went back to count the money. They were locked."

"Xandra." Janeece patted the girl's shoulder. "I believe you. Tell me about Millie Stanfield."

"Millie?" Xandra shuffled through her impressions of the woman. "She's twenty-nine but acts fifteen. Mr. Loving hired her before me. I don't know what kind of a worker she was before, but she's unreliable, and she isn't good with people, which tends to be a negative at restaurants, you know? Men like her, though."

"Men?"

Xandra drummed her fingers over the laptop. "Some of the regulars, the factory guys, ask for her when they come in. Apparently, she frequents the local bars. Barrel House. Lucky's. Mr. Bill's."

"Your colleagues think she had more than a business relationship with Paul Loving."

Xandra met the detective's gaze. "That would explain a lot. But it doesn't make sense. Why would she steal from her boyfriend?"

"Excellent question, one I plan to pursue."

They listened to the thump of clothes in the dryer in the laundry room. Olivia peeked out from the kitchen, waved at Janeece, and asked if Xandra could push her on the swing. Leah scooped the child up and tickled her chin.

"Your sister needs quiet time, Livvie. After we swing, she can read you a story. Okay?"

Olivia clapped her hands and, wriggling free of her mother's arms, pushed through the screen door. Janeece watched the mother and daughter head toward the playset in the yard, her thoughts racing until Xandra spoke.

"Before today, every time I closed my eyes, I saw Reverend Loving on the ground. The blood, the smell, the birds circling above. Now, I see that jackass coming at me with a gun, and all I want to do is kick the shit out of him. Is that normal?"

"Violence is traumatic, Xandra. Cops suffer PTSD as often as soldiers. If you're serious about becoming a police officer, you must prepare to confront the ugliness of the human condition. We don't see the best in people. We spend our days with those who can't or won't follow rules, who prey on others, often because they were preyed upon themselves. It's not a feel-good profession, and the public is always on our backs. But you know what? We keep the peace the best we can and bring those who break it to justice. As for the robbery, try to be kinder to yourself. Take time to process things, to heal."

"How do I do that?"

"Accept what is. Find safe haven with the ones you love. Don't punish yourself for what you couldn't do. Rest and heal."

Xandra kicked at the afghan covering her legs. "I can't do that. My family's at risk here."

"About that. Is J.J. here?"

"No. He's working. So is my father."

Janeece wandered to the wall of family pictures. She peered at the most recent photograph. "Where was this taken?"

Goosebumps prickled down Xandra's arms. "Hinckley. It's a place in northern Ohio where vultures return to roost every spring."

"Did you all go there?"

"It was a family outing." An ache formed in Xandra's chest, tightened until she gasped for breath. She settled back on the couch.

"Did you buy anything while you were there?"

"A few souvenirs. Olivia wanted a stuffed buzzard." Xandra laced her fingers to stop their trembling. "She insisted we all buy something to 'member' the trip."

"What did you buy?"

Xandra clutched the blanket. She had to tell the truth now, wherever that led. "Pins. J.J., Livvie, and I all got one. They were shaped like vultures."

"Do you know where those pins are now?"

"No."

Janeece took out her phone and scrolled to the photograph of the one found inside the stuffed bird. "Does this look like your pin?"

"It looks like the ones we purchased. I don't know if it's mine."

Janeece flipped to the next photo. "Do the initials on the back help?"

Xandra stared at the AB etched into the metal. "Where did you find it?"

"Inside the bird in Reverend Loving's pocket. No one knew it was there until the coroner x-rayed the thing." Janeece tucked the phone away. "Can you think of any reason for your pin to be found on Doris Loving's body?"

"Someone wants you to think I killed her."

Janeece exhaled softly. "That's what I think, too."

The doorbell rang twice, followed by a light knocking. Before Xandra or the detective could respond, Shawn Crowe, wearing an ACDC tee, jeans, and a sheepish grin, stepped into the room.

"Sorry," he pointed toward the entrance, "I didn't know if you were up to getting the door, so I just let myself in."

"Shawn, this is—"

"Detective Janeece Terl, of the Hopewell PD." Terl shook Shawn's hand. "I'll be going, Xandra. We'll talk more later."

Xandra watched the detective drive away, then confronted Shawn. "How's your grandma?"

"Better. Thanks for asking. I'm going to see her tonight." He grabbed a chair, straddled the seat, and rested his arms across the back. His eyes swept from her hair to the bandage, to the top slipped off one shoulder and the yoga pants draped at her hips. Her ringed toes wriggled into the carpet. "Right now, I want to be with you."

"Stop staring." She covered her legs.

"I can't help myself, X. You're just so damn cute."

She held up a finger. "Stop. I look like shit, and I don't want your pity praise."

"This," he moved to kneel beside her, "isn't pity." Cradling her face, he leaned in and kissed her.

"Why did you do that?"

"Because I wanted to. Because when I heard what happened, I freaked. I can't stand that someone hurt you."

"But, Shawn, we're not, I mean, we haven't, anything." Xandra stopped blabbering.

"No pressure, Byrd. I just wanted you to know." He offered his hand, waiting for her to take it. When she did, he lifted it to kiss the bruise left by the IV. They sat holding hands until the voice of Olivia begging for a story interrupted them. Leah opened the screen door, paused when she spotted Shawn, then prodded the child inside. Olivia raced to the couch, crawled into her sister's lap, and eyed the stranger.

"Livvie, this is Shawn. He goes to my school."

Olivia pursed her lips. "I go to preschool. Did you come to visit my sister?"

"I did. We're working on a project together."

"Oh. Well, Xandra's reading me a story now. Do you want to hear it, too?"

"Sweetie," Leah said, "why don't you let your sister visit with her friend while I read to you?"

"But Xandra promised."

"And a promise," Shawn said, "is a promise. What are we reading today?"

Olivia raced to her room, returning with a Curious George book and the stuffed vulture, then nestled between Xandra and Shawn. "This is Buzzy. He's a carrion bird. They do 'portant work in nature."

"Is that so?" Shawn winked at X. "I didn't know that."

Olivia jabbered on about vultures until Xandra started the story. Leah watched from the kitchen, her eyes roving between her daughters and the handsome boy who had come to visit. She thought back to her attraction to Joe, how that unexpected love had produced the grown-up girl before her and given her back the family she thought she would never have again. When tears pricked, she turned away to fuss with the recipe box, searching for comfort food that would ease the dread in her heart. Changes were coming to the Zetts's house.

Leah wasn't certain she wanted them, but she knew that nothing, not even love, could keep her children safe forever.

Forty-one

Although the council meeting wasn't scheduled to begin until seven, cars crammed the lot by six-thirty. Evening shadows washed over the city building, casting bands of light and dark over the sand-colored façade. Janeece and Pete sat in the Vic, observing the citizens streaming through the atrium into the council room. The windows of the chamber opened onto the lot, allowing them a good view of the gathering.

"Too bad we don't have the place wired." Pete chuckled. "We could sit out here and take notes."

Janeece snorted. "Why didn't I think of that? Come on, partner, stay alert and observe."

She held the door for Al and Greta Sanders, an elderly couple she recognized from interviews at the church. They returned her greeting with enthusiasm.

"Terrible thing Paul's trying to do," Mrs. Sanders opined. "The Reverend didn't want houses built on her property. Neither do we." The couple joined other church members, all of whom had come to comment on the proposal. Janeece spotted Joe and Leah, Olivia in tow, at the back of the crowd. Squirming and giggling when she spotted Janeece, the child called to her. The detective waved back, surprised by the longing that rose within her. If she and Henry had a child, who would it look like? Pete jogged her elbow, bringing her back to the moment.

"Loving and Coulter are here." He handed over a printed agenda.

Janeece scanned the single page and sighed. "I hope we don't have to sit through all this other business before they get to the main event."

Pete nodded at the council members filing in behind the dais that held their chairs. "Showtime."

The mayor tapped the microphone, signaled the videographer and the secretary, and opened the meeting. Everyone stood for the pledge of allegiance, followed by the roll call. Only one councilman was absent. The others rustled papers, avoiding eye contact with the public. Janeece didn't blame them. Many of those in attendance cast angry looks at Loving and Coulter and the council. Roy Eisner asked for approval of the minutes, then addressed the audience.

"Welcome. It's good to see so many citizens interested in our local government." Someone hissed. Eisner glared into the crowd. "In consideration of your time and in the interest of all involved with the main subject of discussion this evening, we will dispense with the usual order of business and go right to the development proposal regarding the land located behind and north of St. Francis Episcopal Church. First, however, I want to express, on behalf of myself and my wife and the entire community, our sincere condolences for the loss of Doris Loving, beloved minister, and an upstanding citizen of Hopewell. She will be missed."

The assembly bowed their heads while Eisner recited the Lord's Prayer. After a brief pause, he continued. "This evening Paul Loving and his investment partner Clark Coulter are present to share their proposed plans for the property. This request has been approved by the Zoning Commission. Now, I must say, this is a most impressive strategy for the acreage involved. Besides housing, the developers intend to include several areas of green space as well as a lovely, landscaped entrance. Please give your attention to Mr. Loving and Mr. Coulter and hold all comments until the public portion of the meeting."

The crowd grew restive. One man shouted that he didn't know anything about the meeting until yesterday. "Why weren't we informed before the zoning was approved?"

Eisner gaveled for silence. "The chair of the zoning commission is also present and will share the reasons for granting tentative approval. You'll all have a chance to speak later during the open period. However, if you continue to disrupt these proceedings, you will be escorted from the room. Is that clear?"

Janeece edged up to the front of the room, angling for a better view of Loving and Coulter. Pete circled around back. His gaze wandered over the rows, pausing when he spotted a blonde sitting directly behind Loving. Was that the elusive Millie Stanfield? If so, why was she here?

Loving rose to speak. He first thanked the council for the opportunity to present the plan and then the zoning commission for their conditional approval of the application. Coulter's secretary distributed packets detailing the stages of the development. When Loving mentioned that two hundred homes would be built, angry mutters swept the room. Janeece and Pete exchanged a glance above the heads of the crowd. The murmuring grew louder. Eisner gaveled them to silence. Loving cleared his throat.

"It's not your land, Paul." Mr. Sanders called.

"Too many homes," a woman shouted.

"What about the strain on public services?" another voice demanded.

"And the schools," a man in the back said. The council exchanged wary glances. Eisner once more banged the gavel. Sanders spoke over the noise.

"This is not what Reverend Loving wanted. It's disrespectful. Shame on you, Paul."

A supporter of the proposal rose to his feet. Pete didn't recognize him, but Janeece did. **Gordon Pall, head of the Chamber of Commerce**, she texted. **Figures he'd be on Loving's side**.

Pete jotted the name in his notebook.

"Now, wait a minute," Pall began. "Doris is gone, God rest her soul, and her plan died with her. Since Paul's her only living relative, her property passes to him."

"You don't know that. Show us the Reverend's will." Sanders again.

Pall went on. "This proposal will bring jobs and tax dollars to our community. A silly prayer circle and a burial forest won't."

"That's not for you to decide, Gordon," someone yelled. Eisner gaveled wildly to bring the discussion back to order just as protesters filed into the room.

"Stop the development!" They chanted and waved posters bearing a drawing of a house with a slash through it. Those in favor of Loving's plan confronted the intruders.

"Everyone," Janeece called, "clear the room." She pressed toward the protest group. Eisner roared for order. The crowd separated into supporters and opponents, fists waving, voices raised. Janeece kept her attention on Loving, who looked around in dismay. Coulter crossed his arms and smirked. Pete moved toward the blonde who might be Millie Stanfield, noting a muted, angry exchange with Loving before she hurried away. The man gazed after her, his face a study in despair. The sergeant-at-arms bellowed for the group to disperse.

"Anyone still inside the chamber in the next five minutes," the mayor shouted, "will be subject to arrest."

Unable to reach Stanfield in the crush, Pete rejoined Janeece. Together they watched the protesters merge with the exiting citizens, the signs abandoned on the floor. "You recognize anyone?" Pete said. Janeece shook her head, directing his attention to the front of the room where Loving had cornered Eisner while Al Sanders, the church elder's face a mottled red, confronted Clark Coulter. Despite the collapse of what should have been a triumphant presentation of a winning proposal, the equity man appeared unruffled.

"Why don't you have another go at Loving?" Janeece said. Pete scooted out to wait for the man to leave. He called Kelly, who wasn't crazy about yet another late night, but his wife had gotten used to interruptions to their lives. An hour later, Pete had almost abandoned the vigil when Coulter and his assistant pushed through the doors and hurried to their car. Shoulders slumped, head buried in his phone, Paul Loving trailed after his business associate. When Pete approached, the man shook like a wet cat.

"Sorry to startle you, Mr. Loving. I stopped by your office this afternoon, but your secretary said you were out. May we speak for a moment?"

Loving's eyes darted around the now empty lot. "I've had a bad day, Detective, and this borders on harassment. What could you possibly want to talk to me about?"

"Well, that didn't go as planned."

"Not even close." Loving tugged at his tie. "I had no idea so many people were opposed to what is really a brilliant use of the property."

"And an enriching one for you, right?"

Loving narrowed his eyes. "What are you implying?"

"Mr. Loving, if your sister's property passes to you, it's worth a lot of money and you will be free to develop it as you wish."

"What do you mean if? I'm my sister's sole heir."

"Is it possible the Reverend willed the property to someone else, like the church?"

Loving just stared at him. Pete tried again. "Do you hold the title to the land?"

The man bristled. "That is none of your business."

"Actually, it is. As your sister's only living relative, you stand to gain the most by her death. Unless there is a specific provision in her will—"

"You've seen her will?"

"No. Have you?"

Deflated, Loving rubbed a hand over his head. "It seems to be missing. Mi-, my secretary, went to Doris's lawyer to check. The man claims he gave the original and all the copies to my sister, per her instructions."

"That's curious. No one else seems to know who her lawyer was."

"Name's Steve Glick. His firm's in downtown Lebanon. What lawyer doesn't keep a copy of a client's will?" Loving continued to shake, with rage or guilt, Pete couldn't tell. "Without the original, I'll have to go to probate court. I don't have time for that. I need things settled now. And I want to put her to rest properly."

Pete noted unshed tears in the man's eyes. "Were you close, you and your sister?"

"Growing up, we were inseparable. Before she got all serious into birdwatching and collecting those stuffed specimens. Didn't have time for me." Loving sniffed. "Fancied herself an expert, Dorie did. Plus, she was more religious than me. I'm a businessman. That's what I do. It's all I do. Now, if you'll excuse me, I'm going home and making myself several strong drinks while we try to reschedule this presentation."

"You're going ahead with your plans?"

Loving stared at the ground. "When you're between a rock and a hard place, you do what has to be done."

Pete leaned against the Vic, watching as Loving trudged to his car, sadness and desperation riding the man's slumped shoulders. He wondered how deep Loving's debt must be to force him down such an ostensibly dangerous path.

Forty-two

No dogs barked. No sprinklers whirred. The neighborhood had settled into a late evening coma as Joe pulled into the garage. The collapse of the council meeting followed by three hours of surveillance had taken its toll. He strolled to the curb to retrieve an errant ad flyer when Shawn Crowe drove up, followed by Xandra. Leah opened the screen door and lifted her chin in Xandra's direction, the unspoken question drifting in the still air. *Everything all right?*

Shawn hopped out and opened Xandra's door.

"Thanks for seeing me safely home." She yawned.

"Do you want me to leave? Or do you want to do a bit of sleuthing?"

"Sleuthing?" Xandra bit back a giggle. Shawn shrugged. "Go on in, Mom. We're going for ice cream before UDF closes. Want me to bring you some?"

Leah shook her head. "Should you be going out again?"

"Won't be long, promise." Pursing her lips, she climbed into the Camaro.

"What's wrong?" Shawn said.

"Leah wants to lock me up. She's afraid I'll get hurt again. I seem to disappoint my parents on a regular basis." Xandra flicked away a moth. "Well, maybe not regular, but often. My mom thinks I should choose a safe profession, like teaching. Tell that to the parents in Sandy Hook or Texas."

"What about your dad?"

"My father's ambivalent about my career path."

"It's your life."

"Yeah, but they gave it to me, didn't they?" She settled back against the seat, trailed her fingers out the window to catch the breeze. "Ever wish you had a convertible?"

"Funny you should ask. Reggie and I talked about it once. He was convinced they were nothing but trouble. I sort of agreed, but it would be fun to drive one tonight."

"So, should we go somewhere besides the ice cream store?"

"Do you know where Lynx lives?" Shawn said.

"I do. He, Stuart, and their grandmother have a place behind the shopping center west of the highway." Saying Stuart's name made Xandra's heart ache.

"You've been there?"

"What? Oh, only once. Reggie liked to hang out at our place. I think he had a bro crush on my brother. He probably stole the pins."

"Tell me where to turn, X. After we check out the house, we'll get sundaes." He waited for her to look up. When she did, he traced a finger down her cheek. "You sure you feel all right?"

"I'm good enough." She fiddled with the seat belt until they passed the shuttered Buns N Fries. "Turn at the next light."

Shawn cruised through Reggie's plat. Streetlights overshadowed by the trees that had grown up around them struggled to illuminate the roads, the light dim or totally obscured the deeper they drove into the sixty-year-old subdivision. Hunched over the steering wheel, Shawn searched the left side while Xandra scrutinized the right.

"Are you sure we're on the right street?"

"Keep going. I remember a big tree," she said, "with a tire swing in the front yard. Their neighbor parked a lawnmower trailer in the street. Wait. There. Reggie lives in the third house on the left."

The house was hidden by overgrown juniper bushes. A huge pine dominated most of the front yard. Xandra got ready to get out. "Park here. I'll see if anyone's home."

"Wait." Yanking her back, Shawn drove on.

"You passed it," she said.

"Check your mirror, Byrd."

She leaned toward the side mirror, straining for a glimpse of the house now behind them. A dark-colored SUV with tinted windows idled opposite the Lynx home, the silhouette of a large man visable next to the driver's side.

"That looks like the car that drove by Milo Beck the night I met Stuart there."

"Not a coincidence then."

Xandra took out her phone. She reversed the screen and snapped pictures over her shoulder. "Can we drive by again so I can get the license number?"

"You think that's a good idea?"

"No. Do you have a better one?" She flashed him a grin. He reached the end of the block and eased down the next street, intending to circle back. Orange cones blocked the road, forcing him to make a U-turn.

"If they spot us," Shawn said, "it could be trouble."

Xandra snorted. "If they make us, I'm calling Janeece. Meanwhile, I'll try Reggie again. He must have heard about Stuart by now. Why won't he come forward before the same thing happens to him?"

"Lynx is more interested in avoiding those guys than he is in talking to us." He eased down Reggie's Street, then smacked the wheel. "Damn."

Xandra swore, too. The detour had cost them. The SUV and the man with the binoculars were gone. "Well, at least there's still ice cream."

United Dairy Farmer's reputation for outstanding milk shakes attracted a crowd despite the late hour. Customers crowded three deep at the counter. After a twenty-minute wait, Xandra and Shawn returned to the Camaro, savoring double fudge sundaes and the music emanating from the Camaro's radio when her phone chimed. She relished a final spoonful of chocolate before checking the message.

"Xandra? You just turned three shades paler. What's up?" Shawn grabbed her hand.

"Reggie. He's in trouble." Before Xandra could show him the text, the message grayed out. Shawn tapped the screen. It reappeared, startling in its clarity. **help theyre gonna kill me** A selfie accompanied the message, Reggie, in baggy shorts and a ragged Puff Daddy tee crouched next to Stuart's mountain bike, a bloody, jagged cut carved down his cheek.

Forty-three

Drawn by the starry wonder of the June sky, Janeece leaned back against Henry, searching for a constellation she might recognize. The memory of the contentious meeting at city hall receded, replaced by the image of Olivia Zetts cuddled in her mother's arms.

"Henry?"

"This is nice, Neecie, real nice. You aren't going to spoil it with work talk, are you?" He kissed her neck.

"I was just wondering," she cleared her throat, snuggled closer, "if you might like to make a baby."

Henry stilled. "You aren't teasing, are you?"

She turned to face him. "No, I'm serious. Maybe it's time."

The night drew in around them. Henry tightened his embrace. Inside, her cell phone pinged.

"Don't. Answer. That." Henry said.

"I have to." Janeece kissed him and hurried inside.

Xandra Byrd's throaty voice reached toward her. "Detective Terl? Are you there?"

"I'm here, Xandra," Janeece said. "What's going on?"

"Shawn and I drove past Reggie's, and we saw one of the guys who was spying on me and Stuart at the overlook. And then Reggie sent me a text. He's in trouble."

"Send it to me."

"I already did."

Janeece placed the phone on speaker to search her messages until she found the photo. "Xandra? Why are you whispering?"

"I don't know." Background noise from passing cars blended with the murmur of another voice.

"Are you alone?"

"No. Shawn's with me."

"Where are you?"

"At the UDF on Hopewell Pike."

"Okay, listen to me, Alexandra Byrd. You stay there, do you hear me? Do not," Janeece felt her heartbeat ratchet up, "do not go anywhere until I arrive."

"What if the same guys who killed Stuart find Reggie?"

"We'll find him first, okay? Stay put."

Janeece returned to Henry, who had stepped to her side. "I have to go, babe."

"This," he pointed between them, "isn't over, right?"

"No, it's not. I'm sorry. Can you call Pete while I change? Have him meet me at the United Dairy Farmer Store on the Hopewell-Springboro Pike."

"Should I come with you?"

"Not yet." She pulled on jeans and a Hopewell PD polo shirt. Unlocking the gun safe, she took out her service revolver and badge, then reset the combination. "I hope you won't have to."

"Who is it?"

"The missing Lynx boy." Anxiety percolated in her head. "He's hiding, afraid for his life."

"Want me to call for backup?"

"Not until I know what we're dealing with." She left him with a kiss and a promise and hurried to the car, activating the hood light to speed her passage down the Pike. When she pulled into UDF, Xandra was pacing while Shawn Crowe leaned against his Camaro, phone in hand. Janeece jogged over.

It was closing time. A tired employee swept trash from the lot. The last customers scuffed their way to their cars. Ignoring the stares, Janeece asked for Xandra's phone. The girl brought up the message, shared Reggie's text, then the photos she'd taken outside his house. The images were dark but surprisingly clear. The face of the man watching the house was in shadow, but his height obvious. A second shadow appeared in the final photograph.

"Someone was with him." Janeece sent the pictures on to Pete.

"When I met with Stuart," Xandra said, "two men trailed us."

"This car fits the description of a vehicle seen in the vicinity of Stuart's hit and run."

Shawn draped an arm across Xandra's shoulders. The lights inside the UDF blinked off. An employee came to the door, stuck his head out, and asked them to leave. Janeece flashed her badge, and the kid backed off.

"Detective," Shawn said, "can we get a location for Reggie from Xandra's phone?"

"Maybe. X, did he try to call you?"

Xandra scanned the day's calls, which showed nothing from him, although she did discover one from two days ago. "I didn't know he called. Maybe he left a message."

"Check now," the detective said. "If there is one, put it on speaker."

She had barely activated the recording when Detective Stone arrived. Reggie's voice rang out in the darkened lot. "Sorry about the pins, X, sorry about everything. Don't tell anyone I called." She played the message three times until she realized that she knew where he was.

"That traffic noise in the background." Xandra tapped the screen. "I recognize it. Reggie's at Cox Arboretum."

"How sure are you?" Pete said.

"Positive. J.J. and I take Olivia there to see the ducks at least once a week."

"Okay, say he's there. That's a huge property."

"One hundred and eighty-nine acres, to be exact." Shawn looked up from his Google search. "How will we find him at night?"

"You can't call in a search party," Xandra warned. "He'll run."

Janeece consulted with Pete. "You two are our best bet to find him before those goons do. But you just got out of the hospital. It's not a good idea to go running around in the woods in the dark."

Xandra stared at Janeece. "You can't leave me behind. Please. You have to let me help."

Pete shook his head. "No way. If these men chasing him are the ones who killed Stuart, they're dangerous. We can't risk your safety, too."

Xandra bristled. "Reggie stole my work. I'm pretty sure he stole my vulture pin. Maybe he knows who's trying to blame me and J.J. for the Reverend's death. He owes me. Besides, I'm the only one he'll talk to."

A few stray fireflies straggled across the grass edging the parking lot, their lights dim against the floodlights scoring the front of the building. Shawn wrapped his arms around Xandra, anchoring her body with his own. Stone shuffled his feet. "I vote no, but it's your call, partner," he said. "Whatever you decide, we better get moving."

Janeece's phone lit up. She glanced at the screen.

"What?" Sensing trouble, Pete stepped to her side. Xandra and Shawn moved closer, too. "I sent Xandra's photos to Dayton. One of the officers on night shift checked them against the camera evidence from the hit-and-run. The vehicle's a match."

"That's a break. How do you want to handle it?"

"I messaged dispatch to put out an APB on the car. Let's go get Reggie."

"Okay. Drive separate or ride together?" Pete said.

"Together. That way, we can keep an eye on these two." She tipped her chin at Xandra and Shawn, then waved them into the Vic. Pete exceeded the speed limit down the Pike, crossing from Hopewell into Springboro, then north toward the Mall. When he reached Lowe's, he turned in and parked. Janeece addressed the teens. "Before we get there, a few ground rules. Do you have any reason to believe Reggie is armed?"

"He's never been into guns," Xandra said. "But Stuart had one."

"If Reggie feels threatened, there's no telling what he might do," the detective mused, "but first, we have to locate him. Can you invite him to come out with a text?"

"What do you want me to do?"

Janeece explained her plan. When everyone understood their roles, she ordered Pete to approach the Arboretum. A guard rail blocked the entrance, so he coasted onto the grass and cut the engine. Janeece handed Shawn a flashlight. "Follow us to the welcome center. Do not go any deeper into the park. Do not play hero. Understand?"

"Yes," Shawn said. He grabbed Xandra's hand and led her down the curving drive toward the main building. The ponds to the north glimmered in the moonlight. Paths branched out in all directions, threading among the specimen trees and gardens or leading into the forest.

When Xandra stumbled, Shawn tugged her close. "How are you doing?" he said.

"My head hurts. I don't suppose you have any pain pills on you."

"You didn't bring any?" When she closed her eyes, he rested a hand on her back. "Maybe this isn't the best idea."

"No, it's a good idea. I'm not going back now that I know Reggie's here." They made their way down the walkway.

"You're a better friend than he deserves. Especially after he plagiarized your report."

"Shit." Xandra stopped so suddenly that Shawn almost knocked her down. "I still have that hanging over me."

"One thing at a time, Byrd. Focus." Janeece and Pete, far ahead, separated when they reached the main building. Xandra and Shawn passed between the gift shop and instruction center, heading toward the plant sheds.

"Janeece told us to stop here."

"She did." Xandra kept walking. Shawn followed. The night hummed with the calls of frogs and the fluttering of bats' wings above the arbor walk. When they reached the ornamental grasses, Xandra texted Reggie to meet her at the outdoor pavilion and hurried on to the arched structure, where she collapsed onto a wooden bench. Shawn kept lookout. Fifteen minutes passed before her phone vibrated.

"He's on his way."

"Where are the detectives?"

"Close enough to help, far enough not to hinder." Xandra snorted. "One of my dad's favorite sayings, and trust me, he has a lot of them."

"Your dad seems like a good guy," Shawn said.

"I wish he were here tonight," Xandra whispered. Ten more minutes ticked by. Out among the trees, a rustling. Xandra peeked around the corner of the shelter. A figure staggered from tree to tree, circling closer to their hiding place. Xandra stepped out of the shelter.

"Reggie?"

"Xandra?"

"Yeah. Shawn's here, too." When Reggie hesitated, she moved toward him. "It's time to stop running, Reg. Stuart's dead. We don't want that to happen to you."

Reggie stumbled through the damp grass. When he reached them, Xandra raised her arms.

"God, girl, don't touch me. I probably have lice or bed bugs or something. And I didn't do right by you. Why are you helping me now?"

"Because you asked. Because we care." She cocked her head at Shawn, who joined her. "We need to find out who killed Doris Loving. Someone is trying to blame my brother and me. You're the only one who can help us."

Reggie backed away. Xandra reached for him when a red flash caught her eye. Shawn lunged forward, wrapping Xandra and Reggie in his arms. His momentum carried them to the ground. A bullet smacked into the wall above Xandra's head. Shielding her body with his own, Shawn dragged her back toward the shelter. Reggie wriggled after them. In the distance, Janeece shouted their names. Flashlights wavered across the grounds. The laser dot reappeared, lower on the wall.

"Xandra? Shawn?" Pete called.

"We're all right," Xandra shouted. The shooter dashed from behind the butterfly house and headed into the dense woods. Terl fired twice, but the man kept running. Holstering her weapon, she issued commands into the radio. Minutes passed before sirens echoed down the highway. Police cars pulled into the access road bordering the Arboretum to the north, deploying officers from the West Carrollton and Miami Township Police Departments. Janeece continued to issue orders over the radio. When Pete reached the shelter, he checked Xandra, Shawn, and Reggie for injuries, then escorted them back to the educational center where a command post had been set up. Reggie slumped to the ground, face bleeding, the cloth around his leg leaking blood. An ambulance bumped its way across the lawn.

"No way, man." Reggie struggled to stand. "No hospital. If they found me here, they can find me there."

"Not this time." Pete motioned for the emergency vehicle to stop.

Janeece made her way over to the group, a bullet casing nestled in her gloved hand. "Pete, do you have an evidence bag?"

"What's going on here?" one of the responders asked as he lifted Reggie onto the gurney.

Terl and Stone exchanged a look before glancing at the injured boy. "Someone," Pete said, "wants this kid dead. Reggie, care to tell us who?"

When Reggie shook his head, Xandra wrapped her fingers around his wrist and squeezed. "You are going to tell us, Reggie, or I'm feeding you to the vultures."

Forty-four

The half-moon riding the western sky stippled the surface of the pond in silver. Voices squawked over police radios as first one team, then another, reported their inability to locate the suspect. Disappointed, Terl relinquished command of the search to Miamisburg PD, then escorted Xandra and Shawn to the Vic.

"I want to go to the hospital," Xandra said, pulling free of Terl's grip.

"Not tonight. We're taking you back to Hopewell." Pete hustled the girl into the vehicle, ordered Shawn in, then maneuvered around the police and emergency vehicles and headed south.

Xandra searched for an argument that would change the detectives' minds. "I need to see Reggie. He won't talk to you."

"Calm down, Miss Byrd. You and Crowe failed to follow directions and you put yourselves in harm's way. You are not an official part of this investigation. Detective Terl and I can handle the young man's interview. If we need more information from you, we'll call."

"You always call when you need our help but dismiss us afterward."

"Xandra." Janeece shook her head at the girl. "Now is not the time."

Xandra slumped against the seatback. No one spoke until they reached the UDF. Terl watched them drive away. "They better go straight home," she said.

"That frown says you don't believe they will."

"I know Xandra Byrd. That girl's planning something."

"It's pretty late, and she has classes and work tomorrow, right?"

"That won't stop her. She's a pit bull when she sinks her teeth into an idea. Damn it, I'm tired."

Pete yawned. "Me, too. Any point in going back to the hospital tonight?"

"Probably not, but the girl's right about Reggie's reluctance to talk to us, and we need to set up a security detail before he takes off again or they come back after him. I wounded the shooter, so we should canvas local ERs, see if any gunshot victims turned up tonight." Janeece paged through the texts in her cell. "When Xandra met Stuart Lynx at Beck Park, she said the car with two men inside chased her up Pioneer. The hit-and-run footage confirms two persons in the missing vehicle."

"Not a coincidence. She seemed pretty intent on talking to Reggie."

"Her association with him may put her in danger. Let's alert the guard to keep her away from the boy." She leaned against the window, eyes closed, and sorted through the night's events. A shooter on the loose meant a grilling by the captain and the press tomorrow. If she and Pete could get any information from the boy tonight, they might be able to avoid that unpleasantness. Janeece groaned. She wanted to go home, to rest, to discuss that baby thing with Henry. Her face softened as she recalled the look of surprise on his face.

At the hospital, they stopped at the desk to inquire about gunshot victims, then headed to the surgical wing, where a nurse reported that Reginald Emory Lynx was in the OR to repair damages from a knife attack. Surprised, Janeece asked the nurse to verify the type of wounds.

"Knife before. Gun tonight. Why," she turned to Pete, "would his attacker switch weapons?"

Pete mulled over the question. "Doesn't seem likely. Perps don't normally change weapons. We have a knife used on Doris Loving and Reggie Lynx, a hit-and-run on a boy with a history of minor crimes, and a shooter after Reggie tonight. Do we have more than one bad guy?"

Janeece shrugged. "Who knows? Right now, it's just a kettle of nonsense."

"Kettle? You need to get some sleep, Terl."

"Look it up, Stone. A group of vultures in flight is called a kettle, and that's what this feels like…a whole bunch of birds looking for something to feed on. Nothing about this makes sense. No wonder my head aches."

Janeece returned to the nurse's station "When will Lynx be out of surgery?"

The woman shrugged. "Unknown. The doctor will talk to you when she's finished, though."

Janeece motioned toward the exit. "Let's go home. We'll talk to Reggie first thing tomorrow."

"Actually," Pete followed her through the automatic doors, "there's something else I'd like to do. Look into Paul Loving's financials. That old adage about follow the money might be appropriate here. Any chance of a warrant?"

"Is there probable cause?"

"Maybe. Loving certainly has motive. No one has located Doris's will, and Loving is awfully keen to gain ownership of that land."

"Thin evidence, Pete, but you're welcome to give it a shot with Judge Kirby." Janeece held out a hand. "My turn to drive."

"You're so bossy when you're pissed."

"Give me the keys, Stone."

Forty-five minutes and one preliminary report filed later, Janeece reached home. The nightlight in the hall cast a warm glow over the polished oak floor as she tiptoed around, eventually finding Henry asleep in the lounge on the back porch, hair spiky, his muscled body wrapped in a blanket. She allowed herself a moment to simply watch him breathe. When he opened his eyes and scooted over, she climbed in.

"Did you find the problem child?"

She sighed against his chest. "Reggie Lynx? He's in surgery. Knife wound. Autopsy said Stuart had one, too, on his arm. And someone shot at Xandra, Shawn, and Reggie, but then got away."

"Xandra and who? Neecie, how did that happen?"

She snuggled closer. "Took X and her boyfriend with us to draw Lynx out. Stupid but effective."

"Busy night, then. Any permanent damage to the kid?"

"Don't know. We'll find out tomorrow."

Henry traced her jaw with his fingers, then bent to kiss her. "You too tired to talk now?"

"I'd rather sleep." She yawned, then grinned up at him. "But I don't think you're going to let me."

"Just one question then." Henry shifted her in his arms, molding her body against his. "Were you serious earlier?"

"As a heart attack, husband. Now stop messing with me. I need to sleep."

Henry stood and gathered her up. Above, clouds drifted clear of the moon. The crescent floated in a shadowy Milky Way brimming with stars. Janeece thought about Xandra and J.J. and Shawn and Stuart and Reggie, all the young people caught up in a toxic mix of lies and murder. If she couldn't help them, how would she help her own children navigate a world full of human predators?

Forty-five

Too tired to do more than skim the outline of the group project, Xandra rebanded her notes and stuffed them into the backpack. The research into Paul Loving had yielded scant information. When she contacted the Chamber of Commerce, claiming to be writing a story on him, she discovered no fewer than ten local businesses registered to him and/or his corporation. The man had also filed for bankruptcy twice, then reopened the businesses under new names. She had also checked his tax records. Three of his current holdings were listed as subsidiaries of Clark Coulter Equity. Xandra had no idea who Coulter was. Uncovering the connection was important, but after the robbery at the restaurant and tonight's close encounter with a bullet, she had difficulty concentrating on anything except the look on Shawn's face when he left her at the door. She touched her lips, remembering the kiss he'd placed there, a soft, sweet promise.

Stop it, she ordered as she climbed into bed. *You have no room in your life for a relationship.* The day she moved in with Joe and Leah, she had decided to postpone dating until she figured out who she was and where she wanted to be. All the adults she'd cared about had done nothing but hurt each other. Although Joe and Leah seemed solid now, and the man she'd called Dad for years, Vander Byrd, had found a new love, their pasts were rocky and filled with pain. Even Janeece Terl had a troubled first marriage. "That's not going to be me," she whispered. Before she surrendered to sleep, she rebuilt the wall around her heart, leaving no room for Shawn to squeeze through.

The sun had barely risen when Olivia touched her cheek. "Wake up, Sissy."

"What is it, peanut?" She lifted the sheet so her sister could climb under, then wrapped them both in its cottony embrace.

Olivia opened her hand. Nestled in her palm was a vulture pin. "Member when we went to see the birdies?"

"I do." Xandra examined the pin. The initials OZ were etched into the back. "We had fun, didn't we?"

Wriggling closer, Olivia held up the pin. "I want to wear mine today. Will you wear yours, too?"

"I can't, honey. I lost it."

"No, you didn't."

"Well, it's missing. I've looked everywhere. I think," she hated to lie, but she had no choice, "J.J.'s is lost, too. I'm sorry, Livvie."

"They're not lost. That boy has them."

"What boy?" Xandra propped herself up to look at her sister.

"That Reggie boy. I saw him go into your rooms. When he came out, he had the pins. I asked him what he was doing, and he said he was 'tecting them for you."

"Protecting, you mean?"

"He told me not to tell." Olivia's chin quivered. "Am I in trouble?"

Xandra kissed her sister's curls. "No, baby, you're not. But I will be if I don't get moving. Want to stay here while I take a quick shower?"

"Uh-huh." Olivia curled her hand around the pin and hummed the silly vulture song J.J. had composed on the way home from Hinckley. "Vulture culture, strange birdies. Fly in circles, eat in threes." Xandra found herself humming along, caught in the slipstream of memory. Despite the oddness of the excursion, the family had bonded over the course of the two-day trip. After their return, the connection had not waned. Now, more than ever, she was determined to discover the truth surrounding the Reverend's murder and restore the Zetts family's good name. And that started with Reggie. If her plan worked, she could question him before the police did.

Her parents were awake in their bedroom. She heard voices behind the closed door. But J.J. was still asleep. She hadn't seen much of him the last few days. He'd been working non-stop to build up his savings, trying to make up for what Doris Loving's death had taken from him. As far as Xandra knew, he hadn't found another client willing to give him a chance on a landscaping project. She hated to see him so defeated.

Grabbing a toaster pastry and a juice box, she hurried to the car. A note under the wipers fluttered in the morning breeze. When she opened it, the ink had smeared a little, the words barely legible. *See you in class*. She tucked the dew-damp message in the pocket of her jeans and drove ten miles over the speed limit all the way to the hospital.

Despite the early hour, the lot was nearly full, and she had to park in the last row. Inside, she waved at the volunteer at the information desk as she strolled by. In the surgical wing, she spotted a uniformed guard three doors down from the nurses' station. That she hadn't anticipated. What she needed was a uniform. She returned to the lobby, spotted the cafeteria sign, and wandered down the hall in that direction until she reached a door marked *Food Service*. A woman pushed past, entered, and re-emerged wearing a hair net and a white coat. Good enough, Xandra thought. She slipped inside. Clean uniforms wrapped in cellophane topped with identification tags were lined up on a long table. Xandra walked down the row until she found a badge with a face resembling her own. She slipped into a lab coat, stuffed her hair into a cap, and strung the lanyard around her neck. She stuffed the plastic wrapping in a coat pocket and rode the elevator back to the second floor, then snatched a clipboard from a cart. Clutching the board as though deep in thought, she quickened her pace, stopping short in front of the guard.

"Reginald Byrd?"

The guard hooked his thumbs in the waistband of his trousers. He didn't smile. "No one admitted without authorization."

Xandra held up the ID. "I'm Glory Arsinoe, one of the dieticians on staff. I need to ask about Mr. Lynx's meal choices. Part of our quality control program. It won't take long."

The guard flicked his eyes down the hall, noting the aides carrying trays to patients at the far end. Still hesitant, he thumbed the radio on his shoulder, then stepped aside. "Make it quick."

Xandra pushed through the door. Reggie lay on his back, his bandaged leg propped on a cushion. A line of stitches crawled down his left cheek. When he spotted Xandra, he groaned.

"You're not supposed to be here."

"Yeah. Neither are you." She touched his arm above the IV line. "I don't have much time, Reg. Tell me who's after you."

"I don't know, I swear. Loving had me deliver messages, but that's all I did. I have no idea who they are." He clenched his jaw. "They killed Stuart, didn't they?"

Xandra met his eyes and nodded. "Someone did, yes, and I'm so sorry. But is there anything you can tell me that might explain why they had the Reverend killed?"

He tugged her closer. "There's more than one player in this game, X, and it's too complicated for me to figure out. Stuart had a friend in juvie who had a friend who needed help with something and roped us into his scheme, whatever it was. Might be the same dude in a mask who came after me and Stuart at the Overlook. No clue why. Then those guys in suits tried to find me. And Loving with his stupid envelope. Then the Reverend had me bring that bird to her at the dinner theater."

"Wait. What?"

"The night she got killed and her brother had me deliver that note. After she gave it back, she sent me to the church to get that thing."

"Why?"

"No idea, but whatever else was in that envelope, she kept it."

"You said—"

"I lied, about most everything. I'm getting real good at that."

The rattle of a food cart drew their attention. "I have to go."

"Hey, Xandra, I really am sorry about the paper."

"The paper is the least of it. Why did you steal the pins, Reg?" He looked away, unable or unwilling to reveal that particular secret. "Reg? Please tell me something."

"Ask Millie about the pins," he said. The sounds in the hall drifted closer. Xandra mumbled thanks to the guard and ran back to the restroom. She folded the coat and hairnet and stuffed them back in the plastic bag. She had to return them before the Arsinoe woman reported for work. If she hurried, she could catch Shawn at school, tell him what she'd learned. Reggie's information added a new dimension to the case. If Reverend Loving believed the anonymous threats, she might have known her killer. The words Stuart had said that night came back to her. Birds of a feather. And Reggie believed that more than one person was after him.

Xandra returned the uniform to the Food Service room and left the hospital, her mind working in overdrive. What if both the stolen pins had been inside the stuffed vulture? What if J.J.'s fell out? Did Doris Loving put the pins there? Was it another message? But how did the pins end up with the Reverend? Why did the killer want to implicate Xandra and J.J.? Greed? Anger? Revenge? All motives for violence since humans first wandered the planet. And if someone was after the family, were her parents and Olivia in danger? Throttling down the highway, Xandra imagined vultures circling above her family, drifting ever closer, waiting for a chance to feast on the remains of a home once more broken, this time beyond repair.

Forty-six

Janeece checked on Reggie's status with the head nurse, then greeted the guard outside the room with a cup of coffee.

"Take a break," she said. "I'll stay until your replacement arrives." She scanned the hall, noted which rooms were occupied, and observed an elderly gentleman rolling his IV stand down the hall, one hand clutching the back of his hospital gown. Hopeful the Lynx boy might talk, she took out her notebook.

When she entered the room, Reggie recognized her and pulled the covers up to his eyes. He looked more frightened now than he had last night.

"I have nothing to say to you."

Janeece dragged a chair over and sat down. "I get that, Reggie, I really do, but the thing is, if you don't help us, we can't help you."

"You can't help me anyway. No one can. I have to look out for myself now, and my grandma."

"How is she involved in this?"

"She isn't, but if I talk, she will be."

"If they threatened to hurt her, we can stop that from happening."

Reggie sat up, the IV tube snagging against the bed rail. His voice trembled. "You couldn't save Stuart."

"We might have, if you had come to us sooner."

Reggie buried his head, his words muffled. "I don't know."

Janeece waited, silent and alert, as the boy wrestled with his guilt. The machines monitoring his progress continued their steady beeping. Noises from the hall ebbed and flowed. She checked the time. Nearly nine. The day guard stepped in, greeted her, and returned to his post in the hall. Janeece tried again.

"Why don't you tell me something that's not so tough, like what happened with Xandra's research paper?"

Reggie ran a hand over his head. "Man, that was the start of it. I mean, if I had just told Stuart no and done my own shit, I'd be in class instead of here with my face and leg all stitched up and my brother dead."

"Deep breaths, Reggie." Janeece waited for his panic to subside. "So, you were busy helping your brother with something, and you got behind in your schoolwork."

"It was supposed to be easy money." Reggie pounded the bed. "All we had to do was hang at the church and report on what we saw. Stuart took the morning shift, and I covered the afternoons."

"Who were you supposed to tell?" She kept her voice low, no hint of judgment or accusation.

"See, that's what I don't know. My brother kept that secret. What I know is he met someone in juvie who hooked him up with an older guy who wanted intel."

"Intel? That's not a civilian term. Who were you spying on?"

"The Reverend. Who came to visit her at the church. Who she talked to. Then Mr. Loving started asking me to do things, too." Reggie paused. "The money was good."

"Paul Loving paid you to do errands for him?"

"Yeah, twenty bucks every time. Once a fifty."

"What about your other employer?"

"Paid me and Stuart a hundred bucks a day."

"Damn. I'm in the wrong profession." That teased a smile from the boy. She shook off the chill down her neck and went on. "When did this start?"

"Middle of April. I tried to keep up with my classes, but sometimes we had to do night recons."

Despite the seriousness of the situation, Janeece smiled at Reggie's use of military terminology. He talked like a player in one of those video war games where only cartoon avatars died, proving how ill-equipped he was to be involved in whatever was going on. "Let's see. You and Stuart were spying on Doris Loving for an unknown employer. Your schoolwork suffered, so you passed Xandra's paper off as your own. Then Paul Loving recruited you to work for him. What did he ask you to do?"

He cut his eyes away. "Stuff. Run errands, deliver messages, packages."

He wasn't telling the whole truth. Janeece let it go for now. "And the night the Reverend was killed, did you run an errand for Mr. Loving?"

"I already told you about that." He clenched and unclenched his fists.

"What is it you're not telling me, Reggie?"

His eyes darted around the room. He flinched when a cart rattled by in the hall. Janeece allowed the sounds of the hospital to fill the silence. An aide knocked on the door to ask about his lunch order, promising to return later with a tray. When they were alone once more, she prompted the boy. "What, Reggie?"

"I told Xandra I was sorry."

She sat up when he mentioned Xandra. "When did you see her?"

Reggie squirmed in the bed. "Uh, last night, at the Arboretum."

"Sorry for stealing her paper?"

"Well, yeah, and for taking the pins."

"Pins?"

"She and J.J. and Olivia had these vulture pins from their family trip in the spring. I stole hers and J.J.'s, and I didn't give them to Reverend Loving. But she had them in her hand when I brought her that stuffed bird."

Janeece shook her head as another missing piece slotted into place. "You stole two pins from Xandra and J.J.? How did Doris Loving get them?"

"I don't know." He rubbed his hand over his mouth.

"But you have an idea."

"This is going to sound crazy."

"I can handle crazy."

"See, Millie Stanfield asked me to. Said it was a prank."

"Did you give the pins to her?"

"No. That part's even weirder." Reggie closed his eyes. "She told me to hide them in the desk at the restaurant. And that's what I did."

"When?"

"Monday before the murder, I think. I'm not sure anymore. All the days are mixed up in my head. I can't remember when stuff happened."

"All right. I can check with Millie about the timeline." *If I can find her.* Janeece wrote a note. "Did you see the pins after you put them in the drawer?"

"No, and I felt bad about taking them, so I looked for them the next day. To return them."

"And?"

"They were gone. I'm positive Millie didn't take them. She didn't show up for work the night I put them there, but they were gone the next day."

Reggie closed his eyes. Janeece stood to leave. "Get some rest, okay? We'll figure this out. I'll see to moving your grandmother to a safer location." He muttered a reply she didn't catch before drifting off.

In the corridor, Janeece reminded the guard about admitting no one except medical personnel and Hopewell PD, then placed a call to the station, her mind chewing over Reggie's revelations. She wanted another look at the crime photos.

Forty-seven

The strip mall housing the Chamber of Commerce, along with a sports bar, a tattoo parlor, a hair salon, a pawn shop, and a bakery, drowsed in the June heat. The flowers in the decorative stone urns lining the sidewalk were wilting. Several of the petunias had gone to seed. Pete Stone wedged his car between an oversize utility truck and a soccer mom's van. Inside the Chamber office, he spoke with an intern. The young man checked with someone in the back office, then printed out the entire list of businesses for the city of Hopewell. Using a highlighter, he marked all those belonging to Paul Loving and handed the pages to Stone.

"Ms. Warriner told me to do that." He pointed to the highlighted lines.

Pete shuffled through the pages. "Thanks for your help. In case anything else of interest regarding Mr. Loving comes to mind, here's my card." He tapped the roll of papers against his leg as he left the building. Through the window, Rose Warriner, Chamber vice-president, clutched a cell phone to her ear as she watched him leave.

Next, Pete headed to Hopewell Community Bank. His appointment with the branch manager was scheduled for eleven, which left forty minutes free. When he passed Loving Real Estate, he made a U-turn and eased into the narrow alley behind the office. He followed a brick walkway to the front of the building, where a bell chimed as he opened the door. A blonde head popped out of Loving's office, looked Pete's way, and disappeared toward the back of the building. The bell sounded again. When no one entered behind him, Pete realized the woman had fled out the back. Then he remembered where he'd seen her, the council meeting. Why was Millie Stanfield, the elusive employee of the Buns N Fries, in Paul Loving's office? He started for the rear of the building when Gloria Waller intercepted him.

"Detective Stone, you're back. May I help you?"

Abandoning the pursuit of Stanfield, Pete returned to the desk. "I'd like a word with Mr. Loving."

"He's busy with a client. Let me see when they'll be done. How much time do you need?"

"Fifteen minutes." She gestured for him to sit. Instead, Pete paced the perimeter, re-examining the photos of Loving's sponsorships of local youth teams. The accolades were all at least five years old. There were several shots of Paul and the mayor in fishing gear, holding up a fish or, knives in hand, cleaning the catch on the bank of a river. Pete was paging through an album labelled Denali Adventure when Loving strode in.

"Detective." The man extended a hand. "I hope you've come with good news."

Pete shrugged. "Your sister's body has been released to Anderson Funeral Home, but I'm sure you know that. I understand you'll have to go through probate, though, if a will isn't found. Have you contacted her lawyer?"

Loving pulled free and moved to the refreshment bar, where he poured himself a coffee. "Her lawyer insists he has no copies. He must be lying. My sister left five pages of instructions for her funeral and nothing regarding her estate."

"Did she have another lawyer?"

"Dorie never mentioned him. Or her. And no one has come forward."

"Do you think someone took the will?"

"I have no idea." Loving's voice rose. "Look, if you didn't come about Doris's murder, why are you here?"

"Mr. Loving," Pete pulled out the list he'd acquired from the Chamber, "you have a substantial number of properties and businesses in Hopewell. Many have closed or filed for bankruptcy. Is there anything we should know about your financial situation?"

Coffee sloshed from the mug in Loving's hand. His face grew red, then paled. Motioning the detective to follow, he led the way to his office. Once there, he closed the door and set the mug down. Plopping into his chair, he buried his face in his hands.

"Mr. Loving?"

The man looked defeated. "I haven't had the best of luck recently, but this land deal was going to save me. Doris knew that. Oh, she didn't like it at first, but she knew how much I needed it. Then that kid drew up those plans. He promised to put in everything she wanted. Even a bird sanctuary. When I spoke to her the night she died, she said she had made up her mind."

"Did you send Reggie Byrd to talk to her?"

"You know about that?" Pete waited through Loving's sighs. "I thought if she understood the financial situation, how I could help her develop her ideas someplace else, she would finally see it my way."

"But she didn't."

Loving shook his head. "No. But she swore to think about it overnight. And then somebody killed her. I need you to solve this so I can salvage my business before I lose everything."

"How would that happen?"

The receptionist knocked, then let herself in. "I'm sorry to interrupt, Paul, but your next client is here."

Loving rose, his despair retreating behind the mask of the jovial entrepreneur. "Detective Stone was just leaving, Gloria."

Pete left Loving Real Estate, the image of Millie Stanfield scuttling out of the office merging with Loving's obvious desperation.

Forty-eight

After another unsuccessful attempt to locate Millie Stanfield, Janeece pulled into Beck Park just after one. She had visited the woman's condo building in a complex on Clearcreek-Hopewell Road. The exterior of the three-story units sported a stucco veneer and wood beams that gave it a Tudor look. A large sign advertised two- and three-bedroom townhomes for sale as well as leases starting at twelve hundred a month, a steep price for a woman who, when she showed up for work, served hamburgers and chicken sandwiches for a living. A stop at the rental office revealed little. Stanfield's application included her job history, checking and savings accounts, and no dependents. Millie had listed Xandra Byrd as her emergency contact. Terl wondered if Xandra knew that. The application also mentioned a brother as a reference, but the name was difficult to decipher. Janeece asked for a copy of the form, then went to the woman's address. Although music played inside the dwelling, no one answered her knock. A cat jumped onto the window ledge, rattling the blinds as it pawed the glass. Janeece walked around back. Privacy fences enclosed the yards. The gate to Stanfield's was locked, the slats overlapping, hiding a view of the back entrance. She and Pete would have to make a return trip.

Janeece unwrapped an energy bar as she strolled toward the overlook, mesmerized by the expanse of burgeoning prairie. The land swanned out below the wall, the plants on the hillside still growing into their summer glory. Past the eastern tree line, a pond, property of the homeowners who lived in the development bordering the park, glistened in the noonday sun. To the west, trees shaded the creek that meandered north in wide, lazy bends beneath a steep bank. The campsite lay too far to the south to be seen. Janeece rested on the wall, mulling over what Reggie had revealed during their morning talk. If the bird pins were nothing more than a prank, how did they end up with the Reverend? More important, did the unstained mark on the concrete point to the missing pin? Did someone plant it with the intent to frame Joe's kids? Or did the killer drop it? If so, who carried it away? Janeece didn't like where her speculations were leading.

She worked her way down the switchback to the right of the overlook, emerging from the trees in front of a sign detailing the trails and the distance each covered. Two dog walkers approached, the animals maintaining a rapid pace. She stepped back as they hustled by, then continued south. She passed an elderly couple half a mile down the trail, exchanged greetings, and pressed on. When she reached the back field, she followed a narrow path up a rise, then skittered down to the gravel bank of Pleasant Run. She thought about taking off her shoes to wade when a shadow passed overhead. Janeece spotted the lone vulture and shuddered. Soon the raptor was joined by two more birds. The kettle swooped lower, heading in the direction of the campsite. Janeece sloshed through the creek without removing her shoes and pushed through the tangled brush. Forty minutes later, she stumbled into the hidden camp, startling the scavengers. The birds hopped back but did not fly away. She raised her arms and shouted until, disgruntled, they took to the air.

A young man lay sprawled on the ground where the tent had stood. Flies swarmed his body. Janeece moved close enough to verify the victim wasn't breathing. Reluctant to disturb the scene, she circled her phone in the air until she captured enough bars to call the station. She requested backup, the coroner, and a forensics team, then unholstered her weapon and scanned the forest. No bird calls. Not even the chitter of chipmunks or squirrels. Only the buzz of insects disturbed the quiet. The back of her neck tingled. Was someone watching from the trees? She walked the perimeter, peering into the dense cover. Satisfied no one was hiding in the brush, she approached the victim. There were no signs of a struggle. Squatting, she shooed away the flies to examine the corpse. A hole in the back of the head appeared to be from a small caliber handgun, probably a .38, fired at point-blank range. This was no random act. She slipped on gloves, then tilted the victim's face toward her. Blood and dirt obscured the features. The deceased wore jeans and, despite the heat, a hoodie. One hand clutched a ski mask. The other reached toward a carry-out bag labeled Buns N Fries. A wrapped stack of one-dollar bills spilled out the top. More money lay scattered over the blood-soaked ground. Not a robbery, then, but an execution.

Forty-nine

A sign on the classroom door announced that the computer forensics lecture had been canceled. Xandra shrugged and turned to Shawn.

"Guess we have time to do some digging into our case."

"Our case?" Shawn drew her away from the students crowded around the door. He scrutinized her face. "You talked to Reggie."

"Uh-huh. I went to the hospital and sneaked into his room. He didn't want to talk to me." Xandra shook off the chills creeping down her back. "The bad news? He's in real trouble. The good news? He apologized for stealing my paper, but he refused to say why he stole the pins."

"You're sure he took them?" Shawn pushed through the door to the parking garage and ushered her through.

"He admitted it. If I'd had more time, I think I might have persuaded him to tell me who he was working for."

"So, you almost got caught?"

She pushed her hair back and frowned. "No. I left before that could happen. He did say one curious thing. Reverend Loving asked him to bring that stuffed bird to her at the dinner theater."

"Did he say why?"

"No." Xandra tossed her backpack on the passenger seat. "Want to have lunch at my house?"

"Why, X, are you asking me for a date?" He leaned in, laughing when she pushed him away.

"Get over yourself, Crowe." She tugged the door free.

"See you soon, Byrd." He whistled as he walked away.

She watched him from the side mirror, her firewall crumbling. She circled down the ramp to the exit and eased into traffic, Reggie's refusal to talk nagging at her the entire drive home.

She checked the mail, then stepped inside. J.J. stood by the sink, sandwich in hand, staring out the window. Her greeting startled him.

"What are you doing home?"

"Class was canceled. Are they home?"

"Dad's sleeping. He was out late again last night. This case he's working is a real time suck."

"We found Reggie."

"No shit!" J.J. choked on a bite of turkey. "Where?"

"Hiding at the Arboretum. Reg had a knife wound on his face, and then somebody shot at us."

"This all happened while I was sleeping?"

"Duh. Get with the program bro."

"So, then what?"

"Ambulance took him to Sycamore. Then I went to the hospital this morning." Xandra snagged one of his corn chips. "He confessed to stealing my paper."

"That's something. What about, you know, the pins?"

"Yeah, he took them. Said it was a prank. That Millie Stanfield asked him to do it."

"You believe him?"

"I think there's more to it, but he refused to say anything else. Shawn's coming over, and we're going back to the park. Want to come with?"

Her brother bolted the rest of his lunch. "Can't. I'm due back at work in," he checked his phone, "fifteen minutes."

"You're burning your candle at both ends, J."

"Yeah, well, it takes my mind off the fact that people think I killed Reverend Loving."

"They don't think that."

"Yeah, they do. You don't see how they look at me now. My co-workers act like I'm contagious."

"Bullshit. They don't know anything. Trust me. I'll figure this out and clear both of us."

J.J. shook his head, gulped down a glass of milk, and tugged on his ball cap. "Counting on it, Sis. Hey, tell Crowe to treat you right or he'll answer to me."

"Really?"

"Really, and be careful, okay? Too many people are getting hurt. Someone out there has it in for us. Even Dad thinks so."

"He said that to you?"

"Not exactly, but he's worried. He's trying to resolve all his current cases so he can work on ours."

Xandra watched her brother drive away, goosebumps tap-dancing down her arms. When Shawn pulled up, she ran out to meet him, glad for his company. While they ate, she read through her notes. "The Lovings," she tapped a page, "were fighting over the land behind the church, and Doris ended up dead. However, no one can find her will, which leaves her brother with a claim but no clear title to the property."

"Is that all we know for sure about that?"

"It's not much, is it?"

Shawn rubbed his lower lip. "Why and how did Stuart and Reggie get involved? Did he explain that to you?"

Xandra dropped her head in her hands, recalling her conversation with Lynx. "Stuart was involved with some kid he met in juvie, who had a friend who needed some information. Stuart asked Reggie to help him spy on the Reverend. How that led to her murder I don't know."

"Let's start with that, her murder, maybe try that technique from our interrogations class. Remember?"

Xandra thought back to the lecture on how to assist witnesses with recall. Deep breaths and replay the day. She could do that. "Okay."

"Start at the beginning of the day of the murder. What do you remember?"

"Thursday, Olivia woke everyone up, like always. Mom was still working full days at school. Joe had meetings with two new clients. J.J. had already started work with the city. He didn't add the landscaping job until after the Reverend died." She paused, feeling the loss of the Reverend and J.J.'s hopes all over again. "Everyone was rushing around. I was running late, so I was stressed. After class, I studied in the media center, then drove home to change for work."

"Okay." Shawn shifted closer. "How was work?"

"Let me think." She stared out the window, watched a blue jay chase cardinals away from the feeder. "I arrived twenty minutes early. Checked with the seven-to-three crew about what needed to be cleaned, which supplies were running low, and how busy the morning had been. Our usual scheduled delivery hadn't come yet, so I knew we'd have extra work when it did arrive. Which caused more stress. Anyway, Carson showed up shortly after me. He's good like that. Then Brenda. Emilia didn't get there until after three, as usual, but Reggie clocked in two minutes early. He disappeared down the back hall, returned five minutes later looking puzzled."

"Why?"

"Don't know." Xandra held up a hand. "Wait, I think I do, but let me keep going. Reggie asked Carson if Millie had come in yet. I tried not to roll my eyes at the idea of her showing up on time, but I couldn't help myself. Emilia saw me and laughed. Stanfield showed up thirty minutes late. Her hair was a mess and her makeup smudged. She went to the bathroom to put on her uniform. Reggie kept going over to stand by the restroom, like he was waiting for her. Oh!"

"What's wrong?"

"Nothing." Her eyes popped open. "I forgot he did that."

"Why is that strange?" Shawn rested his forearms on his knees.

"Because he barely spoke to her most days. I remember he grabbed her when she came out and leaned real close. He must have asked her something she didn't like because she shook him off, stuck a finger in his face, and said something nasty. Then like in half an hour, she claimed she didn't feel good and left."

"When's the last time you actually spoke with Millie?"

Xandra thought back over their recent interactions. The phone call when the woman reported she had mono and wouldn't be back for at least a week. Two follow-up texts. Her request to Millie to bring in a doctor's excuse. But the day of the Reverend's murder, they didn't speak about anything but work issues. "You know, I haven't spoken to her since the night of the murder, except once on the phone. But when I asked Reggie about the pins, he told me to ask Millie."

Shawn helped himself to a glass of water, then joined her at the window. "We need to talk to her."

"You're right. And since I don't have to work today…"

"Are you sure you feel up to this?"

Xandra fingered the bruise on her head. "Doesn't hurt much anymore. I just can't make any sudden moves."

"I think that's my cue." He pulled her into an embrace. She glanced toward her parents' bedroom and grinned.

"My dad's not normally a light sleeper, but..." Before she could finish the thought, Shawn kissed her. Xandra startled, then relaxed into his strength, if only for the moment. *Just let me have this one time.* She pressed against him, aware of her body responding to his, when her phone rang.

"Who is it?" Shawn brushed his fingers over her cheek but didn't release her.

"I don't recognize the number." When she answered, Janeece Terl's voice growled at her.

"Xandra, where are you?"

"Home. Mr. Loving suggested I take an extra day off this week. I think he felt sorry for me."

"That was nice of him."

"It was unexpected."

Janeece paused, then cleared her throat. "Can you come to Milo Beck Park?"

"Now?"

"Yes. We've found another body. At the campsite." Shawn raised his eyebrows. "What?"

"Another body," she mouthed.

"Xandra? Are you alone?"

"Shawn's here. Be there soon."

After the detective hung up, Xandra scribbled a note for her father, and they headed to the park. Emergency vehicles and police cars crowded the lot. She and Shawn showed their IDs and passed along Terl's request. The officer in charge waved them through the cordoned-off area. At the bottom of the hill, an officer in a golf cart ferried them to the path by the creek. They splashed across the water and followed the trail through the forest. At the site, yellow caution tape roped off a wide circle around the former camp. Detective Terl stood outside the perimeter, frowning at the chaos.

"Hold up, Xandra." Terl escorted them away from the swarm of investigators. "You sure you're up to this?"

"You haven't told me what this is, other than another dead body."

"I need you to make an identification."

"You think I know who it is?"

"It's possible, and you know not to touch anything."

When Xandra nodded, Terl ducked under the tape and they followed, walking on lengths of plywood laid down to preserve any evidence underfoot. When the detective reached the body, she tugged the girl forward.

"Why," Xandra said, "do people always look so much smaller dead than they do alive?" She shoved away the memory of burying her adoptive mother's miscarriage, of Mimaw's burned corpse, of Doris Loving diminished and bloody on the concrete slab by the trash bins. Gagging at the smell, she took in the worn jeans, the dark hoodie, the hand clutching a ski mask, the bag from the Buns N Fries. When she continued to stare, unmoving, at the corpse, Janeece helped her up.

"That's enough, Byrd."

"Wait." Xandra bent down again to stare at the money spilling out of the bag. She looked back over the body. "It could be one of the guys who robbed me. The younger one. Does the hoodie say Abercrombie on the front?"

Janeece cocked her head. "It does."

Xandra shuddered. "But why is he here? And why is he dead?"

Janeece walked her away from the scene before allowing the techs to return.

"So, you recognize the boy?"

"I didn't see his face. He was wearing a mask, but everything else fits. And the money. Is it all there?"

"Don't know yet, but we will."

"Do you know who he was?"

"We do." Terl consulted her notes. "Ace Farins, sixteen. He recently spent time in the Warren County juvenile detention center."

Xandra exchanged a look with Shawn. "If they were there at the same time, he probably knew Stuart Lynx. That's got to be more than coincidence."

"Indeed." Janeece tapped her notebook against her leg, staring first at Shawn, then at Xandra. "Did either of you visit Reggie this morning?"

Xandra felt the blush creep over her cheeks. "I just wanted to see how he was doing."

"How did you get past the guard?"

She gnawed the inside of her lip, unwilling to reveal what she'd done, but she suspected the detective already knew. "I may have impersonated hospital staff."

"That was risky, and dangerous." Janeece waited for an apology. Xandra met the detective's gaze.

"My brother is a suspect in Doris Loving's murder. I won't apologize for trying to clear his name."

"I'll let that go for the moment. Did you and Reggie talk about the missing vulture pins? Xandra?"

"Not really. He didn't want to say anything, and I had to leave."

"So you wouldn't get caught." Terl waited for Xandra to deny it. When she didn't, the detective continued."

"Did Reggie tell you he stole the pins as a prank? Or that Millie Stanfield put him up to it?"

"Not exactly, but he did tell me to ask Millie about them." Xandra scuffed the dirt with the toe of her tennis shoe. "And just now Shawn was helping me recall the day the Reverend died, and I remembered that Reggie and Millie had some kind of confrontation. It must have been about those damn pins."

"Is there anything you want to tell me, X?"

Xandra clenched her fists. Janeece must know something that she didn't. *Deflect, Xandra.* "Millie. I wonder what her role is in all this?"

"As do I, Miss Byrd." Janeece herded them away from the crime scene. "I especially want to know what happened to your brother's vulture pin."

Fifty

The Hopewell Community Bank bore a sign requesting that, for security, visitors remove hats and sunglasses before entering. Pete chuckled at the suggestion that such actions would reduce criminal activity. In his experience, even more sinister crimes were conducted by white collar criminals who, without ever entering the building, scammed accounts. People who robbed banks didn't have as much success. Tucking his sunglasses into the neck of his white button-down, he strode forward to greet the manager on duty.

"Detective Stone?" Courtney Harris checked his badge and credentials, then escorted him to her cubicle. A yellow folder tied with an elastic band rested next to her computer. Harris handed it to him. "These are Reverend Loving's records for the past five years. As far as I know, she frequented no other financial institutions. All her business and personal accounts are listed there."

"Thank you." Pete released the band and scanned the documents. "I appreciate your promptness in fulfilling the subpoena."

Harris tapped a lacquered fingernail on the desktop. "There is one thing."

Pete noted her hesitation. He replaced the band and settled the folder on his lap. "One thing?"

"Two months ago, her brother opened an account in both their names. He took the paperwork home for her to sign, then returned it to my assistant. At the time, I had no reason to doubt its authenticity."

"What was the purpose of the account?"

"That's just it." Harris looked him in the eye. "There seemed to be no reason or need for it. Reverend Loving was extremely organized. She kept church dealings separate from her own interests, which were substantial. Her parents left both her and her brother quite well off, although they provided for her more than for Paul. I guess they realized his difficulty handling money."

"Would you clarify that, Ms. Harris?"

"You'll see when you go over the statements." She pointed toward the folder. "Loving filed for bankruptcy twice over the last five years. His sister bailed him out both times, but he didn't seem to learn from the experience."

"Why do you say that?"

"This is confidential, Detective, so please don't quote me, but our bank has been instructed not to extend more credit to him without approval from the head office. This new account, the one Doris may or may not have known about, handles more deposits and transfers than any of the other accounts. I'm not at liberty to say more." Harris bit her lip, as if she'd already said too much. "Should you require more information, Detective Stone, I can send you up the chain of command."

Thanking her, Pete urged her to call if she detected any unusual activity in the accounts. She walked him out, pausing at the door. "Perhaps you should ask a judge to freeze the accounts before Paul bleeds off any more of the Reverend's assets."

As the woman walked away, Pete shifted the folder from hand to hand, Paul Loving's history pushing him to the top of the suspect list. He checked his phone. Janeece had sent a text requesting his presence at Milo Beck.

The number of police and medical vehicles parked at the overlook alerted Pete to the serious nature of his partner's request. He jogged the path toward the creek, scampered over a temporary footbridge laid to assist in the investigation, and scrambled up the hillside. The humidity clawed at him. He wished he'd brought water. Finally, through the trees, he glimpsed the white uniforms of the forensics team. Janeece, in conversation with Xandra Byrd and the Crowe kid, spotted him and waved him over. Out of breath, he accepted the canteen his partner offered him.

"What's up?"

Janeece lifted her chin toward the corpse being zipped into a body bag. "We have another victim, a possible acquaintance of Stuart Lynx.

Xandra made a tentative ID of the kid as one of the guys who robbed the restaurant."

"Do we have a name?" He inspected the ground where the body had lain.

"According to JDC records, he's Ace Farins, sixteen, recently released from the same detention center where Stuart Lynx was held."

"Cause of death?"

"Bullet wound to the back of the head. Small caliber. One shot, execution-style. He probably knew his killer." Janeece turned to Xandra. "Care to offer a hypothesis, Miss Byrd?"

Uncomfortable with Terl's question, Xandra cleared her throat. The detective gestured her to go on. "It looks like the bullet angled upward from the base of the neck. Either the shooter was shorter, or Farins was kneeling when he was shot."

Pete nodded at Janeece, then continued to examine the crime scene, noting the numbered markers where items of interest had been found. He identified the holes where the tent had been anchored. Scuff marks indicated movement around the campsite, some caused by the investigators, some by the emergency personnel. Indentations in the soft soil off to the left revealed traces of shoe and boot prints. Squatting, Pete examined them more carefully. He snapped photos, then called one of the tech guys over. "Can you get any good impressions from these?"

The guy looked closer, then nodded. Pete motioned Janeece over. "Farins wasn't out here alone. I identify three sets of prints, one larger than the other two. I'm guessing a male, a female, and our victim."

"There's a significant amount of mud on the boy's shoes. If he arrived with the other two, their shoes will be muddy, too. I'll make sure the techs collect some soil samples." Janeece spoke to the technician, then rejoined her partner.

"Those footsteps lead south," Pete said. "They followed a different path to reach the campsite."

"They didn't come through the park?"

Pete scanned the forested parkland. "No. Now, it doesn't look like much of a path, but there is one there. Someone knew who was staying here. I'm betting on Reggie or Stuart as the camper."

"And the others?"

"Don't know yet, but we have to catch them soon." He scrubbed a hand over the stubble on his cheeks. "I'm tired of finding dead bodies."

Fifty-one

Xandra and Shawn hiked back to the overlook and returned to the Zetts home to find Joe unloading surveillance equipment. Xandra climbed out, then turned to Shawn.

"Do you want to come in?"

He shook his head. "I should check on my grandma."

She started to speak, hesitated, began again. "Thank you. For being there."

"You're welcome, always. Later, okay?"

"Okay." She smiled, shut the door, and jogged up the drive to join her father, who handed her a camera and tripod and slipped an arm around her shoulders.

"More drama?"

"You could say that." As they stowed the gear in Joe's workshop, the discoveries of the day tumbled from her lips. When she paused for breath, Joe scratched his head.

"Slow down, daughter, you're giving me a headache. Sit, start over, and take your time." He settled on one of the counter stools and motioned her to take the other, listening as she recounted the events one more time. When she finished, he scratched his chin. "What can I do to help?"

"Probably nothing."

"Is there something you aren't telling me?" Xandra rarely asked for his advice or his help. Now, she needed it, and he wasn't sure how to process the fierce wave of love and protectiveness that swept over him. When her phone rang, he relaxed, grateful for more time to consider a response. Xandra was even more grateful for the interruption. Soon, she had to come clean about J.J.'s pin or make it go away.

"Shawn? How's your grandmother?" She listened, puzzled, then leaned on the counter. "Wait, you're here, your grandma's fine, and you want to come in? Didn't you just leave?"

"Xandra," Joe tapped her shoulder, "invite the boy in."

Thirty seconds later, Crowe shuffled into the kitchen. "Mr. Zetts."

"Shawn." Joe held a glass of milk in one hand and a bowl of cereal in the other. "I'll be in the workshop if you need me."

Xandra waited until the basement door closed before she gripped Shawn's arm. "What's wrong?"

"I was thinking about that dead kid, and him maybe knowing Stuart, so I called a friend who has an uncle who works at the detention center. My friend called his uncle and found out some things about Stuart and Ace Farins that you should know."

"Tell me."

"Farins was a runaway caught soliciting, but a judge took pity on him. He'd been neglected, abused, shipped from one foster home to another. My guy's uncle works intake, so he never saw the kid with anyone, but logs and videos show an older guy visiting the kid on weekends. Farins must have hooked Stuart Lynx up with this guy."

"He could be the other robber," Xandra said. "Can we find out the dude's name?"

"Your father or Janeece can." Shawn helped himself to a cookie from a plate on the table. "This whole thing is sick, X, and not in a good way. Two murders, three, if Stuart wasn't an accident. Reggie injured. And you, too. I don't like it."

"I'll admit I'm a little spooked." She drew circles in the condensation on her glass. Down the hall, the door to J.J.'s bedroom opened, the muted vocals of Maroon5 spooling out. Yawning, her brother joined them in the kitchen.

"You just wake up?" Xandra said.

"Gotta sleep when I can." He checked his phone. "Have to leave in ten. What's going on?"

After Xandra and Shawn brought him up to date, he grabbed a chair. "What could be worth that much violence?"

Joe clomped up from the basement, a thick folder in hand. "Greed, revenge, jealousy. Strong emotions, all. And murder is the oldest sin in the world. Sorry to eavesdrop, but from what you've said," he inclined his head toward Xandra and Shawn, "it's difficult to see the connection, but it's there. The Lynx boys are the odd men out. Other than running errands for the Lovings, they don't fit in. They're not politicians or venture capitalists or local businessmen. But someone is desperate to cover up one crime by committing another. So, back to basics. What are the motive, means, and opportunity for each of the murders?"

Xandra scurried down the hall to retrieve her laptop. She opened a screen and brought up her notes. "I've been working on a spreadsheet."

Joe scrutinized the data. "Good job, Alexandra. Begin with the Reverend."

She keyed in the timeline to account for what she knew about Doris Loving's movements on the day of her murder. The first blocks identified the members of the church who met with the Reverend that morning. That was followed by J.J. and their walk through the proposed labyrinth, bird sanctuary, and burial forest. The next interaction didn't occur until Reggie delivered the envelope to her at the dinner theater.

"So," Joe said, "there's a gap between four and eight p.m. when no one reported seeing or talking to her. Then brief sightings between eight and eight-thirty. After that, she becomes a ghost. The police probably have statements from those who saw or spoke to her at the theater. I can ask Janeece, but she may not be willing to share that information."

"Does the theater have cameras on the outside of the building?" Shawn asked.

Xandra shook her head. "There's never been a need for them. No vandalism and no attempts at robbery in all the years it's been in operation."

"You checked." Shawn smiled.

"I did."

"Busy girl for one supposed to be recovering from a concussion," Joe said. "What else have you been up to?"

"I had to do something besides lie around and feel sorry for myself." She turned the screen so they all could see. "I created a timetable for the hours I worked at the restaurant and after. Each fifteen-minute segment identifies those present at the BNF with me. I have a code to indicate where everyone was. H for home, R for restaurant, T for theater."

J.J. checked his watch before leaning across the table. "What's the U for?"

"Unknown."

"You have that beside my name, six times."

"Hey." She reached for him. He pulled away. "I know you worked until five that day, but you haven't told me where you were the rest of the night."

"You saw me when you came home."

"Don't act defensive, J.J. Just tell me where you were and what you were doing. I'll fill in the blanks."

J.J. scrubbed his face. "I came home for dinner. Dad saw me."

Joe frowned. "Right, but you went out again, son, for about two hours. You returned around nine-thirty. You brought ice cream for Olivia and Leah and me."

Shawn turned to Xandra's brother. "Doesn't matter what it was, man. You need to tell us."

"I wasn't out killing the Reverend." He paced. "I can't explain it, but I wanted to see the land again, to take it all in, what we were going to do. I thought things were finally coming together, you know. Especially after the mayor…"

Xandra looked up. "After the mayor what?"

Her brother drew a deep breath. "He stopped by the maintenance garage, must have been one-thirty that day, said he wanted to see how things were going with the summer crew. Made the rounds. When he came to me, he put an arm around my neck, playful-like, but he wasn't playing. 'You're not going to mess up those beautiful acres with some damn memory garden, are you, son?' He acted like it was a joke, but he was serious. He said the city plans were more important than the Reverend's."

"Did he threaten you?" Shawn said.

"He implied that if I wanted to keep my job, I should tell Reverend Loving I couldn't help her anymore."

They sat in silence, chewing over the mayor's attempt to bully J.J. and wondering what other threats he may have tendered and to whom. Joe slapped the table.

"We need to find out what happened at the dinner theater," he said. "Before someone else gets hurt."

Fifty-two

The autopsy reports on the bodies of Doris Loving and Stuart Lynx, along with anecdotal notes from the examiners on the scene of the latest killing, rested on Janeece's desk. Gathering them up, she followed Pete into the conference room. On the wall, a magnetic whiteboard displayed pictures of the victims, along with timelines and information collected from interviews. Pete added a photo of the newest victim, Ace Farins, then drew a question mark beside it. Beneath the pictures, a montage of potential suspects: Paul Loving, J.J. Zetts, and Clark Coulter circled in red marker; Roy Eisner, Alexandra Byrd, Reggie Lynx, the unknown robber from the restaurant heist, and the mysterious men in the SUV in blue. Those in red demonstrated the clearest motives, means, and opportunity.

"Do we have more than one killer?" Pete stared at the board. Janeece fiddled with a pen.

"We're missing something." She squinted at the lineup. "If Paul or J.J. killed Doris, what reason would they have to hunt down Stuart? Or kill the kid in the park?"

"Here are the connection points." Pete drew lines from Doris Loving to her brother Paul, Coulter, and J.J. He used a brown marker to link Stuart with the Farins boy, the men in the SUV, the unknown second robber, and Xandra Byrd. "The land appears to be the impetus for the animosity among the adults."

"The mayor seems an unlikely suspect, but his advocacy for Paul Loving's plan at the town meeting raises suspicion."

"The involvement of the young people bothers me. Both the Lovings were manipulating them. Doris used J.J. to further her dream for the land, which placed him in the middle of the controversial deal. Paul used Reggie as an errand boy, and so did the Reverend."

"And Coulter and Eisner were trying to convince the woman to change her mind. Remind me how we know that."

Pete shuffled through the evidence. He pulled out the planner Leah had given them and paged through the dates. "Two calls placed from Coulter's firm to the Reverend the week she died. We have statements from the church secretary that Coulter came to see her while she was walking the woods with the Zetts kid. He left without a meetup."

"Eisner also called her that week. No one knows what they talked about, but she was upset enough to cancel a women's guild meeting for Tuesday afternoon. Leah offered to come to the church to talk with her, but the Reverend said, quote, 'I'm done talking, Leah. Those vultures are not going to win this time.'"

"And she was found with a dead bird on her, one she had asked Reggie to bring to her."

Janeece fingered the coroner's reports. "Let's see what the bodies tell us."

Pete opened the folder on the Lynx hit-and-run. A handwritten note was clipped above the typed report. *Surveillance camera shows a late model, dark-colored SUV swerving from the left lane directly into the victim. License plate was covered by a cloth.* "Stuart Lynx was deliberately targeted, suffering internal injuries, severe brain trauma, a broken left arm, and defensive injuries to both hands. Death occurred upon impact."

"Damn, that's cold." Janeece dropped her head into her hands. Stu Lynx had been a troublemaker, but he wasn't violent or malicious, and he hadn't been in real trouble until he started dealing drugs at school. She scanned the comments by a social worker. *Stuart Allen Lynx is a natural salesman. He makes friends easily, avoids confrontation, and is eager to please. These qualities also leave him open to manipulation by others.* "Sounds like Reggie. Can we get a list of the other young men incarcerated at the detention center at the same time as Stuart and the Farins kid? It's possible our other suspect for the Buns N Fries robbery was there, too."

"According to Xandra, the second guy was older, so I doubt he was in detention with them. Plus there's no way these petty criminals pulled off a hit-and-run."

"You're right." Janeece returned to the report on Doris Loving. "Doris Loving died from severing of the right carotid artery. She also sustained a deep puncture wound to the left side of her chest from a one-sided steel blade approximately six inches long. The strike angled upward from the bottom rib, transecting the left lung. Death from exsanguination. The subject bled out. Contusions on neck indicate she was attacked from behind. The killer was left-handed. No sign of defensive wounds. No skin beneath the fingernails. DNA collected from clothing has been sent to OBCI for analysis. The bird in the subject's pocket was a juvenile specimen of *Cathartes aura*, better known in Ohio as a turkey vulture or buzzard. The bird had been preserved through taxidermy. A tag on the right talon identified the preparer as Todd Willoh, 1645 Brandon Lane, Goshen, Ohio. (See photo)"

"Phone number?"

"Yes. I'll call." Janeece scrutinized the whiteboard. "What did you find out at the bank?"

"Motive." He nudged the folder containing Doris and Paul Loving's financials. "Happy reading."

"One more thing." Janeece fingered the autopsy report. "What happened to the vulture pin belonging to J.J. Zetts?"

"You're convinced it was at the scene of the murder?"

"Photos of blood spatter show that an object fitting the pin's size and shape lay on the concrete, but we didn't find it. Who did?"

"I hope," Pete said, "you're not thinking what I'm thinking."

"Only one reason for Xandra to take it. I so don't want to go there."

They spent the next two hours combing through the notes and witness statements. As Janeece read, she pondered what they knew and what they still needed to find out. A vital link was still out there, one they needed to connect. And fast.

Fifty-three

Shawn parked the Camaro down the block from the UDF. Then, he and Xandra walked to where the Lynx brothers lived with their grandmother. The subdivision dozed in the late afternoon, curtains drawn against the heat. Somewhere in the distance, an electric lawnmower purred. Clouds, backlit by the sun, painted an impressionist canvas above them. Xandra wondered how such beauty could persist among the disasters that men brought upon themselves.

"What are the odds he's here?" Xandra asked. After speaking with her father and brother, she and Shawn had driven to the hospital to coax more information out of Reggie, only to discover that he had checked himself out.

"You're frowning again." Shawn reached for her hand, tightened his grip when she tried to pull away. "What are you thinking?"

"Wondering how I got caught up in this mess."

"You don't feel responsible, do you?"

"I don't know. Maybe. If I had been more observant, I might have seen this coming. Too late now, though, isn't it?" She kicked at a scatter of gravel on the sidewalk. "I'm seeing Penderson and Pierce tomorrow."

"You going to tell them what Reggie said?"

Xandra nodded. "And show them a copy of the note where he claimed responsibility. I hope they'll believe me."

"They have no reason not to. What else?"

"I've been snooping online. Paul Loving owes back taxes on most of his properties, but he keeps buying or investing in new ones. Someone's bankrolling him. I don't understand, with his track record, why anyone would."

"Didn't the Reverend warn you about vultures? And birds of a feather? Maybe she meant her own brother."

"Hold that thought." She walked slower as they approached Reggie's house.

"Keep an eye out for that SUV," Shawn reminded her.

X glanced up and down the block. "You know, when J.J. and I saw Loving in the woods with that Coulter guy, I got the feeling they knew each other pretty well."

"Didn't you tell me Loving's tight with the mayor, too?"

"Yeah. Rockin' Roy, who seems overly invested in the housing development. My mom saw him with Reverend Loving the week before she died. Said Eisner was all red-faced and arguing with her, the Reverend, I mean. Mom had never seen Doris so angry. I wonder if the mayor is one of Loving's investors."

"That would be a major conflict of interest."

"If it came out that he has a personal stake in the game, yes. This is his first term in office."

"Might be his only one. Look." Shawn dragged her behind one of the oak trees shading the street. Reggie was loading suitcases into the trunk of a beat-up Pontiac.

"C'mon. We have to find out what he knows before he leaves." Xandra rushed toward Reggie, who spotted them and started toward the house. His leg, wrapped in a thick bandage, buckled. He caught himself against the hood of the car as Xandra reached him. Hauling him up, she pinned him against the car. "You should be in the hospital."

He cut his eyes at Shawn and licked his lips. "I have to get my grandma out of here before they come back."

"Who, Reg? Who's after you?"

Lynx glared at her. His grandmother emerged from the garage, a box of kitchen supplies in her arms. Shawn hurried to take it from her while Xandra stayed with Reggie.

"You have to talk to me, Reggie, before J.J. ends up charged with murder."

Shawn stashed the box in the trunk, then joined Xandra. Reggie picked a thumbnail. "All I know is what I told you and Terl. Stuart met some kid in detention who hooked him up with an older guy looking to take advantage of some big deal going down in Hopewell. I told my brother to stay out of it, but the dude promised big money in exchange for information. He didn't say anything about the danger."

Xandra refused to be sidetracked by Reggie's tears. "An investor? In juvie? That's bogus."

"No, it was legit, a friend of a friend of Ace Farins."

"You know Farins?" Shawn said.

"Met him once. Why?"

"Farins is dead, Lynx."

Reggie dropped his head in his hands. "Fuck, no." Shawn grabbed him by the shoulders and shook him.

"It didn't stop at information, did it?" Shawn said.

Reggie ran a hand over his mouth. "I couldn't talk him out of it."

"Exactly what," Xandra said, "did he do?"

"The night the Reverend died, Stu told me to hide, that they were coming after me."

"Why?"

"Because I knew something that could ruin the plan."

Xandra frowned. "What did you know?"

"I don't have a clue. Maybe the name of the fool Stuart hooked up with." He edged toward the house. "I also know the last person who saw the Reverend alive."

"You got to give us names, Reggie."

"I don't want any more trouble," he said. "I need to get my grandma somewhere safe." Xandra and Shawn refused to move. Reggie darted a glance over his shoulder and lowered his voice. "Stu met Farins in detention. Ace introduced him to Chad Stanfield."

"Chad Stanfield? Is he related to Millie?"

Reggie dropped his head. "He's her brother."

"Her brother?"

"That's what Farins said, but they didn't act like siblings. More like friends with benefits."

"Yuck. You saw them together?" Reggie bobbed his head in agreement. "But at the restaurant, she flirts with Mr. Loving."

"Yeah, she's a piece of work. Dumb bitch liar." Reggie ducked under Shawn's arm and limped over to help his grandmother load more boxes. "She claimed she and Loving were getting married."

"Double yuck." Xandra said. Shawn buckled Grandma Lynx in. "Reggie, who was the last person to see Reverend Loving alive?"

"Stay out of this, X. These people mean business." Reggie shoved past Shawn and into the driver's seat. "Tell those detectives to follow the money. Greed is responsible for a whole lot of badness. My brother's proof of that, isn't he?"

"Wait." She grabbed the door. "Where are you going?"

"Far enough from here that they won't find us. Stop trying to solve this, X. You, too, Shawn. You're in way over your heads." He yanked the door shut and backed out of the driveway.

Back in the car, Xandra and Shawn talked through the information Reggie had given them. "Do you think the detectives know this?"

Shawn waited for traffic to ease before pulling onto the Pike. A dark-colored SUV passed them, heading toward the subdivision. Xandra glanced at the vehicle as it sped by, then slid lower in the seat. "Shawn, that's the car that followed me the day I met Stuart in the park."

"Want to follow them?"

"No." She shivered. "Reggie got away just in time."

When they pulled into the driveway, Xandra confronted him. "Please, Shawn, I don't want you involved anymore. It's too dangerous now."

He shook his head. "Too late, Xandra. I made my decision days ago. We'll see this through together."

"But there's nothing in it for you. You could get hurt."

"Are you worried about me?"

"Stop. Of course, I'm worried. Reggie's right. We should leave this to the police."

"You don't think our stars will rise if we solve this thing?"

Xandra shook her head. "No. I think they'll kick us out of the program if we get in the way. I don't want that for either of us."

Shawn cupped her face in his hands. When he kissed her, she didn't resist. She wanted this. Shawn Crowe was not part of her plans, but here he was. He liked her and she liked him. Pulling away, she muttered goodbye and fled into the house, Reggie's last words still pinging. *Better safe than dead.* Only one thing could cause more pain. What if J.J. was the last person to see Doris Loving that terrible night?

Fifty-four

Xandra brushed raindrops from her hair and, grateful that she'd stashed the copy of Reggie's note in her backpack, headed toward Professor Pierce's office. She acknowledged Shawn, who had planted himself in the waiting room, but she didn't stop to talk. The office door was closed. She tightened her shoulders and knocked. When the door sprang open, a dark-haired man with green eyes and an easy smile welcomed her in.

"You must be Alexandra Byrd." He motioned her to approach the desk where the department chair was grading papers.

The presence of the stranger unsettled Xandra. She set her pack on a chair and drew out Reggie's confession. "Professor Pierce? Should I come back later?"

"No." Pierce removed her glasses and smiled. "This is my husband, Tuck Cornell. He works with Detectives Stone and Terl."

Xandra eyed Pierce. "Am I in trouble?"

Cornell joined the professor at her desk. "No." Pierce said. "Please sit down. You have something for me?"

"Reggie Lynx sent this to me." Xandra laid the copy on the desk. Pierce exchanged a glance with Cornell.

"May I?" Cornell reached for the paper. "Have you shown this to Pete and Janeece?"

"They have the original. I also gave a copy to Professor Penderson."

"Well done, Miss Byrd." Pierce slipped the note into Xandra's folder. "If Professor Penderson is satisfied, so am I. By the way, I understand the Lynx boy was involved in a shooting, as were you and Shawn Crowe. Where is Reggie now?"

Xandra blinked. How did Pierce know about the shooting and Shawn's involvement? "I don't know."

"That's disappointing. However, this statement should end any accusation of plagiarism, and you can get back to work on your degree."

Xandra shook her head. "My brother is still a suspect in the Reverend's death. I intend to clear his name."

Cornell raised an eyebrow. "Last I heard, you hadn't been deputized."

"I have trouble respecting boundaries when people I love are threatened."

"Nevertheless," Pierce steepled her fingers beneath her chin, "it's not your job...yet. Janeece Terl and Pete Stone are very competent investigators."

"How do you know them?"

Pierce and Cornell exchanged a charged glance. "We worked together on a previous case," the professor said.

"Miss Byrd," Cornell sat next to her, "do you have information about the case that my friends should know?"

She thought about Reggie's disclosure of the Chad and Millie Stanfield connection, the suggestion that Millie and Paul Loving were in a relationship, and Reggie's insinuation that J.J. had been the last person to see Reverend Loving alive. She wound the strap of her backpack around a finger. "Not that I know of. Is my record cleared?"

"You and Mr. Crowe are competing for top honors in your class, so consider this advice." Pierce held Xandra's gaze. "In addition to grades, your conduct in and out of class will be evaluated when considering admission to the academy. You should consider any actions you take with great care."

Xandra blushed. "May I go now?'"

Pierce shuffled through the paperwork on her desk. When she found what she wanted, she held it up. "In addition to the note Reggie sent you, he also sent a letter to Professor Penderson, admitting his guilt and exonerating you."

"So, I did all that worrying for nothing?"

Pierce folded her hands over Xandra's file. "Not for nothing, Byrd. Your help in finding Lynx may finally provide the leads Janeece and Pete need to solve this case."

Fifty-five

Henry carried dinner in from the grille. The fish steamed in the foil, the veggies nicely charred. He kissed Janeece and divided the food onto two plates.

"Whoa," Janeece said, "we feeding an army tonight?"

"You need to eat more, hon. Especially with all these late hours you're putting in." He rested a hand over hers. "I'm worried about you."

She squeezed back, then spread a napkin over her lap. "I know. I'm a little worried myself. This damn Loving case."

"It's a tough one, for sure. Besides," he winked, "if you're serious about the baby thing, you need to keep your strength up for, you know, trying."

Janeece smirked. "That will not be a problem."

"Eat your dinner, wench. Maybe we can start that trying before you have to leave."

•

J.J. fiddled with the clasp on his tackle box, the search for his missing knife an excuse to be alone, to fight the sick feeling in his gut. Terl and Stone were dropping by later to have another informal chat with him and his father. What was he going to tell them? He hadn't harmed Reverend Loving. His family believed him, but how could he convince the others that the final surprise encounter hadn't resulted in her death? He scrolled through his phone until he came to the text Loving had sent that Thursday.

We need to talk. Outside the dinner theater. 8:30

It wasn't the first one she'd sent him, only the most ominous. She had shared her concerns about her brother's plans regarding the land, but she had insisted he keep their conversations private. Now that she was gone, would he be breaking that promise if he revealed what she'd told him? A rap on his door interrupted his musing. He should erase all her texts, smash the phone, destroy any link between them. Instead, he closed the screen and shoved the phone into his pocket.

"Come in, Livvie."

His stepsister peeked around the door, then rushed into the room, lifting her arms for him to pick her up. For Olivia, there was no difference between her half-sister Xandra and her stepbrother J.J. He swallowed the ever-present guilt that surfaced whenever he thought of his mother's suicide. Her death had devastated him. He would always be grateful for Leah's acceptance of him into the new family. She treated him no differently from her biological daughters, even though his blood connection was to Joe. Some days, he thought himself an intruder, an add-on by circumstance rather than love. If they stopped believing in him, what would he do?

Olivia placed her hands on his cheeks and forced him to face her. "Don't be sad, J.J. I love you."

"I love you, too, doodlebug."

She showed him her collar. "I'm wearing my birdie pin. Where's yours?"

"I lost it."

"I'm lucky I hid mine, when that boy stealed yours and Xandra's."

"You saw Reggie take our pins?"

"Uh-huh. I told Xandra." Her mouth drooped. "Don't be mad. He said it was for a 'prise and I shouldn't tell anyone until she 'prised them."

"She?"

"Mossie. No, Missy. No." She pursed her mouth like Leah did when she was thinking. "Millsie. He said he was taking them to Millsie."

J.J. picked her up and headed for the garage. His dad needed to hear this.

•

An orange and gold banner of clouds spread across the darkening sky beyond the tree-lined yards that stretched from the newest sections of the plat to the highway. Joe stowed the lawnmower and returned to the back deck. A chipmunk shimmied up the pole supporting the bird feeder, persistent despite Joe's numerous attempts to thwart the raids. Maybe the inverted cone he'd nailed to the pole today would deter the critter. *Man versus nature*, he mused, *a perennial conflict*. He picked up stray toys, emptied Olivia's wading pool, and pondered the turn his life had taken over the past thirty-six months. Against all odds, he and Leah had found each other again and, with counseling and determination, regained the deep feelings that first bound them together, the love that had resulted in Alexandra. His older daughter was a miracle he didn't deserve. True, she harbored dark memories of the woman who raised her, which increased his own guilt, and he hadn't known she existed until three years ago, yet he believed he should have been able to save her from abuse. That sense of responsibility upped the ante on this current mystery. Doris Loving's murder threatened his children. Alexandra was obsessed with finding the killer. J.J. remained a suspect. Damn whoever had incriminated them.

A bluejay swooped by, protesting the chipmunk's raid. Joe made a mental note to refill the feeder, his nod to the Reverend's favorite pastime, before the meeting tonight. Birds had played an important part in Loving's life and in her death. This latest information, Olivia seeing Reggie steal the pins, added another layer to the mystery. How, he wondered, did everything connect? Leah poked her head out the back door and called his name, Janeece hovering behind her. Leaving the jay and the chipmunk to sort things out, he hitched up his jeans and went inside.

"Hey, Joe." A quick hug. Janeece reintroduced her partner. Joe liked Stone. The man had an easy smile and a no-nonsense grip. Leah set out pretzels and mixed nuts, then corralled Olivia, who was showing everyone her stuffed vulture from the Hinckley trip.

"I'll get J.J. Let me know if you need anything. Come on, Livvie, let's read some books." Leah knocked on her son's door. "Showtime, honey."

When he didn't respond, she went in. J.J. stood by the window, a slender wall of coiled muscle in khaki shorts and a faded tee. "J," she touched his back, "they're here."

"Might as well get it over with," he said. He picked up the plans for Reverend Loving's property and a yellow pad of ruled paper. Kissing Olivia, he thanked Leah and headed for the kitchen. Janeece was speaking when he joined them, her words a clear, precise recital of the facts-to-date. When she finished, Pete took over.

"When do you expect Xandra and Shawn to arrive?"

"X doesn't get home until 10:30, sometimes later," J.J. said. "I guess Crowe will get here about the same time."

"While we wait, let's go over your story, son." Joe rested a hand on J.J.'s shoulder.

J.J. spread the drawings out on the table. He used coasters to weight down the corners, then offered the tablet to Detective Stone. "This is a timeline of my movements the night of Reverend Loving's death. And this," he tossed a piece of paper onto the drawing, "is a message the Reverend sent me that night."

The moment stretched out, silent and tense. Finally, Janeece tapped the note. "Explain, J.J."

"I already told you we met that afternoon, walked the property, made some decisions. Reverend Loving was excited. So was I." He ran a hand through his hair. "I left the church around three, but she stayed behind. Said she had to make some calls. I only saw one car in the lot when I left. Mom needed me to watch Olivia, so I picked her up at daycare, went home for snacks, then took her to the waterpark in Springboro. We were back in time for dinner."

Janeece nodded. "We've checked and confirmed all that."

"Right. Then, um, we watched the news. I discussed the plans with Mom and Dad. I was tired, but I had promised Tim Brownie, my boss at the city maintenance department, I'd help set up signs for the concert in the park the next day, so I went back to work. We finished early, a little after eight, and were just sitting around talking when I got the text from Reverend Loving."

"You went to meet her at the dinner theater," Pete said.

"Yeah. She was standing outside, near the portico where you drop off passengers."

"Was she alone?"

J.J. nodded. "I drove up to the drop-off lane and she told me to follow her to her car. There were no spaces close to where she was parked, so I had to drive around until I found an open spot. Took me about five or six minutes to get back to her."

"What did you talk about?" Janeece leaned toward him, one hand resting on her notebook, the other holding the text message.

"She insisted that no matter what anyone said, she wanted the plan for the land to go forward. And she gave me this." He reached into his pocket and pulled out a business card. Everyone leaned forward. Two sets of numbers had been inked onto the back. Joe spoke first. "What are those?"

"Let me finish, Dad, then I'll tell you what I think."

"Fair enough."

"She shoved this at me and told me to keep it safe. Then she hurried back inside. I thought someone was watching from the shadows under the overhang, but I couldn't tell who it was. I went back to my car. I could see the entrance of the theater from where I parked. I waited for a few minutes, and when no one came out, I stuck the card in my pocket and drove to the ice cream store."

"This means," Pete said, "Doris Loving was alive before nine o'clock and shortly after, she wasn't."

"I didn't kill her. She trusted me. She wanted this," he gestured at the landscape plan, "to succeed. Why would I mess that up?"

Janeece stared out the window before she spoke. "Okay, what do you think those numbers mean?"

J.J. put his hands in his pockets. "I know what they are. They're latitude and longitude coordinates for a specific location."

"Where exactly?" Pete asked.

"Her property, the place where she planned to plant the memorial trees."

"I wonder," Janeece murmured, "if she ever imagined that the first one would be hers."

Fifty-six

The Buns N Fries buzzed with conversation and the clatter of trays being returned to the shelf above the trash receptacle. Xandra wiped her forehead as she worked her way around the supplies she hadn't had time to unpack and stow above the grilling area. A second late delivery meant she wouldn't get home on time for the meeting with the detectives. Carson was doing his best to clear off the dining tables before the next rush while Emilia raced from the drive-thru window to the fryers to complete and hand out orders. Even Millie, who had shown up on time and agreed to man the front register, was hustling to greet customers.

Xandra glanced at the clock and sighed. Why tonight, of all nights, did not one but two busloads of sightseers on their way to Dollywood have to stop for dinner at her restaurant? She would post the closed signs in fifteen minutes and try to make it home by ten-thirty. J.J. had already sent a message that everyone was there except her and Shawn, who had texted **see you after work** with an emoji of a cat wearing a Sherlock Holmes hat and holding a magnifying glass. She shouldn't feel giddy, but she did.

"Xandra," Millie called, "we're out of drink cups."

Setting aside her personal agenda, she grabbed a box cutter, sliced through the tape on the nearest carton, and carried the cups to Millie's station. Then she stuck the cutter in the back pocket of her jeans. She could finish stowing the deliveries before she did the money count.

"Hey, boss." Carson edged past her, angling the mop and bucket toward the utility closet. "One of my kids is sick. Do you mind if I go home right at closing?"

His departure would leave them short-handed, but the man rarely asked to leave early. "As soon as the dining room is clean, you can go."

"Thanks, boss." He hurried back to the dining area as the last of the customers strolled toward the exits. Emilia pointed at the camera above the carry-out window.

"No cars in line, X. Can I close now?"

"Can you help restock before you leave?"

Emilia checked the schedule taped beside the ice cream dispenser. "I'm at the limit for hours. What if someone checks the timecards?"

Xandra scooped a fry box from the floor. The girl had a point. Mr. Loving was particular about obeying the laws in regard to young employees. He probably didn't want the government looking into his business. "Better go, then," Xandra said.

"I'll stay." Millie Stanfield stowed two Buns N Fries specials in a bag and handed it to the semi driver waiting at the counter. Xandra blinked at the unexpected offer.

"Thanks, Millie. I really need to get out of here early tonight," X said.

Millie cocked an eyebrow. "You have someplace to be?"

Xandra ignored the question. Millie Stanfield was the last person she wanted to know about her plans to discuss the Loving case with a room full of detectives, her father, and a guy who might be her boyfriend. No one at the restaurant knew about Shawn, and she meant to keep it that way. She followed Carson to the front of the restaurant, inspected the tables and floor, and gave him a thumbs up. Thanking her again, he scurried out the door. Emilia clocked out and met her father in the parking lot. Millie was scouring the condiments and drink station. Dimming the outside lights, Xandra moved to the registers. Each chore moved her closer to the meeting at home. She was emptying the trash cans when a knock sounded at the back door.

"I'll get it." Millie wiped her hands on a towel and moved toward the back. Before Xandra could stop her, she had unlocked the door, which banged hard against the wall, then slammed closed. There was a grunt, and Millie yelped. Xandra flattened against the menu wall, hand closing around the box cutter, and peeked around the corner. At the back of the restaurant, an intruder wearing the same mask as the previous robber, had a gun to Millie's head. Xandra edged toward the front exit as the gunman prodded Millie past the unpacked cartons toward the fryers, which were still cooling. He spotted Xandra and motioned her to stop, then looked straight into the spy camera above the registers and smashed it with the gun barrel.

"How do I turn off the rest of the cams, bitch?" He grabbed Millie by the neck and aimed the gun at Xandra. She pointed to a panel above the refrigerator. Ordering the women to stay in front of him, he reached up and flipped the switch. The console went dark. "Hands in back, Byrd. And you, tie them tight."

Releasing her hold on the box cutter, Xandra turned and held her hands out behind her. Millie secured the zip ties around her wrists. "Now, the hood," he said.

Xandra opened her mouth, then closed it. Protesting would do no good. *Think, Xandra, think.* Millie shook out a canvas sack.

"Bend over, bitch." The man motioned to Xandra.

"No." She stepped back.

"You anxious for another concussion? Or worse? Just do it."

The thought of being bound and blind terrified Xandra. She retreated until she bumped against the counter. "Millie, don't do this."

Millie cocked one eyebrow, her eyes cold and distant as stars. The man shoved the gun in the waistband of his jeans. He grabbed the sack and stalked toward Xandra. Grabbing her by the hair, he jerked her forward to wrestle the hood over her head. She struggled, stopping only when he punched her. Doubled over, breathing hard, she fought for air as he herded her past the prep counter and pushed her to the floor. Her shoulder banged against the boxes.

"You move," he kicked her thigh, "and the blonde gets it."

Millie still hadn't uttered a word. Xandra breathed through the pain until she was sure she wouldn't faint. She wriggled upright, one elbow brushing the box behind her. With slow, careful movements, she eased the box cutter from her pocket and into her palm, feeling for the tab that would release the blade. In the lobby, the registers clanged open. It had been a good day. There were probably several thousand dollars in cash among the three stations. Whispers drifted toward her. Millie and the intruder? The longer Xandra listened, the more confused she felt.

Bracing herself, she leaned sideways and, cutter in hand, concentrated on carving a message into the cardboard. She etched a letter, traced over it with her thumb, and moved on, hoping at least one of the words would be legible. When the whispering stopped, she closed the blade and slipped it back in her pocket. Footsteps, one set heavy, the other a soft shuffle, alerted her to their approach. The man hauled Xandra to her feet, pressing the gun into her lower back.

"Out. Now." She stumbled forward, tripped, almost fell. Her captor shoved her out the door and into the parking lot.

"The door!" Millie's cry echoed around the lot. The exit banged shut. Xandra smirked. The keys to the restaurant and the ones to her car remained inside, in the desk drawer where she'd tossed them earlier this afternoon.

"You grabbed the keys, right, Mil?" A startled intake of breath. Cursing. Xandra ignored the pain in her wrists and ribs as two things became clear. The robber had planned to take her car, and Millie Stanfield was working with him. "If you didn't, we're screwed."

"Shut. Up," Millie hissed. "Let me think."

Moments passed before the man spoke again. "We're out of time. Decide."

"All right." Millie again. "We'll leave hers here, come back for it later. Just stop talking."

Xandra's mind raced with this new revelation. She pushed back against the man, broke free, and stumbled against the hood of a car. Cursing, he shoved her down, kicked her in the ribs, and moved away. She heard the trunk squeak open. Struggling against the pain, Xandra pulled the box cutter from her pocket. Hands shaking, she scratched H E L P into the side panel of the car. The trunk slammed shut, rocking the car, and the blade slipped free, falling to the pavement. She slid down, shivering as she patted the ground, desperate to find the blade before they did.

"Get her up," the man said. Millie grabbed the front of Xandra's uniform and dragged her up just as her fingers landed on the cutter. She dragged it into her hand, nails scraping the ground, the edge slicing the tips of her fingers.

Fifty-seven

The informal task force huddled around the table in the Zetts's dining room, Janeece and Pete sharing notes while Joe inspected the plans for the Reverend's land. When the doorbell chimed, J.J. rose to answer it. Leah returned from checking on Olivia. "Find anything?" she said.

"All this," he said, "makes Paul Loving the strongest suspect in his sister's murder, but it doesn't explain the other deaths. Maybe they aren't connected at all."

"Maybe not." Janeece drummed the table with her pen. "However, a wise man I know once insisted there's no such thing as coincidence."

Joe acknowledged her compliment by raising his glass. J.J. escorted Shawn Crowe into the kitchen. Crowe frowned. "Where's Xandra?"

"You didn't stop by the restaurant?" Leah set the drink tray on the counter.

"She told me to come straight here." He checked his phone. "It's after eleven. She hasn't sent any texts, and she hasn't called."

Pete scrutinized the young man. "Is that unusual?"

"Since the robbery, she texts me every night when she gets off work." His voice trailed off.

"Shawn's right. She should have been here by now." Leah dialed Xandra's number. The call went straight to voice mail. She raised frightened eyes to the group. Before she could speak, Joe grabbed his keys.

"Let's go."

"Joe, you should stay here," Janeece said.

"She's my daughter, Janeece. I'm going, and the boys are coming with me."

The detective shook her head. "You better behave. Leah, stay in contact with Joe."

"I will. Please, find my girl."

Following Pete out the door, Janeece called the station. "Do we have anyone near the Buns N Fries? No? Okay, send Watkins to check things out."

"Terl," Pete stopped his partner, "I have a bad feeling about this."

"Copy that. Call the employees. Find out what time they left work, ask about anything out of the ordinary they might have noticed tonight."

Moths swarmed the headlights as the two cars wound through the neighborhood and out onto the Pike. The closer they got to the Buns N Fries, the more uneasy Janeece felt. Everything she knew about Alexandra Byrd indicated a young woman who kept her word. That she hadn't returned home and wasn't answering her phone invited a number of scenarios, none of them positive.

At the restaurant, a patrol car idled in the drive-thru lane near the side door. Officer Watkins leaned against the hood, flashlight dangling from one hand. The other thumbed his radio.

Janeece left the car idle as she approached the patrolman. "What have you got?"

"Interior lights are on. One car in the back. Registered to a Joseph Zetts."

J.J. jogged around the building. Ten seconds later, he returned, his face creased with worry. "It's Xandra's. There's no one inside, and the back door of the restaurant is locked."

Shawn swore. Joe scrubbed at his mouth. "Check the trunk."

J.J. laid an arm over his father's shoulders and waited for the detectives to speak. Janeece tapped her foot once, twice, sighed. "Before we go there, Joe, let's check the building."

"I'll take the back," Pete said. "Watkins, we have probable cause to believe a crime has been committed. Break the glass if necessary. Joe, you and the boys stay here until we call you."

Joe nodded. The patrolman waited for Pete to cover the rear exit, then popped the trunk of the police car and pulled out a lock release bar. He inserted the thin rod into the jamb of the entry door, working it back and forth until the lock clicked free. "No need for breaking," he said, "just entering."

Janeece stepped in first, fanning her weapon over the dining area while Watkins checked out the restrooms. They worked their way past the registers and toward the rear of the restaurant, shoes crunching on coins scattered across the floor. When Janeece reached the back door, she unlocked it, waved Pete in, then hurried back outside to wave to Joe, J.J., and Shawn.

"Lights on in the office area, but there's no one here," she said. J.J. eyed the desk where his sister tallied the day's receipts. He skirted past the detectives, bracing a hand against the boxes that crowded the aisle. His shorts snagged on the cardboard.

"Are her keys in the desk?" he said. Janeece opened the top drawer, rummaged through the contents, and held up a chain bearing a tiny skateboard and a set of keys. J.J. swallowed hard. "Those are hers."

"Check the safe." Joe said. "She locks the money away before she leaves for the night."

"You know her routine?" Pete asked.

"We do," J.J. said. The cardboard snagged his shorts again. "Hey, does anyone have a flashlight?"

The patrolman handed his over. J.J. directed the light over the carton, revealing the manufacturer's name and bar code and a message scratched into the cardboard surface. On his knees, the boy traced the crude etching. "I think my sister wrote this."

Hands fisted, mind racing, Shawn squatted to peer at the letters. h e l p m e X "Xandra's in trouble."

Pete's phone rang. He stepped away to speak to the caller, then returned, brow creased with worry. "Carson left early. So did Emilia. Both insist Millie Stanfield stayed to help close."

"The mysterious Millie." Janeece opened cabinets until she located the one that held the security camera and recorder. "Do we need a warrant to play this?"

"I don't." Joe nudged Terl aside, pushed rewind, and cued up the tape at the ten o'clock mark. They stared at the small screen as Millie approached the back door. Watched a masked man slip in, look around, stare directly at the camera. He raised a gun to Millie's head and a moment later, the screen went dark. After a fifteen-minute delay, the recording resumed. The man shoved a hooded figure out the door.

Xandra. Joe swore when his daughter stumbled and disappeared into the night. Millie strolled behind.

"The bastards took her," Shawn said.

"My daughter's tough, Shawn. We'll find her."

"Will we?"

Janeece noted the anguish on Crowe's face, the concern on Joe's and J.J.'s. She nodded toward Pete, who escorted them out of the restaurant.

"Go home, guys," Pete said. "We'll call when we find them."

Shawn protested. Joe held him back. While Pete headed back into the restaurant, Joe stared into the dark, brooding, forested land beyond the streetlights, then turned to the boys. "We're not going home. We're going to find our girl."

"Where do we start, Dad?"

"That Millie Stanfield is in on this. She didn't even blink when the guy came through the door. It's like she anticipated every move."

Shawn pounded the hood of the car. "They must be working together. He's probably the same one who robbed the place before, and she helped him."

"Calm down, Shawn." J.J. checked over his shoulder. Detective Stone was staring at them. "We need a plan."

"I'm good, J." Shawn turned to Joe. "What's our first move?"

"Let's get out of here," Joe said. "We need to consider where they might take her."

"What about the park, Dad? Would he take Xandra there?" J.J. blinked away the sudden rush of emotion. He refused to think about his sister suffering the same fate as Ace Farins.

"It's a start, son. Shawn? You in?" Crowe nodded as he yanked the door open and climbed in. Determined to find Xandra, Joe, J.J., and Shawn raced toward Beck Park, fear and a desire for revenge riding with them all the way down Hopewell Pike.

Fifty-eight

It was stifling inside the mask. Xandra couldn't take a full breath without fibers from the cloth irritating her nose and lips. To distract herself, she concentrated on the sound of the tires on the pavement, noting when they drove from asphalt onto concrete. She counted the stops, memorized the turns, and strained to hear what Millie and the man said to each other. He had removed his mask, his tone a mix of anger and elation. Although she couldn't understand every word, one thing stood out. They disagreed on where to take her. He wanted to go home. Millie demanded they return to the campsite where the Farins kid had died. Xandra shivered. Did they plan to kill her or was something else in the works? The argument grew heated.

"He'll meet us," Millie said. "Then, we get rid of both of them and shift the blame onto them."

"Too risky," the man growled. "Too many bodies to hide."

"We don't hide them. A murder-suicide works just as well. No one knows about you, Rye." The seat back shifted. Millie had moved closer to the driver, unaware she had failed to buckle the rear seatbelt. Unrestrained and unable to brace herself, Xandra slid across the seat each time the car swerved. Her hands tingled. If she didn't free them soon, she'd lose all feeling. At the next turn, she wedged herself against the door, forcing the box cutter to the top of the pocket where she'd stashed it. Her numb fingers gripped the edge, but the blade hadn't withdrawn completely. She yelped when it sliced her thumb.

"You should have knocked her out again," Millie groused.

"You want to carry her to the campsite? Get serious."

Xandra inhaled, exhaled, willing her pulse to slow, her heart to stop pounding. They rounded a corner, and she toppled over. The cutter popped into her palm. She angled the blade against the plastic tie, sawing in short, jerky bursts.

The car lurched to a stop, then turned right. Xandra's stomach dropped as they headed down a hill. Rye slowed, then pulled over. Millie prodded Xandra with the gun. "You fall asleep back there?"

Xandra sat up. One of the ties popped free, and the pressure on her wrists eased. She tucked her arms tighter behind her, shoved the cutter between the seat cushions.

"Here?" Tires crunched over gravel.

"No. Go to Hazel Wood. We can walk to the campsite from there."

"You can't be serious. That's at least a two-mile hike."

"It's doable."

"The gate will be locked."

"Stop with all the negatives," Millie said. When Rye didn't respond, she spoke again, all breathy and seductive. "We're almost home free."

Xandra couldn't see, but her ears worked fine. The heavy breathing made her gag. The front seat banged against her knees. She huddled deeper, sickened by the sounds of Millie and Rye, until her calf slammed against something heavy, a tool or tackle box. She reared back, the second tie on her wrist snapping. She almost put out her hands to catch herself. Her head smacked against the window. She bit her lip against the pain and struggled to right herself. She had only one chance to fool her captors. They had to believe she was still restrained.

Rye put the car in gear, backed out of what had to be Clearcreek Park and bumped onto the bridge over Pleasant Run Creek. When he rolled down the window, Xandra recognized the murmur of the creek that shadowed the road. He was right. They were at least two miles from where Reggie had camped, assuming there was an actual trail. He and Millie acted familiar with the terrain, but tonight was a new moon. They'd need light to find their way. Coyotes would be prowling. Deciding she needed the cutter after all, Xandra slipped a hand along the seat until she found the blade. Teasing it free, she stuck it back in her pocket. It wasn't much of a weapon, but it was all she had.

"Huh," Rye said, "Look at that. They forgot to shut the gate."

"Won't need these then." Millie dropped a heavy tool over the seatback, narrowly missing Xandra's feet. The car lurched forward, the rapid starts and stops jostling Xandra. "Damn." Rye slapped the wheel. "Someone's over by the dog park."

"We'll have to change to your plan, then. Hurry, before they spot us."

Rye reversed through the gate, backed onto the roadway, and sped off. They were closer to Hopewell now. Light from the streetlamps lining the median filtered through the hood. Xandra listened harder, cataloguing sounds along the way. At one point, a bass guitar pounded. Probably a band at the Whiskey Barrel in the strip mall by the Interstate. Were they heading toward the complex where Millie lived? Xandra recalled the layout of the buildings, townhomes in front, garages in the rear. The car eased over a speed bump. Rye cut the engine as they coasted downhill. She heard a large door cranking up. The car pulled forward, and the door banged down behind them.

"Check her wrist ties," Millie said.

"Hey." Xandra squeaked when Rye yanked her out of the car. "I have to go to the bathroom."

He patted her cheek through the hood. "Tough shit. You're going to stay right here until we can move you." He reached around to tug on the zip ties. They pulled free. Swearing, he strapped her wrists with a new set, shoved her onto a chair, and tied her ankles.

"You don't want to do this," Xandra said. She knew the attempt was foolish as soon as the words left her lips, but she had to try.

"What? Can't hear you." Millie's laughter rang out in the confined space.

"I said," Xandra took a breath and shouted, "you don't want to do this."

"I didn't at first," Millie said, "but you just wouldn't let it alone. Now, should I leave the hood on or take it off and gag you? What to do? What to do?"

"I always knew you were a bitch, Stanfield," Xandra said, "but I never thought you were a killer. You'll be lucky if all you get is a life sentence."

"Uh-uh, Byrd. You're not the one in charge here. You and Paul will take the fall, hey, that rhymes." Millie giggled. "You and that douchebag Loving will be blamed, and I will be the wronged and very rich wife."

Rye shuffled closer to Millie. "You mean we, don't you?"

"Of course, love. But we must be patient. The land deal will go through once all the loose ends are tied up."

"What the hell are you talking about?" Xandra said.

Millie chortled. "I'm Mrs. Paul Loving now. Gag her, Rye, use that dog chain around her waist, and put the hood back on." He snatched off the sack and stepped closer. She struggled, but it was no use. The handkerchief cut into the corners of her lips, although he hadn't shoved it deep into her mouth. Then he dragged a length of chain attached to a ring in the floor and fastened it around her waist. Millie checked to be sure it was secure. "Good job, Rye. We'll stay at your place tonight, get some rest before Loving shows up tomorrow."

"You sure he's going to show?"

Stanfield snorted. "He'll show. He can't get enough of me."

The door accordioned down. Desperate for air, Xandra tried a few deeper breaths. The gag chafed her cheeks. She arched backward, reaching for the blade with her fingertips. She worked the cutter back and forth until it stuck up above the pocket, but she couldn't hold on. The box cutter tumbled to the floor. Tears trickled down her cheeks, wetting the ends of the gag. She fought a swell of panic. *Stay calm, X.* She rocked the chair once, twice, three times, bracing for impact. On the fourth try, she tipped over and crashed onto the cement, pinning her shoulder against the floor. Pain radiated up her leg. Ignoring it, she rubbed her cheek against the cement. Working to loosen the sack and the gag left abrasions on her face. Blood trickled down her cheek. Her ear throbbed. Air swirled in from beneath the garage door, sending debris into the bruises. She waited for her eyes to adjust to the dark. Then she jackknifed her body repeatedly, turning the chair in search of the fallen cutter. If Millie and Rye kept to their schedule, she had until daylight to get free. If they came back sooner, she was screwed.

Fifty-nine

In a chestnut tree next to the overlook, an owl hooted. Shawn scanned the field below with the night-vision binoculars Joe handed him. The prairie slumbered, the campsite where Ace Farins had died too far away to be seen even in daylight.

"Nothing moving down there?" J.J. said.

"Only fireflies. Are we sure they'll bring Xandra here?" Coyotes howled in the far southern section of the park, sending eerie echoes across the shadowed land. Shawn shoved the binoculars back at the older man.

"Easy, Crowe." Joe placed a hand on the boy's shoulder. "We have to make a choice, a calculated one. Do we stake out the campsite, or do we go to Millie's place and look there?"

"We might run into Janeece and Pete at Stanfield's." Shawn slumped against the wall. "Damn it. I should have gone to the restaurant tonight."

"This isn't on you, son," Joe said. "And going to the Stanfield woman's place might cause more problems. We aren't law enforcement, and we have no way to get inside her condo. If we alert her and her accomplice, they might harm Alexandra."

"What if they already have?" J.J. shouldered his way past the other two. Retrieving a flashlight from the car, he shouldered a backpack and headed down the path to the right of the overlook. "I'm checking it out while we're here."

Shawn and Joe exchanged a look. "Wait up," Shawn said. Joe retrieved his weapon from the lockbox in the trunk and followed the young men into the night.

* * *

Janeece stared at the sky, identifying the Big Dipper but not much else. Had she failed the Byrd girl? Unable to bear the thought of one more death, she paced while Henry dusted for prints and a tech from Springboro PD copied the surveillance video. The message carved into the box taunted her. Xandra had called for help, and they'd arrived too late. She closed her eyes, desperate for inspiration. *Where are you, X?*

Pete finished his calls and joined her by the back exit. "What do you think they'll do with her?"

"I'm afraid to think about it." Hands in pockets, Janeece strolled toward the hedge separating the Buns N Fries from the dinner theater, the thick bushes a metaphor for all that remained hidden since the Reverend's murder. She toed the first steppingstone in the hidden path connecting the two establishments.

"Talk to me, partner."

"We have no idea who killed Doris Loving, but we have a very good idea who coordinated the robberies at the restaurant. There's a high probability that Stanfield and her accomplice murdered the Farins boy, but right now, neither leads us to Doris's killer, and Xandra Byrd is missing." Janeece waved a hand at the sky.

Pete cracked his knuckles. "This is like one of those connect-the-dots puzzles in a kid's coloring book. Hard to see the whole until the lines are drawn. I'm inclined to think one of the big boys – Loving, Coulter, Eisner – went after the Reverend because the land deal was too lucrative to risk losing. I'm wondering if the Lynx boys were working for someone else in addition to the Lovings. And Reggie said Millie Stanfield asked him to steal the pins, right?' When Janeece nodded, he went on. "Maybe the boys decided to use what they knew to blackmail one of their employers."

"Stuart might blackmail Paul, but I can't imagine either brother putting the screws to someone like Coulter or the mayor. Those men have the means and the muscle to strike back. By the way, do we know where Reggie is yet?"

"Several sightings in West Virginia. Seems Xandra shared stories about growing up there."

"Did she tell you that?"

"No, Joe did. He overheard her tell J.J. and Reggie how easy it was to hide in the mountains. He didn't know if his daughter was serious or simply telling tales, but Reggie believed her."

"This was before he stole the vulture pins?" She felt no compassion for the boy who had betrayed his friend.

"If it's any consolation, I believe he regretted it."

"Maybe, but we still can't find the connection between the land deal and the Stanfield woman."

Pete stared over the hedge at the darkened facade of the dinner theater. "We need to look into her relationship with Paul Loving."

"That would knit those threads together, wouldn't it?" Turning back toward the restaurant, she saw Henry coming their way.

"Neecie?" He squeezed her hand. "How you doing?"

Janeece shrugged. "I'm worried, Henry. Pete and I are heading to Stanfield's condo now. If we don't find her there, we'll go roust Loving."

Sixty

Xandra panted until the pain eased. After repeated efforts, she managed to loosen the hood and slide her head free. She counted to ten, then, dragging the chair with her, inched her way toward the cutter that had skittered away after her first attempt to corral it. Her bloodied fingers throbbed. Thirst plagued her. The abrasions on her face and neck competed with the ache in her shoulder and hip. She'd been forced to relieve herself in her jeans. The pungent smell made her eyes water, but she was beyond embarrassment. Millie and Rye planned to kill her. Had they killed the Farins kid? What about Stuart and the attacks on Reggie? No, someone else had gone after the Lynx brothers. Cramped and shivering, Xandra abandoned her efforts to reach the cutter. Her muscles quivered from fatigue and pain. Despite the cold seeping up through the concrete, she curled her bruised cheek against her injured shoulder and fell asleep.

She woke to an agony of bruises. Fingers of light seeped beneath the door. The interior of the garage began to warm. Her body jerked against the restraints, and her nose nudged the cutter. Somehow, in her restless napping, she had moved closer to the slippery blade. Now all she had to do was turn her body and the chair and gather it in. Footsteps sounded outside. She stopped moving, prepared to feign sleep in case Rye or Millie had returned. Panic stalled her breathing. They would find the cutter, and no one would hear her scream. Maybe she could pound her feet against the adjoining wall, attract the attention of another tenant. But what if the neighbor simply called Millie to complain about the noise? Xandra would lose any chance for rescue. No, she needed to run at the first opportunity. That meant no hood and no zip ties.

Forcing herself to take two deep, calming breaths, she pushed to face away from the blade. With a prayer to whatever god was listening, she extended her arms as far behind her as she could. Her shoulder muscles burned. Gritting her teeth, she stretched farther. Her fingers touched, then grasped the tool. She had barely sliced through the wrist bonds when a door rumbled upward. She pressed harder, fear and despair clouding her thoughts. The ties slipped, then parted. Needles of pain flared up her arms. She almost dropped the blade again. Footsteps crunched past the garage. Voices rose, then faded. One sounded so much like Shawn that a sob worked its way up her throat. But nobody knew where she was. No one was coming to rescue her. She was on her own.

* * *

On this second visit to Millie Stanfield's condo, Janeece Terl pounded the door. Once again, the cat hopped up to the window, meowing and scratching at the glass. Pete rang the bell, listened to it echo inside the house. No one answered.

"I'm tired of this shit," Terl said. "Let's wake the manager." It took three calls and the repeated message that it was an urgent police matter before Gerald Constant, who lived on the premises but was currently spending the night with his fiancée in Tipp City, answered his phone. He agreed to meet Terl and Stone by seven-thirty a.m. at the sales office two buildings over from the one where Stanfield lived. When Janeece hung up, her mood had gone from irritated to furious. She glared at Pete, who crossed his arms and shook his head.

"Nothing easy about this, is there?" When she grudgingly agreed, he focused his attention on the door of the condo. "We could claim extenuating circumstances. We do have reason to believe a woman's life is in danger."

"No door busting yet. I don't sense that anyone's home. Let's go roust Loving, stash him at the station, and make him wait for us. Maybe he'll have more to say after he cools his heels in a hot room."

Pete settled into the driver's seat, tossing his notebook at her as she climbed in. "I'm also curious about those coordinates J.J. shared with us. Maybe the evidence we need is hidden there."

"What were those numbers again?" As Pete recited them from memory, she jotted them in her notes. She rubbed her temples, trying to ease the headache. Dread pooled in her gut. "Where are they?"

"We'll find them." He checked the gas gauge and considered deploying the siren. Although the morning commute hadn't begun yet, time was slipping away.

"I hope so, Pete. Too many people have died already."

"We'll be at Loving's residence in," he checked the speedometer, did a quick calculation, "fifteen." They didn't speak the rest of the way to the two-story monstrosity Paul Loving called home. The house displayed a pillared front porch, twin turrets, a driveway lined with faux-Roman statues, and a four-car garage. A line of stunted crabapple trees bordered the asphalt driveway. Pete noted cameras mounted on top of the cast-iron entrance gates. "Fancies himself a tycoon, does he?"

"It would appear so. Or Loving is afraid of something. I wonder if he's home." Janeece pointed at the garage. One of the doors stood open, the bay empty. Pete approached the front, knocked, then rang the bell. No one came to the door. Janeece rolled down her window to order him back when the click of a lock announced someone on the other side. A round face above a rounder body peeked at him through the opening.

"Buenos días. May I help you?"

Pete held up his badge and ID. The woman backed away, pulling the door with her. "Aye, señor, I'm legal. Mr. Loving has the papers. Por favor."

Pete hurried to reassure her. "I'm not here to arrest you, ma'am. We need to speak to your employer. Is he home?"

The woman kneaded her fingers against her dress, but her face relaxed. "No. Mr. Loving left about ten minutes ago. His wife called for him."

"His wife?" Pete looked at Janeece, who had joined him.

"Sí, officer. Missus Loving called to say she had been in an accident and could he come help her."

"Do you have a picture of Mrs. Loving?"

The woman tapped her cheek. "No, I'm sorry. The wedding photos have not arrived yet. But Mrs. Millie said they would be here soon."

"Millie? Mrs. Loving's name is Millie?" Janeece stepped into the foyer. The housekeeper backed away, eyes wide and slightly teary.

"Pues, Millicent is her name, Millicent Elaine."

The detectives thanked her and ran to the car. Pete gunned the engine, fingers gripping the wheel as pieces of the case reassembled themselves. Janeece ticked them off on her fingers. "We should have seen it. Millie's the missing link."

"The guy with her could be, what, a relative, or a friend who somehow knew the Farins boy, whom Stuart Lynx met at the detention center. But he's probably our mystery man who involved the boys in their schemes."

"Millie, married to Paul Loving! How did she swing that, I wonder? So, if something happens to his sister…"

"And then to him," Pete interjected.

"She inherits the property and the payoff when the housing development is approved."

"That's why she was at the council meeting, to see if the deal would go through."

"She and her partner have Xandra," Janeece stated the obvious, "and they are getting really good at killing."

Sixty-one

Xandra tried to open her eyes, groaned, tried again. She must have passed out. She lifted her head, flexed her fingers. The busted ties fell away from her hands. The garage spun around her. She waited for the vertigo to pass, pulled the gag from her mouth, then bent to free her feet. She pushed to her hands and knees, drew in deep, ragged breaths, tried screaming. All that came out was a croak. Bracing a hand against the wall, she struggled to stand and shuffled her way around the space in search of water, food, a weapon. The chain unraveled behind her, stopping her well short of the garage door itself. She bruised a hip bumping into one of three large barrels stashed along the side wall. Unable to pry the lids free with her injured hands, she continued her slow inspection. On a shelf mounted on the rear wall, she found a screwdriver, the handle sticky with tape, the head blunt from use. She bound it to her calf with her hair tie. Her head throbbed, making it difficult to think. She dragged the chair to its original position before collapsing onto the seat. When her captors returned, she needed them to believe she was still their prisoner, but she refused to replace the hood until she absolutely had to. She examined the ties. If she held the cut ends in her palms, it would look like they'd never been severed. The ones that had secured her feet presented a problem. Using the box cutter, she loosened the stitching on the hem of her shirt. She gripped the seam, tore off a long strip of cloth, cut that in half, then tied each piece to the ends of the ankle ties and reattached them around her feet. If Millie and Rye were in a hurry, they might not notice. If. If. If.

Xandra closed her eyes, took stock of her physical situation. She was dehydrated, her tongue and lips swollen. Her jeans had dried, but the urine smell made her eyes water. She had considered lying down in

Millie's car, but when she tried the doors, they were locked, and she wasn't sure the chain would reach that far anyway.

The garage grew warmer, the air stale and stifling. Hushed voices outside drew her attention, but they soon faded and did not return. The urge to sleep was overpowering. She dozed off, only to wake to the rumble of a vehicle pulling in front of Stanfield's garage. The engine idled, the fumes mixing with the odors in the garage. Before the door clattered up, she replaced the gag, took a deep breath, and pulled the canvas sack over her head. She waited, unable to stop the tremors in her legs, the sick feeling that her time was up. When a hand tapped her shoulder, she flinched. Millie snatched off the hood and wrinkled her nose. "Couldn't hold it, huh?"

Xandra licked her lips but didn't speak. Millie unlocked the doors of her Camry, tossed a man's suitcoat onto the back seat, and locked the car again.

"Unlock the chain. Cut her loose," Rye hissed. He went back outside, backed a van up into the garage behind Millie's car. When he opened the back doors, Xandra stared at the bulky shape of a body wrapped in a tarp stuffed inside. Millie unlocked the chain from Xandra's waist and cut the ankle ties. Xandra concealed the loose ends of the wrist bands in her palms. When Millie cut those, she offered a bottle of water.

"Drink and try not to piss yourself again."

Xandra struggled to unscrew the cap. It rattled as it fell, rolling across the cement. While she drank, Rye re-entered the garage. He showed her the gun tucked in his waistband, then hustled her into the back of the van and followed her in. He tied her hands again, this time in front, and replaced the gag. Then he shoved her down next to the bundled tarp, which heaved upward, tossing her against the side panel. A head popped out. Eyes frantic, muffled shouts leaking from the gag in his mouth, Paul Loving stared at her.

"Shut up," Rye said. He slammed the gun against Loving's head. The man stopped wriggling. "Here, Mills. Use it if you need to."

Millie climbed in. She shoved Xandra closer to Loving, then sat opposite the captives. Rye backed the van out and closed the garage door. Hopping into the driver's seat, he drove off, exiting the development and heading down the Springboro-Hopewell Pike. Fifteen minutes later, he pulled into Hazel Wood Park.

"Anyone here?" Millie said.

"Nope, looks like we got lucky. No one at the dog park, and no walkers on the path."

"Good. Pull in behind the concession stand."

Loving had been silent during the ride. Now, as the van crept forward, he groaned. His eyes opened, and he stared at Xandra, silently pleading, but she had no assistance to offer. The only way to save them both lay in escaping into the heavily wooded hills that connected Hazel Wood to Beck Park. She flexed her fingers, swollen again. With her hands tied in front, she was unable to reach the blade in her back pocket. She might manage to free the screwdriver, but would it be enough to fight off both Rye and Millie? Xandra didn't know how far she could run tied and gagged, but one thing was certain. Millie and Rye would kill her if she didn't. Where were her father and J.J.? Shawn? Did anyone realize she was gone? And what about Terl and Stone? *No one's coming to save you,* an inner voice hissed. *Like always, you're on your own.* Fine. She had grown up in the mountains of West Virginia. These puny southwestern Ohio hills would be an easy climb. She crossed her fingers and waited while Millie jumped out of the van. Rye hauled Loving from the tarp. The man flopped over the lip of the vehicle, landing heavily on the ground. He squealed. Rye kicked him, and Loving whimpered again. "Get up."

"Ill-ee?" Paul Loving choked out around the gag.

Rye jerked the injured man to his feet and dragged him over to the trees. "Get her out," he said.

Millie aimed the gun at Xandra, who scooted forward and dropped to the ground. A horn sounded at the entrance to the park, distracting Rye. When he peeked around the concession stand, Millie turned, too, her hand relaxing its grip on the weapon. Xandra lunged forward, ramming her head into the woman's chest and driving her back against the open door of the van. The gun spurted free, landing in the grass several feet away. Xandra ran toward the weapon and kicked it deeper into the weeds. Then she sprinted toward the trees. Five long strides brought her into the pines that bordered the rear of the concession stand. She crashed through the underbrush, ignoring the branches pulling at her, and zigzagged up the hill into denser cover. Below and behind her, Rye swore.

"Stop her," Millie shouted. Xandra kept going. Her hands were still tied, the box cutter half-buried in her back pocket. She had no watch, no compass, no phone. Everything she needed lay next to her keys in the desk at the Buns N Fries. By now, someone should have found them. Someone must know she'd been taken, although no one would know where she was. She fought the despair rooting inside her. Driven by instinct and the desire to stay alive, she stopped thrashing through the woods and began to creep from one tree to the next. The thick growth gave way to a clearing that offered a view of Hopewell off to the west. She oriented herself, then turned south, and slipped into denser cover, determined not to become the next meal for the vultures she imagined circling above her.

Sixty-two

The manager of the apartments, Gerald Constant, appeared uneasy as he waited outside for the detectives. After he shook hands and checked IDs, he escorted them in. When they asked to see Millie Stanfield's condo, he didn't hesitate before speaking.

"That woman has been a thorn in my side ever since that brother of hers moved in. There's something strange in that relationship. Millie signed for him since he didn't have any credit history of his own. I think," the man lowered his voice, "he's a criminal. But what can I do? She put down a substantial amount of money to lease both places."

"Are you saying she and her brother own two condos in your development?" "Well, yes. I have no reason to make up something like that."

"We'll need to see the brother's place as well," Pete said, as he and Janeece followed the man from the office. "Do you recall which bank Millie Stanfield used?"

"Hopewell Community, of course. They service most of our clients. Paul Loving served as her reference and, well, you know, he wields a lot of influence."

When Constant opened the door to Millie's unit, Janeece motioned him to remain outside. She and Pete drew their guns and stepped into the narrow hall. The cat jumped from the windowsill to wind around her ankles. It took less than ten minutes to determine that the place was empty. The cat continued to meow. Janeece picked it up, then inspected the food and water bowls. Both were empty. She opened cupboards until she found a bag of cat food. Mumbling about irresponsible pet owners, she dished up a sizeable quantity of dry chicken bits and set the bowl on the floor. Then she set about checking the drawers and cabinets Pete hadn't yet opened.

"Nothing here of value. Except for the cat, the place looks barely lived in, but I'll ask forensics to dust for prints and DNA." Pete took the manager aside. "Where's her brother's unit?"

Constant indicated the next building over. "She specifically requested that they not be in the same building. Do you want to see his now?"

"Yes." Janeece headed down the walk. "Something tells me we'll find more answers there."

The odor of grease and dirty socks greeted them when they opened the front door. Weapons drawn, they entered and checked the premises, empty, yet with a story to tell. Takeout bags littered the counters, several bearing the Buns N Fries logo. Pete snatched up a receipt from U-Haul for a dark green cargo van, the license number clearly marked at the top of the page. The signature of the lessee: Millie Stanfield.

"Look at this, Terl."

Janeece read over the contract, then called the station. "Sanders, Janeece Terl here. Stone and I need an APB for a 2017 forest green cargo van, license HQW24157. Driver Millie or possibly Rye Stanfield. Millie may be a hostage but more likely is an accomplice. The suspects are armed and considered dangerous. Our missing person, Alexandra Byrd, may be a captive in the van as well." The dispatcher sent out the request before Janeece hung up. Satisfied that they had a lead at last, she wandered into the larger of the two bedrooms. The closet contained a mix of men's and women's clothing. The bathroom also indicated that a couple shared the space. Returning to the kitchen, she explained what she had found to her partner. Pete frowned. "What's going on here? Incest? Another woman?"

Janeece explored the living room. Two picture frames rested atop the single end table. She picked up the first. "Wedding photo," she said. "Rye and Millie Stanfield aren't brother and sister."

"How old is he?" Pete took the photo and held it up to the light.

"Younger than her, and stupider, I imagine. I'm willing to bet he has a serious juvenile record as well as at least one adult incarceration. Now that we have a name, we can access his records."

"How do you suppose they met?"

Janeece shrugged and picked up the second picture. "Millie and Paul Loving and Roy Eisner in what looks like a civil ceremony."

"Our Millie is a bigamist?"

"Looks like it." After Pete snapped photos, Janeece bagged the picture frames and the rental paperwork. "Hypothesis: Millie Stanfield trolls the bar scene for a guy stupid enough to be manipulated. She concocts a get-rich scheme and cultivates Paul Loving, too. Don't ask me how she finds him, but there must be some connection. Text the techs the address of both condos."

Pete lifted the curtain over the window above the sink and stared outside. "Parking garages are out back."

"Let's check them out. Mr. Constant?" When the manager peeked in, Janeece beckoned him over. "Can you open their garages for us now, please?"

Without a word, the man turned and walked away. They followed him down the sidewalk. Constant rounded the building and headed down a flight of stairs to the garages. The one belonging to Millie Stanfield sat directly behind her condo. Constant overrode the individual owner code and opened the door. Inside, a blue compact sat next to several round storage containers. Janeece used a pry bar to pop the lid on the first one, only to find it filled with wigs, costumes, and fake jewelry. The second bin contained books. Pete picked up the one on top. "'**Cold Cases of the Twentieth Century**.' Looks like Ms. Stanfield was doing research." He sorted through more of the books. "These all have to do with unsolved crimes."

"Apparently, she's more than just a fan of crime drama." Janeece tried the doors on the Camry. Locked. She pressed her face to the window. More fast-food wrappers, predominantly from the BNF, littered the seats. She was about to step away when the beam of her flashlight settled on a man's light grey suitcoat on the back seat. A Chamber of Commerce pin gleamed on the lapel. Dark stains speckled the collar. Blood.

Sixty-three

Headlights strafed the lacrosse fields as a police cruiser pulled into Hazel Wood Park. Officer Watkins paused to examine the gate, then cruised the west area before looping back to the concession stand. He rolled down his window, enjoying the caress of a warm breeze, the odor of new-mown grass. He rolled past the concrete block building, stopping to chat with an elderly man just arriving at the dog park. He failed to notice the van half-hidden among the pines. Back at the park entrance, he contacted the station.

"Hazel Wood checks out. I'm off to Milo Beck," he told dispatch. He marked the log and drove on.

In the forest, Xandra swallowed a sob. She was too far away to hail the patrol car, which would be gone before she could reach the pavement anyway. A distant clang indicated the patrolman had crossed the bridge over the creek. She remained in hiding, listening to Millie whisper-shout for Rye to hurry. The voices sounded closer. She crawled into a thicker patch of honeysuckle as he struggled by not three feet away, dragging Paul Loving with him. Her boss stumbled and fell to his knees. Rye hauled him upright and crept closer. Xandra burrowed deep into the loamy soil, waiting for Rye and Loving to pass. After they staggered away, she pressed forward, wrists aching from the ties, ribs sore. She extended her arms to fend off tall brush and understory branches. She checked the position of the sun, guesstimating the distance to Milo Beck. If she reached the campsite before Millie and Rye and reach the back section of Milo Beck, she had a chance of escaping. Dog walkers visited the park on a regular basis. Retired homeowners from the housing development strolled the path throughout the day. Someone would help her. All she had to do was get there before her pursuers.

Xandra shivered. Dehydration, fatigue, and despair took potshots at her resolve. Her legs were unsteady, the adrenaline rush from the escape fading as the terrain grew more rugged. Birds protested her intrusion. She drew a deep breath and slowed down. "Remember where you came from, Xandra Byrd," she told herself. "You don't need a path to find the way." She edged past a windfall, the tree trunks blown over by the last derecho, and hunkered down beneath the overhang of branches.

"This is stupid, chasing that bitch in here," Rye called out, his words strained, his voice faint. "Can I just shoot him now?"

"That's not part of the plan," Millie hissed.

"None of this was part of the plan. I say shoot him here and get the hell out."

"Give up? After all the work I put into this? No. Besides, we can't let Byrd get away. She knows too much. We have to make it look like a murder-suicide after a botched robbery."

"Yeah, well, my way's quicker and easier. Get up, Loving."

"Listen, we can drive over to the path we used before, hike in, and hide in that old shed away from the campsite, remember?" Millie said.

"Yeah. But what if Byrd doubles back to the concession stand?"

"We'll wait long enough to be sure. If Xandra thinks she can make it, she'll head for Milo Beck, I'm sure of it. We just have to wait her out."

They headed back toward the van. Xandra counted to fifty, then crab-walked away from the deadfall, her muscles protesting each move. She halted, back against a tree, drew her legs up, and rested her head on her knees.

Birdsong woke her. She'd dozed off long enough for ants to climb her jeans. A spider dangled from her knee. She brushed the insects off, alert for voices or movement. Again, she took a deep breath and counted, this time to one hundred, then stood, stretched, and listened harder. Convinced she was alone, she inched forward, careful not to step on branches that would break or into holes that could twist an ankle. Sunshine dappled the spaces between the trees with diamond light. Slipping in and out of the shade, Xandra searched for the creek that would guide her to safety.

Sixty-four

A swallowtail and two monarchs flitted over the butterfly garden next to the trail that wound down to the park. An early morning dog walker arrived at the park, a cockapoo, a husky, and a retriever leading the way. The man nodded as he passed. Joe greeted him, then scanned for other visitors as he adjusted the straps on J.J.'s backpack.

"Your shift, son. Remember," Joe said. "No heroics. Use the walkie-talkie if you spot anything out of the ordinary."

"Not if, Dad, when." Ready to resume surveillance after a two-hour nap, J.J. settled the pack higher.

"Listen, J.J. Send Shawn back. I'm worried he'll force a confrontation."

"And you wouldn't?"

Joe dipped his head. "I promised Terl and Stone not to engage. I have a feeling they'll be along shortly."

"You think Xandra's all right?"

"She has to be, son. Leah and I, our family…we can't lose her." Joe wiped his eyes, then nudged J.J. forward. He watched the boy disappear among the trees before laying the binoculars on top of the wall. He checked his gun, then scanned the fields below.

Emerging from the wooded path, J.J. sprinted onto the newly mown trail, his strides carrying him deep into the high grasses. Joe exhaled to lessen the worry lodged in his chest. His children, how proud he was of their resolve, how he feared to lose them. They had woven themselves into the fabric of his days. Three years ago, he thought he'd lost everything. Anne Marie's suicide still hit hard, but the pain of her infidelity had lessened. She'd given him a son. For that he would always honor her. Now, with Leah and Olivia, his transformation to husband and father had delivered more happiness than he deserved. Was he going to pay for that joy with Xandra's life? Shrugging away the fears, he concentrated on watching the prairie, hoping he had guessed right, that the killers would bring Xandra back to the campsite. The squeal of tires interrupted his concentration. Janeece and Pete arrived, accompanied by two patrol cars.

"Joe!" Janeece sprinted to reach him. "Don't tell me those boys are in the park."

His smile didn't reach his eyes. "Okay, I won't tell you."

"Have you seen anyone?"

Joe set down the binoculars. "No one but normal park patrons. You think he'll bring the women here?"

Janeece shared a glance with her partner and turned back to Joe. "Millie Stanfield is in on this, Joe. Maybe Paul Loving, as well. Fill him in, Pete. I'm going to the campsite." She started down the hill. Joe followed her. Pete brought up the rear.

"Loving and Millie Stanfield are married."

"That's unsettling. And unexpected. You sure?" Joe waited until they reached the bottom of the hill before he asked the question uppermost in his mind. "Do you think Alexandra is alive?"

Janeece followed the path along the cliff. Below the steep drop-off, Pleasant Run Creek flowed on, unmindful of the humans. On the opposite bank, a heron protested their intrusion. "Don't go there, Joe. Not yet. Are you carrying?"

"I am."

"All right. Just remember, you're a civilian here. Don't use it unless you have to."

"Glad to know something I taught you stuck."

* * *

Screened by a stand of thornbushes, Shawn set down the binoculars and rubbed his eyes. He had dozed off sometime in the night, waking when the first glimmer of dawn crept through the trees. The campsite lay abandoned, early morning sun washing the ground in pale lemon stripes. Puddles from the rain a few nights ago lingered in low spots. He decided to move closer. Knees cracking, he rose from his position. He circled the site, then scaled the high ridge that overlooked the camp from the east. Only one narrow path led in from the southern end. That had to be how the Farins kid and whoever killed him got here. If the same people had Millie and Xandra, Shawn figured they'd approach from that direction. Severing branches from a young pine, he fanned them out to provide a blind, then hunkered down to wait. In the distance, he detected the rustle of a large animal moving toward him.

* * *

J.J. reached the streambed, removed his boots to wade across, then put them on again, begrudging the time it took. He checked the compass hanging from the backpack and then the time on his phone. Around him, the woods brooded, silent and waiting. As he started up the hill, he glimpsed a vulture riding high above the denser part of the forest. He fought the urge to hurry. The bird would circle lower if carrion lay below. After a pause to hydrate, J.J. scrambled over a scatter of dead branches. Two miles to go. Wherever Xandra was, she needed him to stay calm. He crept on.

* * *

Xandra plunged through the understory, ignoring the burrs stuck to her jeans, the ache of tired muscles. She made slow progress, unable to count the times she reached an impasse and had to double-back or work around a fall of trees, a rain-carved gully, or a jumble of stones mossy and slick. She was grateful for each trickle of water assuring her she was headed in the right direction, eastward and downhill, toward Pleasant Run Creek. Thirsty, she drank from muddy depressions, too dehydrated to care about contamination. The ties chafed her already abraded wrists, but she ignored that pain, too. She had to get away before Millie and Rye could kill her and Loving, before they could blame the robbery and the Reverend's death on her. She took careful steps, alert for the sounds of company, animal or human. She doubted her pursuers knew much about the forest, but Xandra had gathered that knowledge from childhood. Wounded and hunted, she was still in her element. Millie and Rye were not.

Ahead, a rockfall marked what she hoped was the final obstacle between her and the campsite. Eager to reach the creek, she grabbed for a low-hanging branch at the top of the steep slope. The limb snapped, forcing her to her knees. She scrabbled for a new handhold, missed, and slithered down the embankment. When she stopped sliding, she blinked away tears of frustration, swatting the gnats swarming her face. The cuts on her hands burned. She dug her chipped nails into the soil and clawed her way to the bottom, where she lay spent, peering at the tease of sky visible through the canopy. In the distance, water rushed and gurgled over rocks. She had almost made it to the stream. Where were Millie and Rye? If they had reached the southern trail forged from their previous treks, they would be close to the campsite. She needed to hurry.

* * *

J.J. swept the binoculars over the wooded surroundings. Nothing moved. Where was Shawn? Although his cardinal call wouldn't pass muster with bird watchers, it was the only song he and Shawn both recognized and could imitate. He whistled, waited, repeated the call. Off to his left, branches shook. A chipmunk scampered by. Shawn peeked out from beneath a layer of pine needles.

"J.J.?"

"Here." Xandra's brother dropped and low-crawled into the blind. Not a moment too soon. Down at the campsite, voices grew louder. A man dragged a bound and gagged Paul Loving into the clearing. Millie Stanfield followed. She prodded Loving with a gun.

"Where's X?" Shawn mouthed. J.J. shook his head. His chest ached. His sister wasn't with them. Maybe they had guessed wrong or arrived too late. Xandra might be wounded or lying dead in the forest. He pushed to his knees. Shawn hauled him down.

"Remember what your dad said? Stay quiet and watch." J.J. shrugged free of Shawn's hold, then lay down, his fingers digging into the soil. To the west, where the hillside sloped toward the creek, a rattle of stones.

Below, Loving struggled against his bindings. J.J. raised the binoculars to the western bank of the creek and the hill beyond.

"A deer?" Shawn whispered. J.J. swept right, then left, paused at the wild tangle of purple hair. Xandra. She was alive and heading straight into trouble. J.J. pushed free of the branches and leaped forward.

"Go back! Go back!" He waved his arms as he scrambled his way down to the campsite. Shawn broke cover as well, flanking J.J. as they approached from opposite sides. Startled, Millie relaxed her hold on Loving. The man with her swept his gun from side to side, swearing as he searched for targets. Then he pulled the trigger.

* * *

The report of the gunshot reached Joe, Janeece, and Pete as they neared the path that took them across the creek and up into the dense, unspoiled woodland. Joe stepped into the water, weapon drawn, shaking off Pete's attempt to restrain him. Janeece swore as her shoes filled with water. No matter how fast they ran, they were too far to make a difference. Janeece glanced at the sky, startled by the sight of vultures circling.

Joe didn't stop. He tore at the vines hanging from the old-growth stand of trees, pulling himself up the hill and onto the now well-defined path. Pete and Janeece lagged a few yards behind. They had gone a half-mile deeper into the woods when a second shot rang out. Thirty minutes later, panting, disheveled, and on high alert, they reached the campsite.

* * *

Rye's shot went wild, splintering bark and showering fragments down on Shawn as he barreled into the man. The two pitched forward and rolled, each struggling to put the other in a headlock. J.J. rushed Millie, who whirled to confront him. Paul Loving backed away until he bumped into a tree. He slid down the trunk and stopped moving. Across the creek, Xandra emerged from the brush. She sloshed across the shallow, rocky streambed and crawled up the bank, hair plastered to her face, arms bleeding from a thousand scratches. She spotted Millie aiming at her brother and screamed a warning. J.J. dropped and rolled to his right. Millie pivoted from J.J. to Xandra, holding the weapon with both hands.

"You're not going to spoil this for me, Byrd," she yelled.

"It's over, Millie. You can't kill all of us." Xandra feinted left. Her ankle twisted, and she fell to one knee. Hands tied, range limited, she gathered a fistful of dirt and tossed it at the woman. Millie shielded her face, gun waving, as she clawed her eyes. J.J. inched forward. When he reached her, he kicked out, catching the back of her knees. She screamed and toppled to the ground. Xandra clapped Millie's wrist between her palms and twisted. Millie released the gun as she fought to free herself. J.J. tossed more dirt at the fallen woman. Xandra closed her eyes and, roaring, slammed her head into Stanfield's nose. Bones cracked. Blood spurted.

Shawn and Rye wrestled on, grunting as they strained for control, then sprang apart. Xandra recognized the snick of a switchblade and shouted a warning. Rye stabbed at Shawn, who grabbed the blade. Scrambling to his feet, J.J. sprinted for Millie's gun. He grabbed the butt and knelt to press the barrel against her forehead. "Move and I will shoot. Xandra?"

Xandra wiped her hands, slick with sweat and blood, down the back of Millie's tee and turned to her brother. "J.J. Back pocket. Box cutter."

J.J. grabbed the blade and sawed through the ties. Xandra sighed as feeling returned to her fingers, then took the gun and held it on Millie. Rye and Shawn had risen to their feet, blood dripping from Shawn's wounded hand and Rye's battered face. They circled each other, panting with each move. Rye struck out, slicing Shawn's forearm before staggering back.

"Shawn." Xandra stepped away from her brother. "Get out of the way."

Shawn stumbled back as Stanfield again thrust the knife at him. Xandra set her feet, locked her arms, and pulled the trigger.

* * *

Joe spotted his son first, a knife dangling from his hand. Millie Stanfield slumped next to a tree. Her accomplice lay in the middle of the campground. He wasn't breathing. Xandra cradled Shawn's head in her lap, one of his eyes swollen shut from the fighting, his injured arm and hand wrapped in the uniform shirt Xandra had on when she was kidnapped. Blood soaked the cloth, stained the ground. Joe noted the bruises on his daughter's body, the gun lying by her side, then spotted Paul Loving at the foot of an ancient beech, gag loose around his neck, his left shoulder bleeding. Loving raised his head and tried to speak. All that emerged was a groan.

"Dad." Xandra licked her lips. "We need water." While Joe dug out bottles from the backpack, Janeece and Pete closed in from opposite sides of the clearing. Janeece took one look at the scene and radioed for the EMTs. She laid a hand on Xandra's knee.

"What happened?"

"Rye Stanfield shot Loving." Xandra shuddered. "I shot Rye. All the rest is detail."

Sixty-five

Millie Stanfield, stone-faced and unblinking, stared at the wall of the interview room. Detectives Terl and Stone watched her through the observation window. Joe paced behind them, hands clenched around his phone. He was anxious to start the interrogation. Leah and Olivia waited in the atrium with J.J., who had already given his statement. After Xandra gave hers, he would take them all home.

Xandra and Shawn had been transported first to the Kettering Hospital Emergency Clinic in Franklin. Several stitches and one hydrating IV later, his daughter had ridden with the detectives to the station. Shawn had been Care-flighted to Miami Valley for surgery on the knife wounds on his arm and hand. Although no major vessels had been severed, the damage required extensive repair. Paul Loving's wound was superficial. He had been examined, then released into the custody of his lawyer, who promised to bring him in for a statement later that afternoon.

"She's a cold one," Janeece said. "Joe, if I let you in, do you promise to remain calm?"

Joe grunted. Pete paused in the hall. "You want me to talk to Xandra?"

"I do." She rested a hand on Joe's shoulder. "You trust Pete, don't you?"

Joe worked at unclenching his fingers. He had almost lost two of his children. What he wanted now went beyond justice. All his training warred with his instincts as a father, a protector. He inhaled deeply, exhaled, then nodded at Pete and Janeece to go ahead without him.

"I want to hear what she has to say, but Leah needs me, too. I trust you both. Tell Xandra we'll be waiting for her."

Terl sighed in relief and knocked on the door. The woman didn't react to the detective's entrance, remaining nearly catatonic as Janeece set a notebook and a yellow tablet on the table. She paced the room, passing close to the Stanfield woman, before settling into a chair across from her and switching on the recorder.

"Detective Janeece Terl. Friday, June 10, 2019. 2:21 p.m. Interrogation of Millie Stanfield." Janeece looked at the suspect. "You've had quite an adventure over the past two weeks, Mrs. Stanfield. Or should I say Loving? Perhaps both are correct. You are, of course, aware that bigamy is a first-degree misdemeanor in Ohio, punishable by up to six months in jail. However, that's the least of your problems, isn't it?"

Stanfield blinked. Janeece consulted her notes. "Well, we don't need a confession. We have witnesses and plenty of fingerprint and DNA evidence, so, no mysteries there. Let's see. Kidnapping, two counts of attempted murder of Alexandra Byrd and of Paul Loving, two counts of abetting armed robbery, first-degree premeditated murder of Ace Farins and of Reverend Doris Loving."

Stanfield turned to Terl. "I didn't kill Doris. You can't put that on me."

"No? Did Rye do it for you? Because that would still be on you."

Millie lunged across the table. The cuffs chained to a ring in the table prevented her from reaching the detective. "We had nothing to do with her death."

"Convince me."

Furious, Millie glared at the detective, then sat down and smiled. "I can't say I was sad for her to go. Her and those stuffed birds and her insistence on using the land for church shit."

"Uh-huh." Janeece shifted in her seat. "Well, any information you provide could help when it comes time for sentencing. Do you know who did kill her?"

"Why don't you ask Paul, or those partners of his? Coulter's cold-blooded enough when it comes to business. And that puffed up, macho man mayor, Eisner. The three of them had plenty of reasons to want her dead."

"What about Stuart and Reggie Lynx?"

"What about them?" Stanfield scratched at the tabletop. "Stupid kids. Gullible. Rye got them to provide information about Doris's plans, that's all. Paul had Reggie run errands or something."

"What kinds of errands?"

"Ask Paul. Stupid ass never would tell me what that was all about."

Janeece noted the way Stanfield rolled her eyes, thinking she was smarter than everyone else. "Did you ask Reggie to steal the vulture pins from J.J. and Alexandra?"

"What if I did? It was just a harmless prank." Millie picked at the blue polish flaking off a thumbnail.

"Actually, those pins were an attempt to incriminate the siblings in the Reverend's murder. So, your part in the deception may be enough to charge you with her death."

"It wasn't my idea. To take the pins."

"Whose idea was it, Millie?" The detective waited for the woman to decide whether to speak. When she did, Janeece sat back, stunned. She hadn't seen that coming.

* * *

Xandra sat alone in the soundproof room, waiting to share her account of the events of the past twenty-four hours. Her wrists throbbed. She touched the bandage covering the stitches on the back of her head where Rye had assaulted her. Resting her arms on the table, she considered the odds of suffering two concussions in less than a week. Even in her skateboarding days, she'd never been this banged up. All she wanted was to go home, shower, and sleep for a week. She pulled the yellow tablet closer to read over her written statement. What had she forgotten? She thought back to the March family trip to Hinckley to see the buzzards. The coincidence of that simple family outing connecting them to Doris Loving's murder continued to bother her. The stolen pins. Who knew about them? Why had Millie asked Reggie to steal them? Why did Reverend Loving stuff them in the bird found at the crime scene? The evidence suggested that someone had deliberately planned to implicate her and J.J. in the woman's death. Who would gain from that? The questions swirled, answers forming, then falling apart upon closer examination. The only motive that made sense was revenge. So, who had they pissed off? And just like that, a memory surfaced. Two weeks before Loving's murder, she and J.J. shopping with Joe at the new Kroger Superstore when they ran into the mayor. Eisner marching toward them, hands fisted, mouth thinned. He wagged a finger in Joe's face and swore. "You son of a bitch. How much is she paying you to follow me?"

Joe had escorted Eisner away from them, but she and J.J. watched as the mayor berated their dad. Finally, still red-faced, the man stalked away, his final words a clear threat. "You'll regret this, Zetts." Her father had shrugged it off, refusing to disclose details. All he would say was that the man needed to control his impulses, whatever that meant. She had forgotten the incident as soon as they left the store. Before it could slip away again, she hurried to add the account to her statement. A rap on the door, and Pete Stone stepped in. Xandra folded her hands and waited for the questioning to begin.

Sixty-six

The receptionist at the city building greeted the detectives with a smile. "Janeece. Pete. How can I help you?"

"The mayor in?" Janeece eyed the sign-in book on the counter, noting that a C. Coulter had visited earlier that morning.

"He's about to leave on vacation. You'd better hurry if you want to speak to him today."

Janeece stepped through the metal detector, followed by Stone. They glanced into the conference room, then took the steps two at a time. The door to the mayor's office stood open. Eisner had his back to them, flipping a letter opener shaped like a bayonet between his fingers as he stared at the undeveloped land beyond the window.

"Mr. Mayor?" Janeece approached the desk. Pete remained on alert by the door.

"It was Millie, wasn't it?" the mayor said. "She killed Doris to get her hands on Paul's land."

The detective waited for Eisner to turn. When he did, she gestured toward his chair. He sat heavily and leaned his hands on the desk. The letter opener slipped to the floor.

"No, sir. Millie Stanfield is guilty of many things, but you know she didn't kill Doris." When the mayor directed his gaze her way, Janeece recognized the blank stare of a man caught in his own web. "You asked her to convince Reggie Lynx to steal something personal from the Zetts kids. In a strange twist, he took bird pins. The only thing you need to explain is why."

"I...what?"

Pete laid a warrant on the desk. "It took time, but we finally got permission to check the interior camera footage from the dinner theater the night of Reverend Loving's murder. Many people followed her outside to talk that night. You were the last one to do so. When you returned, you were wearing a different coat and shirt. Can you explain why?"

Eisner swiveled his chair to stare again at the Reverend's land. "Such a beautiful piece of property. Developing it would be a boon for the city and for investors. I need the money that land will bring as much as Paul does, and he promised me a significant cut if I supported his bid, if I lent him money. He couldn't get financing at the bank anymore."

"Answer the question, sir," Janeece said.

Eisner stared at Terl. "Did you know my wife hired Joe Zetts to tail me? That he sent her photos of my girlfriend? And Lena's filing for divorce, planning to take everything I have when she goes. Loving needs the land developed so he can pay Coulter what he owes before that vulture takes all his businesses and carves them up. Paul is desperate for the funds. So am I."

"Who's your girlfriend, sir?"

"Why does that matter?"

"Everything matters." Janeece watched him lean down to retrieve the letter opener. He stabbed the tips of his fingers with the pointed tip. "Marilyn Gugino. She works for Clark. That's how we met."

Janeece decided to let that go for the moment. "As mayor, isn't investing in the land deal a conflict of interest for you?"

"My term's up in six months. I planned to keep the investment secret until after I left office. Until after the divorce was final. No one, especially Lena, needed to know about it."

"Doris Loving found out, didn't she? And confronted you that night? How did you get her over to the restaurant? Did you tell her Xandra needed her?" Janeece said. She took out zip ties and placed them on the desk. Eisner shivered.

"You can't prove anything."

"Pete?" Janeece waited for her partner to move into position behind the mayor. "Roy Eisner, you are under arrest for the murder of Reverend Doris Loving."

Pete recited Eisner's Miranda Rights. Then he bagged the letter opener and followed his partner as Janeece escorted the mayor from his office.

Sixty-seven

Xandra wandered the second-floor hallway, pretending she knew where she was going. She ignored the glances cast her way by other visitors, then lingered outside the room where Shawn was recuperating until a man she assumed was his father peeked out, frowned, and popped back in again. J.J. leaned against a wall by the nurse's station, keeping an eye on his sister and the door to Shawn's room. Neither was certain of the reception they would receive from the Crowe family. After all, Shawn's involvement in the case might affect his chance to attend the police academy, not to mention that the injuries to his arm and hand threatened to permanently derail his career choice. Xandra reached the end of the corridor, whirled, and stalked back to her brother.

"What?" J.J. crossed his arms. "You're making me nervous."

"Maybe he doesn't want me here." She worried her lower lip. "It's my fault he's hurt. Everything's my fault."

"His father saw you and didn't tell you to leave," J.J. said. "Are you afraid to see Shawn?"

"No." She squared her shoulders. "Yes. I don't know."

"Only one way to find out. Go. I'm here if you need me."

She tucked the offering she'd brought under her arm and pushed through the door. Shawn occupied the bed by the window, a privacy curtain hiding all but his feet from view. Mrs. Crowe sat in the only available chair. Her husband rested one hip on the heating unit below the window. The patient in the bed closest to the door was asleep, his soft snores filling the room. Xandra peeked around the curtain. Shawn was sitting up, his injured arm cradled on a wedge-shaped cushion. He looked up, spotted her, and didn't look away.

"Hey," Xandra said.

"Hey," Shawn said. His parents glanced at her but didn't speak.

"You look pretty good," she offered, "for a guy who just had surgery."

Shawn wiggled the fingers on the bandaged arm. "Don't look so scared, Byrd. The doctor says there's no permanent damage, although I will have to go to physical therapy."

Mr. Crowe cleared his throat. Shawn broke eye contact to introduce his parents. Mrs. Crowe stood and reached for her husband's hand. "We're just going to go get something to eat. Do you want anything, dear?" She looked at Xandra as she made the offer. Xandra shook her head. "All right, then? Walt?"

Xandra waited for them to leave before she laid the vulture next to Shawn's arm. "Olivia wanted you to have this."

"Olivia?" Shawn ran his good hand over the soft fur of the stuffed animal. Xandra bit her lip.

"Okay, I did, too. It's not every day I'm rescued by a knight in shining armor."

Shawn extended his hand. She stared at it for a moment before lacing their fingers together.

"I prefer to think of myself as a Cherokee badass. 'Cause I'm a quarter Native, you know."

"That, too." She blinked back tears.

"Does this mean you like me now?" His eyes sparkled with mischief and something else she couldn't read.

"I guess it does."

Shawn laughed. "How about we agree to be co-leaders of our graduating class? After what we've been through, I think that's fair."

She looked away. "We need to talk about that, but not today."

He pulled her closer, his breath stirring the hair that slipped free from behind her ear. "You owe me a kiss, Byrd."

"I do?"

"That's how fair maidens reward white knights in all the fairy tales I know." He locked eyes with her, refused to look away.

"Maybe I do," she said, leaning in.

* * *

Joe and Leah watched the detectives cross the atrium. Janeece had a habit of smiling and frowning at the same time, which told him not everything had been explained by the Stanfield arrests. Pete reached them first.

"You want to talk here?"

"No reason not to." Joe slipped an arm around Leah as they took their seats on the bench. Pete pulled chairs over for himself and his partner. Olivia sat on the floor, drawing a picture for her big sister's friend who was hurt.

"The Stanfields will answer for the robberies, the kidnappings, and the death of Ace Farins," Pete said, "and Eisner for the murder of Doris Loving. We still don't know who did the hit-and-run on Stuart Lynx."

"I should have suspected Eisner." Joe rubbed his chin. "He was so angry when he found out his wife had hired me to follow him around."

"We're going to need your files on that. Are we correct in assuming that Clark Coulter's administrative assistant was the mayor's secret affair?"

"Yes." Joe sighed.

"It's not your fault, Joe," Janeece said. "You couldn't have known he'd come after you through the kids."

"Damn it, I should have known. Do you think Coulter sent his hired guns after the Lynx boy?"

Pete shook his head. "I don't think so. Coulter's a vulture, but he's not a killer. He prefers to pick up the pieces after a business goes belly up."

"Maybe there's another way to find the answer." Leah paused. "Sorry, I didn't mean to interrupt."

"It's okay," Janeece said. "What were you going to say?"

"Remember when I cleaned out Doris's office and found her date book and those threatening letters? I also discovered a second smaller calendar, one the Reverend used to carry in her pocket. I didn't think much of it at the time, and I haven't really studied it, but maybe it contains something we missed, like who she counseled in the months before she died."

"Where is that book?"

Leah opened her purse. "I've been waiting to hand it over."

"I'll log this into evidence. Maybe the final piece of the puzzle is in here." She smoothed her braids. It would take time to sift through all that had happened. "Joe, why don't you and Leah go home? I'll call if anything turns up. Pete and I are speaking with the DA later today. We may need to issue a few more warrants."

"As long as my kids are no longer suspects." Joe waited for her nod. "Good. I'll copy my reports of Eisner's affair and drop them and the photos off this afternoon."

Joe scooped up Olivia and he and Leah headed out. Janeece watched them go. "You know what else, Pete? We need to go digging tomorrow, find out what's buried at those coordinates J.J. identified."

"About time." He followed her to the whiteboard display and the photos of the victims, suspects, and crime scenes. He circled the line between Eisner and the Reverend before connecting the Stanfields to the Farins boy and the robbery at the restaurant. When he took a step back, all the lines intersected around three people: Reverend Doris Loving, Alexandra Byrd, and J.J. Zetts. "And there we have our motive, or should I say motives?"

"Greed and revenge," Janeece tapped the three photographs. "No matter how much we want the world to change, the same old reasons rule. The land was a coveted income source. J.J.'s ideas coupled with the Reverend's vision stood in the way, and Joe's investigation of the mayor turned a cheater into a killer."

"Who sought revenge by going after Zetts's kids."

Janeece tapped the photos of the Lynx brothers. "How do these two fit into that equation?"

Pete leaned against a desk. "Maybe they're nothing more than collateral damage. Pawns in a bigger game."

"And the Farins boy?"

"He knew too much and wanted more?"

"I don't think so." Janeece sighed. "I think the poor kid was simply in over his head from the beginning. When he threatened to pull out or tell, they killed him."

"I have an idea. If my hunch pays off," Pete pulled out his phone, "we might be able to wrap this up tomorrow."

"Marilyn Gugino?" Janeece said.

"Bingo. She relayed orders to Coulter's men. The Lynx boys were the mayor's errand boys, too. He had them mail the threats to Doris. When Stuart got greedy, she offered to take care of things for her lover."

"Do we have any proof?"

"Let's have Cincinnati PD bring Marilyn Gugino in for questioning. Once she finds out Eisner's in jail, she might want to cut a deal."

Sixty-eight

The June sun beat down on the grassy field behind the church. Xandra ran a hand over the foxtails that bordered the walking trail. At the far end, a tractor labored. Although the community continued to mourn the Reverend, life went on. Janeece and Joe walked together, heads bent in conversation. Pete spoke with Leah, who gestured toward the forest. Ahead, J.J. and Shawn disappeared into the trees, shovels on their shoulders. Her brother used the GPS on his phone to locate the coordinates they had discovered among the Reverend's files.

As butterflies flitted over the wildflowers, Xandra considered the tragedies engendered by this plot of land, how the lure of big money had corrupted so many. She grieved for the Reverend and Stuart and for Farins, who, younger and more vulnerable than the rest of the victims, didn't deserve his fate. She didn't spare any compassion for Paul Loving or Millie and Rye Stanfield. Paul deserved his disgrace, Millie her confinement. Barring delays, the woman's trial would be held at the end of summer in the Warren County Courthouse in Lebanon. Xandra looked forward to testifying, especially after the grand jury declined to indict her for the killing of Rye Tinscher Stanfield.

Her hands still shook at unexpected moments. She woke sweating from nightmares of Rye returning to threaten her. The therapist she was seeing said it was a natural reaction to taking a life. She shrugged off the pull of remorse and thought about the upcoming graduation ceremony. At the end of August, she and Shawn would know who had earned highest honors in their class. By then, she would also know if she had earned a spot in the academy. But it no longer mattered. She had decided to leave the nest, to grow beyond Hopewell, at least for the moment. Tonight, she would tell her parents. Then, she'd tell Shawn.

They walked for twenty minutes before J.J. called a halt. He had visited earlier in the day to stake off the proposed fountain area and mark where benches would be placed. The Reverend's plan required the removal of several scrub trees and most of the tangled ground cover. Xandra narrowed her eyes, trying to imagine the vision J.J. saw so clearly. At the center of the roped-off area, the earth looked disturbed.

"Did you do that?" she asked.

J.J. shook his head. "I just cleared the top layer. Someone has dug here, but not recently. If I have the numbers right, whatever the Reverend buried should be there." They formed a circle around the spot.

"You sure you should be digging?" Xandra touched the bandage that protected Shawn's arm and hand.

"What are you now, Byrd? My doctor?" Before she could react, he winked. "I won't overdo it. Promise."

J.J. dug, and Shawn shoveled away the loose dirt. They worked in silence, expanding the excavation little by little. The clang of metal on metal drew everyone closer. Ten more minutes of effort uncovered a rectangular object resembling a safety deposit box. Shawn handed his shovel to Joe, who pried the container free. Pete grasped one end, Joe the other, and they wrestled it out of the hole.

While Janeece recorded the discovery on video, Pete slipped on gloves, released the catch, and opened the box. A manila folder rested inside.

"What is that?" Leah said.

Pete undid the flap and flipped through the contents. "An account of Doris Loving's dispute with her brother, of the standoff with Coulter's investment company, and a record of her discussions with the mayor. Oh, and a copy of her last will and testament."

Leah crouched next to Pete to peer at the documents. "All in Doris's handwriting, including lists of phone calls, emails, and visits to the church by the investors in the proposed land deal. Doris was always so thorough."

"And, J.J.? There's something for you." Pete lifted an envelope addressed to J.J. Zetts. He looked at Janeece.

"Go ahead and open it, Pete."

Prying open the seal, the detective pulled out a single sheet of paper and began to read. "I, Doris J. Loving, being of sound and practical mind, designate J.J. Zetts my legal representative in developing the acreage referred to in my will as church property per our agreement of April 21, 2019. In accordance with that agreement, I have deposited the sum of $15,000.00 in an account at the Union Savings Bank in Kettering as compensation for his services, with an additional $5,000 to be set aside from my assets in case of cost overruns. Mr. Zetts has my full confidence that he will carry out my wishes per our discussions." Pete paused. "The Reverend believed her life was in jeopardy."

"She never said anything," J.J. said, regret causing his voice to break. "I could have saved her."

"No, there's nothing you could have done." Xandra reached for his hand. "You deserve this, J.J."

Janeece cleared her throat. "I believe we have all the evidence necessary to comply with Reverend Loving's wishes. Pete and I will take this back to the station. That church lawyer, Sanders, can file the will with the court. Does it say who she designates as her executor?"

Pete scanned the will again. "Leah, she named you. Did you know?"

Leah raised a hand to her throat. "I had no idea," she whispered.

"Well, Joe," Janeece actually grinned, "your family made quite an impression on Reverend Loving."

Xandra stepped aside, glad, for once, that she wasn't in the spotlight, and then backed into a hard body. Hands gripped her arms, slid down to her waist. A warm breath teased the hair on her neck. "All's well that ends well, right, X?"

She considered shoving him away, then relented. Whatever happened in the future, for this one moment, she decided to enjoy being held by Shawn Crowe.

"You're not resisting," he whispered. "Does that mean you like me?"

She tugged his arms tighter around her. "Don't get cocky, Crowe. I might change my mind."

Sixty-nine

Cicada song accompanied Xandra as she crossed the open space between the buildings at Sinclair. Her last exam over, she hurried to check the list of candidates for the academy. The announcement of top student in the class would have to wait until all grades were in. She fingered the scar left by the zip tie around her left wrist, a reminder of how close she'd come to losing her life. Her mother believed it would fade with time. Xandra wasn't sure she wanted it to. The brand served as a warning to be more alert, to follow her instincts, to never let her guard down again.

Inside Building 19, a crowd had gathered to read the posted grades. She acknowledged the greetings of fellow students but hung back until most of them had left. An arm snaked around her waist, pulling her close. She caught her breath, unclenched her fists, and wriggled. Shawn didn't release her.

"You've been avoiding me, Byrd." His breath tickled her neck. A student passing by smirked. "You should not wriggle like that, woman. It gives me ideas."

She bit her lip, snuggled closer. "Sounds like a personal problem, Crowe. And I've been busy. New management at the restaurant. Practice on the range. Besides, when the grades came out, I didn't want to see you cry."

"Now, why would I do that?" He walked them forward to stand in front of the list. "My student ID's up there right next to yours."

Xandra ran her fingers over the numbers, allowing the breath she was holding to escape. "We did it."

"We did." He turned her to face him. "No matter what happens, we're in this together, if that's all right with you."

She held his gaze. "Not for a while yet."

"What does that mean?"

She dug through her backpack for the recruiting brochure. "I have something to do first."

"You enlisted?"

"Don't look so stunned. I should have trusted the detectives. Instead, I took J.J.'s pin from the crime scene. I have some atoning to do." She flicked the brochure. "The academy is your future, Shawn. I'm taking a different path. Recruiter says I qualify for MP training. If you're still here when I get back, we can revisit the team thing."

"And if I'm not?"

"I'll have to live with that." She hesitated before asking, "So, you free this afternoon?"

"Might be. What've you got in mind?"

"I'm thinking a walk in Beck Park might be nice, one where the vultures aren't looking to feast on dead things, and no one's shooting or stabbing us."

He tugged her toward the door. "I'll follow you," he said. "We birds need to stick together, don't you agree?"

THE END

Dear Reader, if you like a book, please consider recommending it to your friends and posting a review on any social platform. Interested in future Byrd & Crowe mysteries or more novels by this author? Sign up for J.E. Irvin's newsletter at www.janetirvin.com for exclusive information, details on forthcoming books, and giveaways!

===

NewAtlantianLibrary.com or
AbsolutelyAmazingEbooks.com
or AA-eBooks.com

Thank you for reading. Please review this book. Reviews help others find Absolutely Amazing eBooks and inspire us to keep providing these marvelous tales.

If you would like to be put on our email list to receive updates on new releases, contests, and promotions, please go to AbsolutelyAmazingEbooks.com and sign up.

For sales, editorial information, subsidiary rights information
or a catalog, please write or phone or e-mail

AbsolutelyAmazingEbooks
Manhanset House
Shelter Island Hts., New York 11965, US
Tel: 212-427-7139
www.AbsolutelyAmazingEbooks.com
bricktower@aol.com
www.IngramContent.com

For sales in the UK and Europe please contact our distributor,
Gazelle Book Services
White Cross Mills
Lancaster, LA1 4XS, UK
Tel: (01524) 68765 Fax: (01524) 63232
email: jacky@gazellebooks.co.uk

www.ingramcontent.com/pod-product-compliance
Lightning Source LLC
Chambersburg PA
CBHW060953030726
47503CB00003B/849